THE HOUSE WITH NINE LOCKS

ALSO BY PHILIP GRAY

Two Storm Wood

THE HOUSE WITH NINE LOCKS

PHILIP GRAY

Harvill
Secker

1 3 5 7 9 10 8 6 4 2

Harvill Secker, an imprint of Vintage, is part of the Penguin Random House group of companies

Vintage, Penguin Random House UK, One Embassy Gardens,
8 Viaduct Gardens, London SW11 7BW

penguin.co.uk/vintage
global.penguinrandomhouse.com

First published by Harvill Secker in 2025

Typeset in 12.5/16.76pt Van Dijck MT Pro by Jouve (UK), Milton Keynes
Printed and bound in Great Britain by Clays Ltd, Elcograf S.p.A.

The authorised representative in the EEA is Penguin Random House Ireland,
Morrison Chambers, 32 Nassau Street, Dublin D02 YH68

A CIP catalogue record for this book is available from the British Library

HB ISBN 9781787304420
TPB ISBN 9781787304437

Penguin Random House is committed to a sustainable future for
our business, our readers and our planet. This book is made from
Forest Stewardship Council® certified paper.

For my daughter Katja
who helped

Heer Halewijn zong een liedekijn.

Al die dat hoorde wou bi hem zijn.

En dat vernam een koningskind,

Die was zoo schoon en zoo bemind.

Zi ging voor haren vader staen:

'Och, vader, mag ik naer Halewijn gaen?'

'Och neen, gy dochter, neen, gy niet,

Die derwaert gaen en keeren niet!'

Master Halewijn sang a song.

All who heard it went along.

A princess one day heard the air,

She who was beloved and fair.

She stood before her father then:

'Oh, Father, may I go to Halewijn?'

'Oh no, daughter, no, for sure,

Those who go are seen no more!'

From 'The Song of Master Halewijn',
fourteenth-century Flemish
folk ballad

——— One ———

Brussels, February 1952

The dead man had been taken away. The only thing still living in the charred skeleton of the warehouse was a tiger-striped tabby cat with demonic yellow eyes. It showed no sign of having narrowly escaped being burned alive, except for a sooty smudge on the bridge of its nose and a tuft of singed fur at the tip of one ear. The animal acknowledged Major Salvator de Smet with an indifferent stare, before vanishing among the debris.

The cat had seen everything, most likely. It was a shame it couldn't talk. It would have known where the fire started. It might have seen how. It might even have been able to explain how a nightwatchman had come to be inside the building, a man called Verlinden whose heavily pregnant wife was due to receive the news about now: husband and income lost in one night. It would have saved everyone a lot of trouble if that cat could talk.

The site was slowly filling up. The fire brigade seemed in no hurry to move on, and half a dozen officers from the municipal police were wandering about, securing a perimeter and taking names. The rain was easing up, but a cloying chemical stink clung to the air. Where Verlinden had been found, just inside the main doors, lay a blanket, a large purplish smear visible across the top. According to the ambulance crew, the nightwatchman had lived just long enough after their arrival to utter the word *Liesbeth*, his young wife's name.

Major de Smet's deputy, Sub-Lieutenant Toussaint – one week in the job and not remotely useful – was picking his way through the doused interior, his tunic loose around his lanky frame, a handkerchief pressed to his nose like a maiden aunt with an attack of the vapours.

'I don't need a deputy,' de Smet had said, when told of the appointment, but Colonel Bedois, his superior in the federal gendarmerie, had remained unmoved.

'New ministry policy: senior Flemish-speaking officers are to have French-speaking deputies, and vice versa. An issue of public confidence. We must move with the times.'

'What am I supposed to do with him?'

'I don't know – have him take notes.'

'Since when have I ever needed notes?'

De Smet had not been boasting. He had learned his catechism by the age of six, and could enumerate all the kings of Israel in order, along with their lineage and deeds. In his first year at school, he had passed the time learning the latitude and longitude of every major city on the classroom map – Helsinki, 60 degrees north, 25 degrees east; Buenos Aires, 34.6 degrees south, 58 degrees west. Once learned, nothing was forgotten.

'Well, if the worst comes to the worst,' Colonel Bedois had said, 'you could send him to hold your table at the Comme Chez Soi.'

But de Smet did not have a table at the Comme Chez Soi, or any other restaurant for that matter. As everyone in his section knew very well, he ate lunch at his desk, or not at all.

He left Sub-Lieutenant Toussaint at the warehouse and turned his footsteps to a building on the other side of the street. With its sandy brick walls, pitched roofs and circular windows, the Federal Engraving Bureau had the look of a medieval monastery. The presses were elsewhere, but it was on these premises that the printing plates were prepared for all kinds of state issuance: banknotes, bearer bonds, certificates, licences. The possibility that these had been compromised or stolen was what had brought Major de Smet to the scene. A fire at a warehouse, whether an act of God or of criminals, did not interest him at all.

While the fire crew were still tackling the blaze, hoses snaking across the street from the Willebroek Canal, de Smet had surveyed the exterior of the engraving bureau with the aid of a torch. At the rear of the building, a stone's throw from the water, a window with a stout iron frame had been smashed in. On the wall a few metres further on, the word COLLABORATEUR had been daubed in red paint – although unevenly, and in such obvious haste that at first it was hard to read. The sun was coming up now, and, revisiting the site, de Smet could see how the paint had splashed onto the ground, colouring the cobblestones and the weeds. Who was the collaborator supposed to be, he wondered? Surely not the unfortunate nightwatchman. The bureau director then? The new king? Or perhaps Mr van Houtte, the Minister of Finance? Flemings were all collaborators, as far as some people were concerned. They had been too friendly towards the Germans during the occupation: joining their youth groups, working in their factories, spreading their lies. Three thousand death sentences – 242 of them carried out – had not been retribution enough. Still, it was a strange accusation, so unfocused, and yet so violent.

The bureau director, Monsieur Meunier, appeared on the other side of the shattered window. Another over-lunched Walloon, he was red in the face and breathing heavily, as if struggling to digest.

'I've gone through the strongroom, Major. Nothing's been touched.'

'What about the plates?'

'I've checked every one, finished and unfinished. Nothing's missing. We keep daily records of the work, as you know. Everything's logged.'

'What about damage?'

'As far I can see, there isn't any damage, apart from the window. The lock to my office, for example – I've the petty cash in there – not a scratch. I don't think they were after anything, Major, thank heavens. Just a mindless act of vandalism. It's what one should expect from communists.'

'Communists?'

'It's in their nature. Ever since their man Lahaut was killed, they've been working up to it. Mark my words, this is just—'

'Don't tread on the glass, monsieur.'

Meunier cleared his throat. 'I'm sorry. I must get someone to repair this right away.'

'Leave it exactly as it is.'

'But we can hardly—'

'We'll tell you when you can clear it up. Today's payday, isn't it?'

Monsieur Meunier looked at his watch. His staff were due to start work in half an hour. 'Yes, but the cash doesn't come in until three, by armoured van.'

De Smet ran a finger along the buckled frame of the window. A brick would not have done this kind of damage, even one thrown with venom. This was the work of a sledgehammer, a calculated demolition. Access was the only rationale, and yet the director insisted that nothing inside had been disturbed. Had the criminals lost their nerve at the last minute? Had something gone wrong? Or had Monsieur Meunier missed something?

'You've plenty of time to call it off then.'

'I beg your pardon?' The director's face was slightly redder than before. 'Call what off?'

'Payday. Premises not secure, criminal activity in the area, any excuse. Just make sure no one's paid yet.'

'But I can't just . . . My people are skilled craftsmen and much in demand. I can't just withhold their—'

'Your people may know something. A little inconvenience might encourage them to speak up.' De Smet stepped back from the window. He was surprised to discover that he had cut himself. Two fine slivers of glass had lanced into the flesh of his middle finger. They stood up white and glistening, like frost. 'If we're under attack, monsieur, we can't have people thinking it's business as usual, can we?'

The building had spent most of its life as a brewery. Going through it from room to room, de Smet thought he could detect a sour, yeasty smell, especially in the cellars, where an old wooden mash tun still stood in the corner under a rust-streaked iron lid. Even so, the place was clean and tidy: workbenches uncluttered, tools and materials stowed, the powerful lights and magnifiers folded away, all work-in-progress – the artwork and plates – stowed in the director's private office behind modern locks and a two-inch steel door. One of the latest and most important commissions had been a new 500-franc note, but, as Meunier confirmed, the plates had been completed earlier that week, and safely transported to the National Bank of Belgium. If that had been the prize the raid had come too late.

'We run a tight ship here,' the director said, visibly pleased that de Smet could find nothing amiss. 'I suppose in such times that makes one a target.'

Fingerprinting was unlikely to yield much in a busy workplace. The best bet was one of the larger fragments of glass. But de Smet was not optimistic. If the criminals had been careful enough to dis-turb nothing, they would have been careful enough to wear gloves. After twenty minutes, he allowed Meunier to escort him off the prem-ises. Vandalism, protest, politics – perhaps there was nothing more to it than that.

Sub-Lieutenant Toussaint met them outside. After its brief appear-ance, the sun had vanished behind a raft of cloud and factory smog. On the canal, the lights of a passing freighter were bright against the gloom.

One of the firemen was doubled over, retching against the wheel of his truck. The tabby cat had found its way onto the upper floor of the warehouse, and was watching from one of the blown-out windows.

'They were storing paint in there. The fumes . . .' Toussaint coughed. His eyes were red and streaming, and there was soot on his hands. '. . . they would have been lethal.'

It seemed the sub-lieutenant's use of the handkerchief hadn't been completely ridiculous.

'You think it was fumes that killed our nightwatchman?' Monsieur

Meunier ran a hand over his bald crown. 'It would be some comfort to his wife to know the poor man didn't suffer.'

Unless the poor man had a life insurance policy, which in de Smet's experience was unlikely, Verlinden's wife would be worrying about how she was going to pay her rent at the end of the month, and whether she would be giving birth in a dosshouse. Practicalities were always the priority once children were involved.

Toussaint didn't answer the director's question. 'The doors to the warehouse were secured with a padlock. Did Verlinden have a key, sir?'

The director nodded. 'The nightwatchmen are issued with keys to all the buildings on the site, in case of emergencies – except the one to my office. I keep that on me at all times. You're thinking he let himself in, I take it?'

'Could be,' Toussaint said.

'He went in to tackle the fire, I expect,' Meunier said, 'and was knocked out by the fumes. It's not bureau policy, of course. The correct procedure would have been to raise the alarm and wait for the fire brigade. But then, Verlinden had only been in the job a few months.'

De Smet and Toussaint looked at each other. Could it be that the issue of liability was already on the director's mind?

'Verlinden saw distinguished service in the war,' Meunier went on. 'Air-raid defence and so forth. The kind of man we like to hire, when we can.' He shook his head. 'Bloody reds.'

The tabby cat's tail twitched. Meunier went back to his office.

'What did you find?' de Smet said, because it was obvious his deputy had found something.

'I checked the main doors, sir. They were shut when the fire crew arrived, secured with the padlock. It's still there. Verlinden might have got himself into the building, but he had no way of getting out again.'

'Meaning?'

'Padlocks don't close themselves. Someone shut him in.'

They walked back to the car. The Juvaquatre was temperamental, with an engine that was prone to flood. De Smet did not usually let anyone else drive it, but he wanted to think without worrying about the road.

Toussaint turned the starter. The engine didn't flood. 'Headquarters, sir?'

'No. Verlinden's place.'

'The widow? It's a bit soon. She'll be in shock.'

'People in shock don't lie, or don't lie very well. The Dansaert District, 48 Rue des Fabriques. Take the Pont Marchant.'

Toussaint turned out onto the main road. The early-morning traffic was starting to build: workmen on bicycles grinding their way along the quaysides, trucks belching black smoke as they passed – citizens oblivious to the death in their midst.

'You think the director was right about the reds, sir?'

'Monsieur Meunier has no information one way or the other.' De Smet opened the glove compartment. Next to his army-issue Browning lay a pack of cigarettes.

'So it doesn't go in the report?'

De Smet put a cigarette between his lips and reached into his pocket for a lighter. It was a while before he lit up. He could sense in this futile attack an intelligence at work, a purpose.

'It's a fairy tale.'

'A fairy tale, sir?'

'*Little Red Riding Hood*, to be precise.' De Smet briefly examined the cuts on his finger. They were still bleeding. 'You think you know who you're dealing with. You think it's your old grandma. But it isn't.' He exhaled a plume of smoke and looked out across the city. 'It's the big bad wolf.'

Gérard the Devil

—— Two ——

On the afternoon of Adelais de Wolf's eleventh birthday, her uncle Cornelis arrived with a present so big it wouldn't fit inside his car. Adelais would never have guessed it was a present – a wooden crate strapped to a trailer – if it hadn't been for the bright red bow nailed to the top. Everyone crowded to the window.

'Now what's he up to?' Adelais's mother couldn't stop them abandoning the tea table and hurrying downstairs.

Until Cornelis's arrival, the day had passed uneventfully. A week earlier, Mrs de Wolf had announced that they would have a party. Adelais was told she could invite four friends from school. 'Any more and we'll run out of chairs. And we have to invite the Wouters twins. Mrs Wouters was an angel when I was sick, and the boys are exactly your age.'

The Wouters family lived in a house with a refrigerator and a telephone. But the boys never played with Adelais except when threatened or bribed.

Adelais had gone to school that Monday armed with four handwritten invitations. It had not been easy deciding on the recipients, because she wasn't sure if four could be persuaded to come. Maria Goossens, who always had a cold, was a fairly safe bet, and Thilde Somers, who was shy, said she would do her best to attend, even though she had preparatory classes for her first communion; but Lotte Verbeke, who sat next to Adelais in maths, and regularly copied her answers, said she would only come if her friend Edwina de Groote could come too. This was a problem, because Adelais did not like Edwina de Groote, mainly thanks to an

11

incident in the playground a few months earlier, when Adelais had been watching the other girls play hopscotch. Edwina, who fancied herself the best, had tripped and grazed her knee. For no reason at all, she had immediately marched up to Adelais, and said: 'What are *you* looking at? You're always *looking*. Like a little spy.'

So Adelais had not given an invitation to Edwina de Groote. The last invitation had stayed in her pocket.

Even so, attendance on the day had been disappointing. True to her word, Lotte Verbeke had stayed away. Neither was there any sign of Thilde Somers. On the bright side, Maria Goossens did appear, with a blocked nose and a jigsaw puzzle of the Taj Mahal, and so did the Wouters twins in identical home-knitted sweaters, their hair damp and freshly parted, their mother's hands clamped around their shoulders, as if to make sure they couldn't escape.

'What a lovely smell! Is that chocolate?' she cried. 'You lucky boys, Mrs de Wolf's been baking!'

Mrs de Wolf had insisted that Mrs Wouters stay, since there were plenty of empty chairs. But the twins had remained silent and unsmiling, even as they chomped their way through a round of *frikadellen* in tomato sauce, pancakes with cream, and several slices of chocolate cake.

Uncle Cornelis had parked his old Citroën in the alley beside the house. He was not a big man – average height, at best, with a head of wavy dark hair, and deep-set eyes – but he always seemed to occupy more space than other grown-ups, something to do with his loud voice, and his cheerful demeanour. In the interests of speed, Adelais had come down with her walking stick. It meant she could only hug him with one arm.

'There she is, my favourite niece.'

'I'm your only niece, aren't I?'

'I suppose that must account for it. That, and your funny face.' Cornelis kissed Adelais on the forehead, and ruffled her hair so that her topknot came loose. Adelais had untidy, straw-coloured locks that refused to be organised, and her heavy-lidded eyes always made it look like she had just woken up.

Everyone wanted to know what was inside the crate.

'I'll need a crowbar from your father's workshop,' Cornelis said, 'if there is one.'

Lennart de Wolf was standing in the doorway with his arms folded. As a small sign above him made clear, he mended watches and clocks for a living. 'I'll see what I can do,' he said, going into the house, and returning a few moments later with a chisel.

The present was heavy. It took three of them to lift it out of the crate. The first thing Adelais saw was a large leather bucket seat. It was followed by a pair of bicycle wheels next to each other, and a complicated arrangement of metal tubing, gears and chains, attached to a third, smaller wheel at the other end. The mudguards and chainguards were red.

'One careful owner. I hope you like the colour.' Cornelis handed Adelais a booklet. The pages were dog-eared, and there was a round stain on the front cover where someone had placed a mug. On it was written:

THE 'NETLEY'

A LIGHT RUNNING INVALID TRICYCLE

FITTED WITH FIRST CLASS PNEUMATIC TYRES

R. A. HARDING (Bath) Ltd.

Adelais didn't know much English, but she did not have to understand the pamphlet to realise that there had been a mistake. She had suffered two great misfortunes at the start of her life: the invasion of her country by the German army, which had occurred a few weeks after she was born; and the invasion of her body by the polio virus, which had followed not long afterwards. Adelais could hardly remember the Germans now – no one in the family talked about them – but the virus had left her with a permanent reminder: a malformed knee and slack ligaments in her right leg. Walking was possible over short distances, with a stick or with the heavy steel support her father had hammered together, but cycling in any form was impossible. Like hopscotch, it was an activity she could only watch.

Adelais knew she should say thank you, but she found her face growing hot at the thought of having to remind her uncle about her leg, in front of everyone. How could he have forgotten about it? Did he imagine her leg was going to mend itself? She glanced at her father: his frown only confirmed what a thoughtless present it was.

'Thank you very much, Uncle.' Adelais's burning cheeks made it impossible to look at him. 'It's very kind of you.'

Maybe she wouldn't have to explain. Maybe they could take the machine and hide it in a corner of the yard and forget about it – like the china nativity angels Grandma Mertens had once given them. They had stayed on display on the mantel for a week, before mysteriously disappearing. 'They flew back to heaven,' her father had explained eventually, 'where they belong.'

Herman Wouters had no use for discretion. 'Adelais can't ride a tricycle. She's got a funny leg.'

With a *plap* Mrs Wouters's hand connected with the back of her son's head, but he was not deterred. 'It's true!'

Uncle Cornelis squatted down in front of Adelais and opened the booklet. A diagram of the machine indicated its various features. 'This is a rotary handcycle. You don't pedal with your legs. You pedal with your arms – here, see? And I happen to know that you have excellent arms.'

As if to prove the point, he gave them a squeeze. Adelais's arms were as thin and weak as any eleven-year-old's, but at that moment they felt powerful, as if her uncle's words were enough to transform them.

'It's a lovely thought,' her mother was saying. 'But isn't that thing a bit heavy for her? And the roads are so dangerous. Maybe if we wait a year or two—'

Adelais launched herself into the seat. She could already see herself careering down the streets with the wind in her hair, passers-by waving, children like Edwina de Groote jumping out of the way as she crashed through the puddles. On her first-class pneumatic tyres she would fly across the city like a witch on a broomstick. People would turn to look at her, instead of looking away, which they usually did when they saw her limping along. It would be like starring in a film.

She knew what to do: the crank arms were in front of her, at chest height. The crank turned the chain, and the chain turned the front wheel. The whole mechanism could be swung to left or right, like a ship's rudder. Her legs weren't needed at all.

She gripped the handles, pushed with her right hand and pulled with her left.

'That's the idea,' Cornelis said.

The crank began to move. The chain tightened. The tricycle rocked forward an inch or two, stopped, and then rolled back again.

'She can't do it,' Herman Wouters said. This time nobody slapped him.

Adelais tried again, putting all her strength into it, but the crank would not turn more than a couple of inches.

'Told you.'

'Nonsense,' Uncle Cornelis said, 'all she needs is a push.'

He got behind her and planted his hands on the back of the seat. The tricycle began to roll forward. Adelais found she could turn the crank, slowly, painfully. By the time she reached the street she was almost up to a walking pace.

'She won't make it fifty metres.' It was the other Wouters boy this time. 'Not before dark anyway.'

His brother laughed.

But he was wrong: Adelais got as far as the corner of Jan Roomsstraat, which was almost a hundred metres, before the others had to come and push her back.

★

The de Wolfs lived in the eastern district of Sint-Amandsberg. From the little attic room at the top of the house, there was a view across the rooftops and chimney stacks all the way to the three spires that marked the heart of the city. It was in the attic that Adelais's father found her that evening.

Adelais did not often go up there. The stairs were narrow and steep, and Mrs de Wolf had never liked her daughter using them unless she had to. Until recently, she would insist on escorting Adelais whenever she went from one floor to another, even when it was to use the closet. Worse, she would wait outside the door until Adelais had finished, so as to be on hand to escort her back again. She even did this when they had guests. Tonight though, after finishing her puzzle of the Taj Mahal, Adelais had found herself unsupervised. She had stolen some gingerbread and made her way to the attic as the sun was going down.

'What are you doing up here, Ada?' Adelais's father was tall, and had to stoop to pass through the door.

'Nothing.'

Adelais had been thinking about all the sights she was going to visit on her handcycle, once she had built up the necessary strength. On this point, Uncle Cornelis had been encouraging: just as blind people developed sharp hearing, he said, so she would develop strong arms. It was Nature's way. To prove his point, he had set her a challenge when no one else was listening. 'I'll give you three hundred francs if you cycle to the Devil's House and back again, in one go.'

The Devil's House was a fortified mansion on the southern side of the old city. These days it housed the Public Records Office, but many centuries earlier it had been occupied by an aristocrat called Gérard Vilain. According to legend, Vilain had earned the nickname Gérard the Devil because all five of his wives died in mysterious circumstances, one after the other.

Adelais's father was holding something. It was another present, wrapped up in brown paper and string.

'But you already got me the scarf,' Adelais said.

'This is something extra. I don't know if you'll like it. I just thought . . .'

He handed over the gift. Inside the wrapping was a picture inside a frame: a sketch of a stone bridge over a deep ravine.

'It's an etching, with a hand tint. I did it a long time ago, when I wasn't much older than you. I thought we could hang it in your room.'

Adelais said she would like that and her father smiled and went to fetch a hammer and a nail. In truth, the picture was not one Adelais would have chosen for herself. She would have preferred a photograph of Katharine Hepburn wearing slacks, like the one she had seen in a magazine. But she did not mind. She was still thinking about her uncle's challenge. The first thing she had to do was work out the shortest route to the Devil's House. Every day, she would go a little further, setting down her progress in a notebook. Then, the only issue would be how to spend the three hundred francs.

Over the months that followed Adelais stuck to her plan. 'I'm just going to ride around for a bit,' she would say, if anyone asked. Sometimes, for the sake of variety, she would say she was going to play with the Wouters twins, which nobody seemed to think incredible.

'As long as you're back for supper,' her mother would say.

Within a fortnight, unbeknown to her parents, she had reached the big avenue that cut across Schoolstraat. By the end of the summer, she had passed the end of the ship canal in Dampoort. She hid her notebook under her mattress, in case her mother read it, and put an end to the enterprise. But Mrs de Wolf did not find the notebook. If anything, she was more preoccupied than usual with her own affairs. By Christmas, Adelais had crossed the River Leie, just a few hundred metres from the Devil's House.

Uncle Cornelis visited them often during this time, motoring over from Brussels, but nearly always in the evening, and often after Adelais's bedtime. She would hear him talking with her parents late into the

17

night. Sometimes there were arguments. Whenever he saw her, though, he would take her to one side, and ask how she was getting on with his challenge. 'Am I going to leave here three hundred francs poorer?' he would ask, reaching for his wallet.

Adelais could have lied and claimed the money. She had a feeling her uncle wouldn't have minded. Perhaps he even expected her to cheat. But she was not tempted. She dreamed of showing him, of cycling all the way and back, with him following in his car. That way, nobody could doubt her, or call her a liar. And she would have done it, if it hadn't been for the accident.

— Three —

For the last six months, Adelais had been having weekly sessions of experimental physiotherapy. Normally, such treatment would have been too expensive for the de Wolfs, even with Mrs de Wolf putting in shifts at the linen factory, but Ralf Helsen was an old family friend, and only charged a fraction of his normal rate. The doctors at the hospital had warned that the unnatural gait forced on Adelais by her deformed knee might have a knock-on effect on other parts of her frame as it developed: her hips, her spine, even her good leg. That was why every Thursday afternoon after school, Adelais and her mother would take a tram to the neighbouring district of Heileg-Hart.

Dr Helsen's treatment was concentrated on Adelais's back, thighs and buttocks. The gluteal muscles in particular were vital for the development of a balanced posture, he said. They would need to be strong and flexible to relieve the strain on her joints.

Adelais was made to sit upright with one ankle resting on her knee, and lean forward again and again, until her nose was touching her calf. She would have to lie on her front with her good knee tucked under her chin, and hold her bad leg clear of the examination table until it began to shake like a jelly. There were a dozen different tortures in every session, some of them involving contraptions of Dr Helsen's own design, made up of weights, ropes, pulleys and gauges. These would introduce a greater degree of precision to the proceedings, he explained. Sometimes he would coach her through her exercises. At other times, he would wander off to consult a book.

With her mother off shopping, the only distraction during these long sessions was provided by Dr Helsen's daughter, who would walk into the consulting room unannounced. Saskia Helsen was the youngest of five children, and the same age as Adelais. Her older brother and three sisters had been raised with a fairly normal amount of guidance, but by the time Saskia had come along, her parents' capacity for nagging had been utterly exhausted. Saskia did whatever she wanted to do, went wherever she wanted to go, and said whatever she wanted to say. No one ever told her to go to her room, or mind her own business, or watch her tongue. At least, that was how it seemed to Adelais, as she stretched and strained, laid out on the examination table, a slave to Dr Helsen's regime and the implacable demands of her leg.

On the other hand, Saskia knew things that eleven-year-olds didn't usually know. By some distance the youngest in her family, she regularly overheard her older sisters complain about their husbands, and her mother's response. She had a fairly clear idea where babies came from, and why the virgin birth was a miracle. She even knew what sort of woman a *slet* was – all information that was as new to Adelais as it was disturbing.

'Mother says husbands want three things from their wives, and they'll only behave themselves if they get at least two out of three.'

Saskia's head had popped up at the end of the examination table as Adelais was recovering from a stretch. Dr Helsen's youngest had large, startlingly pale green eyes and dark, shoulder-length hair parted on one side.

'So, what are they then?'

Saskia counted them out on her fingers: 'Compliments, conjugals and cuisine.'

'What are conjugals?'

'I think they're like physiotherapy. That's what it sounds like.'

Adelais thought about her own mother and father, and what passed between them. There was always cuisine, if that wasn't too fancy a word for it, but she was fairly sure there was no physiotherapy. As for compliments, her father got very few of those. What he got were complaints, mainly about all the things they couldn't afford. 'What if a husband only gets one out of three?'

'Then he goes off with a *slet*.' Saskia shrugged. 'That's kind of what they're for.'

Adelais did not like the idea of her father going off with a *slet*, but it wasn't an easy thing to picture. The few times she had seen him out without her mother – at a bar or at the archery club – he had always been in the company of other men.

'How's the bet?' Saskia asked. 'Have you got your three hundred francs yet?'

After keeping quiet for several months, Adelais had finally explained Uncle Cornelis's challenge. She had wanted something interesting to say in return for the information about Saskia's sisters and their unsatisfactory husbands. 'Just half a kilometre to go.'

'And half a kilometre back again. So that's actually a kilometre.'

'I suppose it is.' Another kilometre on the handcycle was not a trivial distance. As it was, Adelais completed every trip with gritted teeth. Sometimes her arms were so sore afterwards she could hardly lift them.

'You can always stop for a rest.'

'No, I can't. I have to do it in one go, those are the rules.'

'No one would know.'

'I don't need to cheat. I can do it.'

Saskia went to the window and peered out through the lace curtains. Dr Helsen's was a grand house with four storeys and a facade of classical stonework, like a Greek temple. Adelais's mother said his family had never been short of money.

'Do you think he's right then, your uncle?' Saskia said.

'About what?'

'Nature. Like blind people who can hear like a bat. Less of one thing and more of something else, to make up for it.'

'My uncle's usually right.'

21

Saskia sat on her father's huge knee-hole desk. Dr Helsen was on the telephone in the next room. 'What about boys?'

'Boys?'

Saskia swung her legs back and forth. 'I was thinking, if you didn't want to waste your time on boys, if all they wanted was to be fed and pampered like babies, would there be something else to make up for them?'

'Like being a nun, you mean?'

'God, no. A nun? I'd rather be dead.'

Adelais was shocked. In her household, brides of Christ were spoken of with reverence. Adelais's mother had wanted her to go to a religious school, where all the teachers were nuns. This led to arguments, because her father had been against it. Mrs de Wolf had given in only because the community school was a hundred metres away, close enough for Adelais to get there on her own.

'They have to wear nightdresses in the bath,' Saskia said. 'Did you know that?'

'Nuns?'

'My sister Madaleen stayed at a convent once, and all the nuns got in the bath with their nightdresses on, even the Mother Superior who was at least seventy and almost dead.'

Adelais considered this information. 'Were they trying to save soap?'

'No. It was so they weren't tempted.'

'By what?'

'Their bodies, of course. Tempted to do things.'

'What things?'

'Wash each other or something, scrub each other's backs. That's how it starts.'

Adelais tried to picture the scene. 'My mama scrubs my back sometimes. It's nice.'

Saskia nodded. 'Exactly.'

The clock on the wall said the session was almost over. Adelais picked up her shoes, and began to lace them up. She had a good idea what Saskia was really getting at. She was thinking that a girl with a deformed leg, who couldn't dance, and needed help to climb out of the bath, a girl whose hair was always untidy and whose only friends were sickly or chronically shy – a girl like that was unlikely to find herself a sweetheart or a husband, one worth having at any rate. If Saskia didn't put it like that, it was only because she did not want to seem unkind. But she needn't have worried: Adelais had already decided that boys were not worthy of her attention. What was more, everything she had learned about the older Helsen girls and their unhappy marriages had convinced her that grown men were no better. If anything, they were worse. The wisest course of action was to steer clear of them altogether, and she resolved there and then to do exactly that, forever.

Forever lasted until the following morning, when Adelais struggled into her blue dungarees and set off on the handcycle towards the River Leie. It was then, approaching the Sint-Joris Bridge, that she set eyes on Sebastian Pieters for the very first time and, in spite of his being a boy and of no possible interest, saved his life.

—— Four ——

Adelais had plenty of time to admire the bicycle later, after its rider had been taken away in an ambulance. It was a shiny new Gitane, with drop handlebars, a shimmering blue frame and whitewall tyres. The only thing it lacked, being a racing model, was storage: there was no saddle-bag at the back, and no basket at the front, nothing that would spoil its sleek, aerodynamic lines. That was why the boy had rested his bunch of flowers across the handlebars, and was holding on to them as he sped along the quayside under the dappled shade of the plane trees.

The sight of him brought Adelais to a halt. Bands of winter sunlight were flashing across his face as he leaned into the bend. As she explained to herself later, his speed and the flowers on the handlebars, and maybe even the striking, cobalt-blue bicycle – it was these things that struck her, and not the boy himself, who looked about fourteen or fifteen, and was only more handsome than average if you noticed that sort of thing, which she didn't.

A truck thundered past, horn rasping. A flock of pigeons took to the sky, wings clattering, and the road was empty again. The young man had vanished, along with his bicycle. Nor were they further along the quayside or on the bridge. The only clue that he had been there at all was the bunch of flowers, lying in the gutter.

Adelais didn't know if the pigeons were to blame, but she did know that boys on bicycles didn't vanish into thin air. There were people on the pavement and cars on the road, but none of them had stopped. They didn't seem to know that anything was wrong.

There wasn't time to tell them. Adelais launched herself across the junction. A van with a ladder on its roof swerved to avoid her, sounding its horn. From the quaysides on the River Leie, it was a three-metre drop into the water, but here, by the Sint-Joris Bridge, there was a stone ramp leading down to a towpath. From the top, Adelais scanned the scene: the sun was reflecting off the river, dazzling her, but then she saw the boy, lying half in the water and half out. He wasn't moving. His bicycle lay on the path, the back wheel turning.

Adelais turned down the ramp. It immediately came to her that she had never gone down a steep slope before because Ghent did not have any steep slopes. The handcycle surged forward, as if motorised. The frame began to shudder, the front wheel swaying from side to side. Adelais squeezed the brakes as hard as she could. They squealed as if in pain, but made no difference. She came off the ramp too soon, slamming hard onto the towpath. The front wheel locked. For an instant, she felt weightless. Then the handcycle pitched over on its side, tipping her onto the cobbles.

She looked up. Her vision was slowly rotating, like the back wheel of the Gitane, and there was a sharp pain in her left wrist. The boy had slipped further into the water, which was coloured with red swirls. His head was beneath the surface.

She didn't like to wear the brace when she was on the handcycle. Instead she relied on a walking stick with a crooked handle. It lay in front of her now, its tip pointed at the drowning boy.

Adelais grabbed the walking stick and crawled towards the water's edge. There wasn't time to get up. She hooked the handle of the walking stick around the boy's far shoulder and, with one great heave, rolled him onto his back. Water spouted from his mouth like a whale. Before he could slip under again, Adelais heaved him towards the edge of the towpath, reaching it on the third attempt.

The coughing told her he was still alive. It went on for at least a minute, during which time Adelais found the gash on the boy's forehead: it was an inch long, and crossed the hairline above his right eye. In the course of the struggle, she had got her dungarees wet, and there were smudges of blood all over her blue cardigan. She wondered if she would get into trouble with her mother, or if saving someone's life would count as an excuse. She reached into her pocket for a handkerchief and pressed it against the boy's forehead to staunch the bleeding.

She was adjusting the knot when he opened his eyes. They were chestnut brown, like his hair.

'You.' He blinked. 'Are you—'

'Don't try to talk,' Adelais said, because she had heard people say that in films. 'Help is on its way.'

The boy smiled at her. Adelais could not deny that he had nice teeth. If you had just saved someone's life, you were allowed to notice their teeth. You were also allowed to notice broad shoulders and a strong chin. She was going to ask the boy what his name was, but then he moaned and closed his eyes again.

By this time, they had been spotted from the bridge. A man with a cigarette in his mouth appeared, followed by a man wearing spectacles and a double-breasted suit. The man in the suit said the boy should be put on his side, and as they were rolling him over a woman with a pram came hurrying along the towpath. She removed the bloodstained handkerchief, and wrapped the boy's head in a pink baby blanket, which made him look ridiculous, like a woman at a Turkish bath.

The adults were now in charge and there was nothing more for Adelais to do but limp back to the handcycle which, like the boy, was lying on its side. She examined the front wheel: something had happened to the axle, so that the rim of the tyre scraped against the mudguard when it turned. She was not sure if she could cycle home. She realised that she was trembling slightly all over, even though she wasn't cold.

An ambulance pulled up on the quayside above and the boy was loaded into the back on a stretcher. The man in the suit looked at his watch and left. The woman wheeled her pram away, the baby crying inside. The man with the cigarette was soon the only one left.

'What about the bicycle?' Adelais said.

'Someone'll be back for that,' he said, and sauntered off.

The bicycle looked expensive. Adelais couldn't leave it unattended. What if it were stolen? She had no choice but to wait, but an hour went by, and then two hours, and nobody came to claim it. No one came back at all.

The wind picked up. The sun slowly sank behind the houses. The traffic along the quaysides increased, and with it the noise, until the place where she stood beside the river became a cell of stillness, a forgotten backwater in a busy, important world.

Adelais found herself fighting back tears – tears which she knew were stupid. Her father would know how to mend her tricycle. He mended things for a living. Her wrist was only bruised, and her handkerchief could be washed. If she got into trouble for staying out late, she had an excuse: it was because she had saved a boy's life – unless, in fact, she hadn't. Because it wasn't impossible that the boy had died in the ambulance, or at the hospital from an injury to the brain, or from having swallowed too much riverwater. No, she couldn't boast about saving the boy's life, even as an excuse. That would jinx it. That would tempt Fate. It felt like Fate was involved already.

As dusk was descending, a policeman finally noticed her from the bridge. He pushed the handcycle back up to the road, and took charge of the Gitane. He was unable to tell Adelais about the boy, what had happened to him, or even where he was. He said only that she might be called upon to make a statement, and he took down her name in a notebook.

Adelais pedalled home, her front wheel rasping and squeaking. If the boy was dead, it meant that hers was the last face he had ever seen, hers the last words he'd ever heard – words from a stranger that were not even her own. She wished she had come up with something more comforting or beautiful or wise. More than that, she wished she had found out the boy's name, or at least told him hers.

— Five —

By the time she got back to Schoolstraat it was dark. Adelais pushed the handcycle into the alley and let herself in through the back door. Her mother was going to be angry with her – it was unavoidable – but Adelais could not resist postponing the moment of reckoning. When she heard voices in the workshop she knocked and went in.

Seated at the workbench under a cone of light was Uncle Cornelis. He was staring through the big magnifying glass that her father used to mend watches.

Adelais's father stood beside him. 'Don't you knock?' he said.

'I did knock.'

Uncle Cornelis's attention remained fixed on the object under the glass. Adelais glimpsed metal, threads of bright reflection on polished steel. 'Hello there. Is it time for supper?'

'I don't know, I've been out.'

'Having adventures, were you?' Uncle Cornelis adjusted the magnifying glass and picked up a small pointed instrument.

'Sort of, yes. How did you know I—'

'Squeak, squeak, squeak. That front wheel has taken quite a knock by the sound of it.'

'I think the axle's bent.'

'We'll have to take a look at that.'

'Not now, Ada,' her father said. 'Run along.'

Adelais closed the door and made her way to the kitchen, following the smell of onions and stewed meat. She found her mother standing by the window, biting her thumbnail. She looked anxious, even more so than usual. People used to say Adelais took after her father when it came to her

28

looks, which was not what she wanted to hear. She would have preferred her mother's thick brown hair and delicate features, and her dark, sad eyes.

'Mama?'

For a moment her mother seemed confused. She glanced at the clock. 'Where have you been? It's late.'

Token anger, barely irritation.

'There was an accident. A boy fell off his bicycle and I went to help him. And then the wheel went wobbly on my cycle, and there was nobody to help me get home.'

Adelais sensed that if she got to the end of the story quickly enough, she might escape being questioned about where the accident had happened, or how she came to be there.

'Well, you're back now. Have your supper. No need to wait for the others.' Her mother went over to the range. 'Your uncle's brought us some chocolate.'

On Wednesdays Adelais's mother usually made a big stew, using whatever meat she could get – pork or beef or occasionally rabbit – but always with onions and bacon, and cooked in beer. By Thursday the meat was tender. The dish would last until Monday, eked out with cabbage and potatoes, or bread if there was nothing else.

Adelais sat down to eat. It was lucky she wasn't being questioned about the accident, but she sensed that something wasn't right. 'What's Uncle Cornelis doing with Papa?'

'What do you mean?'

'I saw them in the workshop. Is Papa making pictures again?'

With a clang, her mother replaced the lid of the stew. 'What are you talking about?'

'He gave me a picture for my birthday, the one in my bedroom. Didn't they used to do art together? Isn't that how you met?'

The etching of the bridge was hanging up beside her bed. It was the first thing she saw when she woke up every morning: the warm biscuit-coloured stones.

'You never forget anything, do you?' Her mother wiped her hands on her apron. 'I expect Uncle Cornelis has a watch that needs mending. Now eat up.'

Adelais didn't think her uncle had been looking at a watch, but her mother was clearly in no mood for arguments. Adelais finished her supper quickly and went upstairs to record the day's progress in her notebook. Normally, she would have asked to stay up so that she could spend some time with Uncle Cornelis, but not tonight. She had a feeling he would want more details about the accident and, unlike her mother, he would know at once if she left anything out.

Adelais woke the next morning with a knot of anxiety in her stomach. She threw on her dressing gown and clambered downstairs.

Her parents were at the kitchen table, drinking coffee and reading. Her father had the newspaper, her mother a small booklet that had arrived in the post a few days earlier. She hid it in her apron as soon as Adelais came into the room, but Adelais had already taken a look when it first arrived. It came from a company in the Netherlands that made 'prosthetics and orthotics to order'. Adelais had no idea what the words meant, but the photographs made it clear: they were supports for amputees and people with bad legs. Unlike the support Adelais's father had made, these were sculpted to look like normal, well-muscled limbs, and some even had hinges and springs at the knee so that the wearer could flex without falling. The devices were tailor-made for each customer, which entailed a trip to North Holland. The prices started at six thousand francs. Adelais did not know how much money her parents made between the watch-mending and the shifts at the linen factory, but she knew six thousand francs was more money than they had, because it was years since her mother had worn a new dress, and the last time her father had bought a pair of shoes, they had come from a second-hand stall at the Friday market.

Adelais did not care about the booklet. It was the newspaper she wanted. If the boy on the bicycle had died, the tragedy was sure to have been reported in the press. Unfortunately, her father seemed in no hurry to be done with *De Standaard*. Adelais watched him scan every column from top to bottom, slowly turning the pages between leisurely sips of his coffee. Her mother gave her some bread and butter, and a mug of warm milk, but Adelais immediately began to hiccup.

Her father sighed heavily. 'Oh dear.'

'What is it?' Adelais asked at once.

'Our new king, our king-in-waiting, isn't going to be crowned. He's going to swear an oath to the Constitution, and that's it.'

'No coronation?' Adelais's mother said. 'That is a shame.'

Like most Flemings, Adelais's parents had both voted for the old king to return, but when he did, the French-speaking Walloons had started rioting. They said Leopold had been too friendly with the Germans in the war, which was a lie, Adelais had been told, because he had really been more of a prisoner. In the end, Leopold had given up trying to be king and handed the job to his son, who had been too young in the war to get blamed for anything. Even so, Boudewijn was being told to keep his head down and not push his luck in case the Walloons went back to rioting again.

With a grunt of disgust, Adelais's father tossed *De Standaard* onto the table. Adelais did not wait for permission. She snatched up the newspaper and began searching for news of the boy. There were reports about politics and football matches, and a new 'community' of coal and steel, whatever that was, but nothing at all about a boy falling into a river. It came to Adelais that perhaps *De Standaard*, being a paper for the whole of Belgium, did not bother with cycling accidents, even bad ones, and that what she needed was one of the local newspapers. Unfortunately, her father had stopped taking his to save money.

'Can I go to the Wouters's house after breakfast?' she asked.

Mr Wouters had the *Staatscourant van Gent* delivered every day. Adelais had often seen the delivery boy pushing it through their letter box.

Her mother smiled. 'You've been playing a lot with those boys lately. I'm glad you're getting on.'

Since her last visit, the de Wouters twins had acquired an electric train set, which they had set up in a spare bedroom. Adelais was not allowed to touch the trains or the signals. She was given the task of organising the model farm animals that had been drafted in to enrich the scene. She escaped as soon as she could and went looking for the newspapers. Luckily, Mr and Mrs Wouters had gone out.

Adelais found several editions of the *Staatscourant van Gent* in the scullery, where some of the pages had been used to wrap potatoes, but none of them were recent. A two-day-old copy had found its way under the kitchen sink, next to a bottle of bleach and a box of shoe brushes. In the front parlour there were magazines in a magazine rack, but no newspapers. She went out into the backyard and lifted the lid of the dustbin. She was greeted by the sight of peelings, and a smell of rotten eggs.

She made her way upstairs again. The twins had suffered a derailment, and were arguing about whose fault it was. Their parents' bedroom was on the other side of the landing. Adelais knew it was wrong going into other people's bedrooms, but this counted as an emergency. She eased back the door. On a small table, beside the unmade double bed, lay a neatly folded newspaper.

Adelais's heart was in her mouth as she hurriedly flipped through the pages, taking in the report of a new road, the threat of a tram strike, a council plan to encourage tourism. A local footballer called Bavo van Gorp had broken his ankle. There was nothing about a cycling accident or the death of a boy.

Adelais went back the next morning. She could not search the house this time, because Mrs Wouters was in, but she had already come up with a new strategy. 'Is there any news about Bavo van Gorp's ankle?' she asked.

Mrs Wouters had never heard of Bavo van Gorp.

'The football player,' Adelais explained. 'I expect it'll be in the newspaper.'

At which Mrs Wouters went and fetched the paper for her. She did the same thing the following day, but Adelais found no mention of the accident in either edition of the *Staatscourant van Gent*, even though the boy had nearly drowned. You had to drown completely, she supposed, to get a mention in the local newspapers. All the same, Adelais found the silence disquieting. It was almost as if the incident had never happened. What evidence could she produce that it had? The swelling in her wrist had gone down, and the front wheel of her handcycle had been mended by the time she went to inspect it the next day.

On Wednesday, school ended an hour early because of an inspection for nits. Adelais decided it was time she resumed her uncle's challenge. She set off as usual, but when she reached the river she could not help stopping, if only to see if anything remained of the flowers. She rode up and down the quayside, but could find no trace of them. The idea came to her that if the boy was all right, he might come cycling this way, just as he had before. If she saw him, she would have the final proof she needed that he was still alive.

The old bell of the Sint-Jacobskerk sounded in the distance. The challenge was over for the day. Adelais was supposed to keep going all the way, but she had been waiting on the quayside for twenty minutes. A chill wind blew, tugging at the dead leaves still clinging to the plane trees. A strange loneliness came over her, one she hadn't known before. She tried to imagine what the boy was doing at that moment, if he was out with his friends playing football, or buying flowers at the market to make up for the ones he had lost. Who had the flowers been intended for? His mother? A relative? A sweetheart? She wondered if he had any memory of her, if in that fleeting moment of consciousness, her existence had actually registered. Perhaps, she thought, she had never been more real to him than a figure in a dream.

The next morning, Adelais's father was reading *De Standaard* at the breakfast table as usual.

'Passing angel,' he muttered when he got to the classified section. 'What utter nonsense.'

Adelais did not pay much attention, but her mother was curious. She picked up the newspaper and read the advertisement aloud:

RESCUE AT THE SINT-JORIS BRIDGE

Last Friday our beloved son crashed his bicycle into the River Leie and was saved by a passing angel.
Do you know her name? Telephone Ghent (9) 23 9606.

— Six —

Sebastian Pieters had suffered a broken ankle, a dislocated shoulder, a cranial fracture and a bleed on the brain. According to his mother, he would have to remain in hospital under observation for several weeks, until the doctors were satisfied that the blood in his brain had been reabsorbed and that surgery would not be needed to remove a clot.

'He'll be so happy to see you,' she said, as she escorted Adelais to the ward at the Sint-Lucas Hospital. 'He was babbling about you from the moment he got here. The advertisement was his idea. We thought he'd been hallucinating.'

Mrs Pieters had curled blonde hair and high cheekbones, and everything she had on was part of an outfit, with matching colours and complementary shades. She wore perfume and lived in the district of Zuid, in a big house with a garden on one side and a park on the other. Mr Pieters worked as a director at S.A. Textile des Flandres. Adelais expected her mother to point out the coincidence – her being in textiles as well – but on the day they all met Mrs de Wolf did not mention her factory work. She did not say much about anything. Adelais wondered if she felt uneasy, wearing her old hat and the black dress she normally wore to Mass. She had greeted the story of the rescue with a mixture of joy and bewilderment, as if it were proof her daughter really was an angel. 'Adelais, I believe God was at your shoulder that day,' she had declared. 'He brought you to that place.'

Her father's reaction had been different: 'You should get up to mischief more often.'

Adelais hardly recognised the boy in the hospital bed. His head was wrapped in bandages, his right arm was in a sling, and his right leg was in a cast. He was asleep, a paperback book in his left hand. Several more books lay in a pile on the bedside table.

'I told him to expect a special visitor,' Mrs Pieters said. 'It'll be a nice surprise for him. I need to talk to the doctors. Do you mind waiting?'

Adelais sat down beside the bed, clutching the bag of plums she had brought as a present, aware of heads turning her way. What was she doing here, after all? Had she come just to be thanked? Knowing the boy was alive should have been thanks enough. Why should she put him through the exhausting business of expressing gratitude when he was still sick?

Adelais allowed herself another look at the boy's face. He had long eyelashes, and the line of his eyebrows was curved and fine, like his mother's. His mouth, in which could be detected the traces of a pout, resembled his mother's as well. If he had been a girl, Adelais had to admit, he would have been beautiful, even without his mother's cheekbones.

'Get better soon . . . Sebastian.' It took an effort to say his name, as if it were one of those bad words she was not supposed to know. 'I hope you get your bicycle back.'

According to Sebastian's mother, the Gitane had not been returned, and the municipal police had been unable to help. Adelais had seen a policeman take it with her own eyes, and said so, but Mrs Pieters seemed reluctant to point the finger. 'I'm sure they wouldn't steal it on purpose,' she'd said, leaving Adelais to wonder how they could have stolen it by accident.

She got to her feet. She could wait for Mrs Pieters in the lobby. She had gone a couple of paces when the boy stirred. At the sight of her, he sat up suddenly. 'You.'

She tried to smile, but she was out of practice.

The boy looked as confused as he had at the river. 'Are you . . . ?'

'What?'

He frowned at her stick. His voice was hoarse. 'You're . . . you're limping.'

'I know.'

'Are you hurt? Did you . . . ? Did I run into you? Is that—'

'No. I have a bad leg.'

'Oh, good.' The boy slumped back against his pillow. 'I've got a broken ankle, and a dislocated shoulder. *And* a fracture.' He touched at his bandage. 'Up here.'

'I know,' Adelais said. 'And a bleed on the brain.'

'What?'

Maybe the boy did not know about the bleed on his brain. Adelais held out the plums. 'I brought you these.'

The boy stared at the bag and blinked. The look of confusion returned.

'My name's Adelais.'

'Adelais.' The boy looked at her intently. She felt her cheeks grow hot.

'De Wolf.'

'De Wolf? Is that one word or . . . ?'

'Two words.'

'So you're definitely not . . . ?'

'Not *what*?'

'Sorry. I thought . . .' The boy cleared his throat. 'You see, I thought you were an angel, to begin with, a real one. I thought I'd died and you'd come to take me to—'

'You banged your head.'

'Yes, I did, didn't I?' He scratched at the bandage. 'It still hurts, actually. Especially when I read.' He lifted the paperback book a few inches. 'And my arm gets tired. It's hopeless.'

The talk of angels made Adelais uncomfortable. 'What's the book?' The boy showed her the cover. The title was *Pietr the Latvian*. 'What's it about?'

'Murders, in Paris. And a detective. It's really good. I was well into it before . . .' he gestured towards his plaster cast, '. . . all this.'

They fell silent. Adelais wondered whether she should sit down again or go. 'I could read to you, if you like. For a bit.'

'Yes. I mean, could you?'

'Tell me where you are.'

He handed her the book. 'Chapter Seven. Here.'

Adelais had always been good at reading, but she hadn't done it out loud since she was six years old. She sat down by the bed and cleared her throat. 'Chapter Seven. The Third Interval.'

'Thank you, Adelais,' the boy said.

'I haven't started yet.'

'I don't mean for reading.' He reached for the bag of plums and rested it on his chest. 'I mean, you know, for saving my life and everything.'

Sebastian stayed at the hospital for the whole of January. The doctors were worried about his headaches. After a fortnight, they took his arm out of the sling. A week after that, they took the bandages off his head, revealing a patch of white scalp with a purple scar down the middle where the stitches had been. The cast on Sebastian's leg stayed on, because the break was of a kind that healed slowly. Sebastian said they wouldn't have to worry about taking it off, because he would be dead from boredom long before then.

Adelais visited several times a week. After school she would take the tram. At weekends, provided it wasn't raining, she was allowed to make the journey on the handcycle. The hospital wasn't much further than the Devil's House. She spent her visits reading aloud. They got through the rest of *Pietr the Latvian*, then *The Hanged Man of Saint-Pholien*, which was set around a casino in Liège, then made a start on *The Yellow Dog*. Adelais did not always arrive during visiting hours, but the nurses had a soft spot for Sebastian. As soon as she arrived, they would pull the curtains around his bed so that they would not be disturbed. 'Such a nice young man,' one of them whispered to her, as if it was a secret.

Every visit began with an exchange of theories about the unsolved crime in the story, who was guilty and why. Sebastian's ideas were clever and elaborate, and always wrong, but no matter how exciting the story became, he never read ahead, even though the headaches were fading and his shoulder was mended.

'Do you think he's in love with you?' Saskia asked, after one of Adelais's visits to the physiotherapist.

'Of course not.'

Dr Helsen's youngest was lying across the settee in the waiting room, with her head propped up on one arm. 'I think if he wasn't in love with you, he would read those books for himself.'

'I told you, he can't. It makes him ill.'

'Why can't his school friends come and read to him?'

'They like football and riding bikes. They don't want to hang around a hospital.'

Saskia wrinkled her nose. 'I don't blame them for that. Hospitals smell.'

'Anyway, I like his books. There's always a murder in them. Sometimes there are lots of murders.'

Saskia yawned, but Adelais could tell she was faking. 'You know, I heard that if you save someone's life, then they belong to you forever. Like a slave.'

'Where did you hear that?'

Saskia shrugged. 'Well, maybe not a slave. More like a parent with a child. The parent gives life to the child, so the child is supposed to do what it's told.'

'I can't be like a parent to Sebastian. He's already got parents, and he's older than me anyway.'

'How much older?'

'Two years and ten months.'

Saskia rolled onto her back. 'I suppose he could be like a little brother.'

'Or a big brother. That's how it is, a bit.'

Saskia balanced one knee on top of the other. Her sandal had come undone, and now dangled off her big toe. 'I've got a brother. He's never here.'

'Sebastian'll be out of hospital soon. I don't think I'll see him much after that.' It was something Adelais told herself often. It paid to be prepared.

'So, exactly like a brother then,' Saskia said.

On one of her Saturday visits, Adelais was directed to the Rehabilitation Room, a long, whitewashed space on the ground floor, with gymnastic equipment arranged along one wall. The doctors had given Sebastian a pair of crutches and left him to practise using them. From the other side of the door, Adelais could hear him muttering and groaning, and the familiar thud of rubber ferrules on a wooden floor.

'Everything hurts,' he said, when she walked in. He was wearing a dressing gown and pyjamas. 'They said I've been in bed too long, but whose fault is that? I only did what I was told.'

The doctors had been worried about his brain, that had been the priority, not his legs or his shoulder, but Adelais decided against reminding him. She had never seen Sebastian look so unhappy.

'I thought crutches would be easy,' he said, 'but they're torture. I've already got bruises under my armpits.'

There had been a time when Adelais had used crutches more often than not. She had been in danger of falling without them. It was years before she could balance with the brace and the stick, let alone manage with just one or the other.

'You'll get used to them,' she said.

'I don't *want* to get used to them.' Sebastian slumped down on a bench. 'All I did was fall off my bike. Why do I have to spend months . . . ?'

Adelais sat down beside him. She had been expecting to talk over the latest developments in *The Yellow Dog*, where a shooting and several poisonings had spread panic through the seaside town of Concarneau. She picked up Sebastian's crutches: two bowed pieces of wood with a strut in between, padded with leather. 'You have to let your hands carry your weight, not your armpits,' she said. 'Keep your elbows bent when you hold the handles. Don't reach forward too far — about half a normal stride is enough – and keep the end of the crutches a little way outside your feet so you don't trip yourself.'

'Sounds complicated.'

Adelais handed him the crutches.

With a sigh Sebastian got up again. Tucking the crutches under his arm, he lined himself up opposite the door. 'Half a stride, you said.' He set off again, taking short steps, arms pushing down harder.

'You lead with the good leg,' Adelais said, 'always.'

'Good leg, right.'

He started again, his steps building to a steady rhythm. 'How am I doing?'

'Look ahead of you, not down.'

'Why?'

'I don't know. So you don't bump into things?'

Sebastian went back and forth a few times and stopped at the door. 'Right, come on.' He was flushed, and slightly out of breath.

'Are we going back to the ward?'

'I need some fresh air. Do you mind?'

Adelais followed him down the passage to the front of the building. They passed several porters and nurses, but nobody challenged them. Outside the main doors was an oval of grass, surrounded by a driveway.

'You'll catch a cold,' she said.

Sebastian took no notice. 'What's this?'

Adelais had left her handcycle next to a line of parked cars. 'That's how I got here.'

'Nice.' Sebastian stooped to examine the machine. 'There are no handlebars. How do you turn?'

Adelais showed him the mechanism, how the cranks and the chain pivoted from side to side. 'It's not as fast as a bicycle. But it's a lot quicker than walking.'

Sebastian ran a hand along the bright red frame. 'Can I have a go?' he said.

41

— Seven —

The rain arrived in February and seemed in no hurry to leave. It pooled at street corners and turned the gutters into oily brown streams, sluicing into the rivers and canals, swelling the pungent waters until they threatened to overwhelm the banks. Adelais got wet on her way to school, and returned home with a cough. By supper time, she was flushed and sweating. Mrs de Wolf put her to bed and kept her there for three days, feeding her broth and dark chocolate. Adelais did not mind missing school – or Mass, for that matter. What she minded was having to wait for the next instalment of *The Yellow Dog*.

In the past when she had been ill, Adelais's father would come and read to her, but Lennart de Wolf had taken on some work in Brussels, and was going to be away for a while.

'Who's he working for?' Adelais asked. 'Why can't they come here?'

'Some customers, you have to go to them.'

'Because their clocks are too big? Like a church clock?'

This seemed like a good explanation, but Adelais's mother shook her head. 'It's not a church clock. Now eat up.' Mrs de Wolf had prepared semolina porridge, which she had sweetened with a dollop of jam.

'Then I don't understand.'

Adelais's mother busied herself spreading a napkin under her daughter's chin, and smoothing it out with her fingers. 'Some clocks are delicate. They don't take kindly to being moved.'

'Are they valuable?'

'They are.'

'Who owns them? A collector?'

'Something like that. The important thing is Papa should be well paid for once, if things go well.'

'So the collector's rich then?'

'Very rich. Now eat your porridge before it gets cold.'

Adelais took a spoonful of semolina. It was smooth, with a nutty taste. It was good news that her father had a rich new customer. She wished her mother would tell her more about it, but it was obvious she didn't want to, as if that might jinx it. 'I suppose Papa must be really good at his work, to be trusted by a collector.'

Mrs de Wolf smiled and sat down on the bed. 'You're right. He *is* good. And not just at mending clocks. Before the war . . . well, he made beautiful things. He was much in demand. Your uncle, too.'

Adelais knew that Uncle Cornelis had introduced her parents. He and Lennart de Wolf had been apprentices together in Antwerp. At some point Lennart had decided to set up on his own, because he wanted to be his own boss, whereas Uncle Cornelis had gone to work for the government at a printing works. 'Do you mean they made pictures, like the one I got for my birthday?'

'Most suitors give flowers to their sweethearts. The first present your father gave me was an etching of a rose, tinted by hand. The detail was . . . It was magical. You could see every fibre, every vein, like it was alive.'

'Why did he stop?'

Adelais's mother shook her head. 'Things were different after the war.'

'Weren't they better?'

'For some people. Not everyone.'

'Not for Papa? Why not?'

Adelais's mother sighed. 'Your papa was for the unity of the Dutch-speaking peoples, of Flanders and the Netherlands. Some people thought the Germans might help. It was just an idea, but after the war, well, it could count against you.' She got up. 'I'll take the bowl later. Don't forget to say your prayers.'

'How much longer will Papa be gone?' Adelais asked.

'Just a few more days. A week at most.' Mrs de Wolf stopped in the door. 'It'll be worth it. We'll be able to afford a telephone, maybe a refrigerator. And one or two other things, things we need.'

Adelais knew at once that she was talking about the company in North Holland, and the special supports they made for people with bad legs, supports that cost six thousand francs.

A few days later Adelais came home from school to find the house empty and a note from her mother on the kitchen table.

I have gone to meet Papa in Brussels. There is stew and potatoes in the oven. Please do your homework, lock the doors and get yourself to bed good and early. Do not wait up on any account because I will not be back until very late.

Mama xx

PS – Remember to say your prayers.

Adelais had never been left alone before, not at night. The thought of having the whole house to herself was exciting, at first. She could do whatever she wanted. Nobody would nag her, or tell her off or complain about the way she went about things. She wouldn't have to consider anyone's feelings but her own.

She decided she was hungry. She took the stew out of the oven and put it on the table. The potatoes were overcooked and powdery, but improved by some butter, which Adelais spread over them with a knife. It was raining outside. Water trickled in the drainpipes and gurgled in the drains. The muted call of a mechanical cuckoo reached her from her father's workshop. Then everything in the house was still.

Adelais wondered why her mother hadn't said anything that morning about going to Brussels. Was there an emergency? What if she wasn't back by morning? Should she go off to school, or wait? What if her mother didn't come back at all? Who should she tell, Mrs Wouters or the police? Adelais got out her geometry homework and tried to focus on calculating angles, but it didn't make her feel any easier. The house was too empty, and if she stopped what she was doing and listened, she fancied she could hear someone creeping down the stairs. In the end she decided to follow her mother's instructions and go to bed. Once in her pyjamas, she pulled the blankets up over her nose and listened to the rain as it slowly died away. On an impulse, she grabbed an old rag doll she'd had since she was three, and dragged it under the covers with her.

She was woken by the growl of an engine and headlights in the street. She scrambled to the window in time to see the back of a car as it turned into the alley. She grabbed her stick. It was still dark, and without the brace she was forced to go slowly down the stairs. Voices in the kitchen rose up to meet her. A woman was shouting, sobbing – it couldn't be her mother. Her mother had never sounded like that. Another voice, a man's, broke in. He was trying to calm her down. That voice she knew: it was Uncle Cornelis's. For a moment, Adelais wondered if she was dreaming. It was the kind of situation that had often cropped up in her dreams. In her dreams she was always watching and listening from outside a room, although since the rescue at the Sint-Joris Bridge, those dreams came less often.

She opened the kitchen door. Her father was slumped behind the table. Adelais hardly recognised him: his hair was matted, he had grown a shaggy beard and his eyes were bloodshot. He was supposed to have been working for a rich collector of clocks, but he looked like he had been imprisoned in a dungeon.

Adelais's mother stood opposite, her face in her hands. Uncle Cornelis placed a hand on her shoulder, but she knocked it away. 'Get away from me!'

There was venom in her voice and in her eyes. She raised a hand. She was going to hit him. She was going to strike Uncle Cornelis across the face.

'Mama?'

They saw her. Her mother's arm dropped to her side. She turned away. Her father looked sheepish, spent. Only Uncle Cornelis was unchanged. He cleared his throat and smiled. 'Hello, little one. We didn't mean to wake you, we're sorry. Be a good girl now, and go back to bed. Let the grown-ups argue.'

Adelais didn't move. She wanted to know what was wrong with her mother and father. She wanted to know that everything was all right.

Slowly her father got to his feet. Without saying a word, he went over to Adelais and put his arms around her. His face was rough and he smelled of rancid bacon. Adelais began to make sense of it: the collector of clocks had tricked him, and made him a prisoner – like Robert Donat in *The Count of Monte Cristo* – and somehow it was all Uncle Cornelis's fault.

'Come on, now,' her father said at last, and taking Adelais's hand, he led her slowly back up the stairs.

'Did he put you in a dungeon, Papa? Did he lock you up?'

'Lock me up? Who?'

'The collector. Did he trick you?'

'I'm not sure—'

'You'll tell the police?'

Her father's grip tightened on her hand. 'No. No, we're not telling the police, Ada. It was nothing like that. A mistake, that's all. It was just a mistake.'

They were on the landing when Adelais heard her mother shouting at Uncle Cornelis again: 'Get out! Just get out!'

The next morning Adelais got up quietly and made her own breakfast without waking her parents. When she returned from school everything was back to normal. Her father had shaved off his beard and was hard at work in his workshop. Her mother was in the kitchen, peeling vegetables. She had caught Adelais's cold, and was sniffing, that was the only change.

Adelais wanted to know more about the collector, and what had happened in Brussels, but Mrs de Wolf was not in the mood to talk. Adelais sensed she was disappointed not to have the money from the clock collector, whoever he was. Adelais thought of saying she didn't mind about the custom-made supports, that she was perfectly happy with the one she had. But then she remembered that she wasn't supposed to know about the company in North Holland, because her mother had kept the catalogue hidden.

The following Saturday Adelais took the tram to the Sint-Lucas Hospital. This time she arrived during visiting hours, but when she got to Sebastian's ward, she found him gone.

The sister in charge was seeing to an old man in one of the other beds. 'Ah, you,' she said. 'I'm glad you've come.'

'Where's Sebastian Pieters?'

'Don't worry, dear. He isn't dead. We discharged him the day before yesterday.' The sister led Adelais to a room full of cabinets and sinks. 'He left this behind. Perhaps you could take it to him if you see him.' She was holding Sebastian's copy of *The Yellow Dog*. 'You will be seeing him, won't you?'

—— Eight ——

It rained for the rest of the week, not with the same conviction, but enough that Adelais did not feel like going out on the handcycle. She did not continue with her uncle's challenge, even though the Devil's House was nearer than the hospital. She went to school, sat through the lessons, came home again, and stayed in her room, or up in the attic. *The Yellow Dog* sat on her bedside table, but she did not read on. She didn't care about Concarneau's mysteries now that Sebastian was not there to share them. She knew she should take the book back to him, but Zuid was even further than the hospital. Someone would have to go with her, and Adelais did not want to ask. Her mother always seemed preoccupied or brisk, as if to ward off any questions about the night she returned from Brussels. Nothing had been said about it, and by the look of things, nothing was going to be. There was a silence in the house that was new.

On Saturday morning the clouds lifted, and a bright sun returned. Adelais was alone in the kitchen, colouring in a map of Africa, when she heard the ring of a bicycle bell coming from the street outside. She was not supposed to open the door to strangers while her parents were out. So when the ringing did not stop, she went to the front door and peered out through the letter box. The letter box was halfway up the door and all she could see at first was a pair of bicycle wheels doing a slow turn over the cobbles.

The bell rang again.

'What do you want?'

There was a squeak of brakes. The wheels turned and came towards her. Adelais glimpsed turned-up trousers and the hem of a cable-knit sweater. Then she was looking at a familiar pair of chestnut-brown eyes.

'Why don't you have a telephone?' Sebastian said.

Adelais blinked. 'We're getting one.'

'Good. Because I hate writing letters. It's a bore.'

'I know.'

Sebastian nodded, as if satisfied to have got something off his chest. 'Are you—'

'Have you come for your book?'

'My book?'

'*The Yellow Dog.*'

Sebastian frowned. 'I thought I left it at the hospital.'

'You did.'

'Well, no. I came to—'

'You've got your bicycle back.'

Sebastian looked down. 'No, I haven't. This is an old one, my father's.'

Adelais threw back the bolts and opened the door. Sebastian had been restored to normal. The cast had been removed from his leg, there was colour in his cheeks, and apart from the white scar on his forehead there was no way of telling he had been in a serious accident. 'Are you finished with your crutches?'

'I've still got them for emergencies.'

'And they let you go cycling?'

'I'm supposed to build up my strength, the doctors said so. I'm cycling to Laarne today. That's eight kilometres.'

Adelais felt a faint stab of jealousy. She knew there was an old castle near Laarne. People said they used to burn witches there, but she had never been. No bus or tram would take her that far outside the city. 'I'll get your book,' she said.

'I was thinking you could come with me. There's a place I'd like you to see. It's a bit of a secret, as a matter of fact.'

'Eight kilometres altogether, or eight kilometres there and back?' Adelais said. 'Because that would be sixteen kilometres.'

Sebastian wheeled the bicycle around so that she could see all of it. It was black and, unlike the Gitane, equipped with both a basket at the front, and a pannier at the back. There was food in the basket and the pannier had a folded blanket strapped across the top. 'You can sit here.'

Adelais's parents wouldn't be back for hours.

'It's the castle, isn't it? That's what you want to show me.'

Sebastian shook his head and smiled.

The streets were narrow all the way to the Scheldt. After that, their route followed the river as it meandered towards the south, stark brick terraces and warehouses giving way to fields and farms, with alders and willows crowding the spaces in between. Most of the way, the river was hidden behind a swathe of long grass, but Adelais could feel its presence in the wide horizons and the cool, gusting breeze. She was holding on to the end of the walking stick, which she had hooked over the handlebars of the bicycle. Her left hand was on Sebastian's shoulder.

The road became a track. Sebastian pedalled harder, swooping and veering between the puddles. Adelais let her head roll back, so that she could feel the sun on her face.

'Where are we going?'

'It's a secret, I told you.'

Without warning, Sebastian steered the bicycle through a flooded pothole. Adelais shrieked, though the water had hardly touched her. It felt good to shriek and, apart from Sebastian, there was nobody around to hear her.

Near a village called Destelbergen they left the river and wound their way east, past coppery hedgerows and waterlogged meadows that steamed in the sun. Sebastian stopped to point out the grey turrets of Laarne Castle, but instead of heading towards them, he pedalled on until the hedgerows gave way to an old brick wall. The wall went on for a hundred metres and stopped at a pair of iron gates. Thick tendrils of ivy had wrapped themselves around the bars, so that it was hard to see beyond them. Adelais glimpsed a carpet of sodden leaves and a curving avenue of trees.

'Is this the place? Who lives here?'

'Let's see.'

'How do we get in?'

The gate had been secured with a padlock and chain. Sebastian pedalled on a few metres, to where a poplar had seeded itself into the bank. The wall behind it was bowed and misshapen. The upper rows of bricks had completely fallen away. On the other side of the road, horses were grazing.

Sebastian climbed to the top of the wall. 'Come on.'

'I can't get up there.'

'Give me your stick.'

'It's too high.' Adelais could imagine what her mother would say, the horror and disbelief that she should even think of it.

'Use that foothold, where the gap is.'

'Then what? I could fall.'

'You won't fall. I'll have your hand.'

Adelais considered the hand in question, and the boy attached to it. If she were halfway up the wall and lost her footing, she doubted he would have the strength to hang on to her. He would have to let go or be pulled down on top of her.

'It's all right,' she said. 'I'll stay here.'

'Put your left foot in that gap, where the brick's fallen out. Lift yourself and grab my hand. We can haul you up the rest of the way together.'

Adelais shook her head. 'I'm not strong enough.'

'Yes, you are. I know you are.'

'How?'

Sebastian reached down further. His hand was just above the top of her head. 'If you're strong enough to drag me out of a river, you're strong enough for this. You're the strongest girl I know, and the bravest.'

Adelais looked into his face. He was not smiling. He was waiting. He gave her a reassuring nod. She *had* been brave at least once, under the Sint-Joris Bridge, and nothing so very bad had happened. It was easier being brave when you had Fate on your side.

She handed Sebastian the stick, took a faltering step back and launched herself up the wall.

The house had once been white, but dirt and algae now discoloured the stucco, which had crumbled away in places to reveal the brickwork underneath. Most of the tall windows were boarded up. The rest were shuttered from the inside. For all that, it seemed to Adelais like a palace. Two sets of steps led up to a wide gravel terrace, bordered with a stone balustrade. There were plaster escutcheons over the windows and a balcony above the front door. The first floor was topped by a pediment, decorated with a coat of arms.

Sebastian led the way around the terrace which had been colonised by weeds and several oak saplings. 'No one's lived here for years. The Wehrmacht used it in the war.'

'Who owns it?'

'The Counts of Ribaucourt did originally. One of the countesses got fed up living in that gloomy old castle, and had this built instead. It's supposed to be a hunting lodge, but I don't think there was much hunting. Mostly parties.'

'What about now?'

'It belongs to the city council. But they've no use for it. Too far out for a school or a hospital.'

The house backed onto a wide lawn, flanked with trees. At the centre of an ornamental pond stood the statue of a huntress holding a broken bow. The water in the pool was black and smelled of ooze. Adelais tried to picture the place as it would have been in the countess's day: light blazing from the windows, carriages in the driveway, gardens sculpted and flowering.

They had stopped at the side of the building. A small window was set low in the wall, shedding light into a basement. Sebastian pulled at the boarding. It came away in his hands. 'You have to see inside.'

'What if someone catches us?'

Sebastian got the window open with a practised nudge of his fist. 'I told you: nobody comes here, except me.'

Inside the house it was cold and dark. The smell of damp was everywhere: in the bare, filthy kitchens, in the entrance hall, with its Greek columns and marble floor, on the grand staircase that was wide enough for three people, arm-in-arm. They went in silence, the crunch of grit beneath their feet.

At the top of the stairs, a huge stain discoloured the plaster. Adelais recognised the speckled pattern of mould.

'There's a hole in the roof,' Sebastian said. He was whispering, even though they were alone. 'I put some buckets underneath, but it's not enough.'

Opposite the top of the stairs was a set of double doors, their brass handles shaped like a pair of swans. Sebastian threw them open. 'The ballroom. You have to see it.'

He stepped back to let her pass. Sunshine was streaming in through tall French windows, softened by the dirt on the glass. The beams struck a huge chandelier, suspended above the middle of the floor, and were split into hundreds of rainbow-coloured threads. The room was bigger than Adelais had imagined. Plaster reliefs, white on pale blue, decorated the walls.

'So they were here, the parties.'

'The countess was famous for them.'

Adelais made her way to the windows. Even with the stagnant pond, the view across the grounds was stately. 'It's a shame. They shouldn't let it all fall down.'

'They will though, unless someone buys it.'

'Someone rich.'

'That's right.'

Adelais turned. Sebastian wanted to tell her something, but wasn't sure if he should. 'What? *Is* someone going to buy it?'

Sebastian looked at the floor. 'You'll laugh.'

'Only if you say something funny.'

'I thought . . . I thought I'd buy it. When I'm older. When I'm an architect. It can't cost all *that* much. Look at the state of it. And I'd get investors to back me.'

'What are investors?'

'They put money in at the start, and then take it out again later, only more.'

'How's there more?' Adelais was fairly sure having parties and mending roofs meant spending money, not making it.

'There'll be more because it'll be a hotel, a country-house hotel. There'll be nothing else like it in all of East Flanders. I'm going to call it the Astrid, after the countess. That was her name: Astrid Christyn.'

'What does your father think?'

Mr Pieters was a businessman. He had to know about these things.

'I haven't exactly told him.' Sebastian set about closing the shutters. 'I did ask him if the place would make a good hotel, in principle. He said no, it wouldn't. A hotel has to be in the middle of a city or by the seaside. If it's neither, nobody comes to stay.'

'I'd come to stay,' Adelais said.

'Would you? I'd see you get the best room, with the best view.'

'Can I have breakfast in bed?'

'Of course, with champagne.'

'And a boiled egg?'

'Any kind of egg you like.'

'Not too runny. I don't like them runny.'

'I'll inform the chef.'

'Good. That's settled then.'

Sebastian rubbed a patch of dirt off the window with his fist. 'We'll make it happen one day, shall we? You and me?'

'All right,' Adelais said.

Sebastian looked at her and laughed, as if talk of a hotel had all been a joke.

Adelais frowned. 'You said I'd laugh, but now you're laughing.'

Sebastian fell silent. 'I'm sorry. I wanted to be the first to laugh, just in case. I haven't told anyone about this. I'm afraid they'll think . . .'

'You've got a screw loose?'

Sebastian nodded.

'Well, I think that about you already,' Adelais said. 'So it couldn't make any difference.'

They made their way back down the stairs. Adelais knew now why Sebastian had brought her to the house: because he knew she would listen to his plan. It was a dream that mattered to him, however unrealistic it might seem. She felt a glow of pride, knowing that he trusted her, and her alone, with something precious. No one had ever done that before. Perhaps, she thought, it was another of those privileges that came with saving someone's life.

When they were done inside, they took a tour of the grounds, following paths that had all but vanished under moss and dead leaves. In several places trees had blown down and been left where they fell. Birds took flight from the branches as they approached. Under the shade of a towering beech tree, a pair of children's swings hung from a sturdy wooden frame.

'Who put these here?'

'I don't know, but they're still all right. Get on.'

The seats were warped and slippery, but solid, and the ropes were thicker than her thumb. Gingerly, Adelais sat down, leaving her stick on the ground.

'I'll give you a push.'

'No, thank you. I'm fine.'

Adelais's mother had never encouraged the use of swings. 'If you slip off, I hate to think what would happen,' she would say whenever they went near a playground. Adelais had watched the other children swinging, but never once had she seen anyone fall.

Sebastian took hold of the seat and pulled it back until it was under his chin.

'What are you—'

He let go. Adelais swung forward, then back again, gripping the ropes so hard it hurt.

'Stop! No, I can't—'

Sebastian gave her a hard push, and another. She was going higher and higher, her heart in her mouth. At the top of every swing there was a delicious moment of weightlessness. She wanted more.

Sebastian got on the swing beside her, kicking his legs out to gain greater height, tucking them under as he rocked back. Adelais copied him, daring herself to go as high as he did, then higher. Without saying anything, they settled into a rhythm, one going forward as the other went back. Perfection was passing each other at the lowest point, dead centre, and saying 'hello' or 'good morning', like two casual acquaintances passing each other on a ride through the park.

Aux Quatre Vents

—— Nine ——

Brussels, May 1953

Liesbeth Verlinden had been at the Leopold Hotel, cleaning and making beds, for the last six months. There had been talk of compensation after her husband had been killed at the Federal Engraving Bureau, but the talk had come to nothing. Had he met his end inside the main building it might have been different, but the authorities had determined that Pauwel Verlinden was guilty of contributory negligence, having entered the burning warehouse in contravention of bureau policy. His employers were not therefore liable. The fact that his death might not have been an accident did not make any difference. Verlinden's widow received nothing. An officer of the gendarmerie who had been investigating the death had advised her to hire a lawyer, but Mrs Verlinden had no money for lawyers. Her savings had been just enough to cover the funeral and one month's rent at their apartment on the Rue des Fabriques. She gave birth to her second child, Nikolaas, at a hostel run by the Sisters of Charity of Jesus and Mary.

The Leopold had seen better days. Once grander than its rivals in the Quartier des Quais, its wealthiest customers had drifted away to more modern establishments, equipped with basement swimming pools and en suite bathrooms as standard. The owners of the Leopold had been forced to cut their prices, filling its forty-eight rooms with commercial travellers and the occasional tourist, customers for whom cracked enamel and tasselled curtains were not intolerable. The main problem, as far as the staff were concerned, was that the tips were not as generous as they had been. The cleaning staff, in particular, noticed how the ten-franc notes, left on pillows or bedside tables by departing guests, had become five-franc notes, or even coins. Sometimes there was no money at all. Nor was the management in any mood to make up the difference. As Monsieur Poncelet, the general manager, never tired of repeating, with so many Belgians out of work, anyone with a job should consider themselves lucky.

Cleaning at the Leopold always started with the common areas – the lobby, dining room, stairs and corridors – which had to be swept, mopped and polished well before the guests got up, the work of three hours. At half past nine, it was time to start on the rooms. The decor might be faded and unmistakably pre-war, but Monsieur Poncelet insisted that standards in all other respects should be of the highest order. The beds were stripped, fresh linen supplied every day and fitted with martial precision around the mattresses, bolsters and pillows. A maid who had once decided that the sheets only needed a little straightening had been sacked on the spot. Whether there was a change of guest or not, the floors had to be swept, the surfaces dusted, the windows and mirrors polished. The bathrooms were to be spotless, with fresh towels, soaps and colognes arranged exactly as prescribed. The work was supposed to be complete by one o'clock, at which time the tips were collected and handed over to Monsieur Poncelet for safe keeping. After the kitchens and staff quarters had been cleaned, and after Monsieur Poncelet had completed his inspections, the money was shared out.

On a Thursday, one year and three months after her husband's death, Liesbeth Verlinden was making the beds on the top floor, when a bellboy called Thomas stuck his head round the door. She had been making slower progress than usual that morning, thanks to a fingernail that had split while tucking sheets under one of the heavy mattresses. The pain was intense and the wound threatened to leave blood on the linen.

'I'm almost done. Give me two minutes.' She was sure Thomas had come to deliver a reprimand from Monsieur Poncelet, or worse: a summons.

'There's a telephone call for you downstairs.'

'For me?'

'A Mrs de Bruyn. It sounded urgent.'

Mrs de Bruyn looked after the Verlinden children when Liesbeth Verlinden was at work. She did not own a telephone, which could only mean she had made the call from the telephone box at the far end of the street.

'What did she say?'

'Something about your daughter.'

'Emeline? What's happened?'

Thomas shrugged.

Liesbeth left the bed half made and hurried down the corridor towards the lifts.

'I wouldn't,' Thomas called after her, as she reached for the call button.

The main elevators were exclusively for the use of guests. Staff, Monsieur Poncelet excepted, were supposed to use the back stairs or the small service elevator that hardly ever worked. If nobody had been sacked on account of this rule, it was only because nobody had dared to break it.

Liesbeth could hear the machinery in motion. The sound was getting louder. It was probably a guest, on the way to their room – or Monsieur Poncelet, starting his inspections on the top floor.

She couldn't risk her job. Liesbeth took the eight flights of steps to the ground floor. The telephone was one of two behind the reception desk. The receiver lay on its side. Liesbeth snatched it up, ignoring a disapproving glance from Roland, the elderly concierge, who was going through the post.

'Mrs de Bruyn?'

The line was dead.

'I have to go.'

Roland looked at the clock above his head. 'So soon?'

'It's an emergency: my daughter. Please explain to Monsieur Poncelet.'

'I'll try.'

Without looking up from the letters, Roland held out his hand. It took a moment for Liesbeth to realise that she was supposed to give him the tips she had found. There wasn't time to argue. She reached into her apron and took out a handful of notes and coins. She didn't know if Roland planned to keep the money, or see that it was shared out among the other cleaning staff later that day. She only knew that she wouldn't be seeing a single centime of it.

The attacks had begun around the time they moved from the hostel to a pair of attic rooms on the Rue des Palais. Liesbeth had been woken one night by the sound of Emeline's wheezing. She found the child balled up in a corner of the bed, panic-stricken and flailing as she struggled for breath. The first attacks had only lasted a few minutes, but over the following weeks, they had become longer and more frequent. Liesbeth worried that Emeline had caught an infection in her chest. The rooms were cold and they'd been forced to stuff paper around the window frames to keep out the draughts. But there were no signs of a fever and only occasional fits of coughing. Liesbeth wondered if the death of her husband was responsible. Emeline had seemed to take the news well at the time, if only because, at three years old, she had been too young to understand what death was. But maybe the loss had gnawed away at her from the inside, weakening her system, like a bad conscience.

'She's asthmatic,' Dr de Witte had declared on their first visit. He said there was no treatment and advised against violent exercise.

Mrs de Bruyn's sister had recommended an infusion of butterbur and ginger, but it did not seem to do any good, even when Emeline didn't spit it up. The attacks had gone on getting worse. Liesbeth hated leaving for work in the mornings. She was better than anyone else at keeping Emeline calm, helping her fight the panic that made breathing even harder. As she ran for the tram stop on the Chaussée d'Anvers, she felt certain it was another attack that had sent Mrs de Bruyn scurrying to the telephone. What else could it be but the sight of the little girl slowly suffocating in front of her?

Mrs de Bruyn lived in a basement apartment three doors down on the Rue des Palais, within sight of the elevated rail lines that ran north to Antwerp. A bicycle was resting against the railings outside. The door to the basement was ajar. She could hear Nikolaas crying on the other side.

She found Emeline sitting upright on the edge of Mrs de Bruyn's armchair. A nurse was kneeling on the floor in front of her. Emeline looked deathly pale. Her eyes were bloodshot and she was trembling.

'Remember now, Emeline,' the nurse said, 'pursed lips. Like you're blowing me a kiss. Nice and slow.'

Breathing exercises. Dr de Witte had given them a pamphlet on the subject. Liesbeth took her daughter's hands and did the exercises with her: deep breaths in through the nose, long breaths out through pursed lips. In a couple of minutes, the wheezing stopped. Emeline slumped into her mother's arms. It had been a bad attack, but there had been worse.

Mrs de Bruyn came in from the kitchen, carrying Nikolaas. Some of her grey hair had come loose and hung about her face. 'I sent for the doctor. I didn't know what else to do. You should've seen her.'

She had called Dr de Witte, but Dr de Witte had not come. A nurse had been dispatched instead. Was that because the last bill had not been paid?

The nurse got to her feet. She was a neat, handsome woman of about thirty. Liesbeth noticed that she was still wearing her coat. 'It's the air, if you ask me. Filthier than ever these days, especially around here, with the trains. Not good for a child with weak lungs, not good at all.'

No one had ever suggested that Emeline had weak lungs. She had always been a healthy, active child. But then, that was before.

The nurse made out her bill and, after a moment's hesitation, left it on the table. On her wedding finger there was a gold ring. Liesbeth wondered if she had children of her own.

'I'd think about moving to the country, if I were you,' the nurse said. 'Clean air. Good for the bronchioles. She'd be fine there, after a while.'

Liesbeth Verlinden nodded. 'The country. We must think about that,' she said, trying to sound like it was a practical suggestion, and one that was perfectly well within her reach.

—— Ten ——

They called it a seminar, as if the officers of the gendarmerie were a bunch of students studying philosophy at university, but that did not mean attendance was voluntary. 'Centralised Command Structure – Demarcation and Reporting' was scheduled for nine o'clock, but with two minutes to go, Sub-Lieutenant Toussaint found Major de Smet on the telephone. As soon as he hung up, he began putting on his hat and coat.

'Have you forgotten, sir? The seminar?'

De Smet unlocked the top drawer of his desk and took out a magnifying glass. He owned several, but this one was special: instead of one lens, there were three, sandwiched together. The arrangement eliminated all distortion, even at the edges. Manufactured by the Carl Zeiss company, it had been liberated from a counterfeiter currently serving a thirteen-year sentence at the Maison d'Arrêt de Saint-Gilles. De Smet kept it in a suede pouch, and always polished it after use with two practised swirls of the lens cloth. Toussaint had never yet dared to touch it.

'I haven't forgotten.' De Smet tucked the magnifying glass, pouch and all, inside his coat and pulled on his gloves.

'I was under the impression we were all . . . Didn't Colonel Bedois say—'

'Don't let me stop you, Sub-Lieutenant. If you feel a lecture on . . . what was it?'

'Demarcation and reporting.'

'If you feel that's a good use of your time, go ahead.' De Smet was already at the door. It was a while since Toussaint had seen him in such a hurry. 'On the other hand, if you feel like being useful – now, or at some point in the future – I suggest you come with me.'

★

65

Number 15 Rue de la Chancellerie was a monumental six-storey building in the heart of the city. With bars on its windows and two floors of classical stonework, it was too ornate for a prison, but too austere for a palace. A brass panel to the left of the doors read: *Banque Bruxelles Lambert*.

'What are we doing here?'

A doorman stood by to let them pass, giving de Smet a nod of recognition, although whether to the uniform or the man Toussaint could not tell.

'Answering a summons from Monsieur Declercq.'

'Declercq?' Toussaint's words echoed in the marble-clad lobby. He lowered his voice. 'Who's Monsieur Declercq?'

'A man worth knowing.'

Another bank employee, a young man in a crisp pinstripe suit and shiny shoes, was waiting for them at the reception desk. 'Major de Smet? The *chef des dépôts* is waiting for you downstairs.'

He set off along a corridor towards the back of the building. A flight of stone steps led them down to another corridor, as wide and bare as the first, but lit with electric light. A third corridor ended in a metal grille with a door set into the middle. An armed guard on the other side let them through. The space beyond was wider, with rooms going off left and right, and at the far end, the studded steel doors of the main vault. Toussaint wondered how much money was behind it, how much treasure: millions of francs' worth probably, perhaps hundreds of millions. He wondered what it looked like, that kind of wealth.

A room to one side was furnished with filing cabinets, two large desks and some upright chairs. The young man showed them in and left, closing the door behind him. Toussaint heard keys jangling outside.

Monsieur Declercq was a tall, slender man, with old-fashioned wire spectacles and a beaky nose. He wore a waistcoat with a fob watch, and the cut of his suit, like the rest of him, made no visible concession to the twentieth century. Perhaps, Toussaint thought, he had spent the last fifty years in the bowels of the Banque Bruxelles Lambert and was oblivious to the modern world.

Declercq greeted them in French. De Smet replied in kind. 'So what do you have for us, monsieur?'

Declercq put on a pair of white cotton gloves. He handed another pair to de Smet, and a third to Sub-Lieutenant Toussaint. On a desk, under the light of a powerful lamp, lay a leather document wallet. Declercq opened it and stepped back. There, between two sheets of clear acetate, lay a single 500-franc note.

De Smet sat down at the desk. The front of the note bore an image of the bearded Leopold II, etched – appropriately, Toussaint thought, given the horrors he had inflicted on the Congo – in the colour of dried blood. De Smet drew the light closer. After a few moments, he removed the note from the acetate and laid it down again, reaching into his coat for the magnifying glass. Silence fell, punctuated only by the ticking of an old pendulum clock on the wall, as he began a detailed examination. Declercq stood waiting, his hands folded in front of him, like a pall-bearer at a funeral. Toussaint found his stillness unnerving.

In the Brussels gendarmerie they told stories about Salvator de Smet, his record and his methods. Sub-Lieutenant Toussaint hadn't been in the department a month when he began to hear them. It was said de Smet could spot a counterfeit note with his eyes closed, literally. He could tell a fake from the smell, from differences in the composition of the ink, or the chemical treatment of the paper. Genuine notes and forged ones made different sounds to de Smet's ear when they were folded or crumpled up. It was said de Smet could pick out the forged bills from a stack, merely by running his fingertips over the edge, that he could detect differences in the way the fake notes had been cut, the response of different types of paper to the blade. More than that, he could assign each forgery to the individual who had created it, as readily as an art dealer could attribute a Rembrandt or a Chagall. They might as well have been signed.

Toussaint was sceptical. From what he had seen so far, such extraordinary talents weren't necessary. Forged currency was usually crude. A moment's examination in daylight was enough to spot it. The colours were wrong, the printing was sometimes crooked, most often the shading was achieved not by thousands of tiny points of ink, the fruit of meticulous etching on steel plates, but with a wash, as in a watercolour. Such fakes were not designed to fool a bank teller, let alone an expert. They were for passing in bars, at racetracks and fairgrounds, under cover of darkness.

There were other stories about de Smet, less credible and more lurid. Toussaint heard them in fragments, in snatches of overheard conversation and chance remarks: de Smet had spent the war down a mine in Germany, rather than being sent home like most Flemish prisoners of war; his mother had been a burlesque dancer; his father had died in the Central Prison in Leuven, while awaiting trial for bigamy. It was even implied – nobody would say it outright – that de Smet had drowned a man in Antwerp, some hoodlum who wouldn't talk. Toussaint did not know what to believe. Most of the time, his boss seemed too quiet, too ordinary to have that kind of past. The clean-shaven face, the short hair, the small mouth and hard, humourless gaze brought to mind the greyest of bureaucrats, or a schoolteacher who had long since lost interest in teaching.

Finally de Smet spoke: 'Where was this found?'

'Tournai. Two days ago.'

'Tournai? That's Bastide's branch, isn't it?'

'Correct,' Declercq said.

De Smet sighed. For some reason, it wasn't what he wanted to hear. 'How many?'

'Six that we know of.'

De Smet turned the note over. Leopold II gave way to a painting by Peter Paul Rubens: *Four Studies of a Moor's Head*. De Smet leaned closer, poring over the image with the magnifying glass. Toussaint had never seen him so completely absorbed. There was an intensity – was it an appetite? – that was rare, even for him.

De Smet put the magnifying glass down. That was when it happened: he picked up the 500-franc note and held it to his nose, inhaling deeply, his eyes closing. 'Esparto,' he said. 'French.'

Declercq nodded. 'Indeed.'

Toussaint knew about esparto: it was a type of grass that grew in North Africa and Spain. At mills in Italy, Germany and France it was mixed with wood pulp to make a unique grade of paper – paper used to make banknotes by the National Bank of Belgium, among others. It seemed at least one of the stories about de Smet was true.

'The intaglio work is exceptional,' de Smet said.

'I'd go further.'

'Further?'

'I'd say it's original, in a sense.'

Toussaint laughed. 'Original? What does that mean?'

Declercq looked at him over the top of his spectacles. 'It means, *Sub*-Lieutenant, that the intaglio plates were not copied from existing banknotes, which would usually be the case.' Declercq turned back to Major de Smet. 'I don't believe this level of precision and depth could have been achieved by that means. A banknote of this type is a three-dimensional object. The cross-hatching, the several layers of shading, these can only be rendered with this degree of accuracy by using the original films, or the original plates.'

'All of which are guarded,' Toussaint said, 'and all of which are accounted for.'

'One would certainly hope so,' Declercq said.

De Smet held the note up to the light. 'The watermark's faint. Post manufacture, I'd say. Is that how Bastide spotted it?'

'That and the letterpress,' Declercq said. 'The typeface is imperfect. It's most evident in the 3s and the letter T.'

De Smet looked at the note again. 'I didn't see that.'

'A commercially available typeface, not bespoke.'

'No other flaws?'

'Not at normal magnification.'

'You'll be checking the stacks?'

'As fast as we can, of course. It'll take time.'

De Smet replaced the acetate and closed the folder. 'Perhaps, in the circumstances, it would be best to keep word of this . . . contained, as far as possible.'

'Not my decision, Major, but it will be my recommendation, if it's yours.'

De Smet got his feet. 'It is.'

He took off the gloves and placed them on the desk, his movements deliberate and measured. It took effort to maintain the surface of calm, Toussaint could tell. He put his own gloves next to de Smet's. Obviously, he wasn't going to need them.

'Thank you, Monsieur Declercq,' de Smet said. He tucked the document wallet under his arm. 'Please keep me informed.'

They got as far as the lobby when the silence became unbearable.

'He was wrong about original plates, wasn't he? I mean, they're kept in a vault.'

'Then he must be,' de Smet said.

'So why the secrecy? If there are forgeries in circulation, isn't it better to tell everyone?'

'Not yet.'

The doorman gave them another nod. Outside, it was starting to rain.

'It's standard procedure. If we want people to be on the lookout—'

'This isn't a standard case.'

De Smet handed over the document wallet and unlocked the car. Toussaint climbed in beside him. By the light of the windscreen, the 500-franc note looked like any other. Toussaint wasn't sure he would even have noticed the faintness of the watermark, if he hadn't already been told about it. While de Smet was reversing into the main road, he gave the paper a furtive sniff. There was no doubt: it smelled like money, except that – it was hard to explain – holding it, touching it, gave him a thrill that real money never had. Somehow, the craft that turned paper into gold was more magical, more mysterious, when it was practised illicitly.

'I still don't understand.'

'If the flaws become known, they might be corrected. The letterpress work at any rate. In which case . . .'

'They'd be almost impossible to detect.' Toussaint saw it now, the scale of the crisis de Smet wanted to avoid. Undetectable forgeries could be circulated on a large scale. Bank vaults could fill up with them before anyone realised. 'But so far, there have only been six notes, in one bank branch. Doesn't that suggest a very small operation?'

De Smet overtook a truck on the Rue Ravenstein. The driver of an oncoming Mercedes sounded his horn.

'Perhaps. But Bastide's vigilant. Exceptionally so. What he spots others would miss. My guess is, they already have.'

'What do we do?'

'Every forged note is the start of a trail. We locate as many as possible, we follow them to their source. We hope our adversary gets careless.'

'And if he doesn't?'

'Citizens need to believe their money has value, that their wealth, great or small, is real. They need to believe the state when it says so.' De Smet put on his wipers. For a moment, the road ahead was obscured by a smear of water and soot. 'If for any reason they stop believing, if the spell is broken, then what? What's left?'

A week passed without further sightings of Declercq's counterfeits, then another week and another. De Smet examined and re-examined the banknotes in question, but if he learned anything new he didn't share it. Sub-Lieutenant Toussaint began to wonder if Declercq's notes were really counterfeits at all, and not the result of some sloppy workmanship at the Bank of Belgium. When it came to printing currency, it was not unheard of for mistakes to creep in. The resulting notes were often worth far more to collectors than their face value – which struck Toussaint as a slippery kind of irony. But then, when he had all but forgotten about the whole business, another pair of notes turned up at a bank branch in Brussels, just a few blocks from Federal Police Headquarters. It was followed soon afterwards by sightings in Leuven, Axel, Charleroi and Oudenaarde. Most of the reports came from bank personnel. But here and there other recipients had raised the alarm: a typesetter in Liège, a print dealer in Balen, a customs official in Ostend.

In the room at the top of the building de Smet put up a large map of the country. The location of each report was plotted with a black enamelled push pin.

'How does this help us, sir?' Toussaint asked, because de Smet had never done anything like it before.

De Smet did not look up from the report he was reading. 'There are approximately seventy thousand retail outlets in Belgium, Sub-Lieutenant. With limited resources, we can either stake out a few and hope to be extremely lucky, or look for a pattern in the data.'

'But I don't see any pattern here,' Toussaint said.

'That's because the forger doesn't want you to. He's counting on you being impatient, inexperienced and lazy.' De Smet turned over a page of the report. 'You might at least consider disappointing him.'

— Eleven —

Ghent, 1956

In Flanders they had raised the school leaving age by one year. Adelais had to wait until she was fifteen before she could start looking for a job. The factories in the north of the city, in Heilig-Kerst and the Canal Zone, were the obvious places to start, but few of them had vacancies, and the ones that did would not take her. They did not say so outright, but she was left in no doubt that her leg had a lot to do with it, even though, as far as she could see, the machines on the shop floor were all operated by hand.

'Your friend Sebastian, isn't his father a big wheel at one of those places?' her father said. 'A word from him and you'd be in.'

But Adelais did not want to work at Textile des Flandres. She did not want to ask Sebastian for the favour, and she did not want his father to be her boss. Instead, she went every day to the Wouters's house and looked through the Situations Vacant in the *Staatscourant van Gent*. Unfortunately, almost all the vacant situations were for men with trade skills – electricians and carpenters – or women with shorthand and typing, neither of which Adelais knew. When a new canning factory opened forty minutes away in Wondelgem, she joined the queue of people applying to work there, but by the time she reached the front all the posts had been filled.

Adelais needed to bring in some money. There was still no refrigerator and no telephone. More importantly, the customers coming and going from her father's workshop were fewer now than ever. Some days, her father did not even bother to open up. He got out of bed at ten and shuffled about the place unshaven, demanding to know why there was never anything to eat in this damned house, or why it was impossible to get a decent cup of coffee. Adelais soon discovered that her mother had been cutting back on luxuries, coffee being one. When Uncle Cornelis sent her two hundred francs for her birthday – inside a card that said *Don't tell Mama!* – she had gone out and bought a bag of beans. Helping her father get a proper breakfast in the mornings made her feel a little less useless.

After a couple of months, Adelais had a stroke of luck. Mrs van Hove, who ran the greengrocer's shop at the corner of Azaleastraat, had a cousin who owned a bar in the Canal Zone. Aux Quatre Vents was an establishment where the customers paid for their drinks in advance and were issued with a chit that they handed to the barman. It was a way of making sure nobody ended up drinking for free. The proprietor, a Mrs Claes, wanted someone to man the till, someone who didn't have to be paid very much, but was good with numbers. Adelais, who had always been among the top three in maths at school, fitted the bill perfectly. Even her leg was not a problem. Once installed on the high stool in her booth by the door, she was expected to stay there until the time came to go home.

Adelais was afraid her mother would not approve of her working in a bar, but the only word of objection came from her father: 'Why do all the bars in this town give themselves French names? What's wrong with Flemish names?' He accepted the money she handed over though, all the same.

Aux Quatre Vents occupied a windy corner lot a hundred metres from the Handelsdok. Through the steamy windows, Adelais could see the tops of the steel cranes towering over the quays. For much of the time the place was almost empty, but then a freighter would come down the canal from Antwerp or Holland and it would fill up. In an attempt to attract more local business, Mrs Claes had decided that the decor should have an American theme. Behind the bar was a picture of a blonde film star sitting on a hay bale. On the opposite wall hung a Coca-Cola sign, shaped like a bottle cap, and a display of sports pennants blazoned with the names of places and teams – Cincinnati Red Legs, St Louis Browns, Brooklyn Dodgers – that Adelais could only imagine. The biggest investment had been an old American jukebox. The bar was roomy enough for a small dance floor, which mostly went unused, except on Fridays and Saturdays, when customers came in with their dates. Adelais liked to watch the dancers, even though most of them were not very proficient, frowning with concentration, sweat on their brows – unless they were drunk. The drunk ones laughed like hyenas as they stumbled about.

Now and again, an old Walloon called Albert, who worked on the docks, would come in and play his accordion. Most of the melodies were sad, but Mrs Claes, who was a big, muscular woman not much given to sentiment, said his music reminded her of when she worked in Paris before the war. Sometimes, if there weren't too many customers around, she would sing along in French. It was not clear what kind of work Mrs Claes had done in Paris. Adelais had asked a couple of times, but nobody had given her an answer.

As well as alcohol and coffee, Aux Quatre Vents offered sandwiches and snacks, which were prepared during the course of the day and placed in a glass cabinet at the end of the bar. Sometimes Adelais was allowed to take home what had not been sold. She was glad of the food. Her mother was often out in the evenings, doing charitable works with the Beguines of St Elizabeth. It meant the midweek stews were a thing of the past. Adelais got enough to eat at the bar, but she worried about her father. He had grown thinner in recent years, his face drawn, his clothes loose about him. Often he gave off a sour smell like the crates of empty wine bottles that were stacked around the back of the bar.

Adelais usually took a tram home after work, but sometimes Sebastian would turn up outside the bar on his father's bicycle. During the summer they would ride up and down the riverfronts or mingle with the tourists on the Graslei. At other times, they would go straight back to

Sint-Amandsberg. Adelais never knew when he was going to show up. She had told him not to telephone the bar unless it was an emergency, because Mrs Claes did not like her abandoning her post at the cash register. In any case, Sebastian never seemed to know when he would be free. He had been given a place at the university and had to work hard. He did not mind, he said, because Ghent was the best place in the country to study architecture.

'One day, I'll have lots of rich clients and that's where I'll find my investors for the Astrid.' He would set out his plans as they slalomed along the cobbled streets. 'I just hope it hasn't been sold by then. That would be a disaster.'

Now and again, he would show up with sketches under his arm. They depicted one aspect or another of the hotel – the lobby, the ballroom, the dining room, the gardens – fully refurbished and operational. Sebastian, it turned out, was a skilled draftsman. He would ask Adelais for her opinion on the decor in the bedrooms or the layout of the flower beds and then, a week or two later, would return with a new sketch reflecting her choices. With each new picture, their grand project seemed a little less fantastical. Visions of the Astrid came to Adelais when she slept. She saw wedding parties dancing in the ballroom, and men in dinner jackets drinking cocktails. She saw herself sitting on the swings in the garden, watching hot-air balloons fill the sky. It was painful to wake up from those dreams each morning and find herself back in her bed on Schoolstraat, with another day in front of her like all the others.

Sometimes Adelais dreamed she was the countess Astrid herself, drifting across the ballroom in a long red dress, like Grace Kelly's in *Dial M for Murder*, which she had seen at the Plaza on Veldstraat – except that the countess had been an excellent dancer, by all accounts, and Adelais could not dance at all.

—— Twelve ——

One evening in October, Adelais came home to find a porcelain figure of the Virgin Mary standing on the kitchen dresser. The Virgin wore robes of pale blue and white, and a halo of stars supported by a wire frame. When plugged into a socket the stars lit up. Her mother was kneeling on the floor in front of it. Tears were running down her face.

Adelais did not know what to say. The mother of Christ had wept at the foot of the cross. *Stabat mater dolorosa* – they sang about it in the Sint-Jacobskerk at Easter. Maybe her mother's tears were merely a reflection of the Virgin Mary's, brought on by contemplation of that pitiful scene. Maybe they were nothing very much to worry about.

When she saw her daughter, Odilie de Wolf got off her knees and dried her eyes on her sleeve. 'I'm sorry,' she said, and turned off the electric halo. She picked up the kitchen knife and got on with chopping vegetables by the sink.

The porcelain figure was the first thing her mother had bought for herself in years. It was as if she wasn't worthy to possess anything nice, anything she didn't need to keep body and soul together. But there were plenty of people less kind and hard-working than she was, Adelais thought, and they did not have any compunction about treating themselves.

As she lay in bed that night, it came to her that her mother did not feel valued. That was what lay behind the appearance of the Virgin Mary in their kitchen, and the long hours doing charitable work with the Beguines of St Elizabeth. But it was not too late to change that. Her mother had a birthday coming up. Adelais decided to buy her something special, something she would never buy for herself. Thanks to her job in the bar, she had some money at last. The only question was what to buy.

She found the answer the very next day at the Friday market. There, hanging in a second-hand clothes stall, was a camel wool overcoat. Mrs Wouters had one just like it. It was narrow at the waist, with a flared skirt, and black fur on the cuffs and lapels. Mrs Wouters looked beautiful in it – Adelais had heard her mother say so. How could she not want one for herself? The only difference was that this coat had a large brown stain on the lining, and one of the big grey buttons was missing.

The stallholder wanted more for the coat than Adelais could muster, but she promised to keep it back until the following Friday. Adelais still had some of the money Uncle Cornelis had given her, and with the help of another pay packet, and a fifty-franc loan from Hendryck the barman, she amassed the sum she needed with a few francs left over. After buying the coat and stowing it at the bar, she devoted her free time to the search for replacement buttons. She had tried every shop in the city before she returned, aching but triumphant, with five buttons covered in grey felt. They were not exactly the right size or shade, but close enough that nobody would suspect a switch. Mrs Claes helped her tackle the stain, using a mixture of white vinegar and lemon juice, and when that proved ineffective, lent Adelais the money for dry-cleaning. Forty-eight hours before her mother's birthday, the coat was pressed, spotless and wrapped in tissue paper, just as if it were new.

It was a Saturday. Adelais had arranged everything with her father. He had promised to buy flowers and chocolates, and they were going to make a birthday breakfast as soon as Adelais's mother appeared. Adelais got dressed early, fetched the coat from its hiding place under her bed and took it downstairs. The sun was shining outside and a welcoming smell of fresh coffee rose up to meet her.

She found her father sitting at the table, a vase of flowers in front of him, staring into space. He had combed his hair and shaved, and put on a clean shirt.

'Is Mama up yet?' Adelais whispered.

The coffee pot on the range was boiling over. She grabbed a tea towel and removed it from the heat.

'Mama's gone out.'

'Out where?'

Her father looked at his hands. 'Sister Angelika's ill again. Mama's gone to help out.'

Adelais had never laid eyes on Sister Angelika. She imagined she was old and sickly, but all she knew for sure was that when her mother went to visit her, she usually stayed away for hours. Sometimes Adelais couldn't help hoping Sister Angelika would either get better or die.

'Where is Sister Angelika? Where does she live?'

'Molenberg, I think.'

Molenberg was less than three kilometres away.

'When will she be back?'

Her father got up. 'She didn't say.'

He gave the Virgin Mary an unfriendly glance and left the kitchen without waiting for coffee. Adelais heard the door of his workshop close behind him. She wished she had come down earlier. That way her mother would have seen the coat. She could have worn it to Sister Angelika's. Even if she did have to spend most of her birthday visiting a sick person, at least she would have known about the present and what it meant.

Adelais put the coat on the table and waited for her mother to come back. She read an old newspaper and a magazine that she found in the kitchen drawer. In the magazine she read that an American film star called Cyd Charisse had insured her legs for $5 million, and that she had suffered from polio as a child. A photograph showed her dancing with Fred Astaire in a dress slit open to the waist.

Adelais's mother did not return that morning, or that afternoon. It was not until the following morning that Adelais finally found her.

'The coat's beautiful,' she said. 'But you can't spend this kind of money on me.'

From her tone, it was obvious she meant it. Adelais found herself explaining that the coat was second-hand, that it hadn't cost very much at all, that you could still make out the stain on the lining, that it was only the buttons that were new: things that were all true, but which she had never planned to say.

Her mother smiled, the way people smiled when they were being brave, and said that in that case, it was a wonderful gift. All the same, when Adelais thought about it, what she mostly felt was guilty, as if the coat had been stolen.

'Where was your mother going yesterday?' Saskia said.

They were sitting in the gloom of the Eldorado on Veldstraat, watching *High Society* with subtitles.

'She was visiting a sick nun in Molenberg.'

They were at the interval. An usherette in a gold-braided jacket was selling cigarettes and sweets from a tray. Being a Sunday matinee – tickets half-price – business was slow.

Saskia offered Adelais one of the sugared almonds she had brought from home. 'I meant yesterday morning.'

'So did I. Why, did you see her?'

Saskia sucked noisily on her sweet. 'Yes, but not in Molenberg. I saw her at the railway station. We were meeting my aunt.'

'The Sint-Pieters railway station?'

It would have been a sensible question, if there had been more than one station in the city.

'I saw her get on a train to Brussels. Going that way, at any rate.'

'It must have been someone else.'

Saskia shook her head. 'No. She was dressed like she was going to Mass. I said to my papa, "Look, there's Mrs de Wolf," and he said, "So it is." We would have said hello, but, well . . .'

'Well what?'

Saskia shrugged. 'She didn't look like she wanted to talk.'

The lights went down again. On the screen, Grace Kelly was walking around a swimming pool in a white swimsuit. Her legs looked as nice as Cyd Charisse's, if not as long.

'What time was this?' Adelais whispered.

'About nine o'clock. I would have stayed in bed, but it was sunny and I was bored.'

Adelais tried to focus on the film. Her mother must have changed her mind about visiting Sister Angelika and gone to Brussels instead, or maybe her father had misheard. This was the most likely explanation, Adelais decided, even if, as far as she knew, no one in the family had set foot in the Belgian capital for years – not since her father's job with the clock collector, and the night he had returned to Sint-Amandsberg, filthy and starved like a prisoner.

Saskia plucked another sugared almond from the bag. 'Wasn't it your mother's birthday yesterday?'

Adelais's sweet was still in her hand. 'Yes.'

'And she didn't tell you she was going to Brussels?'

'I didn't see her.'

'When did she get back then?'

'Late.'

'See? If she'd only gone to Molenberg, she'd have been back in no time.'

Adelais found she did not want to talk about her mother any more, but Saskia had a way of getting ahead of her that made it seem pointless to call a halt.

Saskia settled deeper into her seat. 'It's suspicious, isn't it?' She was holding a sugared almond between her incisors, so that she sounded like she was drunk.

'What do you mean?'

Someone behind them went *shush*.

Saskia bit the almond and shrugged. 'You said things were funny at home.'

Music struck up. Now Grace Kelly was on a yacht, singing about love with Bing Crosby. Adelais pretended to listen. A minute ago, there had simply been a miscommunication. Now her mother's birthday absence was connected to everything that frightened her, everything in the past few years that had changed for the worse.

After a couple of minutes, Saskia leaned over. 'You know what we have to do?'

'What?'

'Follow her. Next time she says she's going to Molenberg to visit this nun.'

'I can't do that.'

'It's the only way. You want to know, don't you?'

'It's not . . . She'd see me.'

Saskia nodded. 'That's why I'd have to do it. She wouldn't recognise me, not if I wore sunglasses and a hat. It might be fun.'

The person behind them went *shush* again, louder. This time Adelais was glad. Saskia was being ridiculous, letting her imagination run away with her. Maybe in her family it would be all right to sneak around after her mother or father, but in any normal family, in Adelais's family, it would have been wrong, simply wrong. If they hadn't been in the cinema, she would have said so. Instead she let the matter drop, hoping that by the time the credits rolled they would both have forgotten about it.

'How's Sister Angelika? Is she going to get better?'

Adelais had not been meaning to ask the question. It had slipped out, like a little fish darting between her fingers. She had been lying in bed with the covers up to her chin waiting to go to sleep, when her mother had looked in to say goodnight. It had clouded over in the afternoon and now raindrops were tapping against the windowsill.

'Sister Angelika?'

Adelais nodded. 'You went to see her yesterday.'

'How did you—'

'Papa told me.'

Adelais's mother reached down and stroked her hair. Adelais could not see her face. 'She's fine. You don't have to worry about her.'

'Is she in hospital?'

'No. She's at home.'

Adelais shut her eyes. 'In Molenberg?'

'Yes,' her mother said. 'In Molenberg.'

With that, she kissed Adelais on the forehead and closed the door.

—— Thirteen ——

On the Saturday after St Nicolas, Adelais climbed onto the Netley and cycled as fast as she could to the telephone box at the corner of School-straat. There hadn't been time to dress properly or brush her hair. She had thrown a coat across her shoulders and gone out as she was, her feet bare inside her shoes. It was not yet nine o'clock and the streets were quiet. She crossed the main road without stopping.

The telephone box was occupied. A woman in a striped cloche hat was holding the receiver in one hand and a small dog in the other. She saw Adelais, took in the stick and the pyjamas, and hastily finished her call.

It was Saskia who answered.

'Mama's gone out,' Adelais was still out of breath. 'She was dressed like she does for Mass.'

Saskia yawned. 'Is it Sunday?'

'It's *Saturday*. She had on the coat and everything.'

'The coat?'

'The new one.'

'I thought it wasn't new.'

'As good as.'

'Where was she going then?'

'That's the point. To Sister Angelika again. She left ten minutes ago.'

There was a long pause on the line. Adelais heard the sound of pages turning – the pages of a magazine. As far as Saskia was concerned, the subject of Mrs de Wolf and her secret excursions was no longer exciting, it seemed.

'What are you going to do?' she said finally.

Adelais began to shiver. The woman with the dog and the cloche hat had hurried away because she thought Adelais was mad. Standing outside a telephone box in a coat and pyjamas was the kind of thing mad people did. 'Nothing, I just thought . . . It doesn't matter. Goodbye.'

'You don't want me to follow her? There's a train leaving for Brussels in . . . twenty-two minutes. I could make that.'

Saskia had been flicking through the pages of the railway timetable.

'Yes. Yes, go.'

'All right. If you're sure you want me to.'

Adelais wasn't sure. She didn't like being kept in the dark. It was like being shut out, and that was what she hated most of all.

'I just don't want you to blame me,' Saskia said.

'Blame you?'

'It's something Mariëtte said.'

Mariëtte was the second oldest Helsen daughter. Saskia said she was the prettiest and had always enjoyed the widest choice of suitors. It hadn't stopped her choosing badly.

'What did she say?'

'She said once you know something, you can't go back to not knowing it. And sometimes you wish you could.'

Aux Quatre Vents was quiet for a Saturday. Hendryck the barman put on the jukebox and hummed along as he swept the floor, the limp sliver of a cigarette between his lips.

Once, years ago, someone had told Hendryck that he resembled Clark Gable. He had been trying to capitalise ever since. He had slicked hair and a Rhett Butler moustache – and his own teeth, which put him one up against the original. On the other hand, he was wiry and cave-chested, and had a bald spot that was almost as big as a monk's. Still, he had old-fashioned manners which he had learned working in the hotel trade, and a knowing smile for every female customer who walked in the place. When he talked to Adelais, which was not often, it was usually about some film they had seen. Hendryck loved films – all kinds of films, even the French ones they showed at the Savoy, and the German comedies that played at the Ideal.

'Did you know, Grace Kelly's films are banned in Monaco?' He had already seen *High Society* twice. 'Her Prince Charming's just banned the lot of them.'

'Prince Rainier? Why?' Adelais was behind the cash desk, doodling and watching the clock. She had promised to call Saskia at six. Every time she thought about it, the knot in her stomach tightened.

'I suppose he doesn't like the idea of the common folk gawping at his wife. Either that or her leading men make him jealous.' Hendryck chuckled. 'I mean, Cary Grant? Next to him, Rainier looks like a bus conductor.'

The record changed on the jukebox. A string orchestra struck up a sentimental tune. As he swept, Hendryck's footsteps began marking out a rhythmical pattern across the dance floor.

'What do people do in Monaco?' Adelais said.

'Show off and lose money at the casino. Monaco only exists because rich Frenchmen want somewhere to hide their money. It's one huge piggy bank.'

Adelais had a piggy bank, except that hers was a China tabby cat, lying on its side with one eye open. At that precise moment, it contained thirteen francs and seven cents.

'Who are they hiding it from?'

'Tax collectors, of course.'

Adelais had read about tax collectors in the Bible. In St Luke, they were the ones who beat their breasts and were humble before God. 'What about rich Belgians? Where do they hide their money?'

'Don't you know? That's what Luxembourg's for.'

'Have you been there?'

Hendryck laughed. 'Of course. I have millions in a numbered account. I only work here for fun.'

Adelais watched him dance on with his broom. In spite of his wiry frame and his bald patch, he looked quite graceful. 'Is that a waltz?' she said.

'Can't you tell? Three beats to the bar.'

'I don't know about dances.'

'You should learn. Dancing takes you to another world, if you do it right.'

Adelais looked at the clock again. It was dark outside, but there were still twenty minutes to go. 'I'd like that,' she said.

Hendryck stopped sweeping for a moment and fixed her with a stare. 'If you can put one foot in front of another, *mon amie*, you can learn to dance.'

Adelais called from the telephone box at the end of the Kongostraat. The light inside the box was dim. Adelais could hardly make out the numbers on the dial. The phone at the other end rang and rang, but nobody answered.

The wind blew litter along the deserted pavement. People said the docks were a bad area, but Adelais had never seen any trouble, except drunks getting into arguments with each other. All the same, she felt vulnerable, lit up inside a glass box, like a mannequin in a department-store window. She began to wish she had called from the bar.

She waited five minutes and tried again. Still nobody answered. She did not want to go home yet. She wanted to know what had happened. The thought of going to bed without hearing from Saskia was unbearable.

She decided to wait a little longer at the bar. Her hand was on the handle of the folding doors, when she heard rapid footsteps approaching. Someone rapped on the glass, making her jump.

'There you are. I thought it was you.' It was Saskia, wearing a beret and a raincoat, her face a pale yellow oval.

'You scared me,' Adelais said.

Saskia cupped her ear against the glass. 'What?'

Adelais grabbed her stick and went outside. Saskia had never come down to the bar before. Adelais didn't remember telling her where it was.

'There's such a thing as a telephone book,' Saskia said. 'Anyway, I didn't want Pa listening in. I don't think he'd be very happy with me.'

'Your pa isn't in. Nobody's answering.'

Saskia shrugged. 'They must have gone out to dinner. Talking of which, I'm starving.'

They found a kiosk on the Hageland Quay. Saskia bought blood sausage and chips and sat with Adelais under the plane trees, eating out of a paper bag. Adelais wasn't hungry.

'I didn't recognise her at first. That coat's very smart, and she's definitely lost weight. It was the hat that gave her away. She needs a new one.'

'Where was she?'

'On the platform. It was busy. I wouldn't have seen her if she hadn't walked right past me.'

'She took a train?'

'Same one as last time.' It was cold enough that Saskia's breath made clouds in the air. Adelais's brace felt cold and heavy around her leg. 'There were stops at Aalst and some other place. I was terrified she was going to get off before Brussels. I got off the train both times, just to be sure I hadn't missed her.'

'She didn't see you?'

'I stayed one carriage back the whole way. It was harder once we got off the train. Not so much cover.'

Adelais began to feel sick. It had to be the smell of the blood sausage, or the stale fat in the fryer, mingling with the rank water of the canal. *Once you know, you can't go back to not knowing.*

'Where did she go?'

'She bought flowers in the station, a winter bouquet. You know the ones: red leaves and berries, and little white flowers. I suppose it was a gift for someone.' Saskia held a chip upright between finger and thumb, as if unsure if it was suitable for eating. 'I was a bit surprised at that.'

'Aren't you supposed to buy flowers for sick people?'

'Yes.' Saskia bit the chip in half. 'I was more expecting her to be on the receiving end.' She held out the bag.

'No, thank you.'

'Still, my pa says anything goes these days. You can buy flowers for a man and it's not odd any more. They do it in Spain, and Russia. Of course, it's always all right when it's a woman.'

Maybe the best thing was to call a halt now. Just get up and go. Having Saskia follow her mother, it was shameful.

'What happened after that?'

'She got on a tram, a number 63, towards Schaerbeek. There was a queue, so I was able to keep back a bit. I hadn't a clue where I was going, but I took notes.' Saskia took a small notebook from her pocket and flipped through the pages. 'We went thirteen stops and got off at the Boulevard Léopold III.'

'She still didn't see you?'

Saskia chewed on a mouthful of sausage. 'I walked off in the opposite direction as soon as I reached the pavement.' She tapped the beret on her head. 'Then I changed hats and doubled back. Trouble was, I left it too long.'

'You lost her?' Adelais found she was relieved. She could carry on not knowing. She preferred it that way.

'I saw her in the distance, turning into . . .' Saskia consulted her note-book. '. . . the Rue Henri Chomé. But when I got there, I couldn't see her. It's quite a long street, at least three hundred metres. There's a square halfway along, opposite a cemetery, and a cafe at the far end. I thought she might be in the cafe, but . . .' She shrugged.

'There wasn't a hospital? Anything like that?'

Saskia looked at her. She was still chewing. 'No hospital. Whoever your ma went to see, they must live somewhere on the Rue Henri Chomé. I went round the block a few times, just in case, but I didn't see her again. I could have waited back at the tram stop, but there didn't seem much point. Anyway, I'd have frozen to death.'

It was clear what Saskia thought: that Adelais's mother was having an affair. It explained everything – the absences, her father's drinking, even the guilt. But it couldn't be true. Adelais shook her head. It just couldn't. Her mother and father still loved each other, even if—

'You should check her address book,' Saskia said. 'See if she knows anyone on Rue Henri Chomé. That's the next step.'

Adelais got to her feet. Now she was supposed to rifle through her mother's things, as if she wasn't already disgusted enough with herself. Edwina de Groote had been right all along: *You're always looking. Like a little spy.* 'Thank you, Saskia. Thank you very much. I should go home now.'

'Why? It isn't late.'

'I owe you for the train ticket and the trams.'

Saskia shook her head. 'Forget it. Like I said, it was fun.'

One day in December, Adelais came home to find a priest in the front room. She was used to seeing Father de Winter at Mass, but he hadn't been to the house since her first communion at the Church of Sint-Amandus. Some clergymen made a lot of house calls, but he was not one of them. He had always struck Adelais as a remote figure: tall, with neat grey hair and spectacles with heavy black frames. When he wasn't presiding over Mass or hearing confession, he sat on important church councils and committees. According to Adelais's mother, his work had even taken him to Rome.

He got to his feet when Adelais came in. He was holding a small black prayer book and gave off a smell somewhere between camphor and cologne. Her mother sat opposite him. He asked if Adelais was well, and if she was enjoying her job at the bar.

'Of course, it's just temporary,' her mother said, before Adelais could answer. 'Until something more suitable comes along.'

Father de Winter raised his hand. '*Fac et aliquid operis, ut semper te Diabolus inveniat occupatum.*' Adelais did not know Latin, and neither did her mother. Father de Winter smiled graciously. For a clergyman, he had good teeth. 'St Jerome. "Engage in some occupation, so that the Devil may always find you busy." '

Adelais's mother was ashamed of her for working in a bar. Adelais hadn't realised until then. She made her excuses and left.

'What did Father de Winter want?' she asked later, as she was eating supper in the kitchen.

'The good shepherd cares for his flock, Ada,' her mother said. 'He goes where he's needed.'

'Why's he needed here?'

It was a provocative question, sin being inseparable from life, but Adelais's mother didn't seem to hear her.

Father de Winter came back several times over the festive season, always bringing his black prayer book and his odd ecclesiastical smell. His visits seemed to help Adelais's mother, at least for a while. She was calmer afterwards – not happy, but quietly resolute, as if steeled for some purpose Adelais could only guess at. If she paid any more visits to Sister Angelika, Adelais did not hear about them, and she wondered if Father de Winter was responsible for that too. One way or another, he seemed to know more about her mother than she did, thanks no doubt to her weekly confessions. Adelais considered this unfair. What was the point of having a child, if you couldn't tell them the truth?

One day, as he was leaving, she ambushed Father de Winter at the corner of the alley. 'Is something wrong with her?' she asked him.

Father de Winter stopped. He took a moment to finish pulling on his grey wool scarf. 'Now what makes you say that?'

'She's troubled, I can tell. It's like she's upset with herself.'

'Upset? Why would that be?'

'I don't know. I want to know. Why does she have to pray all the time? Is she ashamed of something?'

Father de Winter pulled the scarf tight. It was neat, like a cravat.

'Shame arises from sin, my child, and sin is in all of us. It is a milestone on the road to confession, to restitution and to redemption. Did they teach you nothing in that heathen school of yours?'

He was evading her question, as she knew he would.

'She didn't used to be like this. She used to be . . . normal.'

Father de Winter's hands were in his pockets. The breath whistled faintly in his nostrils. 'Conscience is a flame, a guiding light to salvation. Sometimes in life it burns faintly, at other times bright. The important thing is that we see it for the gift it is.'

Adelais refused to think of her mother's state of mind as a gift, or a flame. It struck her as more of a sickness. She avoided Father de Winter after that. His homilies, his Christian cheerfulness, his overbearing calm, they worked at the bonds of her family, as if intent on prising it apart. At the sight of him she would ride out on her cycle even when, like most nights, she had nowhere to go.

—— Fourteen ——

Sebastian whooped and looked back over his shoulder. 'They said it might snow, but not like this!'

They were riding his father's bicycle past the towering mass of the Sint-Niklaaskerk. What had begun as a few flecks of sleet had blossomed into a feathery cascade that dimmed the street lights and cushioned the cobblestones beneath the wheels. Adelais buried her face into the folds of her scarf. Sebastian hadn't said where they were going, but from the purposeful way he was cycling, she felt sure he had a destination in mind.

As they approached the Korenmarkt, a smell like burnt sugar reached her nostrils. Stalls had been set up in the middle of the square, selling hot snacks, alcohol and festive gifts. The stepped gables of the old houses on either side had been decorated with strings of electric lights, their outlines bright against the night sky. Choral music played over a tannoy.

'They had these fairs in the old days,' Sebastian said. 'Now they're bringing them back. My father says it's for the tourists, but who cares?'

One of the stallholders was roasting chestnuts on a griddle, sending clouds of smoke into the air. Sebastian bought them a portion each, served in a cone of newspaper. They ate them as they wandered through the crowd, Adelais feeding Sebastian because he needed one hand to wheel the bicycle. Children were already scooping up the snow in their mittens and hurling it at each other. Nobody told them off or got angry, not even the grown-ups who got caught in the crossfire. Some of them seemed to have downed a few drinks already.

One stall was selling painted wooden nutcrackers, carved to look like soldiers, kings and queens. One of the queens had a fur hat, fur-topped boots and white fur stole. 'Look, there's the countess!' Sebastian said, and it took Adelais all her powers of persuasion to stop him buying it.

The choral music on the tannoy was interrupted by a voice announcing something Adelais could not make out. There came a muffled ripple of applause. A folk tune struck up in the middle of the square. Adelais heard an accordion, a violin, a guitar and a drum, then male voices hurled into the night. An old couple began to dance. Others clapped along. When the folk song was over the band switched to a waltz. Sebastian had eaten all his chestnuts and stood watching with his free hand in his pocket. 'My mother's making me join a dancing class? Can you believe it?'

'You?'

'She says a man who can't dance is a social liability. She can be very old-fashioned.'

Adelais wondered if not being able to dance made her a social liability too. 'It doesn't sound so bad.'

Sebastian squinted at the falling snow. 'I told her, I've got more important things on my plate, but she insists.'

It came to Adelais that his nonchalance was affected. The subject was difficult for him, awkward – because of her leg, of course. Dancing was something they could never share.

He shrugged. 'My Saturday mornings are going to be ruined.'

They often went out to the old hunting lodge on Saturday mornings, but Adelais could never stay long because she worked at the bar in the afternoon.

'How many lessons are you having?'

'I've a class every Saturday from January until May. Then there's a dance at the opera house – if you can image anything stuffier – and it's finally over.'

Adelais had never set foot inside the opera house, but she had seen pictures in magazines. The men were always dressed in tailcoats, and the ladies in gowns that went down to the floor. The ballroom was decorated like a French king's palace. The ballroom at the hunting lodge would have looked austere beside it, even if it hadn't been damp and mouldy.

'I suppose you'll have to dress up,' she said.

Sebastian groaned. 'I hadn't thought of that. Damn, I expect I will.'

'I can hardly imagine it: you in a starched collar and bow tie . . .'

Sebastian shook his head as he turned the bicycle around. 'The last time I wore one of those, it gave me a rash. Absolute agony.'

The following Monday, Hendryck the barman was sweeping up. It was late and the only customer left in the place was an old regular asleep in the corner with his mouth open. Hendryck looked up from his broom to find Adelais standing in front of him.

'What are you still doing here? Don't you have a home to go to?'

He had an inch of cigarette stuck to his bottom lip, but it had gone out. Adelais held out her hand. In her palm was a stack of coins.

'What's this for?'

'The jukebox.'

'Help yourself.'

Adelais shook her head. 'I want you to show me.'

'How to work the jukebox?'

'How to dance.' She held her hand up higher. He saw her swallow. 'Can you teach me?'

Hendryck laughed. 'I don't think so.'

'You said anyone could learn.'

'I meant it.'

'So? Why not—'

'I only dance with ladies. And you're just a . . .'

Whatever Hendryck had been about to say, he thought better of it. He turned away and carried on sweeping, working his way around the empty tables until he reached the front door, where he expelled the dirt with three emphatic shoves of the broom. As if he had time to give dancing lessons, he thought. As if people wouldn't think he was getting desperate in his old age, picking up the girl from behind the till, a girl half his age who walked with a stick. The very idea was demeaning.

He was halfway back to the bar when his favourite waltz came on the jukebox. Adelais's face was pressed against the glass, her face lit up by the golden glow of the machine.

She wasn't half his age: she wasn't even a *third* his age. And all she ever did was watch people. She watched them drink and eat and talk, and hardly said a word herself. Most especially, she watched them when they danced.

'You can turn that off,' he said finally.

'Why should I?'

Hendryck sighed and took the cigarette end from his mouth. 'Because we're going to have to start slower than that, with counting. One, two, three.' She looked up at him. 'Just the basics. And you do exactly what I tell you, all right?'

—— Fifteen ——

They began with the waltz. Right foot back, left foot to the side, right foot close. After that, the reverse: left foot forward, right foot to the side, left foot close. The trick was to make a curve with the first step, and make the other steps as small as possible. That way you could keep up with the beat, no matter how fast it was, while making a gentle circle round the floor.

Adelais did not need her stick because Hendryck supported her. He held her right hand with a firm grip, while her left hand rested on his shoulder. Even when she stumbled, which was often to begin with, she was never in danger of falling.

'Stop looking at your feet,' he said.

'I'm afraid I'll tread on yours.'

'Listen to your partner.'

'I am listening.'

'Not that way.' Hendryck held her tighter. He smelled of stale tobacco and pomade. 'Two bodies, one dance. Sense what's coming, feel it. That's why I'm holding you. So you can feel the motion before it even starts. Close your eyes. It'll help.'

'I'll bump into something.'

Hendryck gave her a little shake. 'No, you won't. I won't let you.'

After half an hour, he put the music on. By that time, Adelais's hip was hurting and the brace was biting into her thigh, but she did not say anything. She tried to focus on the music and the motion of her partner's body so that gradually her own steps and his and the music seemed to braid into one. Hendryck was right: it was easier when she shut her eyes, when she trusted him not to steer her into a table or a chair. It was strange: in his arms she felt lighter.

Mrs Claes came out of the back and stood watching, hands on hips. 'What are you up to, Hendryck, you old goat?'

'Instruction.'

'You're too old for her. *Far* too old.'

'Frankly, my dear, I don't give a—'

Adelais lost the beat and tripped over Hendryck's feet. 'I asked him to teach me, Mrs Claes.'

'Did you now? What for?'

Adelais did not have to answer because someone in the kitchen dropped a plate. Hendryck let go of her and went back behind the bar. The lesson was over. He had shown her the basics and that was that. Adelais got her coat and stick.

'Thank you,' she said, as she headed for the door. She wished there was someone else she could ask for lessons, because she was definitely going to need more.

Hendryck was pulling a beer. 'Come early tomorrow, all right? We've got a lot to cover.'

The next day Hendryck put on a different waltz. It was half an hour before opening time.

'You're bending your legs,' he said, after they had taken a few steps.

Adelais had adjusted the joints on her brace so that it hurt less when she went backwards. 'Is that wrong?'

Hendryck shrugged. 'No. It'll come in handy when you learn the tango. A little bounce is good.'

Adelais could not easily picture a tango, but she had a feeling it was not a dance they would be doing at the opera house. She closed her eyes again and focused on the waltz. She tried to imagine dancing with Sebastian, but the smell of tobacco and pomade made it impossible.

When they had been around the floor a few times, Hendryck went back to the jukebox. 'We can start on the foxtrot now,' he said. 'It's a staple, good for anything in common time, if it's not too fast.'

'What's common time?'

With his finger Hendryck drew a square in the air, before planting it on the button marked 'Tuxedo Junction'. It was a favourite with the customers, a band number with a languid melody and an unhurried beat. 'It's just a waltz with one extra step.'

Mrs Claes came out to watch them again. It was hard to tell if she approved. Out of the corner of her eye, Adelais saw her sigh and shake her head, but she looked more sad than angry. Maybe, Adelais thought, the dancing was another thing that reminded her of her years in Paris before the war.

Six paydays later, Adelais went to the opera house. There was only one dance scheduled for May: a charity event for the Flanders Red Cross. A double ticket cost five hundred francs. Adelais had two hundred francs, but she could borrow fifty from Hendryck again, because he knew she was good for it.

'A single ticket, please,' she said.

The woman in the box office had freshly coiffured hair, and wore a tweed jacket. 'I'm afraid not,' she said with a chuckle, as if Adelais had said something comical. 'All tickets are double tickets.'

'But I'm coming alone.'

The woman frowned. Adelais wondered how much she got paid for taking money at the opera house, as opposed to a bar. Judging from her hair and the way she was dressed, it had to be significantly more. 'This is an event for couples,' she said. 'You have to come with a partner, unless you've enrolled in a class.'

'What if you don't have a partner?'

The woman looked slightly disgusted. Then she smiled, which was somehow worse. 'Well, this is not the occasion to find one, young lady, if that's what you had in mind.'

At Saskia Helsen's school, dancing lessons had been part of the curriculum, but she had never mentioned them before.

'I wouldn't mind them,' she said, 'but we're not allowed to choose our partners and I usually get stuck with Bettina Lemmens, who's as tall as an ostrich and dances like a penguin.'

They were queueing outside the Majestic for a film about Vincent Van Gogh called *Lust for Life*. Everyone wanted to see it because the great painter had been born in Zundert only a hundred kilometres away, which, as far as the people of Ghent were concerned, made him practically a native.

Adelais explained about the Red Cross Charity Dance and the double-ticket policy. 'I can pay you back for your half, only it might take me a while.'

She knew she wasn't going to get away with leaving it there. She told Saskia about Sebastian's classes, that she wanted to surprise him at the charity dance. He had assumed that dancing was beyond her, but she was going to prove him wrong. 'I've been taking lessons at the bar. Hendryck says I'm getting the hang of it and he's very tough.'

'Well, I suppose it might be fun. Pa'll give me the cash.'

'Thank you, Saskia. I hate to ask, but I really want to go.'

Saskia smiled at Adelais and took her arm as they shuffled forward in the queue. Once she had tickets to the dance, the only issue remaining would be what to wear. Somehow, from somewhere, she was going to need a dress.

They had gone forward a few paces when Saskia said: 'You told me Sebastian was like a brother to you.'

'I know.'

'So you can't really dance with him, can you?'

'Why not?'

Saskia pulled a face. 'You don't dance with your brother. I've a brother, so I should know. It's, well . . .' She lowered her voice. 'Incestuous.'

'Incestuous? It's only dancing, Saskia.'

She looked over her shoulder. A woman with an ugly brown hat was staring at them.

'It's the thin end of the wedge. Everyone knows what dancing's really for. My pa's got a book about it. It's actually a fertility display. You dance, and after you've danced, you mate.'

Adelais was glad Saskia couldn't see her blush. 'That's not how they see it at the opera house. The woman in the box office was very clear about that.'

'I'm just sounding a word of warning. You don't want him getting the wrong idea.'

At that moment, Adelais was not sure what the wrong idea was.

They were almost inside the building. It looked like there were still some tickets for the Van Gogh film, so they wouldn't have to see Charlton Heston in *The Ten Commandments* instead, which they both agreed was a relief.

'Of course,' Saskia said, 'if Sebastian thinks of you as a sister, he probably won't want to dance with you either. The problem might not arise.'

'There isn't a problem, Saskia. You're being—'

'Isn't he coming with a partner anyway? Who's he coming with?'

'His whole class is going, together.'

'I see.' Saskia nodded to herself, and reached into her bag for her purse. 'An opportunity to play the field. He'll have his eye on someone though, by now. He's a boy, isn't he?'

Saskia did not know what she was talking about, and Adelais got through almost the whole of *Lust for Life* without thinking about Sebastian dancing with other girls, or picturing one that he might like especially – a girl sweeter and prettier than she was. The idea did not make her jealous, in any case. What could be more ridiculous than being jealous of someone who might not even exist? Besides, Sebastian would spare her a waltz or two, and maybe a foxtrot – and maybe a polka as well, if she got that far with Hendryck – and she would have made her point. She would have proved that she was not a social liability. Sebastian wasn't supposed to fall in love with her, or realise that he had been in love with her from the moment they met, because that was the kind of thing that only happened in films — films that cheered everyone up, perhaps, but had nothing to do with real life.

She told herself all this during *Lust for Life*, and again on her way home, and a few more times before she went to sleep. It was deliberate. Someone had once told her that if you thought about your feelings long enough, they would start to disappear.

The House with Nine Locks

—— Sixteen ——

Brussels, March 1957

There was something different about the call from Waregem. Major de Smet took down the information calmly, asking the same questions he always asked, but the way he sat in silence afterwards, it was obvious he had heard something significant.

'Another find, sir?' Lieutenant Toussaint said. 'How many this time?'

De Smet took a long time to reply. 'Waregem: get me the file.' He tossed a key onto the desk. Toussaint picked it up and headed for the door. 'And see if you can find me yesterday's copy of *De Standaard*, the racing page specifically.'

'The racing page?' Toussaint risked a grin. 'Are you going to place a bet, sir?'

The telephone on de Smet's desk rang, and he snatched up the receiver. For an icy moment, Toussaint wondered if he had gone too far. 'You could say that, yes.'

Toussaint took the stairs to the top floor. It was there that de Smet had set up an operations room. It was narrow and bare, big enough for a row of filing cabinets, a desk placed sideways and a solitary chair. The sound of traffic drifted up from the Rue du Marché au Charbon through a small window with one frosted pane. When he wasn't in there de Smet kept the room locked.

A big map of Belgium covered most of one wall. There were now black pushpins at 153 different locations. At each of these, at one time or another over the past four years, counterfeit 500-franc notes of the kind that had first turned up in Tournai had been spotted. Attached to each pushpin was a small paper label, bearing a reference number in de Smet's meticulous hand.

On the wall opposite were more maps of Belgium, on a smaller scale. The pushpins here were fewer in number and connected with lengths of red string. They represented attempts to establish a pattern, to reveal a methodology in the distribution of the notes: times, places, amounts – anything that could be traced to a source, anything that might indicate where their adversary might go next. So far, these attempts had been unsuccessful. With every new report de Smet dropped what he was working on – often in Toussaint's lap – and went to investigate. The result was always the same: the addition of information that told them next to nothing.

The forger had been patient and careful. His target locations, whether towns or city districts, appeared to be chosen at random. From what they could gather he arrived often, but not always, on a market day, when retail trade was brisk. He would visit somewhere between twenty and thirty shops and stalls, making purchases at each. On an average day, de Smet estimated, around thirteen thousand francs would be exchanged. Operation complete, the forger would not return to that location for at least six months.

Larger shops, oblivious to the deception, would use some of the counterfeit notes to pay wages. Smaller operations would exchange them for stock. Eventually, in the days, weeks and months that followed, the counterfeit currency would find its way into banks, where it might or might not be detected. By then it was too late to work out who had first received them, let alone get a description of the individual who had handed them over.

De Smet called it a 'retail operation': slow, labour-intensive, but highly profitable. The alternative was to sell the counterfeits wholesale to criminal gangs who knew what they were buying. In such cases, the best fake notes sold at a quarter of face value. Thousands of notes could be unloaded in a single transaction, but dealing with other criminals carried risks of its own, and the Tournai Forger seemed unwilling to take them. De Smet said it was only a matter of time: their man would go wholesale, sooner or later. He would get greedy. But four years had gone by, and so far they had done nothing but follow in his wake, recording his path to riches, like fans following their idol.

Toussaint unlocked the door and switched on the light. It was cold inside. The air smelled of stale tobacco. On the big map he found Waregem: it lay thirty kilometres south-west of Ghent. Unusually for a town of its size, there were already seven black pushpins in place.

The files in the cabinets were organised alphabetically. Waregem had a file to itself. Toussaint looked over the reports. They were nothing unusual: clusters of counterfeit notes being banked from multiple sources over periods lasting a few weeks. If anything stood out, it was that the totals were high. The information had been provided over the telephone. At no time had the bank employees concerned been interviewed.

Toussaint checked the dates on each report and it was then that he saw what de Smet must already have seen: the last report had come in just two months earlier. According to his own rules, the Tournai Forger had returned several months too soon.

'So he's jumped the gun a bit. How does that help us?'

Toussaint handed over the file, along with the newspaper. One of the gendarmes who guarded the building took *De Standaard* every morning and kept a stack of them behind the front desk.

De Smet took out the reports. 'It's helped us already. A clerk at De Spaarbank was on the lookout for the bad notes. She spotted them at once. A few more months and she'd have forgotten all about it.' He looked at Toussaint over the top of the papers. He wasn't smiling, but the lieutenant could see a predatory eagerness in his eyes.

'You think he's getting careless? It's hardly a blunder.'

'It's a lapse. There may be more.'

Toussaint had been working a smuggling case and wanted to get back to it. De Smet would have another pin in his map, a little anomaly in the timing to spice things up. If that made his day, then fine. Toussaint just hoped he wasn't going to be sent out to Waregem to write the report. He had a double date set up with a couple of typists and a comrade in the Judicial Division and didn't want to miss it. Besides, the Tournai Forger might be clever – exceptional even – but catching him wasn't personal. It wasn't going to validate his existence, or justify his position as an officer of the law.

De Smet had opened the newspaper. Toussaint had never known him to take an interest in horse racing, or any sport for that matter. As for gambling, it was the kind of thing that could tank a gendarme's career. De Smet had said it himself: an officer who gambled was an officer who could be corrupted.

Toussaint turned to go. Out of nowhere, he remembered something: there was a racetrack at Waregem. 'Did they . . . ? Were there races this week?'

De Smet did not look up. 'There were ten, on Tuesday.'

'And you think . . . ?'

De Smet got to his feet. 'Yesterday morning a customer called Eric van Aken deposited twenty thousand francs into his account at De Spaarbank.' He took his overcoat from the hook. 'Four of his notes were forgeries.'

'Four? Is he in custody?'

De Smet gave Toussaint one of the pitying looks that he had grown used to over the years, but resented nonetheless. 'Mr van Aken is a bookie, one of at least twenty bookies at the track.' He pulled on his coat. Toussaint could already see that his plans for the evening were shot. 'That's what brought our man back to Waregem when he should have stayed away: he has a soft spot for the horses.'

Most of the other bookies had already banked their takings at different branches around the region. One of them, a man called Jaspers, still had the cash in a safe at his home in Kortrijk. Another used a safe

108

deposit box in Brussels. In each case, where the cash could be traced, counterfeit notes were found. The forger's trip to the races in Waregem had been a matter of business. He had bet five hundred francs on every horse in every race – that was de Smet's conclusion – placing each bet with a different bookie. It was a great way to lose money, if you were betting with money. But the forger was betting with paper. He ended up with a winning ticket every time. One horse came in at 20/1, another at 18/1. The bets were paid for with counterfeit money, but the payouts were real. None of the bookies had seen anything unusual. None of them could give Toussaint a description. The forger had placed around sixty bets in the course of the day, but nobody could remember his face.

Two weeks later, Toussaint travelled out to the Wellington Hippodrome in Ostend, a flat racecourse two hundred metres from the sea. If de Smet was right, the occasion would prove too big a draw for the forger to resist: a full card of races, twenty-seven bookies and a big crowd to cover an escape if something went wrong. It was their best shot yet at an arrest.

Toussaint and de Smet were in plain clothes. Six gendarmes from the local station patrolled the exits. The perimeter was far from impermeable, especially on the south side, where the track gave onto a nine-hole golf course and a cemetery, but de Smet was convinced it would sink the operation if the police presence was too heavy. The forger was likely to be a regular, and if anything was different, he would notice. It meant de Smet and Toussaint were the only ones watching the bookies.

It was a sunny day with a stiff onshore breeze. Along the front, people had turned out in numbers. Some brave souls were going for a swim. Others were picnicking on the beach or around the course. There was a festive atmosphere, regular announcements from the tannoy adding to the sense of anticipation. Toussaint moved through the crowd, a Beretta heavy in his jacket pocket. Almost everyone he passed was part of a group – couples, families, what looked like a veterans' social club. Walking around on his own, he felt conspicuous.

De Smet was up in the grandstand with a pair of binoculars. It was at his insistence that the bookies had been kept in the dark. If they were told counterfeit bills might be in circulation they would start inspecting every 500-franc note that came their way, which meant holding them up to the light to reveal the watermark. 'Our man only has to see that a couple of times and he'll be gone.'

At twenty minutes past noon, the horses in the first race were led into the paddock. People were still streaming in through the gates, swelling the crowd. At the bookies, queues were forming. De Smet had abandoned the grandstand, and was heading down to the course. He didn't look like much of a racegoer to Toussaint's way of thinking, in his city overcoat and his teardrop fedora. He looked like fun was the last thing on his mind.

Toussaint's superiors said he was lucky to have ended up where he had. Major de Smet had cracked a lot of tough cases over the years. There was a lot he could learn. And Toussaint had learned a lot: the importance of thoroughness, of amassing detail even when it seemed insignificant. He had learned the value of patience and vigilance, of leaving nothing to chance. And yet, for all that, when Toussaint thought of Major de Smet, what he pictured was a spider, pale and bloodless, sitting motionless in a corner of his web, waiting for a tremor that would tell him when to strike.

Two years earlier they had gone after a company accountant called Jens van Marcke. Van Marcke had been swindling his employers, a large import-export firm in Antwerp. He had not covered his tracks very well, but de Smet had found out all there was to know about the man before he was even questioned. In particular, he had found out that van Marcke's mistress was a Yugoslav immigrant, and that she was applying for Belgian nationality. Some of the missing money had not been accounted for. De Smet had got it into his head that there had been an accomplice, someone who had turned a blind eye at the right moment, someone van

Marcke had paid off. If he didn't get a name, van Marcke's mistress would be deported to Belgrade for consorting with a known criminal. Van Marcke insisted he had been acting alone. De Smet had carried out his threat. A few weeks later, by which time the missing money had been found and the accomplice theory discredited, court officials at the Palais de Justice had gone to collect van Marcke from a holding cell at the start of his trial. They had found him dead. He had opened his wrists with a shard of mirror glass. Toussaint had been present when de Smet received the news. The major hadn't registered so much as a flicker of regret, hadn't even paused from his work. 'Is there something wrong?' he had asked, when he caught the lieutenant staring.

The fact was, when it came to de Smet, there were some lessons Toussaint didn't want to learn.

The horses in the first race were still being walked around the paddock. Toussaint watched them for a minute before sauntering off towards the bookies. A dozen of them were strung out opposite the finish line, standing on boxes, their odds chalked up on boards behind them. A French horse, Claire de Lune, was the clear favourite. Most of the bookies had her at 3/2. Toussaint play-acted at shopping around, before joining a short queue for a bookie called Appelman's. De Smet had told him to be patient, to get a good look at who was betting, who was winning, who kept coming back. They had all afternoon to find their man.

Toussaint scanned the faces all around him, trying to fix as many as possible in his mind. It was then he recognised one of the bookies from the Waregem races – the one who lived in Kortrijk and kept his cash in a safe. His name was Jaspers. He was writing a slip for a young man in a blazer. The young man took the slip and handed over a 500-franc note. Before Toussaint had time to think about the danger, Jaspers had taken the note and was holding it up to the sun, squinting at the watermark. He had been caught for three thousand francs at Waregem. He was not going to be caught again.

Toussaint hurried over. Jaspers had to be told, before he ruined everything. The young man in the blazer moved away, clutching his betting slip. An older man in a grey raincoat ambled forward, his nose buried in his race card.

'Excuse me, sir,' Toussaint said. 'Just one second.'

The man in the raincoat looked up at him, smiling absently. He had a lined face and thick dark hair, streaked with silver.

Jaspers was frowning. 'Lieutenant Toussaint? I thought it was you. What's up this time?'

Toussaint grabbed him by the sleeve and whispered in his ear: told him to forget about the watermarks, told him why in as few words as he could.

'All right, understood,' Jaspers said. 'But you're not the one losing out.'

Toussaint turned. He had drawn attention to himself. He would have to make himself scarce for a while.

The man in the grey raincoat was no longer in the queue behind him. He had been there a moment ago, all ready to bet. Now, in his place, there was an old boy with a white moustache and a shooting stick. Toussaint stood on tiptoe and checked the queues at the other bookies. People were flooding into the grandstand, taking their places for the start of the race. He glimpsed the grey raincoat. The dark-haired man was nudging people aside, a man in a little too much of a hurry. Then he was gone.

It was the forger. He had been standing within earshot when Jaspers had given the game away – standing there with his pockets full of counterfeit bills. It hit Toussaint that it was his fault: he had panicked, risked his cover too soon, risked everything.

There wasn't time to think about it. He took off towards the corner of the grandstand. A bell sounded, summoning the horses to post. The crowds were moving against him, heading for the side of the track. He looked for de Smet, caught sight of him in the distance. He had no idea that the whole scheme was blown.

The main entrance to the hippodrome was forty metres away. One of the uniformed gendarmes was there, his hands behind his back. Toussaint ran over: 'Man in a grey raincoat, dark hair. Did he come through here?'

The officer scratched his chin. 'Could have, sir. Maybe that way.' He pointed into the car park on the other side of the gates.

The cars were lined up at right angles to the road. Latecomers were still arriving, but it was quieter than around the track, the noise of the tannoy and the crowd muffled by the wind. Toussaint walked along the row of cars, peering through the windscreens. A couple were necking in the front seat of a convertible. At the end of one row, a family were piling out of a Renault Dauphine. The children were in short trousers. The mother wore sunglasses and a yellow sundress.

A cheer went up from the crowd. The race had begun. The voice on the tannoy became a stream of noise. Somewhere nearby an engine kicked into life.

The engine grew louder. Toussaint turned. A motorcycle was coming towards him from the far end of the car park. The rider was wearing a helmet, but there was no mistaking his face. Toussaint reached into his pocket for the Beretta, flipped off the safety, slid in the first round.

'Stop!'

The motorcycle surged forward. It wasn't going to stop. Toussaint took aim with two hands. The thought flashed though his mind: he had never shot a man before.

The woman in the sundress was suddenly in his line of sight, just the other side of the target. Her children were running up beside her. If he missed his man he could hit one of them.

The motorcycle made a half-swerve around him. Toussaint had one chance. He threw himself at the rider, managed to get a grip on his collar while his left hand found the handlebars. The caps of his shoes scraped across the dirt.

The machine went over. Toussaint hit the ground with a jolt, taking the impact on his hip. He opened his eyes to see that the world had tipped on its side, the asphalt on one side, the cloud-streaked sky on the other. A sharp pain lanced through his head.

He sat up. Drunkenly, the world righted itself. The motorcycle was still on its side, the engine running. Where was the rider? Somewhere behind him a woman screamed.

Toussaint looked back. The rider had picked up his pistol.

Toussaint coughed. 'You're under arrest,' he said.

The rider walked over to him, raised the Beretta and struck him hard in the face.

Toussaint was still on the ground when de Smet found him a few minutes later.

'Did you get a good look at him, at least?' he said.

Toussaint couldn't answer. His jaw felt like it was broken and his mouth was full of blood. The other gendarmes arrived and helped him to the first-aid station. Over the tannoy they were announcing the results of the first race. Claire de Lune had come in fourth.

—— Seventeen ——

Ghent, April 1957

Every year, for the past four years, Uncle Cornelis had sent Adelais two hundred francs on her birthday, tucked inside a card. This year there was no card and no money.

During most of that time, Cornelis had been abroad. He had business in Amsterdam and that was why they had seen so little of him. In fact, if it hadn't been for a couple of family funerals, a wedding and a cousin's first communion, Adelais might not have seen him at all. Still, he had always remembered her birthday, and whenever she had seen him, he had made a point of sitting down with her and asking what she had been up to. What's more, he had never been satisfied with banalities, the way most adults were. He wanted to know what she *really* thought about things, and people – teachers, neighbours, relatives. He would listen and laugh. 'You've sharp eyes, little wolf,' he would say. 'And sharp ears to go with them.'

Adelais had always liked this choice of moniker. Wolves were strong and dangerous, even little ones. And they were pack animals, which Adelais liked the sound of. She was still a child when she saw the small bronze figure of a wolf at the Friday market. She knew she had found her uncle the perfect present, and gave it to him at the first opportunity. Cornelis examined the figure from all sides, before solemnly declaring that he had never received a better gift in his life.

Six months had gone by since she had seen him last, at a christening in the church of Sint-Antonius on Forelstraat. He must have arrived late because Adelais did not notice him until the ceremony was well under way. When it was over, everyone filed out onto the pavement, the baby wailing and hiccupping, his mother struggling to wind him through several generations' worth of christening robes. Adelais found Uncle Cornelis greeting relatives with smiles and handshakes, but when it was his sister's turn she gave him no more than a nod before moving on.

Adelais hugged him and asked if he was coming back to the house.

'Not this time, little wolf.'

'But you never come any more. Why don't you come?'

Uncle Cornelis looked up and down the street. A sharp wind pulled at his hair. These days it was silver around the sides of his head. 'It's complicated. My work's been . . . demanding. I've had to travel. You'll understand about these things when you're older.'

'I understand already. I work for a living, you know. I have a job.'

'You do? What kind of job?'

'In a bar, by the docks: Aux Quatre Vents.'

'Aux Quatre Vents, that's an interesting name.' Uncle Cornelis was trying to sound positive, but it was clearly an effort. To him, she was still a little girl, too young to be serving alcohol to crewmen and dockers. 'So . . . you like this job, do you?'

'I like the pay.' Adelais shrugged. 'It's better than no pay.'

'Of course.'

'I was lucky to get anything. And it's not so bad. I sit behind a till, taking money. There's music.'

Adelais knew what her uncle was thinking: that his favourite niece deserved better. How often had he told her that she was special? As a child she had believed him, the way she once believed in Santa Claus. But she was grown up now.

'All the same, you might look around for a different occupation,' Uncle Cornelis said. 'Something more . . . rewarding perhaps?'

'I'd think about anything if it paid well,' Adelais said. 'That's the main thing, isn't it? If you've money, everything else can be fixed.'

'You've a head on your shoulders, little wolf.'

'Did you have something in mind? I'm not fussy.'

Uncle Cornelis did not answer. Instead, he offered Adelais his arm and led her towards the community hall where a party was under way. 'Tell me,' he said, 'did you ever complete that challenge I set you, on the handcycle?'

'Of course. I went further than the Devil's House. I went all over Ghent.'

Uncle Cornelis reached inside his coat. 'Then I owe you some money, don't I?'

'Never mind about that. I wasn't thinking about the challenge. I was enjoying myself.' Adelais would never forget the thrill of leaving School-straat for the first time, making her way towards the heart of the city all on her own. Reaching the Sint-Joris Bridge in time to save Sebastian was the reward for her efforts, the hidden purpose behind it all – that was how it had seemed.

'All the same, a deal's a deal.' Before Adelais could stop him, Uncle Cornelis had pressed three hundred francs into her hand. 'Honour among thieves.'

'What do you mean?' Adelais tucked the money away in her pocket. She could not deny it: three hundred francs would come in handy.

'I mean, we're cut from the same cloth, you and I.' Uncle Cornelis lowered his voice. 'Your mother might not like it, but it's true. I could tell as soon as I saw you with a baby's bottle in your mouth. When a break comes your way, you grab it with both hands, even if you don't know where it'll take you. Because that's what life's about. That's the adventure. It doesn't come to you.' He stopped and took Adelais's hands. 'Am I right?'

'Right?'

'About you, little wolf.'

'Of course. You know me better than anyone. You always have. You gave me the handcycle because you knew I'd make the most of it.'

'And you didn't disappoint me.'

Uncle Cornelis accompanied Adelais into the hall, but he did not stay long at the party. After a few minutes she saw him slip away as quietly as he had arrived. She hurried to the door in time to see him climbing into his old Citroën. He gave her a sad little wave before starting the engine and pulling away.

A few weeks after her birthday Adelais was making breakfast in the kitchen. It was a Saturday and she had gone out early to buy fresh rolls and a bag of coffee. The dance at the opera house was fast approaching and she had been trying to save money for a dress, but then Saskia had said she could have one of her older sisters' cast-offs. They weren't the latest fashions, but better quality than anything Adelais had considered, and all that would be needed was a little alteration. When the coffee was ready, she went to fetch her father from his workshop. He had to be there, because there had been no sign of him upstairs. She knocked twice and went in.

Her father was lying slumped over on his workbench, snoring. Next to an empty glass sat an earthenware bottle with the stopper off. Adelais picked up the bottle. There was half an inch of genever in the bottom. She gave it a sniff and grimaced. That was when she noticed the letter.

It was different from the bills and notices to pay that were strewn across the bench. The paper was thick and pale blue, with an embossed coat of arms in dark blue at the top. It was the official coat of arms of Belgium. Underneath, in capitals, were the words: MINISTRY OF FOREIGN AFFAIRS.

Adelais slid the letter out from under her father's elbow and read:

Dear Mrs de Wolf,

It is with deep regret that I write to inform you that our consular representative in Amsterdam, the Netherlands, has been notified by the Dutch authorities of the death of Cornelis Willem Mertens, to whom our records indicate you are next of kin.

According to our information, Mr Mertens was discovered at his place of lodging on the morning of 15 April. The cause of death has not yet been determined, but the circumstances are not regarded as suspicious.

We will contact you again in due course regarding the remains. I would be grateful if you would acknowledge receipt of this letter at your earliest convenience. In the meantime, please accept my deepest condolences.

Yours sincerely,

Gustaaf E. Audenaerde

CONSULAR SECTION

Adelais stood for a long time holding the letter. She looked at her father, passed out at his bench, an empty bottle in front of him. Her uncle may not have been a constant presence, but he had always been on her side, always watching, even from a distance. *My little wolf.* One of her earliest memories was of being carried on his shoulders along the beach at De Haan, him breaking into a run while her mother shrieked at him to be careful. She had been able to count on Uncle Cornelis and now he was gone. She hugged herself. The workshop felt cold.

Adelais's tears dripped onto the letter. Cornelis hadn't just been her uncle: he had been her mother's brother and her father's brother-in-law. She was being selfish, Adelais told herself, thinking only about what he meant to her. She wiped her nose on her sleeve and put the letter down. Her gaze fell on the date: *19 April.* The letter had been written ten days earlier. Her parents had known about Cornelis's death for at least a week.

Her mother was standing at the kitchen sink when Adelais came in. The electric lights on the Virgin Mary's halo had been turned on.

'Why didn't you tell me?'

'Tell you what?'

'About Uncle Cornelis.'

'Have you been talking to your father?'

'Papa's asleep in his workshop. I think he's been there all night.'

Adelais's mother picked up a dishcloth to dry her hands. 'You mustn't worry, Ada. He's just—'

'Why didn't you tell me?'

Adelais's mother carried on drying her hands, as if they were unusually wet. 'I was going to. I was just waiting for the right time. I know you've been busy.'

'I'm not a child any more.'

'I know. I'm sorry.' Adelais's mother put a plate of butter on the table, next to the rolls. 'You should eat something.'

Adelais sat down and watched her mother pour her a cup of coffee. 'What happened, Mama?'

'I think he'd been ill for a while, and then suddenly . . .'

'Was it a heart attack?'

'I don't think so. More like an infection. They haven't told us yet.'

'Will they bring him home?'

Adelais's mother turned back to the sink. 'He left instructions. He wanted . . . he wanted to stay in Holland. He must have liked it there, I suppose.'

'Are we going there?'

Adelais's mother shook her head. 'It all happened very quickly, the funeral, everything. Because of his illness. Special precautions. The Dutch are very strict about those things.'

Adelais sat at the table, trying to picture Uncle Cornelis's coffin being lowered into a Dutch grave. The Dutch were Protestants and she wasn't even sure they did things the same way as Catholics. All the same, it seemed wrong that nobody in the family had been there.

'I want to go,' she said. 'I want to say goodbye.'

Her mother sighed. 'The best thing you can do for him now, Adelais, is pray for his soul.'

'But I want to go. I want to say goodbye. I'll pay my own fare to Holland.'

Her mother sat down at the table. 'Ada, I know you were fond of your uncle. I know he was always buying you things.'

'That's not why—'

'But you must believe me when I tell you that he wasn't . . .' Odilie de Wolf shook her head. Her face was flushed. 'He turned his back on God a long time ago.'

Adelais looked into her cup. She hated it when her mother talked this way. She wanted to scream: *I don't care.*

'To tell you the truth,' her mother went on, 'I'm glad he hasn't been here very much these past few years, because . . .' Again, she seemed to have trouble saying what she meant.

'Because what?'

'Because he's . . . Cornelis has *always* been a bad influence. I was afraid he might lead you astray, we both were. I'm sorry, but it's true. You're like him in some ways. He often said so, and I see it sometimes: something dauntless, no fear of judgement. It worries me.'

'What are you talking about?'

'I know Cornelis did nice things for you, but trust me, he never did anything without a reason. There was always a plan behind it, a scheme. He always knew how to get under your skin.'

Adelais stood up. Her mother should have been grieving over her lost brother, but instead she was painting him like the Devil, all because he didn't go to confession and pray four times a day, all because he was *fun.* At the door, she turned. 'I thought you weren't supposed to speak ill of the dead, Mama. Maybe you should take a long hard look at yourself.'

Later that day, Adelais took the handcycle to St Bavo's Cathedral. In the recess to the right of the altar, she lit a candle and recited the prayer of St Francis. She said goodbye to her uncle Cornelis and told him she would see him in heaven, if there was one. She pictured him waiting there, holding in the palm of his hand the little bronze wolf she had given him. After she had watched the candle burn down for a while she went outside, sat under the statue in the square, and cried.

—— Eighteen ——

Sebastian had exams to prepare for, and weeks passed without any sign of him, but then one evening he came by the bar when Adelais was finishing up. Usually he arrived on his father's old bicycle, but he was on foot this time, and he was carrying a satchel full of books over his shoulder. He looked pale and there were dark circles under his eyes. 'I was in the library all day,' he said. 'I had to take a break.'

Adelais was glad he didn't look too good, because she herself was grubby after a day at work, and it was a while since she had washed her hair. These days she wore it in a ponytail, rather than a topknot, but she had more ambitious plans for the dance.

'I can wait if you're busy,' Sebastian said.

It wasn't yet time to go, but Mrs Claes gave Adelais a smile and nodded towards the door. She had a soft spot for Sebastian, just like the nurses at the hospital, which Adelais took as a good sign. Mrs Claes had been around. She knew a bad egg when she saw one.

They made their way down Kongostraat and over the river. In a small, dusty park they bought a bag of peanuts from a vendor and sat on a bench, shelling the peanuts and watching children play in the playground opposite. It was still light and not cold.

'How's your mother doing?'

Sebastian didn't normally ask after her family. That was the kind of small talk they avoided, but then Adelais remembered Uncle Cornelis. Perhaps a death in the family was simply too momentous to be ignored.

'She's fine. The same, anyway.'

'That's good.'

'And yours?'

'Oh, fine. My father too.'

'Good.'

'Well, things have been difficult, actually, at work. Not just for his firm. The whole industry. But it's cyclical, he says. They'll pull through.'

'Cyclical? What does that mean?'

Sebastian made a circle with his finger. 'Goes round and round. The business cycle, you know.'

Adelais nodded. She had heard the business cycle mentioned on the wireless, and some talk of factories closing, but she hadn't paid much attention. 'Your father won't lose his job, will he?'

'Oh no, no. *He* won't.'

Adelais felt like lightening the mood. 'How are the dancing lessons going?'

Sebastian groaned and threw a peanut shell across the path. 'Disastrous.'

'What? Why?'

'I'm not very good. Dangerous, actually. I've trodden on *so many toes*.' Adelais started laughing. 'No, I mean badly. And I almost gave one girl a shiner with my elbow. None of them want to dance with me now. You can see the fear in their eyes.'

Adelais almost said *I'll dance with you*, but stopped herself. She didn't want to spoil the surprise when she turned up at the opera house. Besides, she had already decided that if you wanted someone to think differently about you, it would help if you looked different, not the way she did now.

'You mustn't give up,' she said. 'Promise me.'

Sebastian studied her for a few moments, without answering. Then he popped a peanut into his mouth and looked away.

Adelais recognised the smell as soon as she opened the front door. Father de Winter was in the hallway, pulling on his overcoat. 'Here she is now,' he said.

Her mother was standing behind him. Her eyes were bloodshot, as if she had been crying, but it was the time of year for hay fever and most years it affected her.

Adelais said good evening.

'I've told your mother, if there's anything you want to talk about, you should get in touch.' Father de Winter put a hand on her shoulder. 'I've left my number. There's always someone there who'll take a message.'

Adelais nodded, even though she had no idea what he was talking about. She wondered if her mother had been complaining about her. Since the argument about Uncle Cornelis, she had been quieter and more withdrawn than ever. Adelais didn't like it.

'There's something I need to tell you,' her mother said, as soon as Father de Winter had left. 'Come into the kitchen.'

Adelais had eaten too many peanuts and her stomach felt bloated. She was not in the mood for a sermon.

'Sit down, Ada.'

Adelais sat down.

'I got word today that they're cutting jobs at the factory – the women's jobs mostly. Mine included. The company's been losing money, they say.'

'Does that mean—'

Her mother held up her hand. She was slightly out of breath, as if she had just climbed the stairs. 'It's a good thing, Ada. I believe it's a sign. God has a way of clearing the path for us, and – as Father de Winter said – nudging us along it sometimes.'

Adelais wasn't thinking about God. She was thinking about Sebastian. He must have heard about the job losses. Was that why he had asked after her mother in the park?

'My path is the path of pilgrimage, to Lourdes. I've been thinking about it for a long time.'

'Lourdes? What are you going to do in Lourdes?'

'I shall be a handmaid and help those in need: the sick and the dying.'

'But you already do that here.'

'We must go where we're called, Ada. It's the only way to salvation.'

Adelais did not want an argument. She could tell her mother's heart was set on going, that she would not rest until she did. There was no point in making it harder for her.

'How long will you be gone, Mama?'

Her mother smiled. 'A few weeks. A month perhaps. But the company's given me some money, and . . .' She sat down at the table. 'I've some saved for emergencies. It's all for you. Only don't tell your father about it. Otherwise . . .'

Adelais nodded. Otherwise he would drink it. There was no need to explain.

'You've work now,' her mother said. 'And I'm sure your father . . . His business will pick up.'

'What if it doesn't?'

Adelais's mother reached across the table. 'Have faith, Ada. That's all we need. Trust in Him.'

Two days later, Adelais got up early. She wanted to go with her mother to the station and see her off. She found her father asleep in the bedroom, and the kitchen empty. Her mother had already left.

──── Nineteen ────

The car was parked forty metres from the house, at the end of School-straat. It was black and shiny, and more expensive-looking than the other vehicles round about, of which there were very few in any case. As she passed, on her way to the tram stop, Adelais noticed the three-pointed star above the radiator: a Mercedes-Benz.

The tram was almost full, but she got a seat near the back, next to a heavily pregnant woman. Adelais stole glances at the bulge where the baby was and wondered what it must feel like to have something that big growing inside you, squeezing up your internal organs and wriggling around. The thought made her feel queasy. She didn't look out the back window, which was why she didn't see that the Mercedes-Benz was follow-ing. Nor did she notice it at the Dampoort, where she changed onto a second tram that took her north towards the docks. It was only as she was getting off at her final stop, a short distance from the bar, that she saw it pull over, as if waiting to see what she did next. Even then, she wasn't sure if it was the same Mercedes-Benz or a different one.

It was eleven o'clock in the morning and the streets were empty. Ade-lais set off for the bar. The tram resumed its journey, engine droning, blue sparks dripping from the overhead lines. She heard the Mercedes-Benz coming along the road behind her, but she didn't look round. It was going to pass her in a moment and then she could forget about it. It wasn't about to run her down. Why would anyone want to do that?

The car slipped by, polished bodywork and chrome. The driver was on the other side. All Adelais could see were his arms and shoulders in silhouette. The car was only twenty metres ahead of her, when the brake lights came on, and the car pulled over again.

Adelais stopped. The driver's door opened, and a man stepped out into the road. He had a long face and a high forehead, and his suit was as black as his car. He walked towards her. His skin was shiny, but covered in fine lines, like the skin on boiled milk. They were all across his forehead and radiating from his eyes.

Adelais stopped dead.

'Miss de Wolf? My name is Klysen.'

The stranger pulled out a card from his top pocket and handed it to her. The card read:

FRANZ A. KLYSEN
NOTARIS – NOTAIRE
Muinkkaai 5
Ghent
Tel: (9) 23 1771

Adelais did not know what to say. Notaries were lawyers. Did that mean she was in trouble? Was it something to do with her father owing money? She tried to hand the card back, but the stranger didn't take it.

'Cornelis Mertens was a client. I've been tasked with the administration of his estate.'

'Uncle Cornelis?'

The stranger nodded. Why hadn't he come to the house? Why were they talking in the street? Adelais did not trust him.

'You're listed as a beneficiary in Mr Mertens's will. But there are certain details that I need to go over with you.'

'A beneficiary?'

'As soon as possible.' The stranger offered her a perfunctory smile. 'If that's convenient.'

The bar was on the other side of the junction. Adelais saw Mrs Claes opening up. She felt a little better, knowing she was there. 'I have to go to work now,' she said.

'Of course,' the stranger said. 'What time do you finish?'

'Nine o'clock.'

The stranger nodded. 'Until nine o'clock then,' he said.

It was a Tuesday and business was slow. Sitting on her stool behind the cash register, Adelais had plenty of time to think about the notary and what it meant, his turning up out of the blue, unannounced. In the detective novels she had read with Sebastian, lawyers usually saw people in their offices. They didn't travel out to see them. In any event, why hadn't Mr Klysen simply written her a letter? He obviously knew where she lived. Or was that the problem? Maybe he hadn't written her a letter for the same reason he hadn't knocked on the door: because he didn't want anyone else involved, meaning her mother and father. Adelais remembered the message Uncle Cornelis had written in her birthday card, the first time he had sent her two hundred francs: *Don't tell Mama!*

Between customers, Hendryck the barman had taken on the job of spring-cleaning the shelves, which involved taking down the bottles one by one, wiping them and running a wet cloth over the surfaces. The shelves behind the bar went all the way up to the ceiling and he had to stand on a stepladder to complete the job.

'Hendryck, what's a beneficiary?' Adelais asked. She thought she knew, but wanted to be sure.

'I think it means you're going to . . .' Hendryck sneezed. It was the dust. '. . . get something. Like when someone takes out life insurance. Or you're in someone's will.' He looked down at Adelais from the top of the stepladder. 'Why do you ask?'

Adelais shrugged. What could Uncle Cornelis have left her? She was not even convinced that the notary had been telling the truth. Her gut told her he wasn't to be trusted.

'I was a beneficiary once,' Hendryck said, returning to the shelves.

'My great-aunt Ingrid, mad old crone. She left me a pair of silver candle-sticks and her collection of stuffed birds.'

A few minutes before nine, Adelais looked up and saw Franz Klysen sit-ting at a table by the door. She had not seen him come in. The bar did not usually do table service, but Mrs Claes must have been impressed by the lawyer's car, because she went over and took his order, just as if they were in a cafe. He drank pastis, diluted with water, which was the choice of Walloons and men off the boats more often than locals. He sat with his back to Adelais, facing the door. There was no way for her to leave without him seeing her and she began to wonder if that was the idea. Beneficiary or not, she couldn't help feeling trapped.

At nine, Mrs Claes took over the till. 'Who is that?' She must have noticed Adelais's interest in the stranger.

'He's a notary.'

'A notary? What, are you buying a house?' Mrs Claes laughed, as if that was the funniest thing she'd heard in a while.

Adelais collected her stick and went over to where Klysen was sitting. 'Here I am,' she said.

Klysen gestured towards the chair opposite. 'Please, sit down.'

There were enough customers in the place that their conversation wasn't likely to be overheard. It was better than talking in the street.

'A drink?'

He had hardly touched his pastis. Adelais shook her head. 'No, thank you.'

The notary shrugged and reached under the table for a slim leather case no thicker than his wrist. Adelais watched him flip open the catches and take out a bundle of densely typed papers, some of them bound together with red ribbon.

'Did you know my uncle, Mr Klysen?'

'We met.' Klysen laid out the papers in front of him. 'I'm sure you knew him better.' He clearly didn't want to make conversation. He wanted to see to business and be done. 'At the time of his death, your uncle owned the leasehold on a property. Do you know what a leasehold is?'

Adelais nodded. The house on Schoolstraat was leased. In seven years, the lease would expire and the de Wolfs would be thrown out. It was one of the things she had learned long ago from listening to her mother and father argue.

'The property is here in Ghent.'

'In Ghent?'

'In Patershol, to be exact.'

Patershol: an ancient, rundown quarter on a narrow bend of the River Leie. Her mother had always told her to stay away from it, especially at night. It was at most twenty minutes' walk from the Handelsdok, but Adelais had only been there once or twice, to drop donations of clothes at the girls' orphanage.

'It's an old weaver's place,' Klysen said. 'There's still twenty-one years left on the lease. The contents of the property are also bequeathed to you. This is the leasehold title.' He pushed a document towards her. It was printed on stiff yellow paper, with names and dates down one side and stamps down the other. The name at the top of the contract was Haeck Maris NV. 'My understanding is that the premises are unoccupied.' Klysen reached into his coat pocket. 'You'll need the keys.'

Adelais felt light-headed. It was all happening too quickly and none of it made sense. Uncle Cornelis hadn't lived in Ghent for years, since before she was born. He had been generous, but he had never been rich enough to have a place he didn't live in, not even a place in Patershol. It was a mistake, a misunderstanding – perhaps a trap. Instinctively she looked towards the bar, searching for Hendryck, but he was busy chatting to a female customer in a ratty fur coat.

Adelais stared at the bunch of keys lying in front of her. She counted nine of them: four for latches and five for deadlocks. She didn't want to pick them up. If she picked them up the trap would be sprung. 'What kind of place is it?' she said. 'What kind of house has nine locks?'

He had her sign a couple of papers, and when that was done, Klysen handed over the contract. There was a map attached to the back, which marked the location and boundaries of the property. Inside a box was written the address: *37 Sluizeken.* As far as Adelais could tell, it was right on the river. She waited for the notary to give her the bad news or to explain, at least, what her uncle had been thinking, but all he did once the papers had been signed for was close his case and stand up.

The keys were still in front of her. She knew she should be excited and grateful. She was a beneficiary. But she could not separate her sudden good fortune from the fact of her uncle's death.

'What do I do?' she said.

The notary looked down at her. He must have thought it was a stupid question. 'If I were you, I'd take a look at the place, right away.'

'Right away?'

'I'll drive you. It's on my way.'

Adelais had never been in a Mercedes before. The seats were soft and comfortable, and smelled of new leather. The dashboard was polished walnut, and all the dials and gauges had lights behind them like the aeroplanes she had seen in films. Even the engine hummed with a quiet confidence that was new.

'What do you think it's worth?' she asked, as they headed down Nieuwland, towards the river.

Klysen glanced at her as he changed gear. 'The lease? I couldn't say.'

The keys were in her pocket now, and she wasn't so scared any more. The lawyer was simply doing his job – a job that was well paid, judging by his car.

'You've no idea?'

'I've never seen the place. Like everything, it's worth what someone will pay for it.'

They followed the quayside into Patershol, where houses of every age and design were jammed together along narrow, unlit streets. After a minute, they came to a square, where there was a tram stop and a handful of plane trees standing lopsided, scraps of newspaper snagged around their trunks. A huddled figure was lying on a bench, bottles strewn across the ground. Klysen took a moment to get his bearings, before turning down a street where the stepped gables of old houses were black against the sky. Somewhere beyond the clouds, the moon was out.

'This is Sluizeken.' Klysen pulled over and wound down his window. 'The old weaver's house must be down there.'

He pointed to an empty yard on their left. Adelais could make out a handful of steps, beyond them a path, half cobblestones, half mud. She could not see the river, but she could sense its chill, fetid presence.

Klysen kept the engine running. 'If you have any questions, you have my card. The same applies if you're considering a change of address, for any reason.'

Adelais was not sure what he meant. She climbed out of the car and closed the door. The notary drove away. In the distance, a couple of women were standing under a solitary street light, smoking. They turned and walked to the kerb as the Mercedes went by, as if expecting it to stop.

— Twenty —

Number 37 was the last in the row of old brick buildings that hugged the north bank of the Leie. The property backing onto it was derelict. Between the house and the water was a narrow wooden dock, barely wide enough for two people to pass. Adelais had to push her way through a tangle of spindly bushes to reach the front door, which was wide like a stable's and covered in flaking white paint. The windows were hidden behind heavy wooden shutters. Warehouses towered over the far bank.

Her fingers found three locks: a latch in the centre and mortice locks above and below. She tried the keys one by one, but it was hard keeping track in the darkness. It didn't help that her hands were unsteady. She tried to think about Uncle Cornelis. This was his place, or had been. There was nothing to be afraid of. Hadn't he always been on her side?

Houses around here couldn't be worth much, not if people were letting them fall down. But the lease had to be worth something – most likely more money than Adelais had ever seen. She wished her mother was around to hear the good news. Maybe she'd feel sorry for calling Uncle Cornelis a bad influence.

The lock at the top turned. The next key on the ring fitted the lock at the bottom. There were four latch keys. The first one she tried was the right one. The door opened with a crack.

The air on the other side wasn't damp and mouldy, like the air in the countess's hunting lodge, but neutral, with a chemical edge, like a fresh newspaper. Adelais found a switch. The light came on with a clunk. On the wall beneath the switch was a meter, with brass tokens stacked up on the top. She was standing in a narrow hallway: white walls, a tiled floor, worn but shiny. There was no sign of habitation.

To her right was a door, with locks top and bottom. Adelais went through the keys, until she had found the right ones. On the other side of the door was a spacious room, bare like the hallway: no furniture, no pictures, no rugs. Instead, there were only wooden crates and cardboard boxes, stacked around the walls. She went to the nearest box. On the side was written *Lokeren*. She lifted the lid.

The first thing she saw was a wooden horse the size of her hand. She had seen ones like it for sale in the Friday market. In a white paper bag she found four pairs of pale grey socks. They were pressed flat, new. A cashmere scarf had a label still attached. Under the scarf was a small silver picture frame. There was no picture inside it, only a sticker with the price: BEF125. Under a packet of white lace handkerchiefs were a small bottle of cologne and a stick of lipstick.

Adelais put the lipstick in her pocket and opened another box. On the side was written *Aalst*. She found a box of red tapered candles, a bottle of brandy, a cut-throat razor with a mother-of-pearl handle, a child-sized shirt still pinned to its cardboard backing, a doll in a box, a waistcoat wrapped in tissue paper, a snow globe, a silver bracelet. She opened a third box, and a fourth. They were all the same: full to the top with new things – hundreds of them, thousands – as if Uncle Cornelis were St Nicolas and these were gifts for St Nicolas's Eve. Except that St Nicolas left sweets and toys, not brandy and silver.

Somewhere outside, a dog started barking.

A door led through to the back of the house, to the old kitchen. There was a ceramic stove against one wall, clad with green tiles. Boxes were stacked around the walls here, too.

Adelais saw the iron bars on the inside of the window. Between the bars and the locks, it was clear her uncle had been very anxious to guard his possessions. But why, if he wasn't going to make use of them? How could he afford them all in any case? Had he bought them, or stolen them? She had read about people who were addicted to thieving. They stole for the thrill of it, it didn't much matter what they took. It would explain why he had taken a doll and a child's shirt when he himself had never married, and had no children.

It made sense now, the way Uncle Cornelis had all but vanished from her life. Her parents had deliberately kept him away from her. The story of his working in Amsterdam, was that even true? Had he been here all the time, not twenty minutes away? The thought made her angry. Uncle Cornelis was family. They had no business shutting him out. And now he was dead.

Steps at the back of the kitchen led down into a large cellar, lit by a line of bulbs screwed into the overhead beams. Once it would have been used to store bales of cloth. Now there were boxes, packed into long rows of free-standing shelves. Many were unlabelled and empty, as if ready for use.

Adelais went back up to the front room. Pinned to the back of the door was a picture she had not noticed before. It had been drawn by a child in crayon: a picture of a girl in a red dress, with yellow hair tied in a topknot. Underneath was a fat red rectangle, with *Me, Aged 7* written inside it.

It was not a realistic self-portrait: for one thing, Adelais had never owned a red dress, and for another, she wasn't holding a stick. She wondered how Uncle Cornelis had come to have it, if it had been a commission or a gift.

Two more keys got her into the room above. This time there were no boxes. Instead, there were shelves full of tins and bottles. The labels – ASPHALTUM, TAPEM, GUM ARABIC – meant nothing to her. Lining one wall were workbenches, topped with marble. Along the middle of the floor, under bright lights, stood three machines.

Adelais stared at the black metal, the levers and wheels, the steel-plate frames, and tried to connect them with Uncle Cornelis. He had bought her a handcycle for her eleventh birthday – that was a machine. But when she thought of the Netley, she pictured movement and freedom. These machines were dark, massive, immovable. Nothing about them suggested freedom or fun.

Two machines were the size of a kitchen table. One had a stout steel gantry raised across the centre, the other a cast-iron wheel on one side as big as a bicycle's. The third machine was smaller than the others. It reminded Adelais of a school desk, with an arrangement of arms and rollers on the front like a giant typewriter. She licked the tip of her finger and ran it along one of the rollers. It came up purple black, like a bruise.

Behind the machine hung a wooden cabinet, made up of shallow drawers. The drawers held small blocks of metal, with a single number or letter in relief on one side. At the far end of the room there were cupboards and sinks and, at head height, lines of wires, strung from wall to wall.

On the top floor was another locked door. That was where she found the paper. It was stored in wooden crates along one wall. Each ream was stamped in red with the words SPARTE 1er GRADE – INTERDIT À LA REVENTE.

In one corner was a tatty leather armchair with a high back, in another a camp bed. A khaki sleeping bag and a couple of blankets lay on top. Between them, bolted to the floor, stood a safe with a single dial on the front. Adelais tried the handle, but it would not open. She took out the document the notary had given her, but there was nowhere any mention of a combination.

Uncle Cornelis would have explained himself, if he had lived. It was his death that made a mystery of everything: the house, the safe, the machines, the boxes full of untouched goods. He had simply died too soon.

A tall window faced east. A block and tackle hung from a hook under the roof. In days gone by, Adelais supposed, this was where the weaver had loaded and unloaded his goods. She opened the window and looked out across the river. The dog started barking again. She could not see it, but she felt sure it was on the other side, watching her from the shadows.

What was in the safe? Money perhaps, or jewels? Or something even more precious? Adelais wanted to know almost as much as she wanted to be gone. She locked the door and hurried downstairs. She would telephone Mr Klysen in the morning. Maybe he had the combination, or knew where to find it.

The keys were in her hand again when she remembered the picture that had been pinned up in the room with the boxes, and the words inside the red rectangle: *Me, Aged 7*. What was the date of her seventh birthday? And who, outside the family, would know?

She went back up to the top floor, and tried the combination: 20.4.47. The safe opened first time.

The pistol was lying on a small pile of books. After a moment's hesitation, Adelais picked it up. The manufacturer's name was stamped onto the handle at the bottom of a circular logo: *Beretta*. The weapon was cold and heavy, not a toy, but unmistakably an instrument designed to wound people or kill them. Adelais could not imagine her uncle having any use for it. Hastily she put it back inside the safe.

Most of the books were manuals about printing. Another was a large notebook with a hard cover. It was full of writing and roughly drawn diagrams: references to inking, pressure, chemicals, paper.

On the shelf below, sandwiched between layers of heavy black cloth, she found eight rectangular metal plates, each a little bigger than her hand: two of steel and six of aluminium. She picked up one of the steel plates and turned it towards the light. She saw swirling concentric lines as fine as strands of hair, and patterns that reminded her of skin. She picked up the other steel plate and found herself looking at the image of a man with a long beard next to the faint impression of a heraldic lion. The engraving on the aluminium plates was fainter and less refined. She made out the profiles of four human heads, turned this way and that – or they might have been four views of the same head, a study. The image reminded her of a famous painting, one she could not name. She turned the plate over. Inside a panel were the words: NATIONALE BANK VAN BELGIE. In a panel opposite were two more words: VIJFHONDERD FRANK.

Her pulse was racing. She wrapped up the plates and put them back in the safe. She slammed the door shut, spun the tumbler and hurried out of the house as if fleeing from a ghost. She knew now why there were bars on the windows, why the house had nine locks. She knew what her uncle's machines had been for, as clearly as if the notary had told her himself when he had handed her the keys. This was what it meant to be a beneficiary, when your beloved uncle turned out to be a criminal, a craftsman who had made his fortune printing counterfeit money.

As she hurried away, she heard her uncle's voice in her head: *We're cut from the same cloth, you and I*. As hard as she tried, she couldn't keep it out.

When she got home Adelais found her father in the front room, listening to the radio. He had been drinking red wine and was in an amiable mood.

'Hello, Ada. You're a bit late, aren't you?' His voice was slurred. He beckoned unsteadily with his hand. 'Come here and tell me your news.'

'I don't have any, Papa. Just another day. I'm off to bed.'

Her father picked up the wine bottle and checked the level. He was visibly pleased to discover there was still a couple of inches left at the bottom. 'All right then,' he said. 'Sweet dreams.'

── Twenty-one ──

Adelais woke the next morning with a cavernous feeling in her stomach. She made it to the closet just in time to vomit, though not much came up. She had forgotten to eat the day before and her dreams – whatever they were – had brought her out in a sweat. Standing propped up against the washbasin, waiting for her head to clear, she wondered if anything she remembered of the day before was real.

She rinsed her mouth and climbed back up to her room. The leasehold contract and the keys were under her mattress, where she had left them the night before. The lipstick was on top of the chest of drawers. She lay down and closed her eyes. Pictures of the weaver's house flooded in, along with the questions that had been going round in her head all night – questions she could not answer, but wasn't ready to share.

One thing she knew: as soon as she told her mother or father, they would take charge. She might be a beneficiary, but she wouldn't get a say. Her uncle's wishes would count for nothing – they had passed judgement on him already. The contents of the safe would only confirm their worst fears.

She didn't have to tell them. She didn't have to tell anyone. She could throw the plates in the river. Then no one would ever know. The plates were the only clear evidence of a crime. The manuals and the notebook did not amount to proof. Otherwise, there was only the gun. That could go in the river too.

She got dressed, and made her way down to the kitchen. She had a piece of bread in her mouth when someone knocked on the front door. Before she had got to it, they knocked again, louder. Her father was asleep in the front room. She could hear his snoring from the hall.

She looked through the spyhole. A man in a police uniform was standing on the front step.

Adelais flattened herself against the wall. Had the notary tipped off the police? Why else were they here?

The policeman knocked again. He could probably hear her father snoring. What if she didn't open the door? That might buy a little time – enough time to dump all the evidence in the river. But if the police knew about her, they would already know about the weaver's house. They would be waiting.

Adelais turned the latch.

'Good morning, miss.' The policeman touched at the lip of his white helmet. He was burly and clean-shaven, with a face like a boxer. 'Mr de Wolf, is he in?'

'That's the daughter,' a voice said. A woman wearing a headscarf was standing a metre away. Adelais recognised one of her father's customers.

'He isn't very well at the moment,' Adelais said. The woman guffawed. 'Can I help you?'

The police officer wore shiny black riding boots. 'Mrs Wilmots here says she brought in a clock for repair—'

'My carriage clock,' the woman said. 'A family heirloom.'

'She says she's just spotted it in a pawn shop, on Achterstraat.'

'That's right. Daylight robbery it is.'

The police officer dug his thumbs into his belt. A leather holster hung down on one side. 'Naturally, she wants the clock back.'

Adelais did not know what to do. Most likely, the woman hadn't paid for the repair and didn't look like she was going to. On the other hand, Adelais was fairly sure there were laws about pawning things that didn't belong to you.

'So what we're looking for, miss . . .' The police officer was looking at Adelais's stick. '. . . is the ticket, and the money to redeem the item. If you can manage that.'

Adelais thought about waking her father, but something told her it was better to handle the matter herself. In his state, he was likely to get into a fight and make matters worse.

'I'll look. Just a minute.'

Adelais hurried to the workshop. The place was a mess of papers, bottles and half-finished repairs. She found the pawn-shop ticket sticking out of an overstuffed drawer. There were others underneath. The amount loaned against Mrs Wilmots's clock was seven hundred francs. Adelais went to the kitchen and took her mother's money from its hiding place. She counted it: eight hundred francs. She left a hundred francs and took the rest back to the police officer on the step.

'I'm sorry,' she said. 'The receipts got mixed up. It won't happen again. And Mrs Wilmots doesn't have to pay for the repair.'

Mrs Wilmots was about to say something, but the prospect of a free repair seemed to change her mind. The police officer passed her the money and the pawn-shop ticket. 'We'll leave it at that then,' he said, his tone suggesting it was against his better judgement.

After he had gone, Adelais hurried back to the workshop and checked the other tickets. She hoped her father would find the money to redeem the other clocks he had pawned before their owners missed them because, apart from the hundred francs in the kitchen and nine francs in her pocket, there was no more money in the house.

Adelais found Father de Winter's number and called from the telephone box. The telephone was answered by a softly spoken woman whom Adelais imagined to be a nun. The Reverend Father was not available, she said, but she could take a message. Adelais said she needed to get hold of her mother, who had been in Lourdes for almost a month. The nun told her to call back at noon.

Adelais was at work by that time. Mrs Claes let her use the telephone behind the bar. The same nun answered. Father de Winter had received the message, she said, but had gone out again on urgent pastoral business.

Adelais asked if it wouldn't be better if she went to his office and waited there. The nun did not seem to like the idea of that and suggested she go to confession on Sunday, if her requirements were 'of a spiritual nature'. Adelais explained for a second time that she was trying to reach her mother who had gone to Lourdes. There was nothing spiritual about it. The nun suggested she call back in the morning and hung up.

The following morning, Adelais took the handcycle up to the Church of Sint-Amandus where Father de Winter's office took up most of the vestry.

The woman who sat outside, hammering away at a typewriter, was not in a nun's habit. She wore a plain dress and glasses and her hair was tied up in a bun. Seeing Adelais walk in, she stopped typing and smiled.

'I'm Adelais de Wolf,' Adelais said.

The woman blinked behind her thick lenses. 'Ah yes, the pilgrim's child.'

She made it sound like it was some kind of honour. 'Can I see Father de Winter?'

The woman consulted the watch that was pinned to her bosom. 'I'm afraid the Reverend Father's—'

The door to the office opened. A priest who was not Father de Winter, but who was just as smartly dressed, came through the door. Father de Winter saw him out and turned back to his office. His demeanour was brisk, businesslike: an important man.

'You're due at the cathedral in twenty minutes, Father,' the woman said. 'Shall I telephone for a taxi?'

'Adelais?' he said. 'What can I do for you?'

'I need to talk to my mother,' Adelais said. 'She's been gone a month.'

Father de Winter frowned. 'Of course. Come and take a seat in my office.'

The room on the other side of the door gave off the same musty perfume he did.

'Is everything all right at home?' he asked, as soon as she had sat down.

Adelais nodded. She did not want to talk about the pawn shop, or her father's drinking, or the fact that they were down to their last hundred francs. She wanted to talk about Uncle Cornelis and the house in Patershol, only not with a priest. 'I need to speak to my mother. It's a family matter.'

From behind his desk, Father de Winter nodded. 'I see. Well, I can telephone the Medical Bureau in Lourdes. I believe that's where she volunteered, at least to begin with. What should I say?'

'That I need to speak to her.'

Father de Winter nodded some more. 'Assuming she gets my message, where can she reach you?' He picked up a fountain pen and unscrewed the cap.

Adelais thought about leaving the number of the bar, but that was hardly the place for a private conversation. She imagined the heads turning as she shouted down a bad line about the contents of her uncle's house: the machinery, the plates, the pistol, the means by which a criminal with the right skills could get rich.

'You know,' Father de Winter said, 'the best thing might be to write her a letter, care of the Medical Bureau. They're very good people. They'll make sure she gets it.'

Adelais thought about putting everything down on paper. That did not seem like a good idea either. 'I need to talk to her. When's she coming back?'

Father de Winter replaced the cap on his fountain pen. 'That I can't tell you.'

'She said a month at most. It's been a month already.'

Father de Winter placed the fountain pen on his desk so that it was perfectly parallel with the edge of the blotter. 'There's something you should understand, Adelais: your mother has put her destiny in God's hands. She is determined to be guided by His will. She will leave the shrine of Lourdes and her good works there when she feels it accords with His plan – His plan for her, and for you.'

Adelais felt her face grow hot. If there was a plan, she was not part of it, that much she knew for certain. 'Isn't a month enough? Most people don't go to Lourdes at all. Most people don't volunteer with the Beguines in Ghent. Why does she need to do all these good works when most people don't do any?'

Father de Winter's mouth was pressed into a line, as if it took an effort of will to keep silent. 'I'm sorry, my child,' he said finally, and the regret in his voice seemed almost genuine. He rose from his desk. 'Write your mother a letter. Perhaps she'll explain herself one day.'

Adelais did not waste any time. As soon as she got back to Schoolstraat she sat down at the kitchen table and began a letter. It turned out to be more difficult than she had thought. She did not dare to explain about her uncle's legacy, but she wanted her mother to know that something import-ant had happened. She wanted to persuade her mother to come home, but she didn't want to sound angry or reproachful, even if that was how she felt. Nor did she want to cause her mother pain. If it was true what Father de Winter had said, that God was telling her to stay at Lourdes, how was she going to feel being begged to refuse? Adelais began the letter again and again, but no matter what words she used, they always sounded wrong: too cold, too distant, too imploring or too evasive. With every attempt, her mother seemed more and more beyond reach, a person she no longer knew. Having tears in her eyes didn't make it any easier.

She had all but given up when her father came into the kitchen. He frowned at the sheets of paper screwed up on the table and put a hand on Adelais's shoulder. It was nowhere near lunchtime, but already she could detect on him a smell of wine.

'You miss your mama, don't you, Ada?'

Adelais nodded. 'Father de Winter says she's staying in Lourdes until God says she can come back. What if that's never?'

Lennart de Wolf stumbled slightly and lowered himself onto a chair. His eyes were bloodshot and it was almost as if he had been crying too. 'I know how it looks, Ada. You think she's abandoned us, but she hasn't, not in her heart. She thinks she has no choice, you see, because of . . .'

'Because of what? Because of God?'

Adelais's father shook his head. 'Because of Anderlecht, because she . . . Because sometimes, when we've done things that we—'

'Anderlecht? That's where you worked once, wasn't it?'

Adelais's father blinked. 'That was a long time ago.'

'I know. During the war.'

'Yes, but this was later, much later.'

'What did she do in Anderlecht, Papa?'

Adelais's father picked up one of the scraps of paper and began to smooth it out. He seemed out of breath, in pain. 'I shouldn't have said . . . I swore I wouldn't.' He got up suddenly, steadying himself against the tabletop. 'You don't need to know about this, Adelais. You only need to know that none of this is your fault, none of it.'

Before Adelais could ask him any more questions, he had left the kitchen. A moment later she heard the door of his workshop slam shut.

That night, Adelais sat behind the till at Aux Quatre Vents. The place was busy and the jukebox was on. Hendryck was hard at work pouring drinks. Mrs Claes and one of the other girls were in the kitchen. Adelais took money and wrote out chits, and stared at the strangers as they shuffled in and out. Nobody spoke to her, except to give her their orders, and she didn't say anything in reply. Loneliness felt like a chasm at her feet. One more step and it would swallow her. The thought of the dance at the opera house, of waltzing with Sebastian, was the only happy thing she could think of.

She wished Uncle Cornelis was still alive. She didn't care if he had broken the law. She wanted to see him smile again, the twinkle in his eye. She wanted to hear him call her his little wolf. Why had he made her a beneficiary, perhaps his only one? It could only be because he had loved her. But there was more to it than that. He had made no request, left her no instructions. She was free to do what she wanted, or to do nothing. All the same, the machines, the plates, he had meant for her to have them. He had wanted her to share his secrets, as they had shared smaller ones in the past. But if so, what did he expect her to do with them?

—— Twenty-two ——

Adelais took a tram to Heileg-Hart on Saturday morning. It was a fine, windy day, fragments of light cloud twisting in the sky above her head. She could already feel the tension in her stomach.

She had settled on the dress two weeks earlier. Saskia's sister Mariëtte had once worn it to a wedding. Now she was too fat for it, Saskia said. It was green, with a velvet bodice, cap sleeves and a long tulle skirt. It fitted Adelais well, and all that had been needed was to take up the skirt a little. The first thing she did when she arrived at Saskia's house was to try it on again, just to be sure.

'Those shoes won't do,' Saskia said. Adelais was wearing a pair of brown lace-ups. They were her best pair and polished to a shine. 'They make you look like a typist.'

Adelais was panic-stricken. She didn't have time to buy new shoes, even if she could find the money.

'Calm down,' Saskia said. 'I'll find you something.'

She disappeared for a few minutes and returned with an armful of pumps, court shoes and dancing slippers, together with a couple of pairs with long straps and high heels, which Adelais knew she would never be able to wear without falling over.

'They're not for you. They're for me,' Saskia said. 'I need to be taller tonight.'

'Aren't you tall enough?'

Saskia might have been small for her age, but she could not be mistaken for a child. In the past few years she had developed the kind of figure that Adelais might have envied, if she had wanted men to notice her on the street.

147

'I don't want to dance with my nose in a man's armpit.' She shuddered. 'It's either stick to the short ones or wear heels. And short men are all terrible, like Napoleon.'

Saskia's sisters had bigger feet than Adelais. She tried on pair after pair, but they were all too broad. They would fall off or give her blisters. Fortunately, a pair of black slingbacks turned out to be a decent fit once they had stuffed tissue paper into the points.

'You see?' Saskia said. 'I said I'd take care of it. Now let's go in for the kill.'

'The kill?'

'Nails, locks and lashes. It's what Mariëtte used to say before she got married. But we'd better have a bath first.'

'I've already washed,' Adelais said.

'In a perfumed bubble bath?'

Adelais hesitated. She had never taken a bath at Saskia's house before. She did not even have physiotherapy there any more. Her sessions with Dr Helsen had concluded when she was thirteen.

'Of course, if you want to smell like an onion,' Saskia said, 'be my guest.'

The bubble bath was French and gave off an expensive floral smell. Saskia sat on the bath stool, painting her toenails while Adelais undressed in the corner, wrapping herself in towels for the sake of decency. She was glad to see that the bubbles covered the surface of the bathwater, because Saskia showed no sign of leaving the bathroom. She had grown up in a house full of sisters, Adelais reminded herself, and unlike the de Wolfs, her family had always been rather modern when it came to social convention.

'I can get in on my own,' Adelais said. She had strong arms, thanks to the handcycle.

Saskia did not look up from her toenails. 'Go on then.'

When Adelais had finished soaping herself, Saskia moved the bath stool behind the bath and washed Adelais's hair with a shampoo that was scented with lavender. Adelais tried to relax and enjoy the feel of Saskia's fingers on her scalp, but almost at once, a clock sounded on the landing.

'What time is it? How much time do we have?'

'Plenty,' Saskia said. 'Why are you so nervous? It's just a dance.'

'I don't want to be late.'

'We *should* be late, fashionably late. That's at least half an hour.'

'That's too much.'

Saskia dumped a cup of water over Adelais's head. 'What's the matter? Are you afraid someone'll bag the boy before you can?'

'Sebastian? No. No, it's just . . .' Adelais couldn't think of any way to finish the sentence. She felt about the dance the way she used to feel about exams at school, only this was worse.

Saskia sighed. 'Don't let the water out. I'll have yours,' she said, and pulled her dress over her head.

Adelais could tell her friend was unhappy about something. For a moment, she was tempted to share the news about her uncle's will. There was nothing Saskia liked more than to be let in on a secret.

'Thanks for all this,' she said. 'I'd be stuck otherwise.'

Saskia shook her head. 'Don't be stupid. Only it's *supposed* to be fun. If it isn't fun, what's the point?'

After they had bathed, they went into Saskia's bedroom and started on their hair. When it came to using the hairdryer and rollers, they were guided by a magazine Saskia had borrowed from her mother. *Dry from root to tip for a lustrous shine*, read the article. *Keep hair in motion to avoid singeing.* When the curlers were out, they darkened their eyelashes with mascara, and put on the lipstick Adelais had taken from the weaver's house.

'This is nice,' Saskia said, admiring her lips in the mirror. 'Where'd you get it?'

Something had been written on the lid of the box: the name of a town. All the boxes had one, and every name was different. 'Lokeren,' Adelais said.

'Lokeren? What were you doing there?'

'I wasn't there. It was a present, from my uncle.'

'The one that died?'

Adelais nodded.

Saskia squeezed her lips together and released them with a pop. 'He had good taste.'

She helped Adelais into her dress and led her into her parents' bedroom, where there were full-length mirrors on the back of the wardrobe doors. Adelais hardly recognised herself. She seemed to have twice as much hair as usual. It fell in loose curls down to her shoulders, like Anita Ekberg in *War and Peace*. The green dress made her seem taller, like a prima ballerina. Even the little touches of make-up lent her an allure that was alien.

Saskia came and stood next to her. Her dress was dark blue with white piping, like a sailor suit, and shorter. She straightened one of Adelais's sleeves and prodded at her hair. 'Well, if someone doesn't fall in love with you tonight, they never will,' she said.

They took a taxi to the opera house and arrived half an hour late. A queue of cars was waiting to disgorge its passengers. They made their way into the foyer, which was flanked with urns full of flowers. Most of the guests were young, and well dressed. In spite of all her preparations, Adelais felt like an imposter. Handing over the entrance ticket, she half expected the usher to refuse it and send her away. As they approached the ballroom, something else struck her as wrong: the music wasn't like any of the music on the jukebox at Aux Quatre Vents. It was faster, wilder, and with a beat that would never fit the steps she knew.

Saskia didn't seem to notice. She accepted a glass of sparkling wine from a waiter and took another for Adelais. 'Drink up,' she said.

The ballroom was even grander than Adelais had expected, but she hardly noticed the plaster cherubs, the frescos or the ornate bas-relief. Under three massive chandeliers, couples were dancing – not facing each other, holding each other, but swinging each other around by the arms. It was a kind of dancing she didn't know, a kind she couldn't do. A band was playing at the far end of the room: musicians with slicked-back hair and burgundy jackets.

Saskia drained her glass. 'That's rock'n'roll. Everyone's doing it now.' She hiccupped. 'Looks exhausting, doesn't it?'

Adelais had seen the jive before, but she had assumed it was something reserved for Americans, and then only for films. This dance was not as fast, but it made no difference. She couldn't join in. What was Sebastian going to think of her, coming to the Red Cross Charity Dance just to watch?

She spotted him standing to one side of the room, talking to a group of people his age. The men were in dinner jackets. The women wore dresses with flared skirts that stopped below their knees – perfect for the new kind of dancing. A tall, elegant-looking brunette laughed at something Sebastian said and squeezed his forearm affectionately. 'This was a mistake,' Adelais said, but Saskia had gone to get another drink.

Sebastian's group were making their way onto the floor. Sebastian looked reluctant, but the brunette grabbed his hand and dragged him along behind her. A moment later they were dancing – making mistakes, losing their way occasionally, but laughing and grinning even as they did. The brunette had a long, graceful neck and high cheekbones. Her legs were slender and straight. Her earrings sparkled.

Adelais tried to get away, but Saskia had spotted her cousin Paulina, who had just returned from her honeymoon in Italy. The country had clearly made a great impression on her, because she described in some detail every museum and basilica on her extensive itinerary. Adelais kept her back to the dance floor. That way, between the gown and Saskia's hairdressing, Sebastian might not recognise her. She hadn't counted on the mirrors that were hung around the walls.

'Adelais?' She turned. Sebastian was standing in front of her. 'What are you . . . ? I didn't know you were—'

'I can waltz, and foxtrot, and polka.' The words tumbled out. Blood flooded into her cheeks, like a hot tap going on. 'I'm quite good.'

'Are you? I'd no idea.' Sebastian almost had to shout over the noise of the band. 'You never said—'

'Anyway, I thought I'd . . .' Adelais gestured at the room. 'You know, why not?' She laughed, but it wasn't the kind of laugh that followed something funny.

'Right. Why not?' Sebastian nodded a couple of times and looked out across the dance floor. 'They'll be playing a waltz or two later on. If you like, we could—'

'Yes, all right. The next waltz.'

'Great. Good. Should be fun.' He smiled, and the warmth of it made her happy. 'By the way, you look absolutely—'

'Fine gentleman you are.' The tall brunette was at his side, holding two glasses of wine. She pouted. 'I got tired of waiting.' She handed one of the glasses to Sebastian. Her skin was flawless, her teeth white. 'Who's the bridesmaid?'

'I'm sorry, this is Adelais. Adelais, this is Marie-Astrid, from my dance class.'

'Astrid?'

'Marie-Astrid.'

Adelais nodded. It was like a poke in the guts. Why did the girl have to be called Astrid? Astrid was the countess's name, the name of the hotel they were going to run one day, together. It was *their* name.

Sebastian seemed oblivious to the theft. 'I've known Adelais for years. Ever since—'

'I saved his life.'

Sebastian laughed and stuck a finger under his shirt collar. It seemed to be bothering him. 'That's right. True story.'

'You *must* tell me,' Marie-Astrid took Sebastian's arm. 'Right after this dance. It's my absolute favourite. Excuse us.'

The band was playing a slower number: a lilting melody in common time. Adelais watched Sebastian and Astrid take to the floor and vanish into the swelling crowd. When she saw them again, Astrid's eyes were fixed on Sebastian's and she was smiling. Sebastian spun her around. He was smiling too. Adelais felt something close to panic.

'Do you think he likes her?'

Saskia had just returned from the cloakroom. On the trip she had acquired two more glasses of wine. 'She may be trying too hard. My sister Madeleen always says you mustn't try too hard. She must really like him, though.'

'Why?'

'She's the prettiest girl in the room.'

'He promised me the next waltz. We're going to waltz together.'

Saskia handed Adelais one of the glasses. She seemed to think it was essential to avoid staying sober. 'The waltz is the most romantic dance. You're supposed to waltz with the one you love, like at a wedding.'

'A wedding?' Adelais could feel her heart pounding against her ribs. Marie-Astrid was laughing now, flashing her perfect white teeth. 'She *is* trying too hard, isn't she?'

Between the foyer and the ballroom was another room, ringed with columns. There was a bar on one side and steps going up to a gallery. It was quieter and cooler than the ballroom, and the guests who stood around talking there were older. While Saskia was dancing with Paulina's husband, Adelais went and sat down on the steps. Her face was burning and her head was starting to swim. Her glass was not empty, but she already felt drunk.

Nothing at the dance was how she had expected it. It was noisy and crowded and complicated, and not romantic the way it was supposed to be. And Sebastian did not seem that impressed with the way she looked.

He had been going to say something, but then . . . Adelais's eyes clouded over. Beneath her feet was a pool of black water, like the water going by the old weaver's house. She let go of her stick and grabbed hold of the banisters. She wanted very badly not to fall in.

She took a deep breath, then another. Her vision cleared. A couple squeezed past her. 'Sorry,' she said, but they didn't reply. The man had a cigar in his mouth. He handed Adelais her stick and carried on up the steps without a word.

A smattering of applause came from the ballroom. After a few moments, the music struck up again: a saxophone and drums. Adelais measured the beats in her head: it was a slow three/four time, a waltz. She even knew the melody from the jukebox: 'The Tennessee Waltz'. She got up, and walked towards the sound.

The dance floor was even busier than before. The couples were travelling around the room in a circle. Adelais searched for Sebastian. There was no sign of him, or of Marie-Astrid. She glimpsed Saskia, dancing with a boy who wore spectacles. Watching the couples spin and sway, Adelais felt unsteady again. What had been in her glass? Was it something stronger than wine?

She felt a hand on her arm. 'So how do we do this then?' There was a grin on Sebastian's face, and sweat on his brow.

Adelais hung her stick on the back of a chair. 'Just hold on to me and don't let go.'

'What did you say?' The saxophonist was riffing with gusto. Adelais put a hand on Sebastian's shoulder. He seemed taller up close and smelled of clean laundry. He took her hand. 'Off we go then.'

He led tentatively, as if afraid she might fall, but after a few steps they were moving like the others, being carried along in the gentle current of the music. Things would be different now between them. Everything would be different – the waltz and Sebastian's embrace made that clear. Adelais closed her eyes. The fear began to drain away.

'Where did you learn to dance?' Sebastian said.

'Hendryck taught me.'

'Hendryck?'

Adelais opened her eyes. Saskia was watching her from across the floor, a hard look in her eyes, as if there was something wrong. The blackness hit her again. It was there, beneath her feet. She stumbled. Someone bumped into them. 'Excuse *me*!' a woman said.

'Are you all right, Adelais?' Sebastian's hold on her was suddenly tighter.

'I'm fine,' she said. 'Don't . . . don't let—'

'I won't let go.'

They were still dancing.

'I think the wine, it's . . . there's something—'

'Drunk,' the woman said.

'I'm not—' The ballroom pitched over. Adelais was sliding into the black water. She grabbed hold of Sebastian. His shirtfront gave way, studs and buttons popping.

'For God's sake, what are you doing?' He was exasperated, angry. Everyone was looking at them.

'I'm *not* . . .' Adelais couldn't talk. She was going to be sick. Another couple nudged past them. Someone tutted. They were causing an obstruction. She felt the bile rise in her throat. She had to get clear of Sebastian. She had to sit down.

'She needs the . . . I'll take her.' Marie-Astrid was at her side. The grip of her hand was cold and bony. Her other hand was around her waist. 'I've got you now. Let's get you sorted out, shall we? Where's your stick?'

Adelais made it to the lavatories just in time. Marie-Astrid waited outside the cubicle. Even as she retched into the bowl, Adelais could see her red satin shoes beneath the door. It was kind of the girl to wait, she supposed, to check that she was all right. But she wished she would go away.

With her stomach empty, the nausea began to subside. Adelais got to her feet and opened the cubicle door. Marie-Astrid was standing by the washbasins, prodding at her hair. She smiled at Adelais in the mirror. 'Feeling better?'

'A bit.'

'We only just made it, didn't we?'

'Yes. Thank you.' Adelais went to rinse her mouth. As she bent over the taps, the room swayed gently, as if afloat on a rolling sea.

Marie-Astrid did not seem happy with her hair. She pushed it around some more and sighed. 'He told me the story, by the way.'

'What?'

'Sebastian. How you pulled him out of the river. The angel of the Sint-Joris Bridge. You really did save his life, didn't you?'

'It was a long time ago.' Adelais picked up the soap and began to wash her hands. She wanted to see Sebastian but she wasn't ready for the ballroom again, for the smoke and the heat and the crowd. Just the thought of it made her feel faint.

'Still.' From nowhere Marie-Astrid produced a lipstick and began dabbing at her lips. 'His *life*. Every day, every minute, he has you to thank for it. There can't be a day that goes by without him thinking about that. He owes you everything.'

'Is that what he said?'

Marie-Astrid leaned closer to the mirror. She was beautiful even when she frowned. 'It doesn't give the rest of us much of a chance, does it? How can we compete with that?'

Adelais did not know what to say. Marie-Astrid talked as if they were old friends, friends who talked openly about their dreams and desires. But they had only just met.

Marie-Astrid put her head on one side. 'On the other hand, gratitude. Is that the best foundation for love – or marriage, for that matter?'

'Marriage?'

A couple of women came through the door, talking and laughing. Installed in adjacent cubicles, they went on chattering.

'I suppose that's why you're here, isn't it?' Marie-Astrid said. 'To keep an eye on him. Not that I blame you. He's very eligible, and so sweet.'

'I'm not keeping an eye on him.' Adelais's lipstick was smudged across her cheek. She tried to wipe it away with the heel of her thumb. It came to her stark and clear for the first time that she loved him. It was as simple as that. Having him in her life had made up for everything, for the isolation and the pain. It had seemed like a gift from Fate. Once Fate had given you a gift, it didn't take it back again.

'I don't blame you,' Marie-Astrid said again. 'Not at all. You know how boys are.' She replaced the cap on her lipstick and offered it to Adelais.

The implication was clear: they might be strangers, even rivals, but they were also comrades, women in a man's world. They were supposed to stick together. 'No, thank you,' Adelais said.

The skirt on Marie-Astrid's dress had a pocket hidden among the pleats. She slipped the lipstick inside and stood watching Adelais with a troubled look on her face. 'On the other hand, love's like everything else, isn't it? In the end, it pays to be realistic, don't you think?'

Before Adelais could ask what she meant a lavatory flushed and one of the women came clattering out of the cubicle, smoothing down her dress. Her companion followed. A few moments later, Adelais was alone.

She looked at herself in the mirror. Her eyes were bloodshot. All the make-up Saskia had applied was smudged or smeared. Her hair was wet at the front, and stuck to her forehead in clumps. Even her dress – her bridesmaid's dress – looked ridiculous, like a costume in an amateur play. She saw herself suddenly as Sebastian must have seen her: a child dressed up as an adult, a child playing make-believe. Could it be true, that what Sebastian felt for her – what he had always felt, from the very beginning – was gratitude? Gratitude, mixed with pity?

Her stick had found its way to the end of the washbasins. She looked at it, hanging there, a thick, ugly thing, and a stark fear came over her that it was true. And what had she done by coming to the dance but remind Sebastian of what he owed her, of his obligation – that, and embarrass him in front of everyone?

Adelais pushed the wet hair clear of her forehead and wiped the make-up off with a napkin. Her head was still spinning. She wasn't thinking straight. Marie-Astrid didn't know what Sebastian felt. They had been to the same dancing class. What use was that? It wasn't late. There would be more waltzes to come. What she needed was some air to clear her head. Then she would be steady enough to dance. Sebastian would give her another chance. He might even be waiting for her.

But Sebastian was not outside the lavatories, nor was he waiting in the anteroom with the gallery, or at the bar. Saskia was there instead, laughing with a group of young friends and gingerly smoking a cigarette. She looked tipsy.

Sebastian was in the ballroom with Marie-Astrid. They were dancing cheek to cheek, a waltz. Marie-Astrid whispered something in Sebastian's ear, which made him laugh, then slid an arm around his neck. They danced past Adelais without giving her a glance. Sebastian looked happy. He looked as you were supposed to look when you were dancing with someone you loved. Adelais stood and watched, until she couldn't watch any more. She would have run, if only she could.

The night was clear, with a breeze that brought the gooseflesh up on her arms. She didn't think about where she was going. There was nowhere she wanted to go, not home, not back to the opera house, not to the bar, where by now the usual Saturday-night crowd of dockers and shipmates would be getting rowdy. A tram passed her on the Vogelmarkt, but she didn't climb on. Her hip was sore, and her borrowed shoes were giving her blisters, but the pain kept her from thinking. The bells of St Bavo's rang out the hour as she crossed the Reep Canal. She didn't count the chimes.

Gradually the streets became more familiar. She had been heading east. She came round a corner and found herself on the Sint-Joris Bridge.

Below her, hidden in the shadows, was the spot where Sebastian had almost drowned. A gust of wind brushed the surface of the water, breaking up her reflection. She felt the weight of all the dreams that had been born in that place – dreams that had kept her going, but which were never going to come true. *In the end, it pays to be realistic.* She wanted to hate Marie-Astrid, but she had only been telling the truth: when it came to Sebastian and his life, she had always been on the outside, and always would be.

Adelais turned away from the bridge. She didn't have to think, she could just walk: put one foot in front of the other, focus on the cobblestones and the paving stones and the gutters. She could walk until she was exhausted, and then sleep – it didn't matter where. She could lie down in a doorway if she had to, like the drunks she saw at the bar, when they were too unsteady to get home.

She came to a junction. In front of her was an iron bench. Something about it was familiar. The ground in front was strewn with litter. Plane trees stood on either side, their pale trunks blotchy, as if diseased. A street sign at the corner read: SLUIZEKEN.

She made her way to number 37. She had not been back since the day the notary had appeared. The place was locked up and the keys were still hidden under her mattress at home, but she wanted to see it, to know that it was really there. The house stood tall and silent, a looming shape against the starry sky, almost invisible in the darkness: a house full of secrets and iron machines.

She knew then what Uncle Cornelis had expected her to do – for herself, for her father, for what was left of her family. It was as plain as if he had put it in a letter. Walking back to the tram stop she also saw, with a clarity that made her shiver, that if he hadn't written such a letter, it was only because, as far as he was concerned, there was no need for one.

Alignment

21 June 1957

Dear Adelais,

I've been trying to find you, but you're never at home. I've been to the bar as well, but they said I had just missed you. What can be keeping you so busy? I hope you haven't had to take on another job. I know things can't have been easy lately, what with one thing and another.

There is some news I wanted to share with you. I've decided to cut short my studies at the university. There's a firm of architects in Antwerp that have offered to take me on as an apprentice. I'm sure I can learn more working for them than I can reading books and going to lectures. I can go for the qualifications later, if it works out, and in the meantime, I'll be gaining experience and making contacts, which suits me much better than writing essays (or letters, for that matter!), and I'll be earning money for myself, like you do. I'll miss Ghent, of course. I'll especially miss going out to the old hunting lodge. I can't bear the idea of someone else getting hold of the place, but everyone says this is a great opportunity – even my mother, who thinks I'm barely old enough to tie my own laces.

I've got a train to catch in an hour. I wanted to try and find you again to say goodbye, but there's been so much to do, and I've run out of time. But I'll be coming back often to see the family etc., so you haven't seen the last of me yet.

Wish me luck!

Sebastian

—— Twenty-three ——

Ghent, Summer 1957

Adelais got up every morning at six. She made breakfast with what she had bought the day before and put it on the table for her father. She left the house at a quarter to seven and made her way by tram to the Koren-markt, where she changed onto another tram going north. Most days she reached Patershol at twenty past seven. She kept a lookout for anyone following her, on foot or by car, and made a mental note of the other passengers, especially any who got on at Sint-Amandsberg. If she saw anyone on the second tram who had also been on the first, she got off right away and waited for another.

Once she was on Sluizeken, she went into a newsagent's and spent a couple of minutes choosing a newspaper. The shop overlooked the path that led down to number 37. If anyone were waiting there she would see them. At the house she locked the front door and opened the shut-ters on the top two floors. She studied for four hours, picked up groceries from a corner shop on Sleepstraat, and then took two short tram jour-neys to the bar in time for work. Apart from visits to the public library, where she borrowed books on printing and engraving, she broke the routine just once: to visit the pawnbroker on Achterstraat. She had to check that nothing else from her father's workshop had turned up there. She could not afford another visit from the police. On Sunday evenings, she went to the pictures with Saskia. She avoided going to Patershol at night. The streets were narrow and dark, and every time she went there, the echo of footsteps gave her the impression that someone was behind her.

Everything she needed was in the house. The hard part was knowing how to use it. Uncle Cornelis had made copious notes. They filled a hundred pages of his large black notebook, some written in pencil, others in various shades of ink, but they were not in any particular order. Paragraphs on chemical watermarks and plate preparation mingled with names, addresses and numbers. There were handwritten diagrams and partly printed 500-franc notes, labelled in a kind of code: *Yellow/red reg, Litho underink, XS press to substrate.* Only when she had read the books from the library and been through the manuals did things begin to make sense. Even then, she often found herself at a dead end. The processes were complicated, the jargon impenetrable. Several times she came close to giving up. But then Herman Wouters's reedy voice would pop into her head: *She can't do it. She's got a funny leg.* She would be back on the handcycle on her eleventh birthday, struggling to move off, remembering how badly she had wanted to prove him wrong. *All she needs is a push,* Uncle Cornelis had said, and he'd been right. If he set her a challenge, it was because he knew she could meet it.

At night Adelais dreamed of the presses, that they were working on their own while she slept, slowly filling the old weaver's house with money, until it burst from the windows in a cloud, exposing her secret to the world. On other nights, she dreamed she was with Sebastian, riding through the snow on the back of his bicycle or swinging on the swings at the hunting lodge. Sometimes they were alone on a beach, walking along the shore with the waves breaking over their feet, which had never happened in real life and never would. She woke from those dreams with a cold ache in her chest, one that only hard work would smother.

Adelais was still studying when a letter arrived from her mother. It described the work she was doing at Lourdes for the sick and the dying, and the miraculous power of faith to alleviate their suffering. Father de Winter had assured her that Adelais was coping well in her absence, which she took to be a sign that God approved of her staying on. She enclosed five 50-franc notes, wrapped in silver paper. She did not say when she was coming back.

By this time, Adelais had progressed from theory to practice. She started with watermarking. King Leopold's profile was rendered using a rubber stamp and a solution of polyethylene glycol. According to the notebook, Uncle Cornelis had experimented with dozens of chemicals, from sulphuric acid to linseed oil, but none of them had passed muster. Only the polymer – a chemical from England – produced a lasting effect. Applying it was difficult. The paper had to be dampened, and an exact amount of pressure applied. It took Adelais ten days of practice to get it right. Held to the light, the image was not as bright as on a genuine note, but to see the difference you would need to put one next to the other.

Lithographic printing took her three months to master. Besides some coloured lettering, its purpose was to give the banknotes their background shades, combinations of yellow, magenta and cyan. The plates were made of aluminium, a separate plate for each of the three colours. Her first attempts at a print, using one colour, came out somewhere between faint and invisible. Cornelis's notes helped her diagnose the problem: she had botched the surface preparation and cut corners when it came to inking. She practised over and over again, experimenting with different amounts of pressure. The images began to come through strongly and evenly, but now there were blotches and stains to go with them. Grease from her fingers was trapping ink. She learned to handle the plates with minimal contact. Equipment and surfaces she cleaned thoroughly after every pass. Her prints became sharp and clean, but when she tried to combine them into composite colours, the images came out blurred like double vision.

It helped that Uncle Cornelis had experienced the same problem. He devoted eight pages of the notebook to issues of alignment, to eliminating movement even as paper and plate were crushed together. Perfect alignment, it seemed, was the key to everything. Slowly Adelais taught herself to cut, position and secure with precision, using the full range of instruments that Uncle Cornelis had left behind. Finally, one day in October, the images of the Moor's head bloomed in their usual shades of amber and brown next to the words VIJFHONDERD FRANK in pin-sharp letters that were part magenta and part cyan. Even under the magnifying glass, Adelais could see no trace of blurring. The lithography was perfect.

She had never felt her uncle's presence in the house before, but she felt it then, surrounding her, lifting her. She felt his approval and pride.

'What's that smell coming off you?' Saskia said the following Sunday. 'It reminds me of Mrs Van den Bosch.'

Adelais sniffed her sleeve. They were sitting in the second row of the Plaza, waiting to watch Marilyn Monroe in *The Prince and the Showgirl*.

'Who's Mrs Van den Bosch?'

'My old art teacher. Mad as a sack of ferrets and always covered in paint, even her shoes.'

Adelais had spent most of the day making lithographic prints, concentrating on the front of the note, with its image of King Leopold II and the Belgian lion. She had not attempted this side before, but there were delicate reds and blues behind the emblem of the lion that it would be easy to botch and she had to know she could reproduce them. The fumes from the chemicals and the ink had seeped into her clothes and her hair, but she hadn't had time to change.

'I was cleaning, in my father's workshop. I knocked over some turpentine.'

'Is that why your hands are blue?'

Adelais had added the blue colour last, but in her haste to clean the roller, she had got ink on her fingers. She thought she had wiped it all off, but even in the dingy light of the Plaza she could see it framing her fingernails and discolouring the joints of her fingers. 'I don't know. I must have . . .'

'It's all right,' Saskia said. 'You don't have to tell me if you don't want to.'

The film was starting. Adelais shrugged, as if Saskia was being silly, and tried to appear interested in the opening credits. She wished she had washed her hands properly and changed her clothes. Now she would have to think of something that did not sound like a lie. She couldn't have Saskia thinking she had secrets. To Saskia, secrets were puzzles that existed to be solved. Now that she had left school, she had more time on her hands than ever. Her father had suggested she study nursing or medicine, but that only proved, Saskia said, that he knew nothing about her.

The lights came up for the interval. Adelais rubbed at the ink on her fingers. She was going to say something about cleaning old paintbrushes, but Saskia did not bring up the subject again. She was easily bored and for once Adelais was grateful. She got up and bought them both an ice cream.

'Did you hear about Textile des Flandres?' Saskia said.

'What about it?'

'Sebastian's father, that's where he works, isn't it?'

'Yes.'

'It's in all sorts of trouble apparently. It might have to be taken over by the state. If that happens, the owners will lose lots of money and most of the bosses will be sacked.'

'How do you know this?'

'My father has a patient with sciatica. He belongs to the Chamber of Commerce.'

Adelais thought about Sebastian, working his apprenticeship in Antwerp. She wondered if his giving up university had something to do with the problems at his father's company.

Saskia scraped the bottom of her ice-cream tub. 'Have you seen him at all, Sebastian, I mean?'

Adelais shook her head. Just as his letter said, Sebastian had come by the bar a couple of days after the dance at the opera house. She had seen him approaching and hidden in the kitchens. Hendryck had covered for her, saying that she had left early, but from the tone of disbelief in Sebastian's voice, Adelais had got the impression he knew he was being lied to. He had probably already seen her through the window. Perhaps that explained why he hadn't tried again.

Adelais was still glad she had stayed in the kitchens. It would have been awkward meeting Sebastian there and then, especially since it turned out he was coming to say goodbye. She wasn't sure how she would have reacted, the dance being fresh in her memory. She might have said something that would have made him feel guilty. That was the last thing she wanted.

'Do you think he's still seeing that girl?' Saskia said.

'What girl?'

'The one at the dance. You know, the tall one with the pretty smile. I can't remember her name.'

Adelais put down her ice-cream cup and shrugged. 'Neither can I.'

The intaglio press was the biggest machine, but mastering it proved easier than lithography. The skill and craftsmanship were all in the steel plates, into which the key images and patterns had been carved in almost microscopic detail. The massive iron press forced the dampened paper into the tiny pits and grooves in the plates, absorbing the thick pigment waiting there. The result was a raised image that felt rough to the touch, like fine sandpaper: the distinctive feel of fresh money.

The simplest part of the process proved to be the hardest: wiping away excess ink from the plate. There was some special art to it, to gathering unwanted colour from the steel without disturbing what was lodged in the depressions. Cornelis's notes spelled out the materials to use, but offered no other guidance. Again and again, Adelais's prints came out faint and patchy. She was afraid to increase the pressure too much, in case she damaged the engraving. In the end, she did not have to. After weeks of practice, she learned to cleanse the surface with three fast swipes of a fine cotton cloth, leaving the ink only where it had to be.

The letterpress came last. Its contribution to the banknote was two small serial numbers on the front. The frame was already set up. All Adelais had to do was choose her numbers and slot the movable type into place. Once the type had been inked the pull of a lever did the rest.

On 23 November, a Saturday, Adelais took a single sheet of esparto paper, one she had already cut to precisely the correct size, dampened it with a sponge, and watermarked it with the solution of polyethylene glycol. When it was dry she ran the paper through the lithographic press, adding magenta first, then yellow, then cyan, allowing twenty minutes to dry between each pass: three passes for King Leopold's side, and three for the Moor's. When the lithography was complete, the ink dry, and the alignment checked, she added the engraved images with the intaglio press, first the front, then the back, with another twenty minutes in between for drying. After checking the alignment again, she cut the paper down to size using a scalpel and a metal frame. Finally, she added the serial numbers she had chosen on the letterpress and recorded them in her uncle's notebook.

The bells were striking five when she held the finished note in her hand. It was crisp, pristine. She rolled it gently between her fingers, then raised it to her nose. It gave off a metallic smell. She had been perfectly calm all day. The precision of the work had demanded it. But now that it was done and there was nothing to go wrong, no mistake she could make that would undo her efforts, she found herself breathless, her heart pounding so hard she could feel it.

—— Twenty-four ——

Brussels, December 1957

Lieutenant Toussaint had returned from hospital one tooth lighter and with a metal plate in his jaw. By the time he was fit for duty the Tournai Forger's counterfeits were getting hard to find. Over the summer, the stream of reports from around the country had dwindled to a trickle. During the autumn, they dried up completely. Nor were there any further sightings of the man himself. Copies of an artist's impression had been issued to every bank branch in the country, based on Toussaint's recollection, but it did not help. Now and again, men were apprehended, men who looked a little like the man in the sketch, but, in every case, the investigation led nowhere. After a few months, these incidents dried up as well – either that or the local police stopped reporting them. Meanwhile, on the top floor of Federal Police Headquarters, de Smet's precious maps, with their forests of pins and flags, remained frozen, like useless relics of an old military campaign, long since abandoned.

De Smet showed no sign of letting go. He had to work on other cases like everyone, but his mind was always on the Tournai Forger. Every snitch in the underworld was squeezed for information, though nothing came of it. When the banks lost interest in tracking the counterfeit notes, de Smet began to track them himself. At night – at weekends too, Toussaint suspected – he made his way to the National Bank of Belgium and checked the stacks in the vaults. They always let him in, but there was something unhealthy about it.

'Isn't it possible we've scared him off for good?' Toussaint said one morning, after another visit to the Banque Bruxelles Lambert had yielded a single, shrivelled note, one that the *chef des dépôts* thought had been in circulation for at least a year. 'We know he's cautious.'

De Smet's eyes closed for a moment, as if the suggestion were painful. 'The blade itself incites to deeds of violence.'

'What's that, sir?'

'Homer, *The Odyssey*.' They had reached the car. De Smet weighed the keys in his hand. 'Perfect plates, keys to illicit wealth. Like the song of the sirens: sooner or later, he'll give in to it.'

'Maybe he has enough illicit wealth already.'

'You don't understand.' De Smet was behind the wheel. He started the engine. 'You can never have enough of being alive.'

The advent of the centralised command structure brought with it the promise of new approaches to policing, greater political accountability, and an injection of fresh blood. That, at least, was how the minister and his officials described it. Lieutenant Toussaint saw only disruption and uncertainty, fuelled by rumours and ambiguous statements of intent. In January, Colonel Bedois announced that he would be retiring. His replacement, it was widely reported, would be chosen from outside the ranks of the gendarmerie, which was hard to see as anything other than an insult. There was talk of a new training division, to be manned by long-standing and experienced officers. Everyone knew what that meant: men too old or too stubborn to adapt to the new system would be taken off active duty. Major de Smet had to be a prime candidate, an old dog who had not the slightest interest in new tricks. Toussaint hoped he himself was still junior enough to avoid being seen as an obstacle, but there was no guarantee of that.

Major de Smet's fixation on the Tournai Forger was not helping his cause. Colonel Bedois signed off on the extra police hours involved in the searches and interrogations, but with ever greater reluctance. The affair was well on its way to becoming a cold case. There were more pressing matters: cigarette smuggling, bootleg alcohol, insurance swindles – cases that might not involve master criminals, but where there was an actual prospect of arrests. That wasn't the most damaging part. The plain fact was: de Smet had made no tangible progress. Except for his solitary slip-up at the racetrack, the forger had proved too clever for him. By continuing to pursue the matter, de Smet was only drawing attention to his own failure, when what he should have been doing was burying it. That the forger had quit the scene was a stroke of undeserved luck. But de Smet's pride would not let him walk away. The thought that his quarry had evaded justice – had bested him – was apparently too much to bear. If de Smet was determined to sully his reputation, that was his affair, but Toussaint still harboured hopes of promotion. He decided to speak his mind.

He found de Smet on the top floor. It was almost a year since the last significant haul of currency. De Smet was standing in front of the big map, pulling out the black pins, one by one.

Toussaint felt an unfamiliar pulse of validation. Had de Smet finally come to his senses? 'I expect he fled the country, sir. That's what I'd do.'

'Is it?'

'Or he could be dead. Or maybe he got arrested for something else. That happens, doesn't it?'

'Yes, it does.'

De Smet was never going to admit that he had been wrong, and that his subordinate had been right, but the fact that he was abandoning his maps made it plain enough.

'We may not have caught him, sir, but at least we put paid to his racket,' Toussaint said. 'That's what matters in the end.'

De Smet emptied a handful of pins into Toussaint's palm and went on clearing the map. 'I don't think we've put paid to anything, Lieutenant. Not yet.'

'But we haven't seen a new note in months. It's over.'

De Smet glanced towards a table at the far end of the room. Under the light of an anglepoise, next to a microscope, lay an acetate folder. Inside it was a 500-franc note.

'A straggler,' Toussaint said, holding the folder up to the light. 'It could have spent years in someone's piggy bank.'

De Smet stepped back from the map. The black pins were all gone. 'That note isn't more than six weeks old. The cuts look fresh and there's no trace of oxidation in the ink.'

Toussaint was back at the racetrack, lying helplessly in the dirt, watching the other man pick up his gun and walk towards him. There had been a moment, a moment he did not talk about, when he had thought he was going to die.

'With respect, sir, does that prove anything? If the note was stored in the right conditions, if it had been kept in a stack, you might not see oxidation, and the cuts wouldn't fray either.'

De Smet wanted the note to be new, of course. He wanted to believe the hunt was back on, that he still might win. It had nothing to do with law and order, or justice. It was something he needed, something for himself. That was why he couldn't bring himself to answer.

The thought crossed Toussaint's mind that de Smet might be insane, and he wondered what it would take for his superiors to notice, or care.

— Twenty-five —

Ghent, December 1957

She decided to print more, in case the first one was a fluke. She made them in small batches, four at a time. By the time she was finished she had four dud banknotes, with bald patches where red should have been, and twelve good ones. The good notes had a face value of six thousand francs, more money than Adelais had ever seen before, but only a fraction of what she could produce. There was plenty of paper and ink. If there was a limit, it was drying space: the lines across the back of the room could hold around a hundred uncut sheets. At her current rate, she calculated it would take her less than ten days to print fifty thousand francs.

The next morning she folded one note into her purse and hid all the others in the safe. Even then, it took an effort of will to cross the threshold. Within the confines of the house creating the notes had been an exercise, a game, and she had been learning a craft along the way. It was hard to think of skills, of self-improvement, as the work of a criminal. Once the deception started things were going to be different.

Her destination that morning was Volderstraat, a thoroughfare lined with the kind of shops Adelais didn't usually go into: boutiques, jewellers, perfumiers. She walked up and down, looking for a crowd, but it was early and custom was slow. Looking at the mannequins in the windows and the women who passed her on the street, it struck her how out of place she was. These days fashionable women wore blouses with wide pointed collars, skirts that stopped below the knee, and jackets that stopped at the hips. Adelais's long dress and long coat looked like relics from the war.

'Can I help you?'

The shop assistant made it sound like an accusation. Adelais had wandered into a boutique with bridal gowns in the window. It was a bad choice. Everything was absurdly expensive. 'I'm not sure,' she said.

The shop assistant was in her twenties and wore a surprising amount of make-up. 'What are you after?'

A line of plaster legs, severed mid-thigh, were displayed along a shelf. The legs wore stockings in various shades. 'Some of those?'

'Silk or nylon?'

Adelais had only ever worn stockings in the winter, and they were made of wool. 'Nylon, I think.'

'Sorry, we don't do nylons. Try the Grand Bazaar on Veldstraat.'

The shop assistant had seen through her. She had known instinctively that Adelais was not a genuine customer. What if she'd had the same nose for counterfeit money? What if they all did?

The Grand Bazaar was a department store, the only one in Ghent. Adelais had already walked past it. She had been put off by the sight of a store detective pacing up and down by the main entrance.

She went into a shoe shop and picked out a tin of polish.

'This is for red shoes,' the man behind the counter said when she put it down. 'Is that what you want?'

Adelais had not paid any attention to the shade. She nodded.

'Twenty-five francs.'

The shopkeeper watched her open her purse. He had spectacles and slicked, thinning hair. Her hands were shaking. Her fingertips found the counterfeit note, its crisp edge. She wasn't going to get away with it. The shopkeeper was already suspicious. He would fetch a policeman and it wasn't as if she could run away. Adelais put two 20-franc notes on the counter.

The shopkeeper rang up the sale and handed her the change.

At the Grand Bazaar, business was starting to pick up. Some of the linens were on sale and a handful of women were tempted. They sifted greedily through the sheets and pillowcases, as if searching for treasure. On the other side of the floor, a smart young couple were buying a set of matching luggage. At the counters there was a short queue.

Adelais headed for the Kitchen & Dining section. There were islands of decorative crockery, place mats and glassware, and an electric food mixer on a stand of its own, the kinds of things she had glimpsed at Saskia's house, but never thought to own. She needed something portable and ordinary, something that nobody would think about twice.

A set of painted wicker napkin rings were on sale for eighty-eight francs. She decided they were a present, a perfect present for a great-aunt who lived far away. Waiting to pay, to keep her heart from racing, she tried to picture her imaginary relative and the birthday she was going to have: her great-aunt Magdalena, who lived in England, drank tea and walked her dogs.

The young couple left the shop, carrying their matching suitcases. Adelais stepped up to the counter. The shop assistant was a middle-aged woman with black bouffant hair. Adelais put down the box of napkin rings.

The shop assistant took a long time to find the price tag.

'They're eighty-eight francs,' Adelais said.

'I think this might be a five.' The shop assistant rang a bell, but nobody came to help.

'It doesn't matter. Eighty-eight's fine.'

The store detective was passing. Except for the jacket and tie, he could have been one of the dockers who drank at Aux Quatre Vents.

'Mr Nuyens, could you check the price on these?' the shop assistant said.

'No need to,' the store detective said. 'They're eighty-five francs.'

Adelais opened her purse. She didn't have eighty-five francs, not in real money. A customer with a little girl in tow joined the queue. The shop assistant was waiting for her. They were all waiting.

Adelais fished out the 500-franc note and placed it on the counter.

Where should she look? At the money? At the ceiling? At the people behind her? The little girl stared at her and hid behind her mother's skirts.

Adelais heard the till ring. The assistant was plucking 100-franc notes from the tray, one after the other, followed by three 5-franc coins. She counted them out into Adelais's palm. 'Thank you. Good morning,' she said with a smile.

Adelais's mouth was too dry to reply. She thrust the money into her purse and walked quickly towards the door. It was done. Four hundred and fifteen francs stolen. Four hundred and fifteen francs that belonged to the directors and shareholders of the Grand Bazaar.

She was at the main doors when the store detective's voice boomed across the floor. 'Miss? Just a minute, miss.'

She turned. He was running towards her, red-faced, determined to catch her before she made it to the street, to the getaway car that wasn't there. She closed her eyes. She wanted to be the little girl. She wanted to hide behind her mother's skirts.

'Miss?' The store detective had something in his hand: it was the box of napkin rings. 'You forgot your purchase.'

When Adelais got home that night, she found the house in darkness. She flipped the light switch in the hall, but nothing happened.

She could see her father in the kitchen, rummaging through the drawers and cupboards by the light of a candle. 'I thought your mother kept some money here. I haven't got a centime on me today, Ada. It's . . . most inconvenient.'

He sounded like one of those scrupulously polite beggars Adelais sometimes encountered in the middle of town, the ones who had flowers in their buttonholes and tried to make it sound as if their having no money was simply the result of absent-mindedness, and slightly quaint — certainly nothing to do with alcohol.

Adelais put down her shopping bag and reached into her purse for the change she had been given at the Grand Bazaar. She fed ten francs into the meter. The lights came on with a clunk. She left the rest of her change on top of the meter and went into the kitchen.

Her father was at the table unpacking her shopping bag. Under the electric light he looked older, his stubble white except for a patch on his cheek, his eyes red and rheumy. The bag was fuller than usual. With the money from the Grand Bazaar there had been less need to economise. Besides bread, cheese and a jar of pickles, Adelais had bought some pressed veal, potatoes, a tin of peaches, and a box of dates that had been marked down.

'What's this?' her father said. He had found the box of napkin rings. Adelais had forgotten to get rid of them.

'Nothing,' she said. 'They're a present.'

Her father looked up at her. 'It's not your birthday, is it? My God, I didn't forget, did I?'

'No, Papa, my birthday's months away. It's a Christmas present for Mrs Claes. You know, she owns the bar?'

'Of course.' Her father ran his fingers through his hair. 'Of course. It's Christmas soon, isn't it?'

'Yes, Papa.' Adelais put the napkin rings back in the bag. She would take them to the weaver's house and hide them there, just like Uncle Cornelis would have done. It was better than throwing them away. 'Are you hungry?'

Her father nodded. 'Come to think of it.'

Adelais laid out the bread and cheese, and unscrewed the jar of pickles. Pulling up a chair, she noticed that one of the clocks from her father's workshop was sitting at the other end of the table.

Her father followed her gaze. 'I tried to get some money for that. They wouldn't accept it.'

'You tried to pawn it? It isn't yours, Papa.'

He shrugged awkwardly. 'It's old Mr Geldmeyer's. I haven't seen him for months. I think he's probably dead.'

'You could still get into serious trouble.' There was nothing for it.

She would have to tell him. 'The police were here a while ago. Because Mrs Wilmots found her carriage clock at the pawn shop.'

Her father looked down at his plate. 'That's what they told me. That's why they wouldn't take this one. They said you paid the money to get it out for her. Why didn't you tell me, Ada?'

'I thought it was a mistake. I didn't think it would happen again.'

'You made sure it didn't.'

Adelais picked up a knife and cut some slices of bread. She did not want an argument. She wanted things to be calm and normal: two family members sharing a late supper in the kitchen. No recriminations. No secrets.

The cheese tasted nutty and sharp. She watched her father eat. He showed no sign of enjoying it, of having an opinion about it one way or the other. Eventually he gave up, leaving the food unfinished. 'I'm so sorry, Ada,' he said. He hunched over the table, fists clenched against his forehead.

'It doesn't matter, Papa.'

'I owe money everywhere. I can't seem to be able . . . If your mother were here . . .'

Adelais's mother hadn't kept him from drinking. As far as Adelais could see she hadn't even tried, as if the task was hopeless, or she had ceased to care. It was strange: Adelais's earliest memories of her parents were of two people in love. They used to hold hands and embrace, and smile at each other. Had something happened? Or was love a phase, something that had its season and then faded away, like an old picture in the sun?

Her father shook his head. 'You deserve so much more, Ada. You're the innocent one. What did you ever do? It isn't fair.'

For a moment Adelais thought he was going to cry. She found her purse and took out three hundred francs. They were the last of the notes from the Grand Bazaar. She put the money in her father's hand. 'Here. This'll help, won't it? Only . . .'

180

'Only don't drink it. That's what you wanted to say, isn't it?' Resentment flared from nothing, before subsiding just as quickly. Adelais's father spread the money out in front of him. 'You're right, Ada. It's time to make a change.' He nodded, a resolution building. 'Starting tomorrow, I'm going to clear my backlog, get some new customers. I may advertise in the newspaper. I used to do that, you know, when I was starting out. I'll get some new customers, and lay off the . . . the drink.' He picked up the money and tucked it away in his top pocket. The statement of intent had cheered him up. 'I'll be on top of things in no time. They won't take our house, Ada. Over my dead body. And we'll get a telephone. Every business needs a telephone. Then I'll be giving you money, instead of . . .' He smiled, and tapped his pocket. 'Anyway, we'll call this a loan, shall we?'

'All right, Papa.' Adelais smiled back and said she liked the sound of his plan, especially the part about advertising again. It was plain to see that she believed him – that he would stop drinking and make a fresh start, get back on his feet – and for the half-hour they spent together in the kitchen that night, it was as if nothing was broken in the de Wolf household that could not be mended.

—— Twenty-six ——

After work the next day, Adelais collected four more forged notes from the safe. She had not planned on using them so soon, but she was already out of money. This time she decided to head for Brabantdam, another busy street, close to where Sebastian used to live. Travelling straight from Schoolstraat she arrived with the morning crowd, clerical workers and businessmen moving briskly along the pavements, carrying umbrellas and newspapers. What she needed was to fit in, to look more like someone who might have a few thousand francs on her person.

As she approached her stop Adelais spotted a boutique. The mannequins looked smart and serious in shades of charcoal and navy. She got off the tram and set off across the road.

She did not see the scooter. She heard someone shouting behind her and turned. It was coming round the side of the tram, engine buzzing, the rider wearing goggles and a black helmet.

Adelais froze. The scooter was going to hit her. She saw herself waking up in a hospital, her wrist handcuffed to the bedstead, a policeman standing over her, asking her to explain how she came to have two thousand counterfeit francs in her purse.

The scooter skidded to a halt, then immediately set off again, winding its way around her, as if she were an obstacle that had no business being there, before accelerating away up the road.

The boutique was expensive. Jackets started at four hundred and fifty francs, blouses at three hundred. Adelais wanted more change than that. Besides, the shop assistant seemed suspicious. She clearly thought Adelais had come to steal something and scarcely took her eyes off her.

As she was leaving the boutique it started to rain. A gentlemen's outfitters sold umbrellas for a hundred and sixty francs. Adelais bought one with the second of her 500-franc notes. The shopkeeper gave her a smile and thanked her for the money. Though the rain was coming down harder, she did not open the umbrella until she had turned the corner at the end of the street.

It had been a little easier, buying something she actually wanted, that she would have bought anyway if she could have afforded it. Pretending to be interested when she wasn't, putting on an act, that was hard. She wasn't cut out for it, like those girls at school who couldn't tell lies without blushing.

At a general store, she picked out a picnic blanket and a blue beach towel with an anchor on it. She liked the idea of picnicking on the beach. The two items came to one hundred and seventy francs.

The store owner tutted as she handed over her third 500-franc note. 'Haven't you anything smaller?'

Adelais was too nervous to speak. She shook her head.

The store owner sighed and handed her the change. 'Not quite the weather for it, is it?'

Back on the street, Adelais spotted two policemen hurrying along the pavement opposite. They were headed in the direction of the gentlemen's outfitters. She did not wait to see if they went in. A tram was approaching a stop on Vlaanderenstraat. She joined the short queue of passengers and climbed on.

It was still raining when she reached Patershol. Struggling towards the house with her stick, her umbrella and her shopping bag, she tried to feel good about having six hundred and seventy francs in her purse that weren't there when she got up. It was not so many years ago that she had practised for months on the handcycle to win three hundred francs from her uncle. But it was no good. Things were different now: she needed more than pocket money. She guessed her father's debts ran into thousands and he would only run up new ones if he did not advertise his business and equip himself with a telephone.

She let herself into the house and put the unused notes back in the safe. The trip to Brabantdam had exhausted her. Her hands were still trembling and there was a high-pitched singing in her head. She lay down on the camp bed and covered herself with the beach towel. In two trips she had managed to exchange three notes. At this rate it would take her the best part of a week just to get through what she had already printed. And where was she going to go next time? There were not many places in the city where the shops were plentiful and the merchandise expensive. If she went back to the same streets too soon, she might be recognised. The thought of going back at all filled her with dread.

She couldn't ask her uncle Cornelis what to do, but there was always the notebook. There were plenty of pages she had barely skimmed. She had just opened the safe again when someone banged on the front door.

She did not move. It was just a salesman, most likely, selling brushes or kitchen knives. Nothing to worry about.

Whoever it was banged again, louder. Adelais went over to the window, and eased open the shutters. Down below, she could make out a motor-cycle helmet and a pair of shoulders in a sheepskin jacket – not the usual garb of the door-to-door salesman. And there was no suitcase, no sign he had anything to sell.

He was not a policeman. She did not have to open up. Then it came to Adelais that she may not have locked the door behind her. Had she even remembered to slip the catch?

The banging came again. 'Adelais, I'm getting soaked. Open up, will you?'

Adelais opened the window. 'Saskia?'

Saskia pulled off the helmet and looked up. Wet hair was plastered to her forehead. 'Who did you think it was?'

She was soaked through and shivering. Adelais had to let her in. 'What are you doing here? How did you find me?'

'I've been following you all morning.'

'What? How?'

'On my scooter. My pa got me one – second-hand, of course. I thought you saw me.'

'What are you taking about?' Adelais closed the door. 'That wasn't you who . . . ?'

But it was: Saskia had been on the scooter that had almost run her over outside the boutique.

'I came by your house and saw you getting on a tram. So I followed it. And then, well, it became a bit of a game. You're not angry, are you?'

Adelais was too scared to be angry. Saskia already knew enough to betray her. One telephone call to the police would be enough.

She pulled off her gloves. 'So this is the big secret. This is where you've been hiding out.'

Adelais needed time to think. 'We should get your hair dry.' She led Saskia up the stairs.

'There's that smell again, that paint smell. What is this place?'

They were passing the floor where the printing was done. The door was shut and locked.

'It was my uncle's.'

'The one who died?'

'He left it to me in his will. It's a . . . a kind of studio.'

'An artist's studio?'

'In a way.' For a moment, it seemed like a good lie, one that might stick: Uncle Cornelis, the artist.

They reached the top of the house. A packet of esparto paper lay torn open on the floor. That was all right: artists needed paper. Adelais picked up the beach towel and handed it over. While her friend dried her hair she went to the window and closed the shutters. The rain was easing, but the towers and spires of the city were still lost in the mist. Part of her wanted to share the truth, to tell Saskia everything. The weight of it all, the danger, was too much to carry alone. A different instinct told her that openness would mean disaster, sooner or later. Saskia was not someone who could be controlled, and secrets, once lost, could never be recovered.

Adelais turned. Saskia was kneeling in front of the open safe. All the money was inside, on the shelf, along with the failed efforts that hadn't yet been destroyed.

Before Adelais could stop her, Saskia had picked up a couple of the duds, the ones where the red lithography had gone wrong, and was squinting at them. For a few moments there was silence, broken only by the slow tap of raindrops on the roof.

'Saskia, you said I didn't have to tell you if I didn't want to. Well, I don't want to.'

Saskia wasn't listening. 'These aren't real, are they?' She looked up. 'You made them, didn't you?' She sniffed at the counterfeit note. 'That's what the smell is: ink.'

Why had she left the safe open? If she had only remembered to close it, she might have been able to keep her friend in the dark – not forever, perhaps, but long enough to make the money her father needed. She could stop after that and go back to her old life. Nobody would have to know. She could carry on working for Mrs Claes at Aux Quatre Vents, watch people drink and dance, without fear of being arrested.

Saskia was frowning. 'You can't use these. People will notice. You'll get caught, Adelais. You'll go to prison.'

Adelais came and knelt down beside the safe.

'Is that what you were doing on Brabantdam?' Saskia said. 'Using these? You were lucky they didn't grab you on the spot.'

Adelais reached into the back of the safe and picked up a couple of the notes that were good. She handed them to Saskia.

Saskia looked at them, one after the other, front and back: King Leopold and Rubens, Rubens and King Leopold. Then she went to the window, opened the shutters and held the notes up to the light.

A smile spread over her face. 'Clever girl,' she said.

There was no hesitation. She wanted to join in. It was frightening how quickly she made up her mind, as if there was no risk, no possibility of anything going wrong.

Adelais showed her the plates and the boxes of esparto paper and the machines on the floor below. She wanted Saskia to know that the processes were difficult, that everything had to be done with great care. All the same, she could not deny that an extra pair of hands would be welcome.

'The machinery's all yours. So it's only fair you get more of the loot,' Saskia said. 'What about two-thirds for you and one third for me?'

She was leaning over the letterpress, fingers running over the blocks of movable type. They were set up and ready for the next print run, whenever that happened.

'Fine, if you're sure you—'

'How many notes have you made so far?'

'Thirteen. Twelve in one go.'

'How long did that take?'

'A couple of days.' Adelais explained how the need to keep drying the notes slowed everything down.

'We should get some heating in here and better ventilation.'

'I suppose. Only, that's not the biggest problem.'

'Then what is?'

'Changing the notes. Changing enough of them. It has to be a shop with plenty of cash in the till. And it has to be busy so no one has time to get suspicious.'

'Why would they get suspicious?'

'They just do. A girl flashing 500-franc notes around? She could be a thief. She could be anything.'

Saskia was already on the intaglio press, turning the great iron wheel, a child with a new toy. Nothing was going to put her off. 'You shouldn't spend it in Ghent anyway,' she said. 'Too close to home. You don't want to be recognised.'

'I can't go too far. I have to be at work by noon.'

Saskia watched the roller go back and forth across the bed plate. 'You should give that up.'

'My job?'

'Think what it's costing you, being stuck there when you could be here, making real money.' Saskia looked up, grinning. 'You know what I mean.'

Adelais heard bells. It was time to leave for her shift at the bar. 'If we don't change the notes in Ghent, where are we supposed to change them? How are we supposed to get around?'

'Leave that to me.'

Saskia surveyed the room, hands on hips. She was wearing trousers, and with the sheepskin jacket and the goggles round her neck, she reminded Adelais of a fearless female aviator, of Amelia Earhart.

'Saskia, why do you want to do this? You don't need to take risks. You've got money already, haven't you?'

Saskia scoffed. 'I have what my father gives me, which is what he thinks I should have. I'd like to have my *own* money. It'd be . . .' She shrugged. '. . . better.'

Was the distinction so important? Adelais didn't understand why. But then, there had always been things in Saskia's world that were opaque to her, such as the way having a wealth of choices could become a burden.

'So how many notes could we make?' Saskia said.

'I don't know. As long as the plates hold up, we could keep going until the paper runs out. It's special. I don't know where it comes from.'

Saskia nodded. 'I've heard that. It's only made for banks. No one else is allowed to have it.'

'But we've plenty,' Adelais said. 'Thousands of sheets. Enough for millions of francs.'

As if they were ever going to print that many.

Saskia's arms were folded. She put her head on one side. 'How many millions?'

—— Twenty-seven ——

Saskia's scooter was a white Lambretta with red seats, and it took off a lot faster than Sebastian's old bicycle. Hanging on at the back, Adelais felt an exhilarating rush of terror. She hadn't experienced anything like it since the day she lost control of the Netley below the Sint-Joris Bridge and plunged down the embankment.

Once she had equipped herself with her own helmet and goggles, Saskia let her drive, especially when they were out changing money – or 'Patershol francs', as they took to calling them. It was better for quick getaways: Adelais would keep the engine running while Saskia bought the goods. After the purchase had been stuffed into one of the bags that hung off the handlebars, they would speed away to their next target. Once they had identified the shops, they could usually hit them all and be gone in less than half an hour.

Saskia was not a great one for advance planning. She usually left the decision about where to go until the last minute. She would look at the sky and say, 'I feel like going west today,' and Adelais would consult the map and give her some options. Towns with a market were top of the list, and in Uncle Cornelis's notebook Adelais had found a list of them. Other than that, Saskia preferred to be spontaneous – unless there was something in particular she wanted, like a pair of fashionable boots or a new hairdryer, in which case she would want to go to a big town with shops that stocked up-to-date things.

Festivals and carnivals were ideal. In February they went to the carnival at Aalst, where the men of the town put on dresses for the main parade and the floats were as big as buses. Adelais and Saskia ate waffles and ice cream as they watched them go by, keeping their goggles on as a precaution, before touring the retail high spots armed with eight thousand francs in forged notes. The proceeds went in the safe.

The carnival in Ostend went on for three days in March. There were rides and market stalls and all the shops were open. After an hour at the funfair, followed by buckets of mussels with chips, they went down to the sea and splashed each other. It was the first time Adelais had been on a beach since she was ten. When they had dried off, they got busy changing the ten thousand Patershol francs they had brought with them. The proceeds went in the safe.

In June, they watched the horse riders' procession at Eine, even though the shops were closed. In a cafe Adelais had two glasses of white beer, served with a slice of lemon. In another, she had strawberries with sugar and whipped cream. In July, they went to the World's Fair in Brussels and climbed inside the giant silver atom which stood a hundred metres tall, buying souvenirs on the way out. It was a hot day. Hurrying back to the station, Saskia ran into a bar. She came out again holding two bottles of beer and fanning herself with 460 francs in change. The proceeds went in the safe.

On the last Thursday in August, they rode east to Dendermonde, and watched the famous procession of giants, which they had seen advertised on posters, and which drew an enormous crowd. Adelais watched musicians perform in the market square and danced a waltz with a man dressed like the King of Hearts. Later, she and Saskia visited a dozen bustling shops and changed twelve thousand Patershol francs. All the proceeds went in the safe.

'You know, one day we might need a bigger one,' Saskia said.

Adelais was more worried about the cellar and what happened when the boxes were full. The idea of brand-new things getting damp and mouldy and going to waste also bothered her. One night, she filled two sacks with clothes and some toys and left them outside the girls' orphanage, which was only a few streets away. A couple of days later, she travelled to the boys' orphanage in the west of the city with two more sacks of useful items, because she wanted to be fair.

By that time, Adelais had bought a telephone for the house on School-straat. She had also placed several small watch-mending advertisements in the *Staatscourant van Gent*. For a while, the increased business seemed to galvanise her father. He was up by nine in the morning and Adelais saw a steady procession of satisfied customers collecting timepieces from his workshop. But after a month, things became more erratic. Repairs took longer or were not done at all. Customers started taking their pieces back rather than wait. It didn't matter. Adelais had more than enough money to cover the bills, and it was only when a refrigerator turned up that her father asked where it was all coming from.

'Mrs Claes gave me a pay rise,' Adelais said. 'She has me doing all sorts of things for her now, including her accounts.'

Her father smiled. 'You were always good with numbers, Ada. Stands to reason she'd trust you with the money.'

The truth was, Adelais had stopped working for Mrs Claes, except for Fridays and Saturdays, when she put in a shift for the sake of appearances, and because those evenings in particular felt empty without something to do. The rest of the time, she worked at the printing press, or rode out with Saskia to exchange her counterfeit francs for real ones.

On days without festivals or crowds, when the shops weren't busy, they improvised their own distractions. Saskia wore flimsy dresses under her jacket, cut low at the front. If there was a man behind the counter, she would smile at him and take a long time finding her money, giving him plenty of opportunities to stare. Once, when only partly hidden behind a clothes rack, she hitched her dress up, and adjusted her stockings, just as Adelais was paying. The shopkeeper, a portly man with a bald head, broke into a visible sweat. When it was a woman they were dealing with, Adelais would hurry over at the moment of payment, clutching at her abdomen, and ask in hushed tones if there was a lavatory she could use. 'Do you think she's all right?' Saskia would ask, watching her go. A brief moment of feminine camaraderie would follow, during which five hundred Patershol francs would make their way into the till.

Adelais wondered if any of these performances were necessary, but Saskia seemed to enjoy them. 'I should be in films,' she said one day, as they were climbing back on the scooter. 'Except this is more fun.'

'Is it more fun?'

Saskia had just bought a pillbox hat with a fishnet veil and was still wearing it. 'Much more. And I don't have to kiss anyone I don't like.'

'Clark Gable has false teeth,' Adelais said.

'That's what I mean. Can you imagine?'

'Aren't there some actors you'd like to kiss?'

'Like who?'

'Tony Curtis maybe?' They had just seen him in *Sweet Smell of Success*, and agreed that he was dreamy.

Adelais brought the discussion to an end by revving the engine, and moving off. The fact was, it wasn't Tony Curtis she thought about when she thought about kissing.

One summer evening Adelais used the new telephone to call the Medical Bureau in Lourdes. Father de Winter had given her the number, although he did not seem especially happy about it. She had to go through an exchange, where the operator spoke French, but after a lot of clicks and rattles, there came a plaintive ringtone that sounded far away.

A woman came on the line. She had a cheery, sing-song voice, and spoke very fast. She was sorry, she said, but she had not seen Madame de Wolf for some time. Adelais waited while she scurried off to get more information. When she returned it was with the news that Adelais's mother was on retreat with les Clarisses.

'Les Clarisses? Who are they?'

The woman repeated the name a couple of time, before switching into Latin: 'Ordo Sanctae Clarae.'

At last Adelais understood: the Order of St Clare. Nuns. But just because her mother was staying with them did not mean she had become one of them.

'When will she be back?'

The woman was sorry, she did not know. She offered to take a message.

'What's their telephone number? Can I call her there?'

'*C'est une retraite, mademoiselle.*' The woman sounded slightly scandalised, as if Adelais were a child who had just asked for a brandy. She was sorry, she said again, but telephone calls were not permitted.

They began printing in batches of fifty notes. It took a fortnight to get through each batch. Saskia brought her hairdryer to the house in Patershol and used it to cut the drying time between stages. By the time the last note was printed, the first one was dry. They increased each print run to one hundred notes. The work was exhausting, but they needed less time to complete it. The safe was filling up with the results of their labour, the bottom shelf with the forged notes, the top shelf with what they received in exchange. Meanwhile, the things they bought and did not want – ornaments, fashion accessories, kitchen utensils, linens – piled up uselessly in the room downstairs.

'This is a lot like working for a living,' Saskia said, when they had finally passed the quarter-million mark. 'There must be a way to go faster.'

The counterfeit money created its own pressure. Adelais felt it just as Saskia did. The more they had, the more urgently they wanted to use it, as if neglected notes would spoil. They started heading out earlier in the day, and recording where they had been. It was, Adelais realised, what Uncle Cornelis had been doing before he died. They travelled east via Antwerp and Brussels to Leuven and Hasselt. They went west to Bruges, and south to Kortrijk and Ypres, stopping at smaller destinations on the way. They kept clear of Wallonia. It was too far on the scooter, and they were afraid of standing out among French speakers. Otherwise the whole of Flanders was their hunting ground.

That was what it felt like: every time Adelais climbed onto the white Lambretta and fired up the engine she was a huntress riding out into virgin lands, braving the dangers not for profit, but for sport.

———

As money accumulated inside the safe in Patershol so did the pins in Major de Smet's map at Federal Police Headquarters. Every sighting of the counterfeit money was recorded there, every report logged in his brain. Lying in bed at night, alone or with company, he would try to read the patterns, to find the clues no one else believed were there. As the hours wore on, the ceiling above his head would become the map, clusters of deceit and corruption blooming like fungus over the cracked plaster. In his dreams, the threads of mould crept into the corners and down the walls, spreading and multiplying until they covered his slumbering body, thickening into a noose that closed around his windpipe. He would wake up, gasping for breath, calling his mother's name. He still lived at the flat in Laeken where she had died, strangling herself with a necktie, a bigamist's second wife, unable to bear the shame.

Late on a Friday afternoon, four counterfeit notes were sent in from a bank in Bruges. They were different from earlier ones: the paper was slightly stiffer, and it had acquired a sheen where the ink was thickest. De Smet was tied up with another case. He took two of the notes home and set them down on the desk, which was equipped with a magnifier and lights. After supper – tinned soup, eaten from the pan – he sat down to examine them more closely, in case there were other changes he had missed.

Under the highest magnification, he discovered cracks in the surface of the ink. It had been heat-dried. That explained the extra stiffness:

heat could cause shrinkage in the fibres, making them tighter and harder. De Smet pushed back from the desk. The forger had always been so careful, his operation almost leisurely. Why, after all this time, after almost a year of inactivity, was he suddenly in a hurry?

His thoughts were interrupted by the buzz of the intercom. He checked his watch: nine o'clock. The girl was on time. While she was climbing the stairs, he put her money in an envelope and placed it on the dining table – police rates, of course, but Isabelle did not mind that. Being with a policeman, at least she felt safe, she said.

Isabelle was a little older than most of the girls in the Quartier Brabant, but he liked the briskness with which she went about her work, and she didn't talk too much. She reminded de Smet of an aunt he'd once had – dead now, of cancer – who used to bathe him sometimes as a youngster. An early memory, erotic in hindsight, was of her playfully slapping his hand away when he had tried to cover his privates. He must have been eight or nine. The way Isabelle wore her hair, curled but tidy, short enough to stop short of her collar, was like his aunt too.

His mind was on the forgeries from Bruges, but the girl had been booked, and it had been a while since the last one. They shared a glass of brandy, after which it was time for Isabelle to wriggle out of her dress. She must have sensed his impatience, because they had sex at the end of his bed, without pulling back the covers, his feet remaining planted on the floor. De Smet had to close his eyes to finish. Otherwise his gaze would drift up to the ceiling, where the spots and threads of mould were multiplying in the gloom. It came to him that he never saw his aunt after his mother's funeral. Apparently she thought the suicide was his fault. The stupid woman blamed him for going to the police, as if he was supposed to keep quiet about his father's crimes, as if he was supposed to let the old man get away with them. How was he to know how badly his mother would take it?

After the job was done, Isabelle washed herself in the bathroom, and put her underclothes back on. 'Do you want some company for a bit?' she asked. He had paid for an hour.

De Smet shook his head. The forger was operating with a new kind of freedom. It grated on him. It was as if the gendarme's efforts were irrelevant, doomed. The rulebreaker would always be one step ahead.

'All right then. Do you have something for me?'

'The other room. On the table.'

The girl left. The forger had never heat-dried his work. He was a craftsman, a perfectionist. His only compromises had been unavoidable: watermarks that were not made at the factory during the paper-manufacturing process; letterpress type that had not been created specially by the central bank. Had someone else taken over, someone greedier and perhaps more ruthless? Such things happened in the criminal underworld.

Isabelle was in the narrow hallway, putting on her coat. De Smet pushed past her and went into the sitting room. The 500-franc notes were missing. He turned on the lamp and searched. Nothing.

He heard the front door open.

'Wait!'

Isabelle was halfway onto the landing. He grabbed her by the arm and pulled her back.

'What are you doing?'

He snatched the bag off her shoulder. She hung on to the strap. 'Stop it! What do you—'

He slapped her. She cried out, stumbled against the wall, shielding her face. A shoe came off, the heel broken. 'Don't, don't, please.' She was cowering, begging. Maybe he had hit her harder than he'd meant to.

He rifled through the bag. The missing notes were inside, folded into a side pocket.

'You said I could take it. You said—'

'I said the table, not the desk.'

Her money was still on the table where he had left it. He stuffed it into her bag and tossed it back to her. She didn't argue any more. She backed away into the hall, one hand still clamped over nose and mouth, leaving the heel of her shoes behind. De Smet shut the door.

Back at his desk, he put the first note under the magnifying glass. A fat red smudge had appeared across King Leopold's broad forehead. It took de Smet a moment to realise that he had got the girl's blood on his fingers.

— Twenty-eight —

By the end of winter they had a million francs. By summer, they had two million. Adelais gave up working at the bar altogether. After a day on the road or printing at the house in Patershol, she did not want to sit behind a till, writing chits, watching customers stumble round the dance floor, drinking themselves into a semblance of contentment. Besides, time was money now – and a lot of money at that.

'This safe isn't safe,' Saskia said one evening, as they knelt before the piles of cash. 'If someone broke in, they could take the lot.'

Adelais used to think of the house as a fortress. The doors were sturdy, with locks on each, and there were bars on the ground-floor windows. Her own home was not half as secure. But Saskia was right: it was foolish, gambling everything on locks that could be picked and a safe that could be cracked.

'Where else can we put it?'

Saskia ran a hand over the piles of notes, stroking them as you might a cat. 'A bank vault would be best. But we can't walk in with a suitcase. There might be questions.'

There were bound to be questions – followed soon afterwards by arrests. It was painful to think that even real money was a threat, a false friend if not used in the right way, at the right time.

'What did your uncle do? Didn't he say?'

Adelais looked through the notebook. The notary's name caught her eye: *FRANZ A. KLYSEN, Muinkkaai 5*. Klysen had been charged with handling Uncle Cornelis's estate. He had known enough about Adelais to avoid contacting her at home. Maybe he knew where Uncle Cornelis had hidden his money. *If you have any questions, you have my card*. They had been his parting words. Adelais had a question now, but asking it involved taking the risk of putting herself and Saskia in his power. She did not like the idea of that.

She carried on searching. In the middle of the last page, she found a name and an address. She had been so focused on printing techniques that she had scarcely noticed them before:

M. Antoine Schiltz

Banque Pétrusse

19 Rue Notre Dame

Luxembourg

<u>*Cash deposits accepted*</u>

This was information she was looking for. There could be no doubt. Hadn't Hendryck the barman told her exactly what the Grand Duchy of Luxembourg was for?

They decided to go together, but Adelais did not have a passport, and June had given way to July by the time they were ready to leave. On a warm, hazy morning, they wrapped a quarter of a million francs in silver paper and hid it in the false bottom of a wicker picnic basket, before heading for the station. Saskia had equipped herself with a camera. Adelais had bought a Luxembourg guidebook. Saskia wore a polka-dot sundress that barely reached her knees, and a straw hat with a blue ribbon. Adelais wore slacks that were too loose to be fashionable, but hid her leg brace. Both of them wore sunglasses.

It took six hours to reach the border outside the town of Arlon. A border guard got on the train and went from compartment to compartment, checking documents and offering customs forms, which few passengers accepted. He took no interest in the girls' luggage, or the contents of their picnic basket, although he did take time, between turning the pages of Saskia's passport, to appreciate the view of her legs, which she had shaved for the occasion and made no effort to cover.

The banks were closed by the time they arrived at the Gare Centrale. Adelais had expected a modest, provincial city, but Luxembourg was opulent and stately. The streets were straight and wide, the buildings stone-clad. By comparison, Ghent was gnarled and sooty. The guide-book directed them to the Grand Hotel Central Molitor, which it described as 'historic'. It stood on a long, tree-lined boulevard a few hundred metres from the station and was capped by a dome, as if doubling as a basilica. Adelais had never stayed in a proper hotel before, not one with an oak-panelled dining room, en suite bathrooms, and towels as thick as her arm. Throwing herself on the bed, with its eiderdown pillows, breathing in the smell of fresh linen, she felt as if she had wandered into somebody else's life, the life of someone important or famous. Their room cost a thousand francs per night, and there were fresh flowers in all the vases. It made her giddy.

After supper, they wandered up the Avenue de la Liberté to the heart of the city. Above the old, overgrown ramparts, they found the Rue Notre Dame.

'There's a casino around here.' Saskia had her nose in the guidebook. 'It was the Kaiser's headquarters during World War I, and Franz Liszt gave his last recital there, twelve days before dying of pneumonia.'

'We didn't come here to gamble,' Adelais said, but she had to admit she was curious. As a child, holidaying with her parents on the coast at Blankenberge, she had once found herself outside a casino. She had been fascinated by the bright lights and the sound of music drifting out into the night. Her father had wanted to go in, but her mother had been horrified. As far as she was concerned, casinos were the Devil's playgrounds.

'My father says casinos are a licence to print money,' Saskia said. 'We should fit right in.' And she winked.

Inside, there were several bars and a man playing a grand piano in the lobby. The air smelled of cigar smoke and half the bulbs were dud in the electric chandeliers. Saskia headed for the nearest cage where chips were bought and sold.

'*Bonsoir*,' she said, smiling at the cashier. She had pulled a 500-franc note from the top of her dress and placed it on the counter.

It was a needless risk, especially here, where there was no easy means of escape, but it was too late for Adelais to say anything.

The cashier smiled and handed over three stacks of chips, each a different colour. '*Tout va bien?*'

'*Très bien, merci.*' Saskia took the chips. The cashier put the money in a drawer without giving it a second glance.

They tried their hands at roulette, blackjack and baccarat. The roulette tables were the busiest, and somebody had something to celebrate with every spin of the wheel. Betting on even numbered reds, they went ahead a hundred francs. The wins were thrilling. Half an hour later, they were down almost three hundred. Luck arrived and stayed with them for a while. Then it vanished and refused to return. Adelais could see why people played on and on, waiting for the heady moment when their luck would turn again.

The cashier gave them a sympathetic look as he exchanged their remaining chips for two hundred francs, but Saskia did not seem bothered. 'That was interesting,' she said, as they were leaving.

'Interesting?' Adelais said. 'We lost three hundred francs.'

Saskia shook her head. 'No, we didn't, Adelais. We gained two hundred.'

She was quiet for the rest of the evening.

Monsieur Schiltz was a tidy, well-groomed man, with a strong jaw and a full head of grey hair. A bloom of colour suggested outdoor recreation: golf perhaps, or riding. Adelais could picture him in an advertisement for Scotch whisky or pipe tobacco.

She had telephoned ahead from the hotel, explaining that she was

Cornelis Mertens's niece and was interested in opening an account. Arriving at the bank, she and Saskia were greeted by men in livery, wearing white gloves. They were served coffee with cream and petit fours on a silver tray, which Adelais was too nervous to eat, but which Saskia devoured without any sign of gastric discomfort. After a few minutes, they were ushered into an office on the second floor. The windows overlooked a small square, at the centre of which stood a stone obelisk with a golden figure at the top.

Monsieur Schiltz spoke French with the faintest of German accents. 'We were so sorry to hear about the loss of your uncle,' he said, rising to his feet and offering his hand. 'We should like to express our condolences, if belatedly.'

'Thank you.' Adelais wondered why Schiltz said *we*, when there was nobody else in the room. She also wondered how he knew about Cornelis's death.

'I hope we can offer you the same service and commitment we were pleased to offer him,' Schiltz said.

Adelais nodded. The banker seemed to be waiting for something. She took the bundles of francs from her shopping bag, still wrapped in silver foil, and placed them on his desk.

If Monsieur Schiltz was surprised at this form of deposit, he did not show it. He unwrapped the bundles and swiftly sorted them according to denominations. 'What have we here, a quarter-million or so?'

'A quarter-million exactly,' Saskia said. She had crumbs at the side of her mouth.

'Very good.' Schiltz made no move to count the money. Perhaps it would have seemed rude, or perhaps it was too small a sum to need counting.

'There'll be more soon,' Saskia said. 'Two or three million at least.'

Adelais gave Saskia a look. Why did she feel the need to impress this man? How did she know he could be trusted? Saskia responded with a shrug.

Monsieur Schiltz was watching them. 'Might I suggest two accounts?'

'Two?'

'Joint accounts can produce . . .' Schiltz smiled. '. . . difficulties, and delays. Where people are in partnership, I always recommend separate arrangements when it comes to the proceeds.'

Adelais wondered what he meant; probably that if one partner went to prison, the other could still get at the money. Or was prison not the only danger? She thought of her uncle and the report from the consul: *the cause of death has not yet been determined.* Had Uncle Cornelis had a partner? If so, what had become of him? She thought of asking Monsieur Schiltz, but she was certain he would not tell her.

'Numbered accounts would suit you best, I assume?' he said, taking papers from a drawer in his desk.

Adelais did not know. 'Is that . . . ? Did my uncle . . . ?'

Schiltz hesitated for a moment, then gave a single nod of his head. 'As the holder of a numbered account, you will be known only by a unique number. By law, the bank may not divulge to anyone the identity behind that number.'

Their accounts would cost four thousand francs per year and paid no interest. 'I hope you will agree,' Schiltz said, 'that this is an acceptable price to pay for peace of mind.'

When the paperwork was done he rose to his feet and shook hands with them again. Outside the window, the gilded figure on top of the obelisk stared down at them, holding aloft a wreath.

'We call her the Gëlle Fra,' Schiltz said. 'The Golden Girl. I like to think of her keeping watch over the bank, our own private guardian angel.'

That evening, a storm broke over the city of Ghent. Lennart de Wolf jumped at the first peel of thunder. He had been pouring a glass of genever at the time and most of it ended up in his lap. This made him furious, not so much because of the stain on his trousers, but because there was no more genever left in the bottle.

Lennart left his workshop and made his way to the kitchen. The genever was strong and the floor seemed to roll gently from side to side beneath his feet. The sensation was not unpleasant. With the rain coming down and thunder echoing all round, he fancied he was aboard a sailing ship on the high seas. The genever was an expensive brand – much better than he used to drink – and often left him with no hangover at all. It was quite unreasonable that he should be denied the last glass because of a summer storm.

In the kitchen he found another bottle in the refrigerator, but it was empty. This wasn't right: there had been a good few fingers left when he had gone to bed the previous night. It could only be that Adelais had been drinking it on the sly – little Ada, already on the hard stuff! The thought depressed him. He should never have let her take work in a bar, even if the pay was good. Hard liquor was a slippery slope.

Another peel of thunder rattled the windows. He recalled that Adelais had been away the previous night with Dr Helsen's daughter. They had gone to some festival or other and were staying the night. She could not have been at the genever. He must have finished it himself. The thought that Adelais had not yet been seduced by hard liquor cheered him up. It was something he could drink to, if he could only find something to drink. He searched the cupboards and went to the refrigerator again. It was well stocked with food – dried sausage, bread and fresh butter, vegetables, pastries – but that was all. He picked up the sausage and bit off the end. It was tasty enough, but what it needed was a glass of strong red wine to go with it. If the shops hadn't been shut, he would have gone out and bought a bottle, possibly two.

An idea came to him: Adelais would be at the bar now. She could pick up a bottle before she left. Mrs Claes would probably sell it to her at the wholesale price. She would give her credit, if Adelais didn't have enough money.

The telephone was in the hall. The telephone company had supplied a phone book when they carried out the installation. Lennart flicked through the pages, searching for Aux Quatre Vents. It wasn't easy: his vision was blurred, and staring at the columns of type made him feel queasy.

He found the number in a section headed HOSPITALITY. After four rings Mrs Claes picked up the phone.

'Yes?' There were booming voices in the background, raucous laughter, music. It was a long time since Lennart had been inside a bar. These days, he did his drinking at home.

'I'd like to speak to Adelais.'

'I can't hear you.'

'Adelais de Wolf, please. I'd like to—'

'Who is this?'

Lennart cleared his throat. Had he been mumbling, slurring his words? He didn't think so, but then . . . 'I'm her father. Adelais's father. It's important.'

Outside, the sky flashed white. There was a crackle on the line, followed by the rumble of thunder.

'Adelais isn't here. Hasn't been here in months.'

'What did you say?'

'She's gone. She came into some money or something. Anyway, she quit.'

Lennart hung up. His head felt clearer, as after a shock, but his body wouldn't stop swaying. For the first time that night he wished he was sober – sober enough to make sense of it, to understand what it meant.

He looked at the telephone. Then he wandered back to the kitchen and stared at the refrigerator. The money hadn't come from Mrs Claes – of course it hadn't. How could he have been so stupid? The answer to that question was there on the table, in the form of an empty bottle. But why had Adelais lied to him? What didn't she trust him to know? *She came into some money.* He could only think of one possible source.

He hauled himself up the stairs, rage and alcohol fizzing in his veins.

It had all happened behind his back: his own daughter, cutting him out of the picture, treating him like some delinquent. Cornelis had planned it that way, no doubt about it. The man had never married, had no children, but still thought he knew more about fathering than anyone else. He as good as claimed Adelais as his own, in spirit. It used to drive him crazy. And now, in death, Adelais had taken his side.

There would be documents, papers. Where had she hidden them? He pulled open the drawers in his daughter's room, rummaged through her clothes. He tore down the books from the shelves and rifled through the pages. He knelt down and turned over the little rug beside the bed. Nothing.

The noise of the rain was louder up here, but the storm was moving away, the thunder echoing in the distance.

He should check under the bed. With a grunt, Lennart rolled forward onto his knees and lowered his forehead towards the floor. His gaze fell on two pairs of old shoes, a box of crayons, a jigsaw puzzle of the Taj Mahal in a cardboard box. His vision began to cloud. He felt nauseous. He was about to sit up when he saw, hanging down from the wire base of the bedstead, a fold of yellow paper.

It was a legal document: a lease contract for 37 Sluizeken, Ghent. Cornelis's name was on the document, crossed out. In its place, Adelais's had been added in type.

A house and its contents, no mention of money. Lennart felt the blood drain from his face. How long was it since they received the news from Holland? How many months had passed?

'No.' He got to his feet. 'No, no, no. Not you, Ada, not you.'

The room was turning like the arms of a windmill.

37 Sluizeken – was that where she was? Was that where he would find her? He had to get there. He set off down the stairs. A picture of his wife bloomed in his head, urging him on. But her face became Cornelis's face, and he was laughing.

'You won't take her, you fiend! You won't!'

At the top of the last flight, he caught his elbow on the banisters. The impact spun him round. He lost his footing and fell, head first, somersaulting once, before landing on the tiled floor of the hall.

Adelais found him dead two hours later. His neck was broken. The lease contract was still clutched in his hand.

July 1959

Dearest Adelais,

I learned the terrible news two days ago. It has taken me that time to compose myself sufficient that I can write to you, my dearest child, and offer you such comfort as I can in the light of this calamity. The Lord is our guide at all such times, and He will show the way to those who ask for it. So He has to me.

Father de Winter keeps a close watch over his flock. He has written to me about your strength, resourcefulness and maturity. Such pride, I felt — a sin, I know! — to read those words, and to learn how you cared for your father, putting him always before yourself, and leading him along the path of sobriety and purpose from which he had strayed. It must seem the cruellest of misfortunes that he should be snatched from you now, when so much had been achieved. But, my dearest one, you must believe me when I tell you that even in such misfortune, the hand of our creator is to be found if we but look for it, and with it His love — His love for you, and for me, however it may seem at this moment. At the very least, we will always have our memories of your father. These we can cherish for as long as we live, knowing that nothing can tarnish them.

The Mother Superior here is the kindest of souls. Though I have not entered her order, still she has readily agreed to the singing of a funeral mass for your father here this Friday. I have worked with the Poor Clares a good deal in Lourdes, and indeed they have asked me to undertake some work elsewhere for a while — which brings me to the matter of the funeral itself. Father de Winter will see to the arrangements. Your father will be laid to rest at the Campo Santo Cemetery, where many of the de Wolfs already lie. I would be there but for one thing: I have already promised to join a

Franciscan mission in the Congo. There is a school and a hospital, and they are very short of female volunteers. It is such vital work. The people there have suffered terribly, not least at the hands of our countrymen, even if many will not acknowledge it. Still, I am certain it is God's will that we should make amends when the opportunity presents itself, for how else will the guilt be expunged?

Dear Adelais, I have been torn between keeping my promise and breaking it. I have prayed without ceasing. I have confided in the Mother Superior. She told me to set aside my heavy heart, and leave the answer to God, for it would be given. And it has. We sail from the port of Marseilles next week. I will write to you again before then, of course.

Do not be angry with me. To be without you is part of the cross I have to bear — the hardest part of all. Open your heart to God, and you will come to understand that I have no choice in the matter. I must go where He directs me. This is my penance, and my hope.

With love,

Mama

—— Twenty-nine ——

It took three weeks for the medical examiner to complete his report, and it was not until then that the funeral arrangements could be finalised. He found a concentration of alcohol in Lennart de Wolf's blood of 0.12 grams per litre, quite enough to have affected his balance. His death was ruled an accident. The funeral service went ahead in late August.

Adelais did not feel like company. Alone in the house, she occupied the hours cleaning, starting in the attic and working down. She tidied up her room, ignoring the impulse to leave it as her father had, her books and clothes scattered across the floor. Stripping the sheets off her parents' bed brought a lump to her throat. Their musty scent reminded her of childhood, of days that would never come again. The sight of the bare mattress was bleak and final. She had to close the door.

She avoided her father's workshop for as long as she could. She did not want to look at his empty chair, his workbench, his things – none of them needed any more. She preferred to imagine him in there, working, a magnifying glass screwed into his eye, humming to himself as he used to. Unfortunately, her father's remaining customers started telephoning after a while. Adelais had to tell them to come and pick up their clocks, because the clock mender was dead. Some of them had heard already. Gradually the workshop emptied of timepieces, until there were none left but some broken watches and a pair of wall clocks that had been unclaimed for years.

Three generations of de Wolfs had been laid to rest at the Campo Santo Cemetery on the north side of Sint-Amandsberg. Lennart's plot had been reserved years ago. Besides the headstone, that left the coffin, the flowers and the pall-bearers to be paid for.

The funeral director, Mr Heirwegh, did not waste time describing the more expensive options. 'The Swedish pine is very popular,' he said, showing Adelais a black-and-white photograph in a printed brochure. The coffin was pale and had straight sides like a shoebox. Just underneath the photograph, in small type, was written: *BEF1200. Handles extra.*

'Now don't worry, my dear.' Mr Heirwegh smiled in a way that was meant to be reassuring, but which merely showed off his gold teeth. 'We can assist in an application to a church charity, if funds are a concern. We know them very well. And I understand your mother did a great deal of good work in the parish.'

Adelais nodded.

'And there are the civic authorities, although between you and me . . .' Mr Heirwegh lowered his voice. '. . . I wouldn't turn to them except as a last resort.'

Mr Heirwegh had been well briefed. He knew that Lennart de Wolf had been a drunk, that his wife had run away, that his daughter was, in effect, an orphan with no obvious means of support. He probably assumed the de Wolf girl was destined for the street, or to be a rich man's mistress, provided he could overlook her bad leg. It would have surprised him to learn that she had a numbered account at a private bank in Luxembourg. Adelais would have liked to see his face.

She handed back the brochure. 'What else do you have?'

Adelais opted for a cherry-wood casket with brass handles and a bouquet of white lilies for the top. Together with the hire of a horse-drawn hearse, the cost came to seven thousand francs. She paid the first two thousand in cash on the spot, which seemed to quell any doubts Mr Heirwegh might have had about accepting her business.

From the undertaker's, Adelais took a tram back to Volderstraat, where she had once spent the best part of an hour buying napkin rings. She went up to the ladieswear department in the Grand Bazaar and picked out a black velvet dress with long sleeves and a bow at the neck. She bought black stockings, a pair of black shoes, and a hat with a veil. Standing in front of a full-length mirror, she could not help reflecting that she looked good in them. Black suited her. It seemed to set off her blonde hair – except that her hair was a mess. After she had paid for the clothes, she found a hairdresser and had it cut.

Father de Winter, dressed in purple vestments, presided over the funeral Mass. Adelais sat alone at the front of the church, the other mourners behind her. More people had turned up than she had expected. She glimpsed the Wouters family, Dr Helsen with Saskia, a couple of veterans from the archery club, a cousin and his wife from Maldegem, and several of her mother's charitable ladies. She knew what they must be thinking: where was Mrs de Wolf? Why was her mother not there? During a pause in the proceedings, she heard some-one whisper *Africa*. She was glad. If they already knew, there would be no need to ask her.

Adelais listened to Father de Winter reciting the liturgy and felt nothing, only that she wanted the service to be over. His eulogy had the same effect. It seemed to be something he had taken from a book. Nothing he said truly applied to her father, except a long and tortured metaphor about clock-mending and eternal life.

After the final prayers, the pall-bearers picked up the coffin and carried it out of the church. Father de Winter followed the coffin and Adelais followed him. It was only when they reached the end of the aisle that she saw Sebastian Pieters. His mother was standing beside him, dressed elegantly as ever, but looking older than Adelais remembered her. Sebastian looked uncomfortable in a suit and tie, his hands clenched together in front of him. He tugged at his collar as Adelais approached. She had seen him do the same thing at the opera house. She had to hide a smile.

A westerly wind was blowing through the cemetery, carrying the sound of locomotives from the nearby freight yards. At the interment Father de Winter's voice sounded small, his words insignificant. Adelais watched the coffin being lowered into the hard ground. The cherry wood was rich and lustrous, the handles gleaming – everything new, like the lilies lying on top: the beginning of something, not the end. That was the promise, it seemed to her, or the pretence. But her father was dead and all his dreams had died with him, and she did not believe, as she walked from the grave, that she would meet him again in heaven, or anywhere else.

After condolences had been offered, Dr Helsen offered her a lift back to Schoolstraat, but it was only one kilometre away and Adelais said she'd prefer to walk.

'You don't want to be on your own now, do you?' Saskia said.

'Just for a bit.'

'We could go to the pictures later, if you like.'

'All right.'

'I'll see what's on and call you.'

When the Helsens had gone, Sebastian came over.

'How did you know?' she said, after he had kissed her on the cheek.

'My mother.' He nodded towards the gates of the cemetery, where Mrs Pieters was deep in conversation with Father de Winter. 'She reads the notices in the newspaper religiously. Never likes to miss a good death . . .' He checked himself. 'Sorry, I—'

'It's all right. It's good of you to come.'

He smiled. 'Are you all right? You look . . . amazing, actually – I mean, considering the—'

'You could have left it at amazing, but thanks.'

They started walking.

'Will you be all right?' he said. 'You know, money-wise? I heard—' He checked himself again. Adelais could imagine what he had heard. When it came to news of other people's vices, Ghent turned out to be a smaller town than she had ever realised.

'I'm fine. You don't have to worry. What about you? How's Antwerp?'

They had exchanged the occasional letter, but it was more than two years since they had seen each other. For a long time, she had preferred it that way.

Sebastian shrugged. 'They're working me hard, long hours and not much time off, but, you know, I'm learning a lot. It'll work out eventually.'

'Are you still seeing that girl, Marie-Astrid?'

They were halfway along the east wall of the cemetery, shaded by a line of plane trees. It came to Adelais that it was getting on for eight years since Sebastian had ridden his bicycle off the quayside into the River Leie.

'You won't believe it, but we're engaged.'

'What?' Adelais stopped.

'I was going to write and tell you, but then this happened and I didn't think you'd—'

'Engaged, that's . . . that's wonderful.' Adelais walked on, faster. 'Congratulations, Sebastian. I didn't know things had . . . That's great news.'

'I'm sorry to . . . Today of all days.'

'It's fine. I'm happy for you, both of you. When's the big day?'

'Next spring sometime. It's not decided. I'll let you know, of course.' Sebastian was tugging at his collar again. 'It's a shame you and Marie-Astrid didn't get a chance to . . . You'd like her. You'd be friends, I'm sure.'

'I remember her very well.' They had reached the main road. It ran all the way to Antwerp and bore the city's name. 'She gave me some good advice. I've never forgotten it. Now undo that top button before it chokes you.'

Sebastian took up her suggestion. A few of the other mourners were following on behind them. The rest had already disappeared.

'There was something else in the paper,' he said. 'I don't know if you saw it.'

'Saw what?'

Sebastian looked away up the road. 'The countess's hunting lodge, they're going to auction it, the city council, I mean. They had plans for it, apparently, but they kept falling through. So it's going to be sold, along with a lot of land they don't want. The auction's tomorrow, I think.'

For Adelais it was one more loss, one more piece of her past falling away. But not the biggest, she told herself – the least of them, in fact: a dream of no consequence that the two of them had happened to share. She could as easily picture somewhere else when she pictured happiness.

'Perhaps it's just as well,' she said. 'I hate to think what state it's in by now.'

'You're right, I suppose. It was bound to be sold sooner or later.'

'Yes, it was.'

'And it was never going to happen, was it, the hotel and everything? If we're being realistic.' Sebastian lowered his gaze and kicked the ground. 'Still, we had some good times there, didn't we?'

Adelais watched Mrs Pieters approach. She was coming to claim her son.

Saskia decided they should see *Attack of the 50 Foot Woman*, even though it was showing at the Rex, which was down by the station and further than they usually liked to go. They had already seen *Ben-Hur* and she must have thought a giant angry woman was the only other thing spectacular enough to keep Adelais's mind off the day gone by. It worked. With all the screaming and destruction, as the rampaging giant hunted for her unfaithful husband in her tattered underwear, it was hard to think about anything else.

The next morning, Adelais got up early, put on her black dress and took a tram to the centre of the city. The offices of the city council were on the Botermarkt, in a grand old building with tall windows and rows of black columns on the lower storeys. At the front desk, she asked where the auction of council property was taking place and at what time.

—— Thirty ——

They rode out towards Laarne on the scooter. It took less than fifteen minutes from Schoolstraat. Adelais did not tell Saskia where they were going or why.

'Good, I like surprises,' Saskia had said, as they were swapping seats.

They rode through the countryside at speed. It had been sunny in the morning, but by the time they reached the hunting lodge the sky had clouded over. Since Adelais's last visit, the ivy that was wrapped around the gates had been hacked down. In its place, a sign had appeared, reading KEEP OUT next to a silhouette of a dog's head.

Saskia peered through the bars at the overgrown driveway. 'Who on earth lives here? Sleeping Beauty?' That summer they had seen the Disney cartoon at the Capitole, twice.

'You'll see.'

Saskia examined the padlock and chain that still secured the gates. 'Not unless you've a hacksaw, or a magic spell.'

Adelais reached into her shoulder bag. 'Or a key.'

She opened the padlock and removed the chain. The gates swung open with a mournful whine worthy of a B-movie horror. She climbed back on the scooter. 'Come on.'

'What about the dog?' Saskia said.

'There is no dog.'

The house looked much the same from the outside, except that another window had been boarded up and scaffolding covered part of the roof. The air was clinging and heavy, laced with sickly smells of decay coming from the woods. They walked around the terrace and then into the garden at the back, Saskia playing along, waiting to be told what it all meant.

'It was built by a countess,' Adelais said, 'for parties. She was famous for them.'

'My kind of girl,' Saskia said.

'Let's have a look inside.' Adelais had two more keys for the front door. They crossed the hallway and climbed up the grand staircase.

'It'd be a nice old place, if it was done up,' Saskia said. 'Pity it's a ruin.'

'It's not a ruin. Structurally it's sound. Once the roof's been repaired, it's mainly plaster and paint. Some windows might need replacing, and I expect the drains—'

'All right. What's this about? How do you know all this? How do you have keys?'

They had stopped outside the ballroom. Adelais opened the doors. 'You like it, don't you, the house?'

'Yes. So?'

'I bought it.'

'*What?*'

'At auction. The city council were selling it off. There wasn't much interest, actually. Mostly people wanted the land – farmers, I suppose.'

'How much?'

'It had a really low reserve price and I didn't bid much more than that.'

'*How much?*'

Adelais dabbed at the parquet floor with her stick. 'All of it, pretty much. Yours and mine. I'll pay you back as soon as I can.'

Saskia walked away across the ballroom without saying anything. She was angry, of course, furious. She had every right to be. She should have been consulted, at the very least. If there had been time, Adelais *would* have consulted her – except that Saskia would have said no. No, was the realistic response.

She was standing by the windows. 'This is the hotel your friend wanted to open, isn't it? I remember you told me about it.'

'Sebastian found the place. It was his idea, but he's gone now. I can do it without him. Or we can.'

Saskia went through into the adjoining room, taking in the elegant plasterwork and the classical lines. 'How are you going to explain the money? A girl from Sint-Amandsberg who used to work in a bar? No one will believe it.'

'My great-aunt Magdalena in Luxembourg, she left me everything in her will. A rich eccentric. I'm working on the story.'

'There'll need to be more than a story.'

'I'll get more.'

Saskia shook her head. She was going to walk away, or insist that Adelais cancel the purchase before the money changed hands. Renovating an old hunting lodge, starting a hotel, that was hard work, not her idea of fun. Adelais had hoped she might see things differently once she saw the place. She realised now that wasn't going to happen.

Saskia had reached the west-facing salon next to the ballroom. 'This is where you'd put the roulette table. Maybe two of them.'

'Roulette tables?'

'That's how you'd make this pay. A licence to print money, remember?' Saskia laughed. 'Like having your own bank. You couldn't lose.'

Adelais saw it now: Saskia had been thinking about casinos ever since their trip to Luxembourg: well-heeled people, exchanging cash for chips, and chips for cash, and losing plenty in between. 'There won't be gambling here. It's not allowed.'

'Not without a licence. We could get one. Another draw for the tourists they're so desperate for.'

Adelais did not know what to think. Gambling had never been part of the dream, not the dream she had shared with Sebastian, but she was already beginning to see how it might work.

Saskia walked back into the ballroom. Her face was flushed, her eyes bright. It was how she had looked when she first saw one of Adelais's forgeries: a world of illicit possibilities opening up.

'So . . . ?'

'I have one condition,' Saskia said.

'Name it.'

'Whatever happens, whatever we do here, we keep Sebastian Pieters out of it. Agreed?'

The Countess

— Thirty-one —

Brussels, Spring 1960

At the end of March, Major de Smet received a copy of the report from the Currency Management Department at the National Bank of Belgium. He immediately took it up to the operations room on the top floor of Federal Police Headquarters, ignoring the telephone ringing on his desk.

The report was twenty pages long and consisted mostly of data arranged in tables. It was written in French. A label stuck to the cover read 'Translation on Request'. De Smet flipped to the summary on the last page. It was signed by Monsieur Etienne, the *chef de département adjoint*. In the twelve months to December, it said, 2,407 high-quality counterfeit notes, with a notional value of BEF1,203,500 had been identified by the central bank and destroyed. The condition of the notes covered the full range, from pristine to badly damaged.

It is clear that many of these notes have been in circulation for a considerable period, certainly several years. As such, many are likely to have passed undetected through the retail banking system at various times. On the other hand, the high incidence of freshly printed notes, suggests that this particular counterfeiting operation is not only continuing, but has increased the pace of its activities.

Taking into account these factors, and assuming that the deterioration rates of legitimate and counterfeit currency are comparable, the Bank estimates that when it comes to counterfeit notes of this quality, the number recovered account for between a quarter and a third of the total in circulation.

De Smet turned to the big map. The white pins had multiplied, their clusters growing like tumours across the face of the country, fatter and whiter in Flanders and western Wallonia, but spreading east all the way to the border. There were so many now, so many outbreaks, he could no longer keep the details in his head.

He pictured the millions of counterfeit francs moving unnoticed through the country, passing from buyer to seller, over and over again – doing what currency was supposed to do: facilitating trade, acting as a medium for the exchange of goods. The recipients rarely lost out. By the time their banks had spotted a forgery, it was too late to identify where it had come from. The banks themselves were compensated by the National Bank of Belgium – an incentive for them to report, rather than turn a blind eye. As for the central bank, it had the power to print what replacements it wanted. From an economic point of view, the counterfeits were irrelevant. Their injection into the banking system would no more than compensate for the currency lost every year to washing machines and laundromats. Perhaps that explained the forger's audacity: he didn't consider his crimes to be criminal.

There were times when it seemed de Smet's superiors were of the same opinion. De Smet had decided it was time to make public the forger's activities, to put every retailer in the country on alert. The new man in charge, Colonel Delhaye, had turned down his proposal. A campaign would involve issuing close to a hundred thousand notices, each one needing to be correctly addressed and posted. It would consume too much money and too much manpower. Besides, the last campaign, involving the forger's likeness, had yielded nothing but a burdensome plethora of false leads. What was required, Delhaye had said with nauseating condescension, was 'some good old-fashioned legwork'.

De Smet looked through the tables in the Bank of Belgium's report.

In one set, the biggest monthly recipients of compensation – the branches of retail banks and savings banks – were listed by name. At the bottom of every list was the total of compensation for *Others*, which was always substantial. De Smet could see no use for the information. He already knew where the counterfeit notes had been found and when. But the way the smaller claims had been lumped together under a single heading stuck in his mind. Had he gathered too much information? The idea went against his every instinct. Was it possible that he would see more clearly with less of it?

He spent an hour going through three years' worth of records, pulling pins from the map, one by one. Any report of counterfeit currency amounting to less than three thousand francs, he discounted. Slowly, the forest of pins began to thin, the tumours to shrink. In their place, a picture began to form. It was indistinct at first. It would break apart and become confused, like a radio signal drowning in static, but gradually it solidified. De Smet stood back. It was like a child's drawing: inaccurate, incomplete. But he knew what it was telling him.

Captain Toussaint was on the telephone, making a reservation for lunch at the Comme Chez Soi, when Sub-Lieutenant Masson stuck his head round the door. 'Colonel Delhaye says can you take the lecture on arraignment procedures? The class is waiting.'

'That's Major de Smet's class.'

The sub-lieutenant shrugged. 'He's not there, sir. He seems to be—'

'Have you checked his office?'

'Yes, sir. There was a note on his desk, addressed to you.'

'A note?'

'Yes, sir.'

'Where is it?'

'On his desk, sir.'

Toussaint sighed. 'Well, that is helpful, thank you. Tell the colonel I'll be there in a minute.'

Toussaint apologised to the restaurant and crossed the hall to de Smet's office. The material on arraignment procedures was in a folder. The note lay on top. It read: *There is a pattern. Check the files. De Smet.* Toussaint put the note in his pocket and hurried to the lecture room where the new recruits were waiting.

For forty minutes, he rambled through the subject of the day, picking up what he could from de Smet's file, improvising from memory. As soon as the class had been dismissed, he hurried up to de Smet's operations room on the top floor. It was dustier than other parts of the building, and the windowpanes were covered with a film of brown dirt. The cleaners could hardly ever get in because de Smet kept the door locked most of the time. Toussaint looked around for some clue as to what de Smet had found.

The big map had changed: at least three-quarters of the pushpins had gone. Most of those that remained were in groups, connected with string, like constellations of stars. The files from the last two years lay open on the table. The largest reports of counterfeit currency had been marked in red. Toussaint remembered going through a similar exercise years earlier, near the start of the investigation. It had yielded nothing significant. But looking at the map now, he saw that the constellations were arranged in a circle. They reached out, irregular and uneven, sometimes overlapping, from a hollow centre, a centre where there were now almost no stars at all.

The forger had made a small mistake. He had been tripped up by an excess of caution, by the fear of being recognised perhaps, of breaking the law too close to home. That was where de Smet had gone. At the heart of the hollow centre was the city of Ghent.

Assistant Commissioner van Buel offered little by way of comment. Forty-five years old and overweight, he sat on the other side of the table at municipal police headquarters, taking notes, his cigarette smouldering unattended on the edge of a red glass ashtray.

De Smet passed over the sketch from Ostend.

'This is who you're after?'

'It was. He was seen three years ago. Someone else may have taken over since then.'

'Who saw him? You?'

'Another federal officer.'

'But he got away.'

'Yes.'

Van Buel shook his head, his breath wheezing through flared nostrils. 'I don't recognise him. I'll pass this around though.'

'I'd like to look through your arrest files.'

'All right. You want to narrow it down? This is a big city.' Van Buel cracked a smile. 'We get a lot of public urination.'

De Smet did not laugh. 'Crimes against property, smuggling, fraud, false accounting, receiving stolen goods – and anything involving counterfeit money, of course.'

'Of course.'

'Or any other type of forgery, including documents, bonds or contracts.'

Van Buel was writing again, taking everything down, word for word. It was, de Smet realised, a subtle form of mockery, although outwardly cooperative. Resentment of the gendarmerie was rife among municipal officers. They resented the federal police the way provincial cities resented the capital, and for much the same reasons.

'So these counterfeit five hundreds, how are we supposed to spot them?'

De Smet took a sample from his pocket and slid it across the table. 'You won't, unless you're expecting them. The watermark's too faint, but not by much.'

Van Buel frowned and picked up the note. He squinted at it, turned it over. 'Now, that is good.' He held it up to the light. 'Christ, yes.'

De Smet could not help feeling a glow of pride. 'As I explained, our man hasn't passed many of these notes in Ghent, not for the past two years. That's how we know he's here.'

'Not fouling his own nest, you mean?'

'Exactly. But there may be other ways to track him.'

'Such as?'

'We believe he's enriched himself to the tune of several million francs in the past few years alone. That kind of money has a habit of surfacing. It's hard to hide, especially from other criminals. What's the use of money if you don't spend it?'

Van Buel had stopped writing. 'Maybe. But you said he was careful.'

'He is, usually.'

'Then millions or not, I wouldn't expect him to flaunt it. In this town, trust me, anything conspicuous, it'd be noticed.'

Commentary: BRITISH PATHÉ NEWSREEL – June 1961

All across Europe tourism is booming, and the ancient city of Ghent, the historic capital of Flanders, wants its share. Local rival Bruges may have a head start when it comes to reputation and accommodation, but Ghent is brushing up – and catching up – fast.

Ghent's many miles of canals and rivers are being dredged and cleaned. Factory discharges are making way for pleasure boats and quayside cafes. Professional guides, fluent in many languages, offer the visitor expert insight into the city's artistic and cultural treasures. The soot of ages is being scrubbed from castles and cathedrals, and new tourist accommodation, from youth hostels to first-class hotels, is opening its doors.

Take this splendid example a few miles to the west. During the war it played reluctant host to officers of the German Luftwaffe. No surprise, they left it in a right mess. Now this belle époque beauty has been lovingly restored, and today serves as Ghent's newest luxury hotel. Nestling in the bosom of lush Flemish pastures, guests at the Astrid Christyn enjoy elegant interiors, fine dining, and the thrill of a night at the gaming tables. Such investment carries risks, but – look there! – Lady Luck has certainly smiled on this happy punter. Ghent will be hoping its bet on tourism pays off too. Fingers crossed – or as they say in Flanders, duimen maar *!*

— Thirty-two —

Flanders, July 1961

Regular guests call her 'the countess', and many go away thinking she really is one. Most nights at ten o'clock, by which time the band is playing, she strides into the ballroom, dressed in silk, in embroidered Chinese jackets with tapered trousers or slender gowns that reach to the floor. A glass of champagne is always waiting for her. Hendryck, no longer just a barman, but also a deputy manager, sees to it personally, uncorking the bottle with a flourish at one minute before ten. The band – usually a quintet – recognises the signal and segues into a favourite waltz. The countess cuts a striking figure. No one in the room, men and women alike, can resist watching her as she takes to the floor. She dances with Hendryck if nobody else has had the courage to ask. More usually, her partner is a guest or one of the regular evening visitors: the president of the Chamber of Commerce, the regional chairman of Kredietbank, which has reportedly lent the hotel several million francs, or Mr Reimond Huybrechts from the city council. Mr Huybrechts is a particular favourite, although to onlookers it isn't obvious why. He isn't distinguished or elegant or a good dancer. What the onlookers can't appreciate is Mr Huybrechts's role as chairman of the licensing panel, where he has had the vision and the good judgement to lend the countess his support. Without it, some say, the hotel might never have opened.

These days the countess wears a bespoke orthotic on her right leg, crafted by a specialist company in Holland. Where once there was iron and wood, now there is aluminium and moulded foam rubber, together with ratchets and springs that grant her a freedom of movement that was never possible before. When she takes off her support at the end of each day, she no longer finds deep, purple-red depressions in her flesh, but a rosy bloom. Her leg and hip still get tired, but for a couple of hours – sometimes more – she moves without the aid of a stick, like anyone else. On the dance floor, she is acknowledged to be an expert: light, agile, strong. For most of her partners, one dance is never enough, but the countess is in demand and one dance is all they get.

Whether partnering his employer or not, Hendryck's talents don't go to waste. He considers it part of his role to request the pleasure with any female guest who looks likely to welcome the gesture. Older ladies in particular appreciate his proficiency and his greying matinee-idol looks. A lady from Ohio, travelling with a female companion, once slipped a ten-dollar bill into his top pocket at the end of an evening, with her room number written across the back. He wasn't quite sure, he said afterwards, if it was a big tip or a small down payment.

After a dance or two, the countess collects her glass. It never needs refilling. She takes a sip and raises it to the portrait that hangs behind the bar. Many guests assume that the subject – a young woman with short red hair and green eyes, and a rosy blush on her cheeks – can only be the original countess, Astrid Christyn, the aristocrat who built the lodge, and who gave the hotel its name. The staff and the locals know better: the lady in the picture is not an aristocrat, but Adelais de Wolf's great-aunt Magdalena, the reclusive Luxembourger whose bequest made the hotel possible. It was painted when the lady was young – as young as Miss de Wolf is today.

The toast is a cue for Rolf, the retired docker now in charge of hotel security, to open the doors into the gaming room. He and the countess exchange a few words, then he steps back to let her pass.

The gaming room was once a dining room, with a table down the middle that would have seated thirty, if not more. In its place there are now two roulette tables, laid end to end, with blackjack available on demand beneath the tall south-facing windows. The croupiers are women, all scrupulously professional. Two of them were recruited from the casino in Luxembourg, which is being closed to make way for an art gallery. Another couple have experience working at the casino in Blankenberge. It is one of the features of the Astrid Christyn – one of its attractions, some say – that most of the employees, like the owner herself, are young women.

The countess spends an hour or so chatting with guests and visitors, making them feel at home. She pays special attention to foreign visitors – Dutch, French and Italians are the most numerous, but the English-speaking clientele is growing. She makes a point of learning about their businesses and itineraries. Thanks to the newspapers she reads every morning, she is thoroughly au fait with current affairs, whether local or international. She is concerned about the Cuba situation, following the failure of the American-backed invasion. She is intrigued by the possibilities of space travel, now that the Soviets have put a man into space. She is on hand with reliable restaurant recommendations, and information about Flemish festivals and cultural attractions.

At around eleven o'clock, when the gaming tables are at their busiest, she moves on to the cage, which is simply a counter on the landing with a polished brass grille around it. On busy nights, the general manager, Miss Helsen, is always on duty there, buying and selling chips. The conversation lasts a few minutes, then the countess returns to her guests. Her presence always seems to lift the mood. Champagne flows, the band outdoes itself and is applauded for every number. On warm nights they open the French windows and let moths flutter and dive around the big chandelier.

At midnight, like Cinderella, the countess slips away, usually to bed, but sometimes into the garden. On fine nights, she walks around the ornamental pond with its statue of Artemis, and along a path that passes beneath the beech trees.

The swings are still there, still sound, even though children are a rarity at the Astrid Christyn. She sits down and watches the house, its windows bright, music drifting out across the grounds, where it mingles with the sound of the breeze in the branches above. After a while she starts to swing, back and forth, going higher and higher, just as if she's eleven years old again, visiting for the very first time, but only when she's certain nobody is watching.

—— Thirty-three ——

Saskia looked after the cash. At school, she had never been much interested in mathematics, in arithmetic, geometry or algebra, but when it came to money it was different: the subject brought her a thrill that numbers in the abstract never had. Watching the gaming tables, calculating the odds, selling chips, even doing the books at the end of the week, gave her an unfamiliar sense of power. The fact that the business had two sides – one legitimate, one criminal; one transparent, one hidden – made it all the more enjoyable. They were breaking the law and no one suspected a thing. The two of them had the whole world fooled. What could be more delicious? In fact, if it hadn't been for the illegal side of the business, for the secrets she and Adelais shared, she might not have bothered with it.

Adelais slept in the basement of the Astrid Christyn, next to the kitchens, in what had once been a servant's room. It was small and the bed took up most of it, but it was always warm, and the appetising smell of baking bread and pastries woke her in the mornings, spurring her to get up and start seeing to her guests. On Sundays, she would dress in dark clothes and ride into the city. She had her own scooter now. A pale blue Vespa, it was not as fast as the Lambretta, but it got her to St Bavo's in time for Mass. The church in Sint-Amandsberg was closer, but the cathedral was on her way, and besides, if she went to Mass at the Church of Sint-Amandus, she might have to talk to Father de Winter afterwards. No doubt he had heard about the gambling at the Astrid Christyn and did not approve. Perhaps he thought she should have shared Great-Aunt Magdalena's legacy with the Church. Whatever the reason, she found him unusually grave and tight-lipped these days, as if in some way she had disappointed him.

After Mass, Adelais rode to the weaver's house, taking a circuitous route through the narrow streets. Sometimes Saskia was waiting for her, sometimes she would come later. They spent a few hours together, working on the presses, before gathering up the notes that were dry and ready for use. After they had been checked for flaws, some of the notes were sealed in an envelope and hidden inside the silk lining of Adelais's Gucci Constance handbag. The handbag went under her seat on her ride back to the hotel.

There was another safe at the Astrid Christyn. It was built into the back wall of the office, but the Patershol francs did not go in there. Instead, they were kept in the locked drawer of a desk, which had been equipped with a false bottom, like the picnic basket they used on their journeys to Luxembourg. All the money in the safe was clean, and the correct amounts were always there. They even let Hendryck have the combination, although he was hardly ever called upon to use it.

On busy gaming nights, at half past eight, Saskia would collect the float from the hotel safe, while Rolf waited outside the door: thirty thousand francs was usually enough. Before leaving the office, Saskia would exchange part of the float for counterfeit notes and hide the proceeds in the desk. Rolf never came in, unless told to. Like Hendryck and the rest of the staff, he had no idea what was going on. It had to be that way, but sometimes Saskia liked to speculate about what he and the others would do, if they ever found out. Who among them would accept a slice of the profits, in exchange for keeping quiet? Who would go straight to the police? She had asked Adelais these questions, but Adelais never wanted to talk about things like that.

In the cage, Saskia put the Patershol francs in their own compartment. Cash came in during the course of the evening, less of it went out again. The croupiers told stories about the tricks crooked casinos could employ, but there was no need to cheat at the Astrid Christyn.

The house always won in the end. As the night wore on, the gamblers who had done well, and those who had not lost everything, stopped by the cage to sell back their chips. By that time, Adelais had identified the best targets: the drunks, the heavy spenders, and the foreigners on the verge of moving on. Their chips would be repurchased using Patershol francs. The notes would disappear into their wallets, to be exchanged days or weeks later at the border or the airport or at a bank in their home town, in Amsterdam, Lille or Milan. There was no need to visit shops any more. The gamblers at the Astrid Christyn carried their counterfeit money all over Europe, where there was little or no chance of it even being recognised.

As chairman of the licensing panel, Mr Huybrechts's endorsement had made all the difference. An overweight, avuncular man with a red face, it was lucky that he supported the city council's embrace of tourism, and even luckier that he suffered from persistent lumbago, a condition for which he received treatment at Dr Ralf Helsen's surgery. Saskia had often seen him come and go. He swore that her father was a miracle worker, the only man in Ghent who could alleviate his discomfort for any length of time – which, in Saskia's opinion, made his condition sound a lot more mysterious than it really was. 'Of course he has back trouble. With a belly like that, it's a wonder he can stand up.'

In spite of his condition, Mr Huybrechts gave a lot of time to his work. Bars, restaurants, hotels and places of entertainment were thoroughly investigated for their suitability, and this did not stop once a licence had been granted. Mr Huybrechts made visits throughout the year, making sure the food and drink were up to scratch, that the hospitality was of a standard that did credit to the city, and would enhance its growing reputation as a travel destination.

Mr Huybrechts adored the Astrid Christyn. He adored its ambition, its elegance, its unashamed *joie de vivre*. He also adored dining with Miss Helsen at a table reserved for his visits, and dancing with Miss de Wolf as he used to dance with Mrs Huybrechts. Most of all, he adored the extra sessions of physiotherapy with Dr Helsen, for which he rarely, if ever, received a bill.

Adelais wanted the hotel to be viable in its own right, but it became clear within weeks of opening that it needed to be bigger. The stable block would give them six extra rooms, but completing the renovations would cost at least another million francs. They did not have another million francs, and it was unlikely anyone would lend it to them, given that they were in debt already. What they had was the gaming licence and the operation in Patershol, the two going hand in hand. They made the difference between profit and loss.

Mr Huybrechts was considerate enough to avoid the busiest nights of the week. He could usually be counted on to show up on the first Wednesday of every month, but when August came around, there was no sign of him.

'Perhaps he's gone on holiday,' Adelais said, as she watched the dining room filling up. 'It's that time of year.'

'I bet he's had a heart attack,' Saskia said. 'One too many puddings.'

They were glad of the free table in the dining room, because the hotel was fully booked and things were busy. A steady stream of cars had driven out from the city, drivers and passengers intent on gambling. They drank heavily and lost heavily at the tables. It was one of those nights when the Astrid Christyn could have turned a tidy profit without the need for Patershol francs.

They hardly noticed the stranger at first. Adelais had been heading for the ballroom when Nadia, the youngest of the croupiers, caught her eye and nodded significantly in his direction. It meant there was something about him she didn't like. Nadia was reliable and sharp, and had taken on all kinds of work at the hotel, including a morning shift at the front desk, and waitressing when it was required. Adelais had learned to trust her judgement.

The man wore glasses and a suit with a waistcoat. He was wandering around the tables with an unlit pipe between his teeth, as if trying to decide if it was worth placing a bet or not – which did not make a lot of sense, because he hadn't bought any chips. As far as Adelais could tell, he was on his own.

She was still watching the stranger when Hendryck appeared at her side, holding an empty bottle of champagne in each hand. 'What happened to Mr Huybrechts?'

'I don't know.' It had not occurred to Adelais that Mr Huybrechts's absence and the stranger's appearance might be connected. 'Who is that? Have you seen him before?'

'Conradt van Ranst. He's on the licensing panel. Says no to everything.'

Van Ranst was standing over Nadia as she raked in the chips and paid out on the wins, slowly tapping the stem of his pipe against his teeth. Nadia looked nervous.

'What's he doing here?'

'Gaming licences are renewed every year. Ours is coming up, isn't it, in a few weeks?' Hendryck grimaced. 'They say he trained for the priesthood when he was younger. Too much of a prig even for them.'

Van Ranst was not as neat or as perfumed as Father de Winter, but something about him did remind Adelais of her parish priest: an understated but unmistakable air of self-worth. It was as if he possessed knowledge that no one around him shared, or was fit to share.

'He tried to shut us down once, the bar I mean,' Hendryck said. 'It was just before your time. Mrs Claes had to hire a lawyer.'

'How could he shut her down? On what grounds?'

'He claimed we were selling untaxed alcohol to the customers.'

'Were you?'

'Stuff comes off the boats now and again, cut-price. You can save some money if you don't ask where it's been. Not that he could prove anything.' Hendryck shook his head. 'Fact is, he just didn't like her – Mrs Claes – that was the nub of it. Doesn't like women in general, especially when they're in charge.' Hendryck caught the look on Adelais's face. 'Women are also the weaker sex *morally*, Miss Adelais, as well as physically. That's what you have to remember.'

'Do I?'

'It was Eve who tempted Adam, and look what that led to.'

'Knowledge.'

Hendryck laughed, but the laugh was short-lived. 'I wish that bastard would clear off. I don't fancy crawling back to Mrs Claes. She hasn't forgiven me for leaving.'

—— Thirty-four ——

The next morning, Adelais telephoned the city council and asked for Mr Huybrechts. Saskia had guessed right: a week earlier, the chairman of the licensing panel had collapsed outside the Cour St Georges after a heavy meal and been taken to hospital. Though he was now out of danger, the doctors had recommended a sabbatical, and it was thought unlikely that he would return to his position for at least six months.

A few days later, a letter arrived at the Astrid Christyn Hotel, addressed to Adelais. She read it in her office three times, while a cup of coffee went cold on her desk.

Commercial Licensing Department
Ghent City Council
Botermarkt 1
Ghent

7 August 1961

Dear Miss de Wolf,

It is my duty to inform you that following an informal inspection of your premises, a number of egregious irregularities have come to light, which cast into doubt the suitability of your establishment as a venue for gambling as delineated in your current gaming licence (No. 2787c/60).

1. Visitors to the gaming rooms are given little or no warning that their participation in games of chance may result in financial loss.

2. The ready availability of alcohol in the vicinity of the gaming area appears calculated to impair the judgement of participants, rendering them more likely to place bets in a reckless and ill-advised manner.

3. Given that significant sums of money change hands, the predominance of female staff represents a palpable lack of security for guests and visitors. These arrangements make the hotel a conspicuous target for criminal activity.

4. The vetting of staff, which should be rigorous, appears wanting. One of your staff received a fine for disorderly conduct in the town of Blankenberge eighteen months ago. Another was a long-time employee at an establishment in the docks where contraband alcohol is believed to have been sold.

5. Insufficient paper records appear to be kept of transactions in, and adjacent to, the gaming room. This creates unacceptable opportunities for embezzlement.

As you will know, the Astrid Christyn has attracted a good number of visitors from outside Flanders and Belgium since it opened for business. While this might be welcome in itself, nothing could do more damage to our city's moral standing than that these visitors leave Ghent feeling that the city has taken advantage of them. It is only fair to warn you therefore that it will be my recommendation to the Commercial Licences Panel that the current gaming licence is not renewed. You may wish to share this information with the relevant staff in advance so that they may seek alternative employment.

Yours sincerely,

C. VAN RANST

Senior Administrative Officer

Saskia took the letter to the window. Opposite, men were tearing broken tiles off the old roof of the stable block. The building was letting in water, and without repairs the interior structure would rot.

'He must want a bribe. With Mr Huybrechts out the way, it's his turn.'

Adelais had a headache, the result of several bad nights in a row. 'Hendryck knows him. He isn't the type to be bought off with a few free meals.'

Saskia shook her head. She wore make-up all day now. It made her look older. '*Our city's moral standing*? What's he talking about?'

'He trained for the priesthood.'

'A bribe it is then.'

'I'm serious.'

'So am I.'

Adelais put her head in her hands. She had been working to a plan, precarious, but feasible. All they had to do was keep going for a while. Once they had finished expanding the hotel and paid off the bank, the Astrid Christyn would be a viable business – maybe even a good business. She would not have to take risks any more, or keep secrets, she could simply work and run the hotel, and dance with the guests now and then. Now, one man was going to wreck everything. 'We can't offer to bribe him. It would only prove his point. Ask Hendryck.'

Saskia came over to the desk. 'Then why send a letter? Why give us warning, if he just wants to sink us?'

'He couldn't resist it, the pig. I expect it gave him a thrill.'

The men on the stable block were hauling stacks of tiles up to the roof, using a pulley. Their booming voices echoed across the yard. Adelais was tempted to send them home, there and then.

'You could grovel.' Saskia perched on the edge of the desk. 'Promise to address his concerns. Thank you, sir, for bringing them to our attention, et cetera. Promise to get rid of the staff he doesn't trust.'

'That means Hendryck, for one. We can't do that to him. It isn't fair.'

'We need the gaming, Adelais. I don't want to go back to riding around the country on scooters, even if it was fun at the time.'

It was their rule never to mention the illegal side of their affairs when in the hotel, not even when they were alone. Adelais had learned from her years working at the bar how easy it was to piece together a person's life, even to guess their secrets, from snippets of overheard conversation. Neither of them had ever broken the rule before.

Saskia was fanning herself with the letter. It was mid-morning, the humidity building. In the gathering clouds there was the promise of rain. 'What we need is for Mr Huybrechts to make a miraculous recovery.'

'You want to pray for him? Light a candle at St Bavo's?'

'I'd try anything if I thought it would work. Although . . .' When Saskia's eyes narrowed, her whole face changed: the doll-like openness was gone. In its place was a fleeting vision of cruelty. '. . . if I *had* to pray for something, I'd rather pray for van Ranst to die. It'd be a lot more satisfying.'

'I suppose.'

'People like him, they love spoiling things. They live for it.' Saskia dropped the letter and wandered back to the window. A burly, shaven-headed locksmith called Ingels was fixing new locks to the doors of the stable block. The previous year, he had put in most of the locks in the main building. Saskia had seen him selling cigarettes to the other work-men on the sly. She had no idea where he got them, but then, locksmiths could get in anywhere, if they put their minds to it. They could help themselves. 'It's a pity we can't just . . . get rid of him.'

'What?'

'Or scare him off. It wouldn't take much, I bet. Bullies are always cow-ards underneath.'

'What are you talking about?'

'You have to stand up to bullies like van Ranst. It's a well-known fact.'

'You want to threaten him?'

Saskia shrugged. 'He deserves it, that's all. And . . .'

'And what?'

Saskia ran a finger along the windowsill. 'I can't stand to see him hurt you like this, Adelais. I won't let him.'

'Prison would hurt a lot more.' Adelais shook her head. 'I wish you could be serious. This isn't a joke.'

'I know.'

245

'We could lose everything.'

'I *know*.'

'*You'd* be all right though, wouldn't you? You've got a rich family, you've got choices, not like . . .' It was a mean thing to say. Immediately Adelais wished she could take it back.

Saskia was looking at her. 'I've made my choice, haven't I?'

The silence was shattered by the crash of tiles landing in the skip.

'What we need is a lawyer.' Adelais's head was throbbing. 'That's what Mrs Claes did: she got a lawyer. And we should tell some of our customers what's going on, the important ones. They might have influence with the city.'

'It's worth a try. They might stand up for us.' Saskia turned back to the window. The shadows around her slowly dissolved as a cloud went across the sun. 'They love damsels in distress. And that's what we are, both of us. It's not like we're a threat to anyone.'

She was trying to sound positive, but even through the fog of pain, Adelais could tell she was not convinced.

—— Thirty-five ——

On the night before the Feast of the Assumption, Conradt van Ranst attended a vigil Mass at the Sint-Niklaaskerk. On his way out, he was dismayed to find an old acquaintance beaming at him from the ranks of the congregation, as it shuffled out into the square. Years ago, he and Jens Blommen had been fellow students of theology, and generally reckoned the stars of their class. Van Ranst had taken the high road to the seminary, which a crisis of faith and the prospect of celibacy had forced him to abandon after a year. Blommen had remained in academia, rising to a senior position at the university, where he lectured in philosophy. Van Ranst, now a mere local government functionary, avoided him.

'Conradt, so good to see you,' Blommen said, taking van Ranst's hand between both of his own, a gesture van Ranst found unnatural and repulsive. 'Where have you been hiding?'

Van Ranst could think of no satisfactory answer to this question, based as it was upon the belittling assumption that he had been invisible. 'How are you, Jens?' was all he could manage.

'Oh, quite well, busy, busy. Between my students and this little lot—' – he gestured towards a handsome woman wearing a gingham raincoat, and a clutch of well-groomed children – 'I've hardly time to turn around.'

The handsome woman smiled at van Ranst, but in a way that made it clear that she had no desire to join the conversation. Van Ranst had met her twice before, when she and Blommen were first married. Her name was Carolina. Clearly she had forgotten him.

'Annet not with you tonight?' Blommen asked.

'Annet? No, sadly not. A summer cold. You know how they can be. She wanted to come, but I insisted she stay in bed.'

'Rotten luck. Well, do send her my best wishes.'

'I will, thank you,' van Ranst said.

Blommen clapped him on the shoulder. 'We must catch up properly sometime. We have *so* much to talk about. Like the old days, eh?'

Van Ranst watched Blommen take his wife's arm and rejoin the worshippers walking towards the bridge. Carolina Blommen said something to her husband, doubtless wanting to know who he had been talking to. Blommen's answer was a brief one, a few words at most, because a moment later he was talking to his eldest child, saying something that made the boy laugh.

Van Ranst watched them disappear before heading north across the square. He made his way through the Korenmarkt, where the gutters were still choked with detritus from the summer festival – streamers, paper flowers, food wrappers – and crossed the river on the iron footbridge, where young couples and tourists loitered in the darkness, admiring the illuminated facades of the Graslei. It wasn't until he was halfway down Jan Breydelstraat, where the road was barely wide enough for a car to pass, that the insistent sound of footsteps planted in his mind the possibility that he was being followed.

Outside the Hotel Gravensteen, he looked back the way he had come. Fifty metres away, a man had stopped to light a cigarette. There was nobody else on the street. The man wore a flat cap and a jacket with the collar turned up. By the glow of the flame, his skin looked like wax. He took a puff and tossed the match away. Van Ranst expected him to move on, but instead, he stayed right where he was, staring into the window of an antique shop, even though, like all the shops on the street, it was dark. After a few moments his head turned and he was staring at van Ranst – staring, but not moving.

Van Ranst hurried away. Footsteps echoed behind him, but he couldn't be sure they weren't his own. He reached the far end of Abrahamstraat and looked back again. Why would anyone want to follow him? It made no earthly sense, unless the idea was to rob him. But these days, there were far better prospects among the tourists milling around the city centre.

A light came on somewhere above him. A woman laughed, the sound carrying out into the night. A window banged shut, waking a dog opposite. It barked a few times, whined, and fell silent.

The man was a hundred metres away, just beyond a street light. Van Ranst could see the cigarette glowing in his hand. Was it the same man or another one? What if there were two of them? What did they want?

Should he run? Van Ranst's black leather shoes weren't made for running, and the other man would be faster. He had to hold his nerve, act as if everything was normal. Prinsenhof was just ahead. It was usually busier. There might be a policeman on patrol, or a taxi he could flag down.

He went round the corner. Nothing moved on the cobbled street ahead but a sheet of newspaper turning a somersault in the gutter. Van Ranst lived on Zilverhof. The turning was two hundred metres away. He could bang on a door and ask for help. But the houses were dark and shuttered. Would they even answer at such an hour?

Van Ranst took off, running as fast as he could. The cobbles were worn and shiny. His feet slipped. He didn't dare look back. Halfway to the corner, the street opened out a little. He heard an engine. A band of yellow light panned across the houses on his left. A car was pulling out of a garage.

'Help! Help me!'

The engine was loud, van Ranst too out of breath to shout again. He waved his arms, caught sight of a woman behind the wheel. She saw him running towards her and stared for a second, before gunning the engine and accelerating away in a cloud of exhaust. How could she do that, just leave him to his fate? Did she think he was some kind of maniac?

Van Ranst kept running. There were footsteps everywhere: behind him, ahead of him, they echoed up and down the street. He reached Zilverhof, coming to rest against an old red postbox. His chest heaved. His lungs were on fire. This was when they would attack him, when he was defenceless. He pressed his back to the wall and waited.

The footsteps had stopped. Nobody came round the corner. All van Ranst could hear was his own breathing. He risked a look back along Prinsenhof: it was just as empty as before. It was the same in every direction: a quiet, respectable quarter of the city, shuttered for the night.

He straightened up. Perhaps he had been a little quick to assume the worst. Just because someone was going the same way didn't mean they were deliberately following you. What a sight he must have been, tearing down the road in his three-piece suit, as if the Devil himself were at his heels. No wonder that poor woman had driven away. He had seen her before. He did not know her name, but he knew she worked in a hospital. Most likely, she had been heading off for her night shift. She would have recognised him too, as a neighbour. Yet she had still refused to help. It was going to make for a very awkward encounter, the next time he passed her on the street.

He reached his house. It had turned into quite an eventful evening, one worth recounting to his wife. Annet had an appetite for anecdotes and trivia, especially when they involved people she knew. It was only when he opened the front door that he remembered: Annet was not there. Nearly two months had passed since the day she walked out, and he could still forget that it had happened. Part of him refused to believe it – or believed she would come back at any rate. But standing in the hallway under the glow of a single bulb, the rest of the house in darkness, her loss felt as permanent and irrevocable as death. He felt a rush of panic at the thought that he might never speak to his wife again.

What he needed was a drink. After a scare like that, he deserved it. He went to the drinks cabinet in the sitting room and poured himself a brandy. When that was gone, he poured himself another. It was a Monday night, but that could not be helped. He needed to calm himself, to head off the bitter mood that was creeping over him.

It was not his fault that Annet had not produced any children. The doctors had been more or less unanimous on that point: statistically, male infertility was rare compared to the other kind. Either way, it had been a grave disappointment, and not just for the usual sentimental reasons. The fact was – van Ranst had to admit he *was* at fault for not having seen it sooner – Annet was a shallow and unserious woman. Having children was her one chance to make a genuine contribution to society. If she missed it, all that was left was being a devoted wife, and she was not even very good at that.

With the brandy, he began to feel more optimistic. He decided to run himself a hot bath. The pipes were soon rattling and rumbling, the taps gushing like waterfalls. Van Ranst undressed. Annet would come back to him sooner or later. She would grow tired of living with her aunt in Roeselare – a dreary sort of town, if ever there was one – and begin to dream of home. He would be magnanimous too, once she made the first move. He took his marriage vows seriously, unlike a lot of people these days. And besides, his encounter with Jens Blommen had been an uncomfortable reminder of how embarrassing it was to have an absent wife, one who did not even have the decency to be dead.

Van Ranst dropped the last of his clothes on the chair and climbed into the bath. It was a good-sized tub and he was able to stretch out, so that only his head and his toes were above the water. He found himself thinking about the Astrid Christyn and the young women who ran it. If Miss de Wolf wanted to squander her inheritance trying to run a hotel that was her affair, but the gambling? How it had ever been allowed was a mystery. Reimond Huybrechts had been the main advocate. Van Ranst shuddered to think what hospitality, what manner of favours Miss de Wolf and Miss Helsen had lavished on the man to win him round – except, if he was being honest with himself, it wasn't really a shudder that went through van Ranst's body. It was more of a tingle, concentrated in the vicinity of his groin.

The young women would have had his letter by now. Soon he would have theirs: a humble, beseeching letter, promising to raise standards, and do better in future, if only he would reconsider. He would have to disappoint them eventually – the idea of young women in charge of a gambling establishment flirted with indecency – but the idea of them metaphorically kneeling before him, as they had perhaps knelt before Reimond Huybrechts, sent another tingle of excitement to his loins. He had reached down to more fully investigate the effect when he saw, reflected in the steamed-up mirror opposite him, a ghostly white face.

He screamed and tried to rise from the bath, the image already imprinted on his brain: white skin, a tiny pink mouth, a curly blond moustache and eyebrows, a pair of wire spectacles with dark green lenses.

Van Ranst's hand slipped on the side of the tub. He crashed down into the water again, sending a surge over the side. The pale face was there again, looking down at him this time. It was a mask, one of those worn by the Gilles at the carnival in Binche. He had seen them on his honeymoon. His wife had taken a photograph, had even bought him a Gilles de Binche mask, though he had refused to wear it.

'Annet?'

The Gille slowly shook his head. A hand in a rubber glove reached out and pushed van Ranst under the water. It was a strong hand, not like Annet's, a hand strong enough to drown him. Panic took him. Somehow he got hold of an arm, a hand. He bit down hard.

The Gille yelped. For a moment van Ranst was free. He rose up, coughing. 'Please, please, please, please, please!'

The hand planted itself on his head. He was helpless.

'Conradt van Ranst.' The stranger sounded like a judge pronouncing sentence, except that there was a coarseness in his speech that a judge would never have had.

'You've got the wrong man.' It was all van Ranst could think of, the one possibility of reprieve.

The hand pushed him under the water again. He was going to die this time. He was going to die and be left to rot in his bathtub. Van Ranst fought, tried to turn, get on his knees, but the hand – two hands now – held him in place.

Suddenly, they let go. Van Ranst surfaced. It came to him that he was being deliberately tortured to death, like one of the Christian martyrs he had studied at the seminary. 'What . . . what have I done to you?'

The Gille bent over him. The mask wore an expression of mild surprise. 'At the next meeting of the licensing committee, Mr van Ranst, you are going to be in a very good mood.'

'W-what?'

'You are going to say yes to every application, no matter where it comes from, no matter what it is. Got it?'

Van Ranst was shaking. He managed to nod.

The hand came down on his head again. 'What are you gonna do?'

'Say yes, say yes. Everything. Say yes. I will, I will.'

'Or else I'll come back and the finish the job. Understand?'

'Yes, yes, unders-s-s- . . . Understand.'

The hand was gone. The mask drew closer. 'Remember, I can find you anytime, anywhere, Mr van Ranst. You won't keep me out.'

Van Ranst heard footsteps on the stairs. A gentle draught cooled his wet skin. The front door closed with a click. He lay in the water, shaking, his breath coming in shuddering pulls. He was not sure how long he lay there, but by the time he was calm again, the water was almost cold. He looked down and realised from the colour that at some point in the struggle he had lost control of his bowels.

The next morning, Staaf Ingels went early to the Astrid Christyn Hotel. He parked his van outside the service entrance and wandered over to the stable block, carrying his toolbox. It was a still morning, quiet but for the hum of the extractor fan in the kitchens, and the shriek of swifts overhead. The roofers had not yet arrived.

Saskia Helsen was inside, wearing a blue print dress. Her face looked puffy and she was not wearing make-up. Ingels had the impression she had not slept very well.

'So. Did you . . . ?'

Ingels nodded.

'You conveyed the message?'

'He got it.'

'You're sure?'

Ingels shrugged. Saskia handed him an envelope. He opened it and counted the notes. 'I'll need another five thousand.'

'We agreed the price.'

'The bastard bit me.' Ingels held up a hand. There was a bandage round it. 'I might need shots.' He let the hand drop. 'Five thousand francs. Call it a down payment on next time.'

'There won't be a next time.'

Ingels nodded towards the gaming room. 'Like those odds, do you?'

A truck rolled into the driveway. The roofing crew had arrived.

'Wait here,' Saskia said.

She made her way through the hotel via the service entrance and let herself into the office. There was a chance Adelais would be up by now, but the kitchens were usually her first stop, followed by the dining room. Saskia went to the safe, and dialled the combination.

There was enough cash inside, but five thousand was going to be missed. She had already taken money from the cage on successive nights, making a noticeable dent in the takings. What could she say to explain the shortfall in the safe? Nothing very credible came to mind.

She heard Hendryck's voice greeting one of the guests, a clatter of pans from the kitchens, the sounds of the Astrid Christyn coming to life. Saskia closed the safe, reached for her keys and unlocked a drawer in the desk. Concealed in the usual place was a stack of Patershol francs. She counted out ten of them and stuffed them in her pocket.

—— Thirty-six ——

Adelais found the city council's letter waiting for her on the desk. It had been three weeks since Mr van Ranst's unannounced visit and she had been dreading bad news. The envelope had already been opened. Saskia had got to it first, but she hadn't been in any hurry to share its contents. It had to be a bad sign.

The letter was brief and impersonal. The licensing panel had extended the gaming licence at the Astrid Christyn for another year. At the bottom was an illegible signature and an official stamp. Adelais read it three times, just to be sure she hadn't misunderstood.

She found Saskia in the kitchens, helping herself to breakfast. 'Have you seen this?'

Saskia nodded, her mouth full of fresh croissant. 'Good, isn't it?'

'Good? I thought we were done for.'

Saskia shrugged. As usual, she had made herself a large *café au lait*, which she drank out of a bowl, like a Walloon. 'He must have been out-voted, that awful man.' She slurped her coffee. 'What was his name?'

'Van Ranst, Conradt van Ranst. His letter seemed so final, like it was all decided. He can't have changed his mind.'

'Maybe someone changed it for him.'

'What do you mean?'

Saskia turned back to the ovens, where the morning's fresh bread and pastries were keeping warm. 'I mean, nobody likes a spoilsport, do they? And he was certainly that.'

'Maybe. Or maybe your prayer was answered.'

'What prayer?'

'Your prayer for Mr Huybrechts's recovery. Maybe this was his doing.'

Saskia helped herself to another croissant. 'Well then, you have me to thank, don't you?'

After lunch, Adelais put on her new red raincoat and rode her scooter back to Schoolstraat. She did not usually visit the old house during the working week. There was always too much to do at the hotel. Even on Sundays, there was no guarantee she would go. She went to pick up mail, hoping for a letter from her mother, or from an old friend – Maria Goossens, perhaps, who had recently married an accountant from Drongen, or Sebastian Pieters – but there had not been any letters of a personal sort for months. Sometimes she cleaned, but without her father or anyone else to mess up the place, the job did not take long. All she had to do was wipe the gritty windowsills and mop the floors. Perhaps even that much was unnecessary, but she did not like the idea of her mother coming home to a filthy house. It might have been empty and the lease nearing the end of its life, but 57 Schoolstraat was still the nearest thing they had to a family home.

Several letters had arrived from Africa during the previous year. None of them indicated how long Adelais's mother intended to stay there. They were brief, incoherent, and took anything up to six weeks to arrive. Adelais had written back, but had said nothing about the hotel. Her mother would know the story about Great-Aunt Magdalena was a fiction of course, and the truth was out of the question, certainly in writing. She would be appalled to learn what Adelais had done. But that was too bad. Her mother had no right to complain. None of it would have happened if she hadn't taken off, leaving her daughter with no support but an alcoholic father and a couple of thousand francs.

Adelais let herself in through the front door. The only thing on the mat was a flyer for a new restaurant on the Antwerp road. The Netley was parked in the hallway where she had left it, partly blocking the bottom of the stairs. She knew she should get rid of the old thing, but she had a feeling it would be hard to sell, and the thought of a junkyard was too much. She stopped for a moment and ran her hands over the handles, trying to recall the excitement she had felt when she first got hold of them, that sense of anticipation, of exciting new possibilities. The machine had never gone much faster than a gentle trot, but that had been enough to set her pulse racing. It felt like a long time ago.

She went through the house, checking that nothing was amiss. In the pantry she found a pool of water on the windowsill, a speckle of dead thunder flies floating on the surface. The bottom of the frame had warped, leaving a narrow gap under the sash. Adelais plugged it with some old rubber bands and made a mental note to repair it later. The rest of the house was unchanged.

The last room she went into was the workshop. Nothing had changed in there either and yet something felt wrong. It took Adelais a while to realise that the old wall clocks had wound down. For the first time ever the room was completely silent.

Her father never let clocks wind down, not even old clocks like these that nobody wanted any more. It was bad for the mechanisms, he used to say. They were made for movement. Adelais got as far as the door. If she was to wind the clocks, she would need the keys and where would she find them? It would be easier to leave the clocks as they were, telling different times, both wrong. With no one to see them, how could it possibly matter?

The workbench had drawers. The remnants of a system were still discernible: tools and spare parts in one, receipts and invoices in another. But the system had broken down over time, so that in some drawers, everything was mixed up. She went through them one by one. In the bottom drawer, a promising brass key peeped out from under a creased piece of paper.

The writing caught her eye. The hand was distinctive, familiar. The same hand had written the notebook Uncle Cornelis had left in his safe.

It was one page of a letter. The rest of it was nowhere to be found.

. . . she can get, if her years are not to be spent in the shadows, watching life go by, but never fully taking part. It makes me angry to think about it. She deserves much more. Tell me, Lennart: why should we always play fair in a world that isn't?

I know Odilie is still upset about the Anderlecht business. It didn't work out as we'd planned, but that was bad luck, not the work of God. Can she be made to see reason? I like to think that all she needs is time. If not, don't let her way of thinking infect Adelais. The girl is too clever and brave to be condemned to a life of martyrdom and penury. I look at my beautiful niece and I see in her everything I have ever liked about myself, and nothing that I have ever disliked. If I had such a daughter, there is nothing I would not do for her, nothing I would not risk.

Consider what I have said, and what is at stake, and talk to Odilie when the time is right. In the meantime, I will wait patiently to hear from you.

Your friend and brother,
Cornelis

—— Thirty-seven ——

At the end of the Tolhuisdok, the ship canal split in two, one part winding its way beneath the Muide Bridge and into the docks further south, the other narrowing as it passed by the small island where the old toll house stood. According to the tip-off, a Dutch-registered Kempenaar barge called the *Volharding*, would be tying up on the north side of the island at around ten o'clock. Along with its legitimate cargo of barley and vegetable oil it would be carrying at least twenty cases of untaxed spirits, and an unknown quantity of cigarettes.

At half past nine that night, Detective Sergeant Colpaert of the Ghent Municipal Police took up his position on the west side of the canal, a hundred metres from the only road bridge connecting the island to the rest of the city. There was scant cover on the embankment – some spindly bushes, laced with brambles – but the street lighting was on the other side of the road and he would be hard to spot at any distance. Anyone moving twenty cases of spirits would need a van or a truck, and that would mean coming back over the road bridge. Officer Wagenaer was waiting at the corner in an unmarked car. Their orders were specific: they were to follow any suspect's vehicle to its final destination, and only move in for an arrest once the location had been established.

At seven minutes to ten Colpaert saw lights approaching over the water. The *Volharding* was on time. He trained his binoculars on the canal to his left, watching as the vessel slowly took form: the low profile, the upturned prow, capped with white – it reminded him of a jutting chin – the wheelhouse at the stern, sprouting masts. He squatted down. The growl of the diesel engine grew louder, until it drowned out everything else. Colpaert could feel his heart beat faster. It was his first time in charge of an operation. Watching the massive barge draw near, he felt like David taking on Goliath. He had to remind himself that this was a small-time smuggling case, and these were small-time crooks. They weren't going to come at him, guns blazing. Arrest or no arrest, he was not going to make the front page of the *Staatscourant van Gent*.

The engines slowed and went into reverse. The dock on the island was illuminated by two lamp posts, one at either end, just bright enough to reveal its position. The barge made a slow sweep towards the nearside of the canal, before turning hard to port. For the first time, Colpaert saw its name written in white letters on the stern. The vessel came within a metre of the quay. After a minute or so, a couple of men arrived and helped tie it up. Job done, they disappeared again.

For a long time nothing moved. The *Volharding*'s engines continued to turn over, providing electrical power. Colpaert looked up and down the road. Traffic was sparse. Nothing went over the bridge onto the island and nothing came the other way. Crouching in the darkness, he began to feel cramp in his legs. It was starting to rain.

After half an hour, the engines cut out. Colpaert spotted a handful of men walking away from the barge. They were headed towards the foot-bridge that led to Heilig-Kerst and Patershol, where there were plenty of bars to relieve them of their pay. None of the men was carrying anything bigger than a kitbag. A single red light burned above the stern of the barge.

Colpaert wondered how long he was supposed to wait, how long before the tip-off could be called a dud. He could radio from the car, but that would mean breaking cover. He was on his feet and starting to climb the embankment when he became aware of another sound: another engine, this one much smaller and quieter than the *Volharding*'s. He ducked down again and scanned the canal. A launch was pulling away from the island, a dim yellow lantern slung from its prow. Colpaert had been told to expect a van or a truck. But what if the contraband was being moved by boat?

The grass was wet and slick. He slipped and fell as he hurried up the embankment. He beckoned frantically at the car, but Officer Wagenaer was too busy enjoying a cigarette to notice. He did not turn on the ignition until Colpaert banged on the bonnet.

They raced south across the link canal and turned east on the main road towards the Handelsdok. The rain was coming down harder and the lights on the loading cranes were blurry in the darkness. All along the quays, barges and freighters were tied up. It was hard to get a clear view of the water. They travelled for a few hundred metres along the quayside and pulled over halfway down. Colpaert climbed out of the car. He could not see or hear the launch. It could only mean it had turned the other way, not south, but north into the Houtdok and the wasteland of old factories on the other side. By road, it was a long way.

He ran back to the car. 'Turn round, quick.'

'Are you sure, sir?' Officer Wagenaer pointed further down the Handelsdok. The launch was going by on the water, its lantern a yellow dot in the distance. It was moving faster now, its propeller kicking up white foam at the stern.

They drove ahead to the Dampoort and watched the launch pass under the bridge. From there it turned into a narrow canal that served as a connection to the River Leie.

'Step on it. We're going to lose him.'

They were getting close to the middle of the city. Scores of small boats were tied up on the opposite side of the river. If the launch slipped in among them, Colpaert wasn't sure he'd be able to pick it out. He craned his neck out of the passenger window, squinting into the rain. He had just spotted a telltale plume of foam when a truck pulled out of Munichstraat into their path. Officer Wagenaer hit the horn, but the truck rumbled on, maintaining the same contemptuous pace. By the time they could overtake, it had been several minutes since they had seen the launch. At the next bridge, Colpaert got out of the car again. The river was straight, the view unimpeded for several hundred metres.

Along the quays, small boats had given way to houseboats and barges, but nothing moved on the water as far as he could see. The launch had vanished.

He had followed it on a hunch and then lost it. And what if the hunch had been wrong? At that very moment the contraband could be moving by road from the Tolhuisdok unobserved, a tip-off wasted. It would take some explaining.

As if on cue, the car radio crackled to life: headquarters wanting an update on the progress of the operation. Colpaert climbed back into the car and unhooked the microphone. He was muddy and wet. The rain beat down on the roof.

Just below the bridge, in the window of one of the houseboats, a light went on. Maybe he couldn't see the launch because it was right beneath his feet.

Colpaert put the microphone back on its hook. 'Turn off the engine,' he said.

Colpaert had expected a bigger haul of contraband than the one they found. He had pictured stacks of champagne crates and vintage brandy, Scotch whisky by the barrel load, Cuban cigars and Russian vodka. The launch, which had been tied up under the bridge, held twelve cases of whisky and six thousand American cigarettes. The houseboat held another four cases of whisky, three cases of French brandy and two cases of liqueurs. The man arrested at the scene was a tough-looking customer, but he had no criminal record. The address in his identity book, a grimy one-bedroom apartment in the southern district of Veldwijk, yielded nothing but a set of lock-picks and twelve thousand Belgian francs in cash.

At noon the next day, having filed his arrest report, Colpaert sent a sergeant to fetch the prisoner and made his way to one of the interview rooms in the basement. Questioning the suspect was not going to take long. The man was not in enough legal peril to finger his associates, or provide much in the way of information. His associates were probably foreigners anyway and beyond the reach of Belgian law. Still, the questions had to be asked, the answers – or lack of them – written down and filed before the matter could be left to the courts.

Colpaert was still on the stairs when the sergeant returned. 'Prisoner's already down there, sir.'

'What?'

'Interview room. He's already there.'

'Why?'

'Assistant commissioner's orders. Some gendarme's turned up from Brussels.'

'Brussels?'

'A major, no less. Came like a shot.'

Colpaert wondered if there had been a mistake. Was the man he had arrested more important than he thought? Maybe he was going to see his name in the *Staatscourant van Gent* after all.

He hurried down to the basement. Outside the interview room, Assistant Commissioner van Buel was talking to a federal officer in uniform. The man had short grey hair and enough pips on his shoulder to indicate seniority. He was reading from a file while van Buel talked. Approaching, Colpaert realised that it was probably his report.

'Sir?'

Van Buel turned. 'Major de Smet, this is Detective Sergeant Colpaert. He made the arrest last night.'

De Smet did not look up. 'Good work.'

'Thank you, sir.'

'Your report doesn't say anything about resisting arrest.'

'No, sir. We had our man cornered. He came quietly enough.'

De Smet removed the report from the file and handed it to Colpaert. His gaze was unflinching and without warmth. 'You might want to recall that differently, Detective Sergeant. We'll have to see.'

'Sir?'

Colpaert looked at van Buel, but van Buel merely sucked his teeth for a moment, before opening the door to the interview room. 'You have the first crack at him, Major,' he said.

De Smet pulled up a chair and sat down. The door closed behind him. The man on the other side of the table was shaven-headed, his skin marked with the kind of scars you didn't get from acne. He sat with his arms folded, arm muscles bulging through a threadbare blue shirt.

De Smet took out a notebook and pencil. 'Your name is Ingels, correct? Staaf Ingels.'

The man nodded. De Smet wrote the name on his pad.

'And what is your profession, Mr Ingels?'

'Locksmith.'

De Smet looked up. 'Locksmith. Since when?'

'Forever. I was apprenticed at fifteen.'

'Where?'

'Here. To Jasper Middelkamp of Ledeberg. He's dead now.'

De Smet wrote down the name, then showed it to Ingels, to be sure he had the spelling correct.

'You work exclusively in Ghent?'

'Pretty much. There's work enough these days.'

'And yet you feel the need to supplement your income by trafficking in contraband.'

Ingels shook his head. 'I told the other one: I'm not saying a word without a lawyer. It's my right.'

De Smet smiled. 'It is, of course. But then, I'm not interested in your sideline, Mr Ingels. What I'm interested in are these.' He reached into the file and took out a cellophane bag with a label attached to it. He emptied the bag and spread out the contents on the table. They were banknotes. For the first time during the interview Ingels looked worried.

'You recognise these, I expect? They were found in your apartment.'

264

'It's my money then. You can give it back.'

'There are ten notes in all. Why don't you tell me where they came from?'

Ingels stared at the notes with a frown on his face, as if trying to interpret the number, words and symbols printed on them. Slowly a knowing smile crept over his face. 'So this is your way of asking for a cut. You should've come right out with it.'

Outside, Detective Sergeant Colpaert was startled by a thud from behind the door, followed by a muffled scream. He hurried towards the interview room, but Assistant Commissioner van Buel stepped into his path.

'Resisting arrest, Detective Sergeant,' he said. 'It's all in your report. Now go and write it.'

Reluctantly Colpaert turned around. The last thing he heard from the interview room was Ingels shouting something about a hotel.

—— Thirty-eight ——

It was the week of the film festival and the hotel was busier than ever. There were businessmen, as always, but instead of tourists the Astrid Christyn's guests now included producers, distributors, directors and critics from a dozen different countries. They rode in and out of town in taxis and limousines, conducted interviews on the terrace and in the conservatory, and jammed the hotel switchboard with endless phone calls.

At night so many cars turned up that the hotel had to open a parking area on the lawn. From nine o'clock onwards the gaming room, ballroom, and bar all hummed with activity. Most of the film people turned out to be accomplished drinkers and champagne was their favourite refreshment. On the first night of the festival the hotel got through seven cases and was down to its last bottle. It was a desperate struggle to restock in time for the following night. When they were not in the mood for champagne, the festival-goers ordered a plethora of exotic cocktails that only Hendryck knew how to make: daiquiris, old-fashioneds, mai tais and manhattans. The band played every night until two. Gambling hours were extended until three, with the city council's consent. The evenings were mild and dry, which was just as well since it meant the windows could all be opened, thinning out the cigar smoke that seemed to accumulate above the gaming tables, where the staff had to work diligently to keep ash off the baize.

'I don't want to tempt Fate,' Saskia said one night, as they counted the bar takings behind the locked door of the office, 'but I think it's fair to say we're on the map.'

Adelais nodded. Underneath the exhaustion was a growing sense of relief, of optimism. 'We are. We're definitely on the map.'

266

'And it's a *world* map. Mr Bamberg's from New York.' Saskia wrote down a number in the ledger and placed the money in the safe. 'You know, if every week was like this, we wouldn't need the Patershol business at all.'

Adelais did not say anything, and not just because it would mean breaking the rule of silence they were supposed to observe. Every week was not like the week of the film festival, and there were still the works to complete and the bank to pay off. Added to that, the film people were the ideal recipients of Patershol francs: they were unfamiliar with the currency, spent freely and mostly lived abroad. That night the cage had been stocked with thirty 500-franc notes from Patershol. By the end of the evening, only one of them was left.

'On the other hand,' Saskia added, 'it doesn't hurt to have a little extra, does it? You never know when your luck's going to change.'

On the Thursday evening at ten o'clock Major de Smet's Juvaquatre pulled up outside the hotel. It was the oldest vehicle among thirty or so lining the driveway and would have been conspicuous, with its narrow hood and bulky wheel arches, had anyone been taking note. De Smet, like Captain Toussaint beside him, was dressed in a jacket and tie. They found a space to park outside the stable block and walked round to the front, squinting into the floodlights playing over the facade.

'Try to look like you've come to enjoy yourself,' de Smet said. 'Blend in.'

'Yes, sir,' Toussaint said, thinking de Smet should take his own advice. The man had never looked happy in his life – or so rarely that it was impossible to picture.

They walked across the entrance hall, catching a courtesy nod from a girl at the front desk, and wandered up the main stairs, following the sound of a band playing 'Calcutta'. A female cashier was selling chips from behind a metal screen. De Smet handed over a thousand francs, Toussaint five hundred. Toussaint's purchase got him eight white chips – the lowest denomination – and three red. The cashier counted them out for him in a sing-song voice, as if he were a child or a simpleton. Maybe she thought someone with a mere five hundred francs to spend could only have wandered in by accident. He would like to have come back with a ton of chips, just to wipe the patronising smile off her face.

More cars were pulling up outside.

'Keep an eye on the cage,' de Smet said. 'Only don't move in, no matter what. Got that?'

Toussaint knew what he was thinking: he was thinking about the race at Ostend and how Toussaint had blown the whole operation by letting himself be spotted. As a precaution, he checked that the gun in his waistband wasn't showing.

In the ballroom nobody was dancing, but there was a crush at the bar. The people were stylishly and expensively dressed. They talked and joked in French, English, German. Nobody was speaking Flemish. Next to them, Toussaint felt conspicuously drab.

De Smet handed him a long glass. The contents were pink and cloudy. 'What's this?'

'I don't know. It's what they're drinking.' De Smet nodded towards the bar, where a jowly American with a cigar was telling a funny story to a party of younger people. The pink cocktail looked like a child's drink, but the American didn't seem to care.

Toussaint scanned the other faces in the room. A stocky, barrel-chested character in a dinner jacket stood by the entrance to the gaming room, but he didn't resemble the man who had broken his jaw. No one did.

'The roulette's through there,' de Smet said. 'From the end of the second table you'll have a view of the cage.' Toussaint pulled the chips from his pocket. 'Don't lose that all at once.'

De Smet spent a few minutes listening to the band and studying the Astrid Christyn as it went about its business. He watched money changing hands at the bar, people getting ready to gamble, juggling chips between their fingers, the alcohol and the music breaking down their inhibitions, displacing reason with euphoria. He had never been a gambling man himself. He had always seen gambling for what it was: an organised swindle that preyed on the desperate and the innumerate, without regard for the consequences. But then, these people seemed happy to bet against the odds. It could only be that the thrill of a win they didn't need outweighed the pain of a loss that didn't matter. Theirs was the privilege of wealth.

He checked his watch: it was a quarter past ten. The pop of a champagne cork caused a gentle stir at the bar. Seconds later, the barman was moving towards the doors with a champagne flute on a silver tray. The American took the cigar from his mouth. 'Here she is,' he said, and everyone turned to look.

Her dress was a Chinese design: narrow at the waist and full-length, with a Mandarin collar and no sleeves. The silk was deep blue, the floral pattern pale gold. For a moment everything else in the room seemed dowdy, mute. Her blonde hair was tied up in a half-bun, but with long curls falling loose about her temples. She accepted the glass of champagne. De Smet thought she must be one of the film people: an upcoming star perhaps, fresh from a triumphant premiere in the city. But the way she greeted people was like a hostess greeting guests. De Smet found it hard not to stare. He heard people muttering her name: this was the young owner, this was Miss de Wolf. He had not expected her to be so striking. He took a mouthful of the pink cocktail. He was glad to find that it was strong.

The band had dropped the tempo and was playing a waltz. A man with silver hair asked Miss de Wolf to dance. She nodded and offered him her hand. The waiter was on hand to take care of her glass. The couple took to the floor and soon others had joined them. Some of the film people, the men in particular, seemed to think the music was old-fashioned and hung back, but most of the guests seemed enchanted. They found partners and dragged them onto the floor.

De Smet turned his back on the dancers and walked through to the gaming room. As directed, Toussaint had taken up a position at the far end of the first roulette table, with a clear view of the cage. De Smet went to the other table. He placed a chip on red and a chip on even. The croupier, another blonde woman, this time in a waistcoat and bow tie, smiled at him and spun the wheel.

'*Rien ne va plus.*'

The other gamblers at his table were all men and spoke to each other in French. One of them wore a corduroy jacket with a rollneck sweater underneath. The roulette ball bounced around the track before landing in one of the pockets.

'*Rouge, trente-deux.*'

Toussaint's table was busier. It meant he could hang back from the betting without looking conspicuous. He glanced at de Smet and shook his head. De Smet could see more people coming up the stairs. How many had come to play?

'*Monsieur?*'

The blonde croupier pushed a stack of chips towards him. Both his bets had been good, but his glass was empty. He put the chips in his pocket and went back to the ballroom. Miss de Wolf was dancing with a different man now, a younger one, and the band was playing 'Mack the Knife', a saxophone spinning out the melody. De Smet had always liked that tune. He went to get another drink from the bar.

He had not noticed the portrait earlier. The sitter had short red hair and green eyes, and was looking away to her left. She was beautiful, de Smet thought, with neat, pretty features and rosy cheeks, but there was fragility and a touch of sorrow in her gaze.

'You know, that's the lady made all this possible.' The words were English. They came from the American. 'Great-Aunt Magdalena.' Before de Smet could respond the man had offered his hand. 'Scott Bamberg, Lopert Pictures.'

They shook. Bamberg's younger companions had slipped away to the dance floor and the tables.

'It's actually quite a story,' he said. 'Like a movie, almost. Are you in movies, Mr . . . ?'

'De Smet. No, I'm not.'

'Well, she was this millionairess – you wouldn't know it from the picture, would you? I mean, where are the jewels? Anyway, she never had kids, or they died or something. Then she gets old and she's in Luxembourg or—'

'Luxembourg?'

Bamberg laughed. He had been drinking for a while. 'Tax haven, right? Fiscal paradise? I wish we had those stateside, but with the IRS, forget it. They got Capone, you know? Anyway, there's no kids, just a nephew, right here in Ghent, name of de Wolf. Except he's a drunk and his wife spends all day on her knees – praying, that is, not the other thing. Religious nut. Real happy family, with one kid, a daughter who the old lady's never met. The kid doesn't even know her great-aunt exists, until one day up comes a lawyer to this bar she works in – yeah, she works in a bar, down by the docks, can you believe it? – and he gives her the news this old lady has left her everything, including the painting. Overnight, she's rich. Unbelievable, right? Fairy tale.'

De Smet nodded. He was glad when his drink arrived. He had a good command of English, but it was hard to follow what Bamberg said – he spoke too quickly and used strange words. The barman gave him a disapproving look, but the American didn't notice.

'That's not the end of the story,' he said. 'She uses the money to buy this old pile. Some countess built it during the belle époque, but then the Nazis took it over in the war and wrecked it, like a ruin. This de Wolf girl puts every penny into restoring it, a real labour of love. And this kid is like twenty-one years old, or something.'

'Miss de Wolf?'

'I tell you, where I come from, kids would spend a windfall like that on convertibles and pot. Start a business? Forget it. So the hotel opens and it's the best thing to happen to this old town in forever. That's why every night, no exceptions, Miss de Wolf raises a glass to Great-Aunt Magdalena – which is gratitude in my book, and something else we don't see enough of these days.'

To illustrate the point, Bamberg raised his glass to the painting. De Smet turned back to the dance floor. Miss de Wolf's partner was showing off, his steps too big, too complex. Miss de Wolf was struggling to keep up. There was a film of sweat on her brow. De Smet saw her briefly wince, before hiding the pain behind a smile. The role of the man in a dancing partnership was to make his partner look good, that was something his mother had taught him – his mother who loved to go dancing more than anything, who had met her fraudulent husband and fallen in love on a dance floor.

'Of course, if I had my way, Miss de Wolf would be in movies,' Bamberg said. 'Except for the leg, of course.'

'The leg?'

Bamberg leaned closer. 'The right one. She walks with a cane sometimes. And there's some kind of support under there.'

De Smet had not noticed until that moment: there was a discreet metal bar rising from the back of Miss de Wolf's right shoe and disappearing beneath the hem of her dress.

'They say she fell off a horse when she was a kid. It was a bad break.' Bamberg suddenly snorted with amusement, as if he had just said something funny, but if there was anything amusing in his choice of words, de Smet was damned if he could see it.

'Mack the Knife' drew to a close. The guests clapped. De Smet found himself standing opposite Miss de Wolf as she separated herself from her partner. The pink drinks had been stronger than they looked. He could feel the alcohol begin to affect him.

'May I have the honour, Miss de Wolf?'

She looked startled, but mustered another smile. 'Of course.'

The band played a slow number. De Smet got a sense that it was for her benefit. De Smet hadn't danced in years, but it didn't matter. His mother had taught him as a boy, and the old steps were still as natural to him as walking. Miss de Wolf was light in his arms. Her hair – or was it her skin? – gave off a delicate perfume, quite different from the smell that came off Isabelle and the other girls in the Quartier Brabant, who doused themselves with cheap scent to mask the smell of sweat. It was a shame he had to bring her bad news.

'I was just talking to an American,' he said. The bad news could wait a little longer.

'Mr Bamberg?'

'He told me how you rebuilt this place. A labour of love, he called it.'

'Mr Bamberg likes stories. He's in the film business.'

'So he said. Is it true about the house?'

'It was a crime to let it rot. We'd always dreamed of restoring it.'

'You've done a fine job. You must have spent a lot of money.'

'Less than you'd think.'

De Smet liked the firmness of Miss de Wolf's hold, the way she danced close to him, so as to feel precisely the motion of his body. It was correct and uncompromising. In the past, when he had danced with young women for the first time, he had found them tentative, their bodies slack, or held at too great a distance. The result was sloppy and unsatisfying. Miss de Wolf gave herself to the dance, to him, if only for as long as the music lasted.

The number drew to a close. There came a smattering of applause. Miss de Wolf was looking at him. 'I haven't seen you before. Who are you?'

De Smet bowed his head. 'Major Salvator de Smet, at your service.'

'Have you come to try your luck at the tables?'

De Smet shook his head. 'I don't believe in luck.' He let go of Miss de Wolf's hand and reached into his pocket.

While Adelais was dancing, Saskia made her way to the tables. The brunette inside the cage waved her over. Her name was Renilde. Her page-boy haircut gave her a youthful look, but she'd had ten years of experience at the Blankenberge casino before she joined the Astrid Christyn.

'Over there, you see? The man with the gin sling and the scar.'

Saskia looked. A man was standing by the first roulette table. He was tall, with sandy hair and an angry-looking scar along his jaw. He was not talking to anyone. 'What about him?'

'He's been watching the cage pretty well since he got here. Tries to look like he isn't. He came with another man, older. I think he's in the ballroom.'

'Are they playing?'

'This one bought five hundred in chips, hasn't placed a bet yet.'

As if to prove Renilde wrong, the man leaned forward and placed forty francs on the baize. Saskia wandered over and stood beside him. He had bet twenty francs on the middle column and twenty francs on black. The ball settled on red 10. He lost both stakes.

'Bad luck,' Saskia said. The man looked at her. 'Do you have a light?'

He put down his drink and fumbled in his pocket for a box of matches. Saskia had decided some time ago that she did not care for cigarettes, especially the yellow stains they left on her fingers, but she did like the air of sophistication they lent her, like the women who smoked in films. While his hands were still cupped around the flame, she saw him steal a peep down the front of her dress.

'It's your first time here, isn't it?' she said.

'Is it that obvious?'

Saskia laughed. 'Are you in Ghent for the film festival?'

'No, just business.'

'Don't you like films? I go every week, or I used to when I had time.'

'I like them, sure.'

'Then you should go while you can. They've got films showing this week you won't catch anywhere else. There's a new Buñuel, a new Ingmar Bergman. And there's a French film called *Lola*, about a single mother who works in a nightclub. I liked it.'

Every time he looked at her his gaze dipped to her lips. '*Lola*, right.'

'And then there's *Last Year at Marienbad*. Everybody's talking about that.'

'Are they? What's it about?'

Saskia shrugged. 'No one knows, not even the director. Well, I hope you find something to your taste – and your friend's as well.'

'My friend?'

'The gentleman you arrived with.'

'We're not friends, exactly.'

'No?' Saskia frowned thoughtfully. She raised a hand and gently grazed Toussaint's jaw with the tip of one finger. 'I hope he didn't give you that scar.'

Adelais followed Major de Smet onto the terrace, where they would not be overheard.

'Your establishment has been passing counterfeit currency, Miss de Wolf. We recovered a number of forged notes from an individual who says he got them here. I'm inclined to believe him.'

In her mind and in her dreams, Adelais had lived this moment a hundred times, although never here, outside the ballroom, with music playing, and people dancing under the light of the great chandelier. In her mind, the police came banging on the door, or lay in wait for her at the weaver's house.

'I don't understand. It isn't possible.'

'Ten 500-franc notes. Five thousand francs, notionally. Payment for work, he says.'

'Work? What kind of work?'

'Work on the building. You've hired a great many tradesmen over the last year, I'm sure.'

'I don't . . . I don't see how—'

De Smet raised a hand. 'I expect you've been paying most of them in cash. It's perfectly normal, after all.'

'Yes, but—'

'And you receive cash from your customers. Especially in there, at the gaming tables. It all goes into the same pot, I assume.'

Adelais nodded. An instinct told her to say as little possible.

'So if someone was to buy chips using counterfeit notes, the hotel might well end up paying them out again, to a tradesman.'

It was too much for Adelais to take in: the tradesman, a large payment in Patershol francs. A payment like that was never supposed to happen – they had a system, carefully designed. For all the confusion, one thing was clear: de Smet was not accusing her of anything, not yet.

'My staff are very experienced, Major. They can tell counterfeit money from the real thing.'

De Smet seemed to find this amusing. 'I'm sure that would be true most of the time, but not in this case.' He reached into his top pocket and pulled out a 500-franc note. 'See for yourself.'

Adelais held the note to the light, turned it over, and then over again, squinting at her own work, as if seeing it for the first time. De Smet watched her patiently. The thought crossed her mind that he was playing with her, that he knew.

'I need more light. I can't—'

De Smet took the note from her. 'It wouldn't help. These counterfeits are perfect in almost every way. There's never been anything like them, not in this country. They're the work of a perfectionist, a craftsman of exceptional dedication.'

'You know his name?'

De Smet laughed. 'If I knew his name I would have no need to trouble you, Miss de Wolf.' His expression darkened. 'I know *him* though, his mind. I've followed him for eight and a half years.' He glanced at the statue of Artemis, armed with her bow. 'Tracked him, you could say.'

Adelais swallowed. 'And he's been here? Are you sure?'

De Smet nodded. 'Your establishment's ideal for his purposes: rapid turnover, quick dispersal of currency and to a very wide area. And he likes to gamble, this man. It's the one weakness that we know of.'

'I'll make sure the staff are informed,' Adelais said. 'We'll be on the lookout from now on.'

'He could be here tonight. His notes could be in the till already – a disturbing thought, I know, but we should check, just in case. It's busy and the forger loves a crowd.'

'It gets busier later,' Adelais said. 'Most customers arrive around eleven.' It was all she could think of: to buy some time. Saskia would have stocked the cage with at least six thousand Patershol francs, ready to be exchanged for chips, probably more. Most of them would still be there. It was not something that could be explained away.

'Nevertheless—'

'Besides, most of these guests have been coming all week. They're with the festival. I don't see any strangers.'

De Smet was already making his way to the gaming room. Adelais followed. She needed to stop him, to hold him up, to reach the cage ahead of him. But he wasn't giving her time.

They nudged their way through the gaming room. Nadia watched them go by. She could tell something was wrong. Adelais thought about fainting, falling. How much time would that buy her? Maybe no time at all.

Saskia had taken over the cage from Renilde. Adelais introduced her to Major de Smet. 'The major thinks some of our customers might be passing counterfeit money.'

'No, really?' Saskia sounded surprised, as surprised as if she had just read a spicy story in the newspaper. 'I can't believe that. They all seem so nice.'

'He wants to see the cash we've taken so far. I explained that we'll have much more later.'

'You'll have to forgive my impatience,' de Smet said. 'I won't hold you up for long.'

She could demand he produce a warrant, refuse to cooperate. But that would be as good as a confession.

Saskia reached for her keys and opened up the cage. De Smet went inside, and rang open the till. In a few moments, Adelais knew, it would all be over.

A stranger walked up to the cage. He had a scar along his jaw and looked deathly pale, as if he had just been sick. As he leaned on the counter, Adelais glimpsed the handle of a pistol sticking up from his belt. Another gendarme, in case of arrests. She should have known there would be more than one.

'Miss de Wolf?' De Smet held up a handful of 500-franc notes. Adelais watched him through the bars of the cage. Soon she would watch the whole world that way. She stepped closer, chin up: the countess, one last time.

De Smet raised the notes towards the electric light above him. 'You see the watermarks?'

Adelais nodded.

'They're bright and clear, with distinct edges. That's how you know these notes are genuine.'

The gendarmes showed no signs of leaving, although the younger one looked sweaty and out of sorts. He found a seat in the gaming room and went back to watching the cage. De Smet hung around the hotel entrance, watching guests and gamblers come and go. Occasionally he followed them up the grand staircase and watched them buy their chips. Neither of the gendarmes had another drink.

Adelais passed Saskia at the bar. 'Kitchens, ten minutes,' she said, smiling, as if it were a joke.

Adelais went down the back stairs. Saskia went down the front. The kitchens were closed for the night, silent but for the hum of refrigerators.

'There were Patershol francs in the cage. What happened?'

Saskia looked excited and pleased with herself. 'I hid them of course.' She lifted the hem of her skirt. A sizeable stack of notes was tucked into the top of her left stocking.

'When? How did you know to—'

'Captain Toussaint. He couldn't resist bragging about how he got his scar. Hot on the heels of a master criminal: the Tournai Forger, he said.'

'Tournai?'

'Trying to impress, of course, like they all do.' Saskia adjusted her stockings, making sure the forged currency was secure. 'He as good as told me why they were here. So I knew what had to be done.'

'He was watching the cage. He didn't see you?'

'He was watching the cage up until the moment he staggered off to the gents.' Saskia caught the expression on Adelais's face. 'Daddy has all sorts of stuff in his surgery. Some of it can come in handy in an emergency. I keep it in the first-aid box. Didn't you notice?'

'What sort of stuff?'

Saskia smoothed down her dress. 'Does it matter? Chloral something. Hydrate, is it? I think it's what they used on Janet Leigh in *Touch of Evil*. All it took was a friendly drink on the house and he was out of the way for a good ten minutes.'

'You *drugged* him?'

'No, I asked nicely if he wouldn't mind looking the other way.' A car pulled up outside. A sweep of headlights lit up the kitchens. 'We should get back. Business as usual, right?'

'Right.'

'We'll talk later.'

Adelais hung back. She wasn't ready to go back to playing hostess, as if everything was fine. They'd had troubles before, but now they were dancing on the edge of disaster. 'They've been hunting us all along, Saskia, from the very start. They're hunting us now.' Her heart was racing, her breath short. She didn't want Major de Smet to see her that way. He would guess the reason.

'Come on, relax,' Saskia said. 'They're hunting for a big brute of a man, the man who broke the captain's jaw. We could *dress* in Patershol francs and they wouldn't realise. They'd be too busy imagining what's underneath.'

'De Smet's not stupid.'

'But he's a man. I saw the way he was looking at you.' Saskia sighed. 'Stop worrying, will you?' She put her arms around Adelais and pulled her close. 'We're way ahead of them. And you've got me to protect you. You'll always have me.'

Outside, car doors opened and closed: well-heeled people come to play, their voices and laughter loud in the night. Adelais left Saskia and went back up to the ballroom. At the bar she asked Hendryck for a glass of wine.

'Something wrong?' he said, as he uncorked a bottle.

'The police are here, the federal police. It seems we've had a master criminal in our midst.'

Hendryck laughed. 'Show me a joint that hasn't.'

Adelais drank her wine. It helped her feel steadier. When one of the film people asked her to dance, she accepted. The band was playing a tango waltz. She had to concentrate on following her partner's lead and gradually she was able to stop feeling frightened about the gendarmes and how close they had come to discovering her secret. Instead, once the dance was over, she found herself thinking about Janet Leigh in *Touch of Evil*, and the way Captain Toussaint had looked when he emerged from the lavatories that evening. Slowly, the ugly notion began to form in her mind that once – at a dance four years earlier – she had experienced very much the same thing.

—— Thirty-nine ——

Adelais didn't fall asleep until dawn. Even then, bad dreams woke her: dreams of panic and dread, played out against the insistent music of the band – dreams of Salvator de Smet, of being at his mercy, cornered, naked. She was glad she couldn't remember most of them.

She got up early and went straight up to the office. The guests were all asleep. A clattering from the kitchens was the only evidence of activity. She went to the desk and took out the cash ledger. There was another in the safe at the old weaver's house, where she and Saskia recorded the exchange of counterfeit currency, but this ledger recorded only the Astrid Christyn's legitimate transactions. Except at the cage, where cash was exchanged for chips, the two kinds of money were never supposed to cross.

The hotel had employed dozens of tradesmen over the past two years: builders, carpenters, decorators, roofers. Adelais went through their bills, hoping something would fit with the five thousand francs the police had found. She was still searching an hour later, when Major de Smet's car pulled up outside. It was raining heavily and the head-lamps were on. Adelais watched de Smet climb out: he was in uniform and had come alone. He shut the car door and stood for a moment, looking at the scaffolding that covered half the stable block. The rain did not seem to bother him. He put on his cap and walked around to the front of the hotel.

Adelais felt her pulse begin to race, but the panic was short-lived. Last night's near miss, the bad dreams, it was if they had sapped her capacity for fear. She was calm enough to function, to play the countess, even if it was a brittle calm. She poked at her hair in the mirror, straightened out her blouse and walked into the entrance hall with a smile on her face.

The uniform was immaculate, braid and buttons bright against navy-blue serge. It struck Adelais as faintly preposterous, like a costume from a light opera. In the daylight, de Smet seemed older. There were bruises on the knuckles of one hand and a jagged white scar. She had not noticed them before.

'I apologise for the intrusion, Miss de Wolf. Could we talk in private?'

Adelais led him into the office and closed the door. The cash ledger was still open on the desk, beside it a year's worth of bills. What was the gendarme going to tell her now? Had another stash of Patershol francs been found? Did he want to search the hotel?

She offered him coffee. He refused it. They sat down on opposite sides of the desk. Adelais wished she had taken more care of her appearance that morning. The dark circles would give away the lack of sleep.

De Smet produced an envelope and placed it in front of her. 'The forger's very likely to come back here. I expect it's only a matter of time. I have reason to believe the base of his operations is here in Ghent.'

'How do you know?'

'Call it a pattern. It isn't cut and dried, but it's there.'

The envelope contained a sketch, folded in four: a rough-shaven man staring straight ahead.

'He might look something like this,' de Smet said.

At first, Adelais saw no resemblance to anyone she knew, but after a few moments she began to recognise the eyes, the position of the cheek-bones, the hairline. The nose was too broad and the mouth too small, but she knew who it was meant to be. 'I'll make sure everyone sees this,' she said.

'It mightn't be much help,' de Smet said. 'I've a feeling someone else is running the operation now.'

Adelais looked up. 'What makes you say that?'

De Smet hesitated. 'Details, Miss de Wolf. They wouldn't be of interest. The fact is, I came here this morning to warn you.'

'Warn me?'

'To be careful. If you spot someone passing counterfeit notes, don't under any circumstances try to apprehend them. Do nothing. Accept the notes, carry on as usual and notify the municipal police. They're aware of the case.'

'We have our own security on hand, Major, and always during gaming hours.' It was something Adelais felt the countess would say.

'I'm aware of that, but this individual is a professional criminal. The fact that he's skilled makes him no less dangerous. He will prove ruthless and violent if the need arises. You can be sure of that.'

De Smet spoke with such conviction, it was almost as if he knew what he was talking about.

'You told me you don't know who you're looking for. How can you be sure he's . . . dangerous?'

De Smet looked towards the window. Rain was splashing against the sill outside. 'Criminals operate outside the law, Miss de Wolf, and without the protection of the law. A capacity for violence is all the security they have. If they don't understand that at the outset they learn it, sooner or later. It's a question of survival.'

'Then we'll take your advice,' Adelais said, 'if it comes to that.'

'Good. I'd hate to see you get hurt.' A polite, tempered smile appeared on de Smet's lips. 'I enjoyed our dance last night very much. You dance with great skill and precision, in spite of your . . . disadvantage. I find that admirable.'

De Smet regarded Adelais steadily. He was expecting a reaction, a show of appreciation for his generous words. Adelais managed to return his smile. The rain had brought a chill to the air. She could feel it on her spine. 'Thank you, Major.'

De Smet got up. Saskia had been right about one thing: it had not even occurred to de Smet that the source of the counterfeits could be two young women. That blindness had protected them. For the moment, it still did.

'One thing, Major: the man we paid with the forged money. He's out of pocket, isn't he? We owe him five thousand francs. It wouldn't be right to leave things as they are. If you could tell me—'

De Smet held up a hand. 'You don't have to worry about that, Miss de Wolf. Your man won't need the money where he's going. He's a locksmith by day and a smuggler by night. And he got caught.'

It was the last day of the film festival, and most of the guests were checking out. By noon their beds had been stripped, their luggage cleared from the entrance hall, their cars and taxis driven away. Saskia arrived late and kept herself busy taking money at the front desk. Adelais had no opportunity to talk to her. Half an hour later, by which time it had stopped raining, she had disappeared. Her scooter was still parked outside, but there was no sign of her in the hotel. Eventually, Adelais found her in the grounds. She had put on a raincoat and was sitting on one of the swings under the shade of a beech tree. Adelais had never seen her there before.

'Why do we keep this old thing?' she said, as Adelais approached. 'It's not like people bring their children here, is it?'

'Maybe they will one day.'

Saskia wrinkled her nose. 'Wrong ambience. This playground's for grown-ups.' She straightened her legs and pushed off gently. 'Still, you come out here sometimes, don't you, when no one's looking?'

Adelais dabbed at the ground with her stick. The grass was carpeted with wet leaves. They were slippery, treacherous. She could not risk a fall.

'What was it for, Saskia, the five thousand?'

'What five thousand?'

'The five thousand you gave the locksmith.'

'Locks, I should think.' Saskia pushed off again, harder and higher.

Adelais had to step out of the way. 'What makes you so sure it was me, anyway?'

'We have a system: Patershol francs never go in the safe. We never mix them with hotel money.'

'I know.'

'We're the only ones who know where they're kept. So if you didn't give them to the locksmith and I didn't, then he must have got them for himself. He must have broken into the house, and—'

'All right.' Saskia's heels hit the ground. She stopped dead. 'All right. I paid him with the wrong money. My mistake. I was in a hurry to get rid of him. I didn't know he was going to get himself arrested.'

'Paid him for what?'

'Most of it was my own money, real money: ten thousand francs. The extra five was a kind of bonus.'

'*For what?*'

Saskia laced her hands together and dropped them in her lap. 'A bit of persuasion. Well, a threat really. We did talk about it, Adelais. Don't you remember?'

'The licensing man? Van Ranst? I never agreed—'

'I know. I didn't *ask* you to agree, because it had to be done and there was no other way. So I kept you out of it, which is where you prefer to be, isn't it? Ignorance is bliss.'

'What are you talking about?'

Saskia started swinging again. Adelais wished she would stop.

'Come on, Adelais. I love you, but you've never been one for awkward questions, have you? Like Patershol: your uncle put together the whole operation and you don't stop to ask how he did it. You don't ask what it cost, or even where the plates came from. What's the story there?'

'There was no one I could ask. Who could I ask?'

'Someone must know something.' Saskia squinted up at the beech tree. Fat raindrops were dripping from its branches. 'But it's better not to find out. What good would it do? And why should you anyway? It's not as if you've done anything really bad. It's better to leave it alone, and it's better I didn't make you choose.'

'Choose?'

'Between scaring off that awful man from the council and losing everything we've worked for.' Saskia let the swing slowly come to a stop. 'In the end, you would have agreed.'

'I wouldn't. I'd never—'

'Oh, don't be stupid, Adelais. Wake up.'

'You took a terrible risk.'

'A calculated risk, as my father would say. And it worked like a charm, didn't it?' Saskia jumped off the swing and set off towards the hotel. 'You know, just once, Adelais, just once, I wish you could just say thank you.'

Late that afternoon, Adelais emptied the desk of counterfeit money. She changed into a pair of trousers, put on her raincoat, and set off for the city on the Vespa. If de Smet came back and searched the hotel, she wanted to be sure he found nothing. She didn't tell Saskia what she was doing. Saskia seemed to relish their narrow escape: outsmarting the police, outsmarting everyone. She might not agree to stop the operation, even to pause. She liked the thrill of it a little too much.

The sky was heavy with cloud. Adelais went fast, skirting the large puddles that had formed in the road. The notes were in the Gucci handbag, slung across her shoulder. She watched for de Smet's car. Maybe he needed to catch her with the counterfeits in her possession. Maybe everything he'd said that morning had been designed to make her do exactly what she was doing. She thought about turning back.

She had just crossed the Scheldt, when a car swung into the road behind her, its tyres squeaking on the asphalt. It was an old-fashioned model, but she couldn't tell if it was de Smet's or not. Adelais twisted the throttle. In less than one kilometre she would reach the outskirts of the city. She could lose him there or lose the bag. The car hung back. In the twilight it was hard to make out the colour. De Smet's had been black, but this looked paler.

She was going too fast when she hit the junction, too fast to stop. The blast of a horn brought her head round. A truck loomed up on her left, hydraulics hissing. It was going to hit her. Adelais braked hard, turned. She felt the back wheel lose its grip, a sickening, frictionless moment, like free fall, followed by a lurching impact as the scooter slewed across the road on its side. The truck thundered past, showering spray from its tyres.

Shards of glass on the ground: a broken wing mirror. She heard voices. A man appeared, crouching over her, then another. She felt no pain — nothing broken, she felt sure. They were asking her questions: was she all right? Did she need an ambulance?

They were helping her up, getting the scooter upright at the same time. Her stick was still hanging from the handlebars. She reached for the handbag: it was gone.

'The bag, my bag!' One of the men was holding it. He had picked it up off the road. She snatched it back from him. 'I'm fine. I'm fine. I don't . . . I don't need any help.' The man asked if she was sure. Another pushed the scooter to the pavement. Someone hit their horn. The men shrugged and shuffled away. They thought she was mad. The car that had been behind her was nowhere to be seen.

Adelais took a deep breath. Her raincoat had an oily smear above the hem. Her trousers were torn at the shin. She was shaking. On the near side of the junction a large poster advertised a new film at the Capitole. Audrey Hepburn, wearing a black cocktail dress, stared down at the scene. Adelais stared back. She knew Audrey Hepburn from *Roman Holiday*, the story of a princess who ran away. It had once been her favourite film.

In her hand, the film star held a cigarette in a long holder. Her eyes were wide and her mouth slightly open, as if surprised by a question she could not answer.

It was almost dark by the time Adelais arrived at Sluizeken. The river was moving again, swollen by the rain. She parked the Vespa and stood on the narrow dock, clutching her bag, watching the water slide by, swift and silent. It had been years since she had first stood on that spot, but for almost the first time since then she had no clear idea of what to do, no guidance, no help. She heard Saskia's words in her head: *you've never been one for awkward questions*. Was that true? Saskia herself had changed. Even before today, Adelais had sensed an unspoken reproach in much of what she did. She had proved a disappointment because she would not open her eyes.

Adelais had almost forgotten the feeling of loneliness. She felt it now. She wished there was someone she could confide in, someone like Sebastian who would listen, someone like Uncle Cornelis who understood. But it was too late: she had deceived everyone who had not left her, everyone except Saskia. There was nobody else left.

She turned her back on the river and made her way along the dock. The weaver's house waited as it always did: windows shuttered, its old brown bricks etched in soot. At the door she pushed a key into the lower of the two deadlocks. It would not move. She took out the key and felt along its edge with her finger: it was the right one. She tried again, tugging at the door handle to free the mechanism. The door rattled against the frame. Neither of the deadlocks had been turned.

She never left the house without turning the deadlocks. One well-placed kick would get through a latch. She even used them when she was inside, working.

She found the latch key and opened the door. The house was in darkness.

'Saskia?'

She had not seen the Lambretta, but maybe Saskia had parked it further away.

She switched on the light and made her way up the stairs. Outside, the braying of a police siren grew louder before slowly fading away. As she climbed she thought she detected a musky smell, one less harsh than the smell of ink.

The door at the top of the house was wide open. Adelais stood frozen on the landing. Nothing stirred. She could make out the crates of paper, the camp bed, the pile of blankets – everything just as she had left it.

She turned on the light and hurried to the safe. It was locked, as always. She entered the combination, forcing herself to go carefully so as not to miss a number. The safe had held around eighty thousand francs in real money. More important, it held the plates.

The tumblers aligned with a familiar click. Adelais pulled down on the handle and opened the door. The plates were there on the bottom shelf, where she had left them, wrapped in cloth. Next to the plates lay another fifty thousand Patershol francs, bagged up, ready for transport. The legitimate currency lay uncovered on the upper shelf beside the Beretta.

Nothing had been disturbed. Only one thing was different: sitting on top of the cash, where she could not fail to see it, was a small bronze wolf.

Rue Henri Chomé

—— Forty ——

Brussels, October 1961

After lunch, Captain Toussaint picked up a copy of *Le Soir* on his way back to Federal Police Headquarters, only to find that Lieutenant Masson already had one.

'Good afternoon, sir,' he said. He had been hovering outside Toussaint's office.

'Good afternoon.' Toussaint's head was still not back to normal after the night in Ghent, and his unhappy encounter with deceptive foreign cocktails. He had been hoping to spend at least the next half-hour quietly catching up on his reading.

'Sir, I was wondering . . . Have you seen the report on page 4?'

'What report?'

'About the new banknotes? The new one thousand, and the new five hundred?'

Toussaint snatched Masson's paper without bothering to open his own. It was a report, set across two columns at the bottom of the page.

. . . An image of Flemish cartographer Gerardus Mercator (1512–1594) has been chosen to adorn the BEF1000 note, while the Renaissance artist Bernard van Orley (1492–1542) will adorn the BEF500 denomination. The new designs, which are unusual in not representing royalty, past or present, were nevertheless approved by the King.

The new notes are expected to boast a number of special security features, recently developed in Switzerland and Germany. These include metal 'security threads' running through the paper, and 'microprinting', which involves the use of fine-scale text or patterns that are often invisible to the naked eye.

'Thanks to these new techniques,' said Bank of Belgium governor, Camille Gutt, 'the Belgian franc will soon be as immune to forgery as the Swiss franc or the German mark.'

The new notes are expected to enter circulation late next year. Existing notes in BEF500 and BEF1000 denominations will cease to be legal tender roughly six months later.

Toussaint sat down. He and his department reported regularly to the Bank of Belgium. There were joint committees and official liaisons, covering a range of financial crimes, from tax evasion to securities fraud, but nobody had given them advanced notice of the new bank-notes. Here he was, having to read about it in the newspapers like an ordinary member of the public, as if he couldn't be trusted. It was humiliating.

Toussaint closed Masson's copy of the newspaper and slid it across the desk. 'So they went with Mercator in the end. I thought they would. Where would we be without maps?'

When he was alone, Toussaint read the newspaper report again. He wondered how de Smet was going to take it – not just the fact that he had been kept in the dark, but the wider implications. In eighteen months' time, the counterfeit notes they had been tracking all over the country would be worthless. They would not be accepted at shops or casinos or racecourses. It wouldn't be possible to exchange them for any-thing, individually or in bulk. They would be gathered up, shipped back to the Bank of Belgium, and destroyed. After nine years, the operation would be at an end.

Where would that leave the Tournai Forger? Where would it leave de Smet?

Toussaint got up and went to the window. Litter and brown leaves were dancing in spirals along the Rue du Marché au Charbon. The news was grounds for satisfaction, he reassured himself, at least from a law and order perspective: the state had reasserted its control over the currency. The forger's scheme had been neutralised. He would have to find something else to do, and the financial crimes section of the federal police could devote its resources to other matters. De Smet could close the file and move on, knowing that the season of master forgeries was over.

Case closed, but not solved. Who was he kidding? Nine years of investigation and not an arrest to show for it, not a single suspect named, it was a glaring example of federal police ineptitude, if that's what you were looking for. And plenty of people were. For Colonel Delhaye it would present a perfect opportunity to impose himself on the department by cutting out some dead wood. He would have got rid of de Smet years ago, if it hadn't been for his reputation.

Toussaint picked up the newspaper and climbed the stairs to the top floor. De Smet was standing in front of the big map, sticking blue push-pins into the Franco-Belgian border. He had cut himself shaving and, unusually for him, the top button of his tunic was undone.

'More sightings, sir?'

'Two *bureaux de change*. They use the same bank in Kortrijk. The bank traced the notes.'

'They've turned up at a few of those foreign exchange places.'

'Yes, they have. Those big hauls in Zaventem?' De Smet tapped a pair of pushpins on the east side of Brussels. 'I'm thinking they came the same way: *bureaux de change* at the airport.'

'So . . . what? Our man wants foreign exchange now? What's that about?'

De Smet had one more pin. He took his time finding the right place to put it. 'Either he wants foreign exchange or his marks do. I'm thinking the latter.'

Toussaint had the newspaper behind his back. 'Meaning?'

'Meaning they're travellers, tourists. On their way home. Selling back their Belgian money at the border.' De Smet planted the pin on the port of Ostend, where a car ferry plied back and forth to Dover. 'The question is: where did they come by the forgeries?'

'You're assuming they weren't sold counterfeits in the first place,' Toussaint said, 'at a *bureau de change*. Isn't that the best bet? Put a man on the inside, somewhere like the airport, you could shift hundreds of notes to unsuspecting tourists. It's perfect.'

De Smet looked at him, a glimmer of respect in his eyes. It did not last. 'The pattern's too diffuse. Most visitors leave the same way they arrive. That means they use the same bureau. If the notes were coming from just one of those, we'd see it sooner or later.' He stepped back from the map. His lips were pale and chalky. He looked unwell. 'We should put men at all the busiest *bureaux*. One stroke of luck is all we need, one tourist with a handful of fake notes and a good memory.'

Toussaint tried to imagine getting approval for an operation of the size de Smet was talking about: hundreds of extra man hours expended in trying, against the odds, to tackle a problem that was invisible to the general population, and which would soon cease to exist in any case.

He handed de Smet the newspaper. 'Page 4, sir.'

De Smet opened the newspaper and read in silence. After a minute he closed it again, folded it, and handed it back. There was no trace of a reaction.

'Well? Sir?'

De Smet seemed lost in thought. A cup of black coffee had been resting on the filing cabinet. He picked it up. 'The *bureaux de change*. That's where we should be watching.'

Toussaint wondered if de Smet had read the right article. 'This changes everything, doesn't it, sir? In a year or so—'

'A lot can happen in a year.' De Smet's attention had returned to the map. 'We must redouble our efforts. Crimes have been committed. This won't wipe them away.'

The crimes wouldn't be wiped away, Toussaint thought, but the means to solve them would. Even if they had a suspect, without the counterfeit currency how could they hope to secure a conviction? They might get by with witnesses and sworn testimony, but where were they going to come from?

Toussaint tried to think of something positive to say. 'Maybe, with time running out, the forger will get sloppy, push his luck.'

De Smet grunted. Maybe, Toussaint thought, the case was not as important to him as it seemed. Maybe the fact that his adversary was about to be deprived of his livelihood was satisfaction enough. Or maybe the old man was finally losing his mind.

Toussaint tucked the newspaper under his arm and left. De Smet went on staring at the map, at the thousands of snippets of data that had been plotted, grouped, connected and configured over its surface: an effort that had yielded clues and insights, but not yet the break-through that he hungered for, never the face or the name of the man who had eluded him. Eight and a half years of data, about to be rendered useless.

He hurled his cup at the map. It shattered. Coffee ran down the paper, and dripped onto the grey linoleum. The officers on the floor below rose from their desks, thinking someone in the building had discharged their weapon.

—— Forty-one ——

When she held him, it was as if the years of fear and anxiety were draining out of her. The sensation was overpowering. There was no room for curiosity, for questions about how the miracle had come about. She didn't want to question anything, unless it turned out to be an illusion or a trick.

'You're here. Are you really here?'

'What do they say about bad pennies?'

How many times during those years had Adelais asked herself what her uncle Cornelis would do? How many times had she longed for his guidance? She allowed herself to look at him. He looked back with an apologetic smile on his face. 'I expect you're angry with me.'

She hugged him again. 'I'm not. As long as you're alive.'

He laughed. 'Well, I'm not a ghost. At least, I don't think I am.' He slapped himself on the cheek. 'No, solid enough.'

'I talked to you every day, in my head. I tried to imagine what you'd say. They told me you were dead. Was that a lie?'

'No, of course not. They were simply . . . misinformed.' Uncle Cornelis fixed Adelais with a stare. There were lines around his eyes that she did not recognise, and his eyebrows were greyer and wilder than she remembered. 'And they have to stay that way. You can't say a word.'

'Not even to—'

'Not to anyone. I'm six feet under and always will be. Promise me, Adelais?'

'I promise. Does that mean you're not staying?' Adelais had been picturing everything the way it was, as if getting there was no more difficult than winding back the hands of a clock.

'Just for a few hours this time. I must be gone by daybreak, like the rest of the undead. But I'll be back.' Uncle Cornelis smiled, but the smile faded. 'I was sorry to hear about your father, Adelais. I wish I could have—'

'It's all right.'

'I wanted to be there, I really did, especially when I heard your mother wasn't . . . I mean, she couldn't—'

'She was in Africa. She still is.'

'Right. Africa. Of course.'

'Helping sick people. There are a lot of sick people there, she says.'

'Still, having to shoulder all that alone . . .'

'It was a while ago. It's behind me now.'

Uncle Cornelis nodded. 'My little wolf.' His fingers brushed against her cheek. 'You know, I think what we need right now is a drink.'

Uncle Cornelis separated himself from her and began to search. They were on the ground floor, where she had found him surrounded by boxes. Adelais had tried to keep the room as well ordered as her uncle but Saskia had tossed things in any old how. She didn't care if they repeated themselves, buying the same items from the same places.

'If I'm not mistaken . . .' Uncle Cornelis found a box labelled *Eupen* and took off the lid. He rummaged around inside before pulling out a clear glass bottle full of a yellow liquid. 'Here we are: a very fine eau de vie.'

Adelais did not like eau de vie, but she was not about to say so. Uncle Cornelis unscrewed the top of the bottle and sniffed the contents.

'Wait,' she said. 'We've glasses somewhere.'

Uncle Cornelis waited while she went from box to box. She found a set of six coloured shot glasses in the box marked *Bruges*, although she was fairly sure they had bought them in Mechelen.

Uncle Cornelis poured out two large measures and handed one to Adelais. 'Here's to life after death.'

They clinked glasses. Adelais gulped the liquor. It tasted like medicine and burned as it went down. Before she could stop him, Uncle Cornelis had filled the glasses again. He was dressed in a heavy woollen jacket with patches on the elbows, like the men who worked the docks. She wondered if it was a disguise, or if it was on the water that he now earned his living. In the past, he had always struck her as dapper and comfortably off.

'We got a letter,' she said, 'from the Ministry of Foreign Affairs. There was a body.'

'Not mine, fortunately.'

'Whose was it?'

Uncle Cornelis scratched a patch of red skin on the side of his neck. 'In these situations it helps to have the services of an undertaker. Bodies are their stock-in-trade, after all.'

'They gave you a body?'

'Sold. Nothing's free in the Netherlands.'

'It wasn't missed?'

Uncle Cornelis shook his head. 'Closed coffin. I think what they buried – the family, I mean – was eighty-five kilograms of old books.' He shrugged. 'Books never arouse suspicion, and they're usually cheaper than bricks.' Uncle Cornelis emptied his glass and carried on rooting through the *Eupen* box. 'You have to have an escape plan, Adelais. You can't wait for things to go wrong and then improvise. If you go on the run without a plan, chances are you'll get caught.'

'I don't have an escape plan.'

'Didn't Franz Klysen give you his number?'

'The notary?'

Uncle Cornelis had pulled a brown leather waistcoat from the box and was holding it up to himself. It looked at least a size too big. In his time away he had lost weight. 'That would've been the place to start. Klysen can always get hold of me.'

'He didn't tell me that.'

'How could he? He didn't know if you could be trusted. You might have told the police. Of course, I assured him that wasn't going to happen, but he doesn't know you like I do.'

300

The waistcoat seemed to satisfy him. Uncle Cornelis folded it up and packed it away in a canvas bag, which was already nearly full. He plucked a cashmere scarf from another box and a pair of gloves from a third. Socks and a blue cotton shirt took up the last of the space. He slung the bag over his shoulder and tucked the bottle of eau de vie under his arm. 'Come on. I want to see what you've done to my machines.'

They made their way up to the next floor. Uncle Cornelis had his own keys. It felt strange, watching him use them, as if the house was still his, as if he had never left. Adelais wondered if she should give the house back to him now. But how could she do that if he were still legally dead?

'Why did you do it? Why did you need to escape?'

Uncle Cornelis had his back to her. It took him a while to find the right key for the deadlock. 'The gendarmes were getting a bit too close. I made a stupid mistake and one day they were waiting for me – nearly caught me too. Then I saw this sketch they had of me pinned up in a savings bank – a surprisingly good likeness. I was afraid they'd eventually match the picture to a name. That's why I had to die.' He looked at Adelais over his shoulder. 'You need anonymity in this line of work and mine was compromised.' He found the key he was looking for and turned the lock. 'Still, my weakness became your strength, you could say. All this time, they've been looking for someone like me, not someone like you.' He opened the door. 'I go by the name of Hartman these days, just so you know.'

'The gendarmes were at the hotel,' Adelais said. 'Last night.'

Uncle Cornelis was still for a moment. 'What did they want?'

'We paid someone with the wrong kind of cash, a tradesman.'

'Tut-tut.' Uncle Cornelis switched on the lights.

'The police showed me that sketch.'

'Did they? Well, that's good, isn't it?'

'Is it?'

'It means they're still in the dark. Were you scared?'

'Yes. I don't think I showed it though.'

'Did they say they'd be back?'

'No, but it's . . . it's different now. I'm afraid they're watching.'

'I doubt that. The gendarmes have bigger fish to fry. Still, it doesn't hurt to fear the worst. Keeps you on your toes.'

Uncle Cornelis put down the bottle, and went over to the intaglio press. He began to inspect it, testing the rollers and the mechanism, running his fingers over the surfaces. He seemed to like what he found. 'You've looked after these presses. We should get a good price for them.'

'A good price?'

Uncle Cornelis went over to the lithography press, and planted a hand on the heavy steel gantry. 'We won't be needing them much longer.'

'Why not?'

'Because King Leopold II is on his way out. The old five hundred's for the chop, the note, I mean. There'll be a new design next year, and a few months after that . . .'

Adelais felt dismay and relief in the same moment. It was hard to know which feeling was stronger. 'I haven't seen anything in the newspapers. Are you sure?'

Uncle Cornelis nodded. 'They've been working on the new designs all year. They'll be using new machines, new premises, everything. And this new paper, with metal inside it, God knows how you'd get hold of that.' He picked up the bottle. Glass rattled against glass as he poured himself another generous measure. 'I ran into an old boy from Anderlecht. He told me all about it.'

'Anderlecht?'

'The Federal Engraving Bureau. I worked there for years when you were a child.'

Adelais was still holding her empty glass. When Uncle Cornelis offered her a refill she covered it with her hand. 'The plates I've been using, is that where they came from? You stole them?'

Uncle Cornelis laughed. 'I *could* have stolen them, as it happens, but I'd have been caught in no time. And it would've been pointless. If the director had found he was missing a plate, he would have changed the design before a note was printed. But they searched and searched, the gendarmes and all, and found nothing amiss.'

There was a gleam in her uncle's eye. Adelais could tell he was proud of himself, proud of whatever trick he had pulled off at the Federal Engraving Bureau.

'So you copied them? Is that what you did?'

Uncle Cornelis turned the lever on the lithography press. The steel gantry rolled slowly over the baseplate with a sucking sound. He rolled it back, faster. The gleam in his eye had gone. He scratched at the angry red skin on his neck. 'It doesn't matter.'

'I want to know.'

'Another time, Adelais.'

'Don't you trust me?'

He looked up sharply. 'I trust you more than anyone, little wolf.'

'Anyone except your lawyer. You let me think you were dead.' Adelais could not help it. There were suddenly tears in her eyes. 'I thought you were dead.'

'So you *are* angry with me.'

'I lit a candle for you. I cried. If you knew . . .'

Uncle Cornelis walked over and took hold of her hands. 'The truth would have been a burden, Adelais. And you were so young. I couldn't risk it. In my place, what would you have done?'

Adelais sniffed. 'The same.'

'It won't happen again, I promise. We're partners now, you and me. We've been partners since the day you first walked in here, even if you didn't know it.'

Once the presses had passed muster, they went up to the top floor. Uncle Cornelis opened the safe and took out the bronze wolf. 'This goes back in my pocket. I never go anywhere without it.'

'Where are you going?'

Cornelis hesitated. It was clearly against his instincts to share that kind of information. 'Rotterdam. I'm taking a train. And a few thousand of the francs you printed. Don't worry, I know where to change them.'

He opened one of the bags of Patershol francs and held a note up to the light.

Adelais could not help feeling nervous, waiting for his verdict. 'What do you think?'

Uncle Cornelis smiled and stuffed a handful of notes inside his coat. 'You need me to tell you? You buy yourself a palace with these beauties and you want my opinion?'

'Yes, I do.'

He closed the safe, and stood up. 'They're perfect. And the Astrid Christyn? Your own little casino? I believed in you – always have – but I never guessed you had that much ambition.'

Adelais had never thought of herself as ambitious. Ambitious people wanted to live in big houses and drive expensive cars. All she had ever wanted was to belong, to take part. 'How did you hear about it, Uncle?'

'The Astrid Christyn Hotel? Everyone's heard about it. You're in all the guidebooks. A taste of the belle époque – I've read about it in magazines. It must have been a lot of work.'

'I had help.'

Uncle Cornelis nodded. 'I know. Miss Helsen, the doctor's youngest. That's a big family, isn't it? And a rich one, I've heard. But the hotel, it makes money, doesn't it?'

'Thanks to the gaming. We need more rooms.'

'Klysen's been asking around. You finish the work on that stable block, pay off the bank, and he thinks the place could easily fetch twenty million. More likely thirty. We just have to find the right buyer.'

'The right buyer? But—'

'Not a bad pay-off for a little illicit printing. And you know it can't go on forever.'

'What about Saskia?'

Uncle Cornelis shrugged. 'Whatever she put in, we'll triple it.'

'I don't want to sell the hotel.'

'It's just a business, isn't it?' Uncle Cornelis studied Adelais for a moment. Then he took her hands again. 'Little wolf, that's the plan. We cash in and move on. It's safer that way. Besides, you don't want to spend your life pandering to tourists day and night. Don't worry, I've found some new opportunities. We just need some capital to break in.' He looked at his watch. 'We'll talk about it next time. I'm sorry, but I have a train to catch.'

'So soon?'

'I'll be back in a week or two. Meantime, keep doing what you're doing. And remember, I'm proud of you.'

Uncle Cornelis slung his bag over his shoulder and went down the stairs. By the time Adelais caught up with him, he was outside, keys in hand, waiting to lock the door.

— Forty-two —

Uncle Cornelis was never wrong. When he set her a challenge, it was because his instincts told him she could meet it. He knew what she was capable of, better than she knew herself, and his faith in her was expressed not just in words, but in deeds. He was proud of her, the way a father should be, and everything he had done for her had been directed at a single aim: to set her free. Adelais's mother hadn't seen it that way: there was a selfish motive behind everything he did – that was what she had said. *He always knew how to get under your skin.* But her mother had left, and it was Uncle Cornelis who had returned.

She rode back to the Astrid Christyn. Looking from the driveway at the lights that burned in the windows, at the pale smoke drifting from the chimneys, Adelais was struck by its beauty. But that did not change the facts: she had her uncle to thank for the place, for everything. How far would she have got without him? If selling it was part of his plan, it would have been foolish to object, and wrong into the bargain. Uncle Cornelis had been her invisible partner, but, more than that, he was the only family she had left.

She pulled up at the side of the building and switched off the engine. Saskia's Lambretta was still there. The sound of the band – a trio this time – was just audible. They were playing a tune she liked. She climbed off the scooter and felt a sharp pain below her left hip. She had grazed it when she fell. Now it was starting to stiffen up. Maybe it was time, she thought, to let someone else take the decisions, to be a passenger for a while. She would get used to it. It might even come as a relief. The hardest part was going to be keeping Saskia in the dark – but that would be temporary, perhaps a matter of weeks. Besides, she was much more practised these days at keeping secrets.

Saskia found her in the kitchens, drinking a glass of milk. 'What happened to the scooter?'

Adelais had forgotten about the broken wing mirror. 'I came off on my way into town. Going too fast.'

'My God, are you all right?'

'I'm fine. A little stiff.'

'Is that blood?' Saskia was pointing to where it hurt. A dark stain had appeared on the fabric of her trousers.

'I don't know.'

'I'd better take a look.'

Adelais did not feel strong enough to refuse. She hobbled to the old servant's room where she slept, while Saskia went and fetched the first-aid box. She took off her trousers and examined her hip: there was a mass of purple bruising and some raw skin, but no blood. The stain was oil. All the same, Saskia made her lie down and insisted on bathing the area with warm water and cotton wool, before swabbing it with disinfectant.

'You don't usually go fast. Why the hurry?'

'I got scared. I thought the police were following me.'

'The police?'

'That man, de Smet. He wasn't though.'

'I wouldn't put it past him. He gave me the creeps.'

Adelais laughed. It made her hip hurt. 'Me too.'

'And then?'

'What?'

Saskia was still dabbing Adelais's hip with disinfectant. 'Where were you going?'

'Patershol. I cleared out the desk, in case the police come back here and search. I should have told you, but—'

'You think they'll come back? Why would they?'

Adelais yelped. The disinfectant had reached a patch of raw skin. 'They won't. If anything they'll drop the whole thing. They're making new banknotes, starting next year.' She turned her head to the wall. She had just made a mistake, but there was no way to correct it.

Saskia sat back on her haunches. 'That's big news, Adelais. How long have you known?'

'About an hour. I saw it in a newspaper.'

'Do you still have it?'

Adelais sighed. 'Trust me, Saskia. I know what I saw.'

Everything went back to normal, but nothing was the same. For a quiet time of year, business was good. Press coverage of the film festival had rubbed off on the hotel. A steady stream of guests checked in for a night or two, to drink in the faint aura of celebrity. The gaming room continued to do brisk business. Saskia calculated that by year end it would be possible to pay off a third of the bank debt.

'What do you think we could get for this place,' she asked, 'now it's a going concern?'

Adelais said she had no idea. She avoided conversations about the future of the Astrid Christyn and what the two of them might do. They made her uncomfortable. For the same reason, she began to avoid Saskia altogether, throwing herself with all the energy she could muster into managing the hotel. By day she did paperwork and acted as an informal travel agent for the guests, booking excursions and buying tickets. By night she dressed in silk and danced in the ballroom between glasses of champagne. Sometimes she drank too much and had to go out onto the terrace to clear her head. She caught Hendryck giving her quizzical looks as he poured her third or fourth glass. Perhaps he thought she was being irresponsible. She wanted to tell him that it didn't matter. The Patershol francs were all locked away in the weaver's house and Uncle Cornelis had everything else worked out. In a little while she would be gone to a new venture in a new city, and the Astrid

Christyn would belong to someone else. All she had to do was trust him and play along.

One Saturday she woke early, drenched in sweat. She had been dreaming of dark streets and black water, some unnamed horror lurking in the shadows, the sound of a woman weeping that she could neither escape nor follow to its source. She got up, drank a glass of water, washed and dressed, but the sense of dread refused to dissipate, as if the darkness of her dream was spreading from her brain into the world around her. It was the wine. It could only be the wine. It had given her nightmares before. What she needed was fresh air. Fresh air would clear her head, make it possible to function, do what had to be done.

She went outside. It was a still, overcast morning, with a faint chill in the air. She crossed the road and struck out across the meadows, giving no thought to the direction. Cattle watched her go by with unwavering attention. She walked until her way was barred by a deep ditch. The towers of Laarne Castle were a few hundred metres away behind a screen of trees. As she approached, a flock of crows took off from the roof and flew away towards the east.

Adelais looked down into the water. The woman she had heard weeping, she had not seen her, but she knew who she was. Even in the dream she had known. But what was she weeping about? Why wouldn't she explain?

Adelais heard her father's voice: *She has no choice, you see. Because of Anderlecht.*

Anderlecht. Adelais saw it now: that was the place in her dream, the place no one would tell her about, where somehow everything had changed for the worse, for her mother, for all of them. Anderlecht, where Uncle Cornelis had once worked creating money for the Belgian state – until he started doing the exact same thing for himself.

Perhaps Saskia was right: she hadn't been brave enough to ask questions until now. It had always been easier to pretend they did not exist.

The city public library was a low-rise neoclassical building on Ottogracht, a hundred metres from the little park where she and Sebastian had eaten peanuts one evening, while he told her about his disastrous dancing classes. The memory still made her smile. The newspaper archive was housed in an annexe overlooking an abandoned chapel. The papers were bound into black binders, but only a handful of titles were considered worthy of inclusion.

Adelais started with *De Standaard*. It was what her father used to read. She was not sure what kind of story she was looking for, but she had an idea when it would have appeared. Major de Smet had been very specific about when his investigation had begun: he had been on the trail of the Tournai Forger for eight and a half years. That meant whatever trick Uncle Cornelis had pulled at the Federal Engraving Bureau had taken place before that. Adelais started with editions from the spring of 1953 and worked backwards.

For seven hours she turned pages, until her fingers were black and the library was closing. There were crime reports in almost every edition, but nothing about the Federal Engraving Bureau, or missing plates, let alone Cornelis Mertens. The operation, whatever it was, had gone unreported.

She did not give up. Adelais went back to the library the next day and started on *De Nieuwe Gazet*. Most of the crimes it covered were in Antwerp and northern Flanders. After leafing through a couple of dozen copies, she turned to *Het Laatste Nieuws*. It carried more crime stories than *De Standaard*, and the reports were longer, following up with court appearances and sentencing.

Adelais's vision had begun to blur and the closing bell was ringing through the building, when a short report caught her eye. Beneath a photograph of a burnt-out building, the headline read: ANDERLECHT ARSONIST STILL AT LARGE. The edition was dated 21 March 1952.

The funeral took place yesterday of Pauwel Verlinden, 37, who died at the hands of arsonists in the district of Anderlecht last month.

The district coroner recorded a verdict of unlawful killing, but as yet no arrests have been made. Federal police are investigating. The involvement of Marxist revolutionary groups has not been ruled out.

Verlinden was employed as a nightwatchman at the Federal Engraving Bureau. He died when a warehouse on the site was engulfed in flames, after what police believe was an arson attack. The main building was also broken into and defaced with slogans, although nothing of value was stolen.

The bureau director, M. Roland Meunier, reaffirmed yesterday that the work of his department, which plays a vital role in the preparation of official state documents, has not been compromised by the attack.

'I can reassure the public that we, who carry out the essential business of government, will never be deterred from the performance of our functions,' he said.

Verlinden was laid to rest at the Saint-Josse-ten-Noode Cemetery in Schaerbeek. He leaves behind a widow and two children.

—— Forty-three ——

She took a taxi from Brussels-Centraal. It was a grey morning, rain-clouds approaching, driven by a sharp east wind. The journey took fifteen minutes. The traffic thinned as they went, the houses growing smaller and dirtier, the people fewer. The driver studied her in the mirror. What was it that brought a smart young woman to the wrong side of Anderlecht, to the abandoned workshops and vacant lots? Why was she travelling alone?

'You have family around here, miss?' he asked, as they crossed the canal on the Pont Marchant, but she did not seem to hear him.

Where the warehouse must have been there was a solitary brick wall, windows blown out, and a square of rubble, bordered by a chain-link fence. On the other side of the yard, a row of cars and bicycles revealed the location of the Federal Engraving Bureau. Adelais asked the driver to wait and climbed out of the taxi.

A van was parked at the side of the building, where doors stood open. Workmen were loading filing cabinets and boxes into the back. More were being wheeled out on trolleys. Adelais walked over. 'Excuse me. Is this where Pauwel Verlinden worked?'

A man with a cigarette in his mouth was standing in the back of the van. 'Who's that?'

'Pauwel Verlinden. He was nightwatchman about—'

'Never heard of him. Try in there.'

He nodded towards the doors. Adelais went inside. She found herself in a hallway with a counter at one end and a guard at the other.

Behind the counter sat a man with glasses and grey hair. 'Yes?' he said.

'I'm trying to find the address of someone who used to work here, eight or nine years ago.'

'Personnel records are confidential.' The man looked Adelais up and down, took in the stick at her side. His tone softened. 'You could make a request in writing. Are you a relative?'

'That's right.'

The man sniffed and nudged his glasses up his nose. 'Who are we talking about?'

Another trolley of boxes trundled past. Adelais heard voices outside. The workmen were talking about her.

'Pauwel Verlinden. I just want to—'

'Verlinden's dead, if it's the nightwatchman you're talking about.'

'I want to find his wife. It's important.'

The man frowned. 'That was years ago, miss. She could be anywhere by now.'

'I don't know where else to start.'

The man hesitated. He leaned closer and was about to speak again, when a man in an expensive-looking suit brushed past the guard and came towards them. He was giving orders to the workmen in a loud voice and looking at a fob watch on a chain. Adelais guessed he was the director, Roland Meunier, or his successor.

The man at the counter leaned away again. 'In writing, miss. That's the best I can do.'

Adelais left the building. The first spots of rain were peppering the cobbles outside. The taxi driver was smoking, one arm hanging lazily from the rolled-down window. What was the good of asking for information in writing, when she was not entitled to it?

'Miss?'

One of the workmen was older than the others. He wore a leather apron and a shirt with a starched collar. He beckoned Adelais over.

'You want to know about Verlinden?'

'I need to find his wife.'

313

'Liesbeth?'

'Do you know where she lives?'

The workman shook his head. 'They used to live in Danseart, on the Rue des Fabriques, but that was before. I heard she moved out to the Quartier Brabant, after she had the baby. It might have been the Rue des Palais.' He picked up a box from his trolley and handed it to the man in the back of the truck. 'Don't work for a lawyer, do you?'

'No.'

'Pity. They never gave her a penny after the fire, and her with two kids. Said he shouldn't have been there or something. I reckon she had a case, but lawyers cost money.'

'They never caught the arsonists, did they?'

The man in the truck laughed. 'Not a chance.'

The director appeared in the doorway. He fixed Adelais with a stare and came marching over. Adelais did not wait to be interrogated. She crossed the yard to the taxi as fast she could.

'Excuse me! Just a moment!'

Adelais did not stop. She climbed into the taxi and told the driver to go.

The Quartier Brabant was a French-speaking district north of the city centre, where the streets were narrow and straight, and the housefronts caked in soot. The Rue des Palais began at a busy junction of roads and tramlines and ran north for five hundred metres before passing beneath the main railway. The houses grew shabbier as they went. Some of the windows were blocked up with cardboard. The air had a charred, sulphurous smell.

'What's the number?' the driver said.

Adelais did not have a number. 'Just take me to the end.'

At intervals, she saw women dressed in evening clothes, wandering aimlessly along the pavements. They leaned over to peer inside the taxi as it went past, before straightening up again. One of them smoked ostentatiously, like a teenager at a party, another carried a red umbrella. Beyond the railway lines, the road continued for another four hundred metres, before reaching a canal. Adelais saw no children. It was not the kind of place where children belonged. The worst parts of Ghent were not as grim.

The taxi driver pulled over. 'This is it. You getting out here?' He was becoming impatient. Adelais had been in his cab for three-quarters of an hour.

At a corner, one street over, was a stall selling flowers. The old woman behind it had a shawl over her head.

'One more stop,' Adelais said.

The taxi took her south and east along avenues lined with trees and flanked by parkland. On the Boulevard Léopold III they turned into a narrower road where the apartment buildings were finished in a blank, modern style. The cemetery lay behind grey walls, with a cobbled forecourt just inside the gates. A rusty sign on one of the gateposts set out a long list of what was prohibited, which included singing and the removal of flowers. Adelais had bought white and yellow chrysanthemums. They were the only blooms that looked fresh.

She paid the driver and climbed out of the taxi. The rain was holding off, but the wind was strong. It tugged at the flowers, as if intent on tearing them from her hands. A path wound its way past a stone colonnade and clusters of yews to a grid of old stone tombs. At the far end was an area of open ground, dotted with newer graves, with here and there a pile of freshly turned earth.

A caretaker was at work on the verges, cutting back the ragged grass with a pair of shears. Adelais walked over. 'Can you help me? I'm looking for Pauwel Verlinden.'

'Verlinden?'

'His grave.'

The caretaker tossed a clump of grass into a wheelbarrow. 'What is it, his birthday?' He nodded towards a corner of the cemetery, where three people stood in front of a headstone: a woman and two children.

The woman wore a scarf and an old-fashioned brown coat. The boy, maybe ten years old, wore short trousers and a sweater that was much too big for him. The girl, older, was thin and pale. She clung to the woman's arm, as if afraid of losing her.

The woman was holding a bouquet of flowers no bigger than her hand. She stooped down and placed it against the headstone. Adelais saw the hardship in her face, in the drawn cheeks and the lines come too soon. Their eyes met, but even then it was hard to look away.

Adelais left the cemetery still carrying the chrysanthemums. She would go back when Mrs Verlinden and her children had left. She dared not explain to them who she was.

Fifty metres further up the road stood a cafe. Adelais took a table by the window and ordered a coffee. As she waited, she wondered what would happen if Liesbeth Verlinden came into the cafe too. Would they talk? Would Adelais ask about her husband's death and what had happened since? Or would she sit in silence, as if there were no connection whatever between them, nothing of importance that they shared?

Adelais had not noticed the name of the street before. It was displayed on a small blue sign on the building opposite: Rue Henri Chomé. She had never been to this part of Brussels before and yet the name was familiar. It took her a few moments to remember: it was to the Rue Henri Chomé that her mother had gone, the day Saskia followed her. It was on the Rue Henri Chomé that she had disappeared.

It had been Saskia's belief that Odilie de Wolf had a friend, or a lover, living on that street. She had bought them a gift of flowers outside the station. Adelais knew now that Saskia had been wrong: her mother had been visiting the cemetery. She had travelled to Brussels to put flowers on Pauwel Verlinden's grave.

—— Forty-four ——

October gave way to November and Adelais heard nothing more from Uncle Cornelis. She began to wonder if he was ever coming back. The hotel was less busy than it had been, but work continued on the stable block. It looked like the new rooms might be ready in time for Christmas.

Adelais watched the progress from behind the desk in the office, workmen coming and going, carrying piping, boards, spools of wire, followed by tiles and porcelain. In a week or two it would be time for painting, for the curtains and furniture. The Astrid Christyn was on the cusp of viability. She had often imagined this moment, the feelings of happiness, satisfaction, of pride. She had taken a childhood fantasy and made it real. How many people could say as much? She stood before the window, day after day, but the feelings refused to arrive. All she could think about was the nightwatchman and the family he had left behind.

She was sorting mail behind the front desk when Uncle Cornelis finally telephoned. It was a Tuesday morning. The line was crackly and he sounded far away.

'Are you alone?' he said.

'For the moment. Where are you?'

Adelais's words echoed around the hotel lobby.

'I'll be visiting in a week or so. I have good news.' The tone of Uncle Cornelis's voice was cheerful, but forced, as if he were selling something.

'Perhaps I should take this in the office, Mr . . . Hartman.'

'It won't take a minute. Just listen.'

Adelais leaned across the counter. One table was still occupied in the

317

dining room: Mr and Mrs Briggs, a middle-aged British couple touring Flemish culture in low season, eating their devilled eggs in silence.

'Go on then.'

'I've found a buyer.'

'For what? The hotel?'

In the dining room Hendryck was sweeping crumbs from the tables into a polished metal pan, watching Adelais out of the corner of his eye. She had never dared to confide in him, not completely, and now the chance was gone.

'First things first,' Uncle Cornelis said. 'I'm talking about our other line of business. They'll take whatever we can supply, provided there's enough of it.'

Adelais did not like the idea of strangers getting involved. It felt dangerous. 'I'm not sure. We've never—'

'I know. But times have changed. This time next year, remember?'

'You always said—'

'I'll keep you out of it. How many items can you make over the next couple of weeks? They need three hundred, give or take.'

'They? Who's they?'

Uncle Cornelis didn't answer. It was a stupid question to be asking over the telephone.

'Can you do it?'

'Maybe. How do I explain being away all that time?'

'You'll think of something.' Uncle Cornelis's breath pushed against the mouthpiece. Adelais sensed an unfamiliar urgency. In the past, he had always been calm. 'It'll be worth it. I told you, Adelais: new opportunities. This'll get us started.'

Adelais wanted Uncle Cornelis to spell out what the opportunities were, where they would lead, and who they would be doing business with, but now was not the time.

Saskia was coming up the drive on her Lambretta. Adelais could hear the familiar buzz of the engine.

'What are they paying?' Adelais did not want to know. She wanted to make her uncle tell her something, to concede something. They were partners.

Adelais heard a click on the line, a faint cacophony of a hundred voices talking at once, then silence.

'It isn't so much a sale as an exchange,' Uncle Cornelis said.

'An exchange?'

'There are other currencies besides money. I'll contact you in ten days or so and tell you where to go.' Outside, the Lambretta's engine cut out. 'I'll explain everything when I see you. We're almost there, little wolf. Almost there.'

'Wait,' Adelais said. 'I need to know about—'

But Uncle Cornelis had already hung up.

Saskia came through the front door, her helmet under her arm. 'Anything wrong?' she said, running her fingers through her hair.

Adelais worked by night. At the weaver's house she turned all the locks behind her and laboured at the presses until her body ached and her vision became too blurred to see. Without anyone to help her, the printing went slowly to begin with, but she had learned to anticipate every problem, every possible mistake, and soon she found herself slipping into a routine, operating with the efficiency of a machine and with as little need for reflection. Every drying line in the house was soon full, every surface covered with the notes her uncle needed. As she worked through them, adding layer after layer of pattern and colour, she thought of herself on the handcycle he had given her for her eleventh birthday, and the challenge he had set her: to reach the Devil's House and return without stopping. The wheels of the presses became the wheels of the invalid tricycle, and the pressure they brought down on the paper reminded her of her struggle with the pedals, the effort it had taken to make them move. She had built up strength on that machine, strength that had enabled her to save a life, Sebastian's life. She refused to think of it as anything other than a gift of love – a gift she was honour-bound to return.

After the third night, Saskia found her asleep at the desk in the hotel office. 'My God, you look terrible. Are you coming down with something?'

Even in her addled state, Adelais saw her chance. 'A touch of flu. Maybe I should go home for a bit.'

'Yes, go home,' Saskia said, 'or we'll all catch it. Christmas is coming. We can't afford an epidemic.'

With a show of reluctance, Adelais removed herself to Schoolstraat. Every morning for the next six days, she telephoned the hotel to say she was not coming in, before returning to Patershol. There was a danger that Saskia would turn up at the weaver's house and realise she had been lied to, but it was a small danger. She had no obvious reason to go there and, with Adelais away, she would be busier than usual at the Astrid Christyn.

On the sixth day Adelais added the letterpress numbers and stored the finished notes in one of the last empty boxes in the cellar. As she gathered the counterfeits into bundles of fifty, she felt a familiar glow of pride. There had never been anything like them, de Smet had told her. *They're the work of a perfectionist, a craftsman of exceptional dedication.* It was something, after all, to reach the pinnacle of your craft, to be the best of the best.

When the notes were stowed away, she cleaned off the plates and put them back in the safe. The Beretta was where it had always been, on the bottom shelf. For the first time in years, she picked it up, weighing it in her hand. It felt heavy. She was sure she would need both hands to fire it. She eased down the latch with her thumb and released the magazine. She wanted to be sure that it was loaded.

— Forty-five —

Major de Smet went up to the top floor of Federal Police Headquarters to find his operations room stripped bare. One of his filing cabinets was out in the corridor, the other had vanished completely. The maps had been torn down from the walls, leaving only a couple of scraps still clinging to the pushpins that nobody had bothered to take out. The desk and chair were gone. The telephone lay on the floor, disconnected, the wire wrapped around it. A civilian in blue overalls was measuring the walls with a sprung-metal tape measure.

'What is this?' de Smet demanded. 'What the hell do you think you're doing?'

'Colonel's orders.' The civilian was making notes in a notebook. He did not look up. 'Whole floor's been reallocated.'

'To what?'

The civilian tucked his pencil behind his ear and retracted the tape measure with a noise like a falling guillotine. 'They told me, but I've forgotten. It's all got to be clear by three o'clock.' He looked at de Smet and frowned. 'News to you, is it?'

De Smet recalled a memorandum some weeks past, something about a new trafficking section to be established on the top floor. He had not paid much attention at the time. He had assumed it was a formative idea, that he would be consulted before any important decisions were made. 'You can start putting it all back,' he said.

'What?' The civilian laughed. 'Are you serious?'

'Deadly.'

'Well, I'd have to hear that from Colonel Delhaye, I'm afraid.'

'You will. Now get started.'

The civilian looked like he was going to argue some more, but something in de Smet's demeanour made him change his mind.

The meeting lasted seven minutes and Colonel Delhaye smiled throughout. His smile was supposed to be infectious, to infuse the encounter with good humour, acceptance and comradery: two old soldiers, following orders – even orders they did not like – because that was the lot of old soldiers. It was all de Smet could do not to strike him, to wipe the stupid grin off his shiny, dissembling face.

De Smet's section was to be folded into a larger team, encompassing financial crime, trafficking and narcotics. A Major Briyon from the customs service had been appointed to head the operation.

'Of course, I'd have preferred to see one of our own in there,' Delhaye said, 'but the word from above, you know. They want a fresh start, new perspectives.'

'My investigations are being disrupted. I'm close to a breakthrough.'

Colonel Delhaye's smile became radiant. 'Oh, good.'

'Criminals aren't going to wait while we reorganise our . . . perspectives.'

'Oh, indeed.' Colonel Delhaye offered de Smet a cigarette and lit one for himself. 'But I'd let the new man sort that out. His problem. It's time you moved on. You've done your bit – and done it well, I might add.'

There had been talk for some time about early retirement. A couple of senior officers had already left. It was not clear if they had been given a choice.

Colonel Delhaye leaned back in his chair. 'I think you'll be pretty happy with the terms I've negotiated on your behalf. It wasn't easy. You know what the bean counters are like. But I wrung it out of them in the end.' He took an envelope from his desk and passed it over.

'I have cases to clear up. I'm not going anywhere.'

Colonel Delhaye shook his head. 'You don't want to be answering to

Major Briyon. These young Turks, they love to throw their weight around. It'd be . . . humiliating.'

'If he doesn't get in my way, I shouldn't—'

'I think the danger is, you might get in *his* way. The whole counterfeiting business, it's not really a priority any more. And we wouldn't want a situation: old guards versus new brooms. The truth is, I don't think we'd come out on top of that one.'

'We?'

Colonel Delhaye's smile briefly faltered. 'You.'

De Smet opened the envelope. He found it hard to read what was inside, hard to focus on the words or the numbers. They meant nothing.

Colonel Delhaye's smile had returned. 'We'll give you a proper send-off in the new year. You know, you're still something of a legend around here. Past glories and all that. It would be a shame to leave under a cloud.'

Toussaint was on the telephone when de Smet arrived back at his office. The captain covered the mouthpiece, and offered him the receiver.

De Smet did not feel like talking to anyone. 'Who is it?'

'Monsieur Meunier, from the Federal Engraving Bureau? He says—'

De Smet took the receiver. 'This is de Smet.'

'Ah, Major, you're keeping well, I trust?'

'Well enough.'

'Good. It's probably nothing, but as I was explaining to your colleague, I thought I should call it in, just in case.'

'Go on.'

Meunier cleared his throat. 'We're moving out of our existing premises, as you know. That is to say, the bureau is setting up elsewhere – at the bank, in fact. Centralisation.'

'I'd heard. So?'

'Well, not that it's relevant, but in the middle of it all, someone turned up asking about Pauwel Verlinden. You remember the case? Tragic business.'

'I remember it.'

'Normally I wouldn't trouble you but you never did make an arrest, did you? I mean, the federal police. The case remains unsolved. I thought perhaps she might be connected in some way—'

'So who was it?' De Smet took a paper and pencil from the desk.

'A young woman, early twenties, I'd say. Blonde, well dressed. She was wearing a red raincoat. It struck me right away as a statement.'

'A statement?'

'A political statement.'

'I see.'

Meunier cleared his throat. 'She claimed she was a relative of Verlinden's. She was looking for the widow, wanted her address. Important, she said. Of course, personnel records are confidential. She went away empty-handed.'

'What was her name, this young woman?'

'I don't know.'

'You didn't take it?'

Meunier sounded mildly affronted. 'I didn't deal with her personally, Major. I merely observed her leaving the premises. She got into a taxi.'

De Smet put the pencil and paper back on the desk. 'Is that all, monsieur?'

'Well, yes. Oh, there was one other thing, now I think of it.'

'Yes?'

'There was something wrong with her leg.'

'Her leg? What do you mean?'

'She was walking with the aid of a stick.'

De Smet took the first train to Ghent, but by the time he arrived at the Municipal Records Office, it had closed for the day. He hammered on the door until a caretaker appeared at the grille. De Smet held up his identification and demanded to be let in.

The birth, marriage and death certificates were stored in the north wing of the building, in rows of shelves, the highest of which were accessed by ladders. A man in overalls was dragging an electric polisher over the tiled floor. Along the middle of the room was a line of desks and reading lights. The air was cool and smelled of old books.

At the time of the warehouse fire, Monsieur Meunier had supplied the federal police with a list of employees at the Federal Engraving Bureau, going back five years. De Smet had gone through it, looking for possible connections to the criminal underworld or to radical political groups. None had been found, an outcome that hadn't surprised him, given that the bureau used the same vetting procedure as other government services. The list was with him now, along with the vetting data. He knew most of the names by heart. If anyone called de Wolf had worked at the bureau, it had been long before the fire.

The birth certificates were separated according to year and arranged alphabetically. De Smet did not know when Adelais de Wolf had been born, and it took him a while to find the record. One thing about it struck him right away: next to Lennart de Wolf's name, under the heading TRADE OR PROFESSION was written ENGRAVER.

That was not all. Odilie de Wolf's maiden name was Mertens. There were two men with that name on the list of employees: Johannes Mertens had left the bureau three years before the fire; Cornelis Mertens had still been an employee at the time. It took twenty minutes and the recovery of two further birth certificates, to establish that Cornelis and Odilie Mertens were brother and sister. Adelais de Wolf's uncle had been working at the bureau when Pauwel Verlinden was killed, and now his niece, the daughter of another engraver, was searching for the dead man's widow.

De Smet sat alone in the north wing, sifting the pieces in his mind, the sound of the electric floor polisher slowly receding down the corridor. A coherent picture refused to form. There were too many gaps. Even the connection between the de Wolfs and the Verlindens struck him as tentative, perhaps even coincidental. Ten years had gone by. What kind of unfinished business could wait that long?

He spread the birth certificates out in front of him. He thought through the details of the attack that had claimed the nightwatchman's life: the arson, the clean getaway, the pointless break-in that resulted in nothing being taken. All the while, the word ENGRAVER worried at his thoughts, like a ragged nail.

He found a telephone and called the Federal Engraving Bureau. He caught the director on his way out.

'Tell me about Cornelis Mertens. Does he still work for you?'

'Mertens? No, he left years ago,' Meunier said.

'How many years?'

'Oh, seven, eight, nine. Something like that.'

'Where did he go? Do you know where to find him?'

De Smet heard voices in the background. It sounded like someone in Meunier's office – a secretary or assistant – was volunteering information.

'Of course, of course,' Meunier said.

'Well?'

'I'd forgotten, Major, but Cornelis Mertens is no longer with us, sadly. That is to say, he's dead. He was living in Holland, died of blood poisoning or something.'

'When was this?'

Meunier consulted his assistant again. 'About four or five years ago. Why are you interested, Major? Has it something to do with . . .' He lowered his voice. '. . . the Verlinden business?'

'You still have his file?'

'Mertens's file? I expect we do. We have archives, although at this moment exactly where . . . We're moving, as I said. Between premises.'

De Smet found it a struggle to remain courteous. 'I'd appreciate it if you could locate the file as soon as possible, Monsieur Director.'

'Of course, Major, of course. I expect it's still here. These old buildings: so many nooks and crannies. You'd be amazed what gets hidden away. The new premises are much more functional, but there's something to be said for character, don't you agree?'

De Smet headed back to the north wing to collect his papers. The caretaker had switched off the lights in the corridor and was standing by the main entrance, jangling his keys. The man in overalls had finished his polishing and gone.

De Smet set about returning the birth certificates to their places. He was on a ladder, Lennart de Wolf's certificate in his hand, when Meunier's words came back to him: *So many nooks and crannies. You'd be amazed what gets hidden away.* That was when he saw it, not little by little, but in a cascade: the scheme, the conspirators, the execution – all at once, everything making sense. His hands gripped the ladder. The sinews in his arm clicked. Colonel Delhaye was going to look pretty stupid retiring a senior officer who'd just cracked the hardest case in counterfeiting history. He wouldn't be smiling then.

Patience, skill, audacity: it was a magnificent plan, like no other de Smet had come across. There could only be one author – the hallmarks were unmistakable. But, for now, it was just a theory, a possibility. He would need evidence, and evidence might be hard to come by. Still, thinking of the operation, sharing in the knowledge of it even ten years on, de Smet felt privileged, like an art collector at the most private of viewings. It was almost going to be a shame to tear it all down.

The Yellow Dog

— Forty-six —

November 1961

Snow came early that year. The staff and guests of the Astrid Christyn Hotel woke up to find the grounds covered by a white blanket, bright and unmarked except for animal tracks across the back lawn and the footprints of birds on the terrace. It was too early for Christmas decorations, at least as far as the interior was concerned, but Hendryck identified a promising fir tree beside the main gates and set about decorating it with electric lights, in readiness for the season. The kitchen staff got busy on a festive menu, and warm drinks – mulled wine, hot chocolate, spiced coffee – were offered at the bar.

Not all the guests were happy with the change in the weather. Mrs Hofman, a pretty blonde Dutchwoman who wore an expensive fur, started complaining the moment she arrived: the snow was slippery on the hotel steps, she said, and her shoes, which had cost five hundred guilders, weren't built for mountaineering.

Her husband was an affable, red-faced man twenty years her senior. 'We'll just have to buy you a nice pair of boots, dearest,' he said, patting her on the arm, as they stood at the reception desk.

The Hofmans had a large room overlooking the stable block. Mrs Hofman was unhappy with the view, and they were given a different room overlooking the woods on the other side – which was also less than satisfactory on account of the dawn chorus, which disturbed Mrs Hofman's sleep. Her suffering did not end there: the mattress was too hard, the room was too cold, and the hot water was too hot.

When Mrs Hofman was not complaining, she was shopping, while her husband attended business meetings in the city. In the evenings she drank cocktails and gambled stupidly. She accused Nadia of cheating at roulette and delivered an impromptu lecture on the shady practice of ball-tripping, which she had read about in a magazine. She threatened to call the police before her husband, chuckling indulgently, dragged her away. Their lovemaking that night was reportedly loud and percussive, which surprised everyone except Renilde, with her ten years of experience at Blankenberge. 'The worse she behaves, the more he likes it,' she said with a wink, and slapped her own backside in a gesture that Adelais was at a complete loss to understand.

Adelais concentrated on running the hotel. She tried not to think about the old weaver's house, the iron machines standing silent behind its locked doors. She tried not to think about Uncle Cornelis, and the future he had mapped out for her. Above all, she tried not to think about the Verlindens, the sickly daughter and the ragged boy. She kept these thoughts at bay, the way the walls of a castle keep back a siege.

It helped that there was a lot to do. The Astrid Christyn was filling up again. Christmas looked like it would be busy. The bar helped too. With a drink or two inside her, and an adequate partner to dance with, Adelais could confine her reflections to the present, or to times in her past that remained untainted.

On the first Saturday of December it snowed again. The flakes were large and soft. They drifted out of the night sky, circled each other in the glow of the hotel lights, before settling noiselessly on the window-sills and the terraces. Watching from the ballroom, Adelais thought back to another snowy night six years earlier: riding to the Korenmarkt on the back of an old bicycle, the Christmas market in a snowstorm, the smell of roasting nuts and burnt sugar, the people singing. That had been the night Sebastian told her about his dancing classes, the night she decided she would be his partner at the opera house, and perhaps forever. As if all she had to do was learn the steps. Her heart had always insisted Sebastian was to blame for not returning her love. Now her head disagreed: her feelings for Sebastian hadn't just deepened over time, they had changed. It had been naive of her to assume that his feelings would change in the same way, at the exact same pace.

She wondered what he was doing at that moment, if it was snowing in Antwerp, if he was watching the flakes come down just as she was. She hadn't heard anything about the wedding. She supposed it had taken place some time ago, and that it had been a strictly family affair, as many weddings were. Marie-Astrid could have had a baby by now. She pictured Sebastian as a father, wondered if it would suit him, if it would make him happy. When she saw him standing at the other end of the ballroom, dressed in a creased grey suit, gazing at his surroundings the way tourists did in St Bavo's Cathedral, she was not surprised at all. She assumed he had simply wandered in from her thoughts, and would vanish again, as soon as she blinked.

It had been less than two years since their last meeting, but Adelais could not help noticing how he seemed to have aged. His cheeks were drawn, and faint lines had appeared around his eyes. His hair was thinner and his forehead higher, and his voice had a husky edge to it, like someone who has just woken from a long sleep. The way he spoke was different too. Even as he expressed wonder at the restoration of the hunting lodge, delight at every detail, from the plasterwork on the ceiling to the polished marble floors, there was hesitation in his voice, a diffidence that was new. He was not a boy any more, Adelais realised. He was undeniably a man.

'I should have telephoned ahead, I'm sorry. I just heard, and I—'

'Don't apologise.'

'I'd heard about the Astrid Christyn, but I had no idea this was the place until tonight, when my father said . . . I'd have come earlier, if I'd known.'

'It's fine, really.'

He looked up at the chandelier and the freshly painted cornicing. 'What you've done – it's a miracle. It's miraculous.'

Adelais was blushing. She hoped nobody could see it, because it was ridiculous. She was blushing as she had at the opera house when she first saw Sebastian with his future wife.

'I had help,' she said.

Saskia was standing by the entrance to the gaming room, watching them. She was wearing earrings and a black cocktail dress, and her hair had been styled into a flipped bob, like President Kennedy's wife. She shook her head and turned away.

'There were times we could have used a good architect,' Adelais said.

Sebastian's smile faltered. 'Well, I . . . I don't do that any more, actually. I gave it up.'

'Architecture? Why?'

He shrugged. 'Well, it wasn't . . . It turned out to be less interesting than I'd thought. I mainly worked on underpasses. And the occasional footbridge. Load calculations, a lot of load calculations. If you're a fan of pre-stressed concrete, I'm your man.'

'So that firm you were in, you left?'

'It got awkward there. Various reasons.' It was obvious Sebastian didn't want to talk about it. 'I'm teaching now. Art, literature and history. Twelve-year-olds, mostly. I haven't got a permanent post yet – no qualifications – but I'll get something soon, with any luck.'

'You're a teacher now. Do you like it?'

'Actually, I do. For once, I feel . . . useful.' He cleared his throat. 'We should drink to the Astrid Christyn. We should drink to your success.'

Sebastian reached for his wallet, but Hendryck was already on hand with two glasses of champagne. As they drank a toast, the band began to play a slow waltz. Adelais wished they had stuck with something faster. It was as if they were both now back at the opera house, a single dance away from disaster. *Love's like everything else. In the end, it pays to be realistic.*

'Isn't Marie-Astrid with you?'

'Marie-Astrid?' Sebastian looked into the bottom of his glass. 'No. No, we're not . . . we're not together any more. It wasn't ever really—'

'You were going to get married.'

'I know.' He shrugged. 'We didn't.'

The room was stuffy and crowded. It was difficult to hear and difficult to breathe. 'You broke off the engagement?'

'She did . . . Well, it was mutual. For the best anyway.'

'I didn't know. I'm sorry.'

Sebastian laughed. 'Don't be. Marry in haste, repent at leisure. Isn't that what they say?'

'Yes, it is. Will you excuse me for a moment?' Adelais coughed. Some champagne must have gone down the wrong way. She headed for the lobby. She needed air: deep breaths of cold air. She needed to be still, for everything inside her to settle, like the snow on the windowsills. She needed to remember that in this place she was the countess.

'He's got a bit of a nerve, hasn't he, showing up unannounced? What does he want?' Saskia was standing at the top of the stairs. Perhaps it was the dress, or the Kennedy hairstyle, but she had never looked more elegant.

'He came to see the place.'

'I heard his parents have been taking in lodgers since the old man got the sack. That house in Zuid? They're living on one floor.'

'A lot of people have money troubles.'

'And his fiancée dumped him. Marie-Astrid, wasn't it? She gave him the push.'

Saskia seemed to think that the worse the news, the better Adelais would like it. 'How long have you known about that? Why didn't you tell me?'

Saskia shrugged. 'You know, rumours. Besides, I didn't think you'd care. You don't care, do you?'

'For God's sake, Saskia. I haven't seen him in years.'

'Well, I'll see he gets a tour then, shall I? And you can entertain Mr Rykert from Kredietbank. He's almost finished dinner and he'll be expecting a dance.'

Adelais was busy entertaining her guests. One of the kitchen staff showed Sebastian around the hotel, before calling him a taxi for the ride to the station. He planned to take the last train back to Antwerp. With twenty minutes to wait until the taxi arrived, he put on his overcoat and went out into the grounds. He paused outside the stable block, where the building work was almost complete, then walked the length of the avenue that ran beneath the beech trees to the boundary. Snow lay over everything. The trimmed yews below the terrace reminded him of giant shaving brushes. In the middle of the ornamental pond, Artemis had acquired a white beehive. Sound was muffled, except for the crunch of his footsteps and the band playing in the ballroom.

He was surprised to find that the swings had not been taken away. He swept the snow off the seats, tested the ropes, one by one, and sat down. The hunting lodge looked more beautiful that he had ever imagined it. His father had told him it was money from some wealthy de Wolf relative that had made the restoration possible, but it had surely taken more than that: it had taken Adelais herself, her strength, her tenacity. When Adelais's mind was made up, there was no giving up, no turning back. He had always loved that about her, and her directness too – and her curiosity, and the way she managed to be rude to him in a way that somehow never hurt. There were, come to think of it, a lot of things he had always liked about Adelais de Wolf. But he had never dreamed they would take her this far. With all his knowledge of who she was, he had still underestimated her: what she could do, what she could become. He wished he could have been there to see the transformation take place, in the house, and in her. Now the chance was gone.

He got off the swing and followed his footprints back along the path.

A woman was standing on the terrace, wrapped in an overcoat and smoking a cigarette. 'So what do you think?' she said.

Sebastian recognised Saskia Helsen. She had greeted him briefly earlier, before handing him over to the cook.

'The hotel? It's amazing. A dream come true.'

'Your dream. At least it was, wasn't it?'

Sebastian looked over the grounds. There was a tinge of blue on the snow, a reflection from the sky. 'I suppose so, to begin with.'

'So how does it feel, having someone else get there first? Hard? Mixed feelings, at least.'

'No.'

Saskia tilted back her head and exhaled a cloud of smoke. 'Oh, come on.'

Sebastian dug his hands into his pockets. 'You must have seen the way it was: rotting away. It was tragic. Now it's saved . . .' He shrugged. 'I'm relieved. I used to feel guilty every time I left. Adelais must have felt the same way.'

'No, she didn't.' Saskia dropped her cigarette and stamped it out on the terrace. 'She saw an opportunity and took it.'

'If you say so.'

'And if there *was* a feeling involved, it would be the feeling that she didn't need you, and that this would prove it, beyond any doubt. She's succeeded there too, hasn't she?' Saskia gave Sebastian a smile and turned away. 'Your taxi'll be here in five minutes. Make sure you don't miss it.'

Sebastian was too stunned to respond. Saskia disappeared into the dining room, leaving him alone. He asked himself if it could possibly be true: that Adelais had restored the countess's hunting lodge, had realised the dream they'd shared, in a spirit of defiance, of retaliation? If so, it could only be that she had felt wronged.

He looked out over to the pond. Artemis did not seem unhappy with her beehive. She wore it with serenity, as if enjoying the joke. Sebastian remembered Adelais's first visit, when he had told her about his plans. She had promised to come and stay when he opened the hotel. She had asked him if she could have breakfast in bed. The thought of it always made him smile.

Saskia Helsen was wrong: there was no spite in Adelais, no appetite for revenge. Her memories of this place had been precious to her, just as they had been to him. They had shared something enchanting and she hadn't wanted to let it go. Instead, she had brought it to life, made it real, and everlasting. That was the Adelais he knew: a girl who never gave up.

Sebastian looked back at the hunting lodge, once more radiant against the dark sky, and the idea took hold — an impossible idea, but one he could not keep back — that she had saved it as much for him as for herself. It was a testament to her love, a monument to the life they should have shared. The sudden sense of loss was overwhelming. He sat down on a stone bench. They had met as children and that was how he had gone on thinking of her. The difference between them was that she had grown up. She had grown to love him, love him like no one else, and he had simply missed it. He buried his face in his hands. He would have given anything to go back, to tell her was sorry, that the best days of his life had been spent with her, that he wished he had never left. But it was too late now, far too late. His return had been like a spectre's at the feast. All Adelais wanted was for him to be gone. If there had been any doubt about that, her friend had erased it.

He got to his feet. He'd planned to say goodbye to Adelais before he left, but that would mean interrupting her again, another awkward moment. It was better to slip away.

The band had come to the end of a number. A clatter of applause followed him as he made his way slowly to the front of the hotel. Cars were lined up along the driveway, polished paintwork frosted with snow. From an upstairs window came a peel of laughter. Sebastian turned up his collar. The world felt cold.

Somewhere out of sight an engine spluttered to life. A scooter came round the side of the building. For a moment, he thought it was going to hit him.

The scooter pulled up beside him. The rider wore a helmet and goggles. 'Get on.'

'Adelais?'

'*Get on.*'

Sebastian gestured towards the road. 'I've got a taxi coming.'

'No, you haven't.'

'But I—'

'I cancelled it.'

'What?'

'I can take you.' Adelais revved the engine. 'Do you want to catch that train or not?'

Sebastian climbed on the back of the Vespa. There was more room than on his father's old bicycle, but not much. He hung on tight to Adelais as they took off down the drive. Just ahead, beside the gates, was a tall fir tree, decorated with a spiral of electric lights. They had not been turned on when Sebastian arrived.

'Adelais?' He leaned forward. 'I missed you. I wanted you to know.'

Adelais tapped the side of her helmet. He would have to speak up.

'I said, I missed you.' Sebastian was shouting. 'In Antwerp. I never—'

Adelais pulled over and took off her helmet. 'Start again.'

'I *said*, I missed you. Are you deaf?'

'No. I heard what you said. I just like hearing you repeat it.'

Sebastian did not feel cold any more. 'Shall I repeat it again?'

'No need.' Adelais put an arm around his neck, and kissed him.

After a couple of minutes the scooter's engine cut out.

— Forty-seven —

Adelais woke up early. Sebastian was asleep beside her in the narrow bed, his arms crossed, one hand tucked under his ear, the other resting on her shoulder. She sat up slowly, feeling the chill air on her skin. Sunday morning. Everything in the hotel was quiet. Outside, fine eddies of snow spun past the window. It felt strange, not waking up alone. Like the snow and the silence, it felt like something borrowed from a different life, a life she had stopped daring to hope for long ago.

She eased herself out of bed and pulled on her dressing gown. When the brace was back on her leg, she went into the kitchens and made coffee, heating a pan of milk on the range. The fresh bread would not arrive for another half-hour, but Saturday's was still edible. She cut some slices, spread them with butter and honey, and took everything back to the room on a trolley.

When Sebastian opened his eyes, Adelais was sitting on the floor, watching him over the rim of a large mug. He smiled at her and stretched, his feet banging against the footboard. 'This bed isn't fit for a countess. You need a bigger one.'

'It was good enough until now.' Adelais handed him a mug. 'Coffee?'

'Thanks.' Sebastian slung his legs over the side of the bed, covering himself with the sheet to hide his nakedness. He pointed at the plate on the floor. 'Is that honey?'

'You prefer jam?'

'No. Honey's fine.'

Sebastian was obviously hungry, unless he ate so that he wouldn't have to talk. Adelais did not mind. There wasn't anything in particular she wanted him to say.

After a while, she stopped watching him and looked down at her toes. 'So, have you done that before?'

Sebastian's mouth was full. 'Done what?'

'You know. What we did, last night.'

'Oh. That.' Sebastian took his time chewing and swallowing. It was a question that apparently needed careful consideration. 'Actually, no.'

'*Actually* no?'

'I mean, no. Never.' Sebastian started rearranging the pillows. 'In spite of my years. Why, was it . . . wrong?'

'Do you mean, immoral –' Adelais tried not to laugh – 'or just unsatisfactory?'

Sebastian picked up a pillow and made to swing it at her. 'I'm sorry I spoke.'

Adelais had expected to feel different afterwards: enlightened with secret knowledge, wiser and worldlier. The idea seemed foolish now, given how earthy and simple sex had turned out to be.

'What about Marie-Astrid?'

'What about her?'

'Didn't you . . . ?'

Sebastian put the pillow back at the head of the bed. 'She said she wanted to wait until we were married.'

'So you waited?'

'I did. She didn't.'

Adelais frowned. 'How did that work?' Sebastian looked uncomfortable. 'It's all right. You don't have to tell me.'

'It doesn't matter. You may as well know.' Sebastian picked up his coffee. 'She had an affair with one of the partners in my firm: Mr van Roy.'

'Your boss?'

'Kind of. For all I know, it's still going on. That's why I had to leave. It got too awkward, and they'd have got rid of me anyway, sooner or later.'

'But your boss? How could she do that?'

Sebastian shrugged. 'Oh, he's very rich. Houses all over the place. A flat in Paris. And keeps himself fit.'

'Is he married?'

'A widower, or so he claims. Nobody ever met his wife though. I wouldn't be surprised if he didn't make her up, to get sympathy.'

'From women?'

Sebastian brought a hand to his forehead. 'Poor wounded soul. They want to ease his pain.'

Adelais took a sip of coffee. 'I wouldn't. I'd increase it.'

Sebastian laughed. 'I was pretty furious. It was humiliating. And all those lies. But, you know, once the anger had burned out, I felt relieved. I wasn't going to spend my life keeping Marie-Astrid happy. I wouldn't have to worry about disappointing her. I spent two years doing that. It took Mr van Roy to put an end to it.'

Sebastian held out his hand. Adelais took it. She lay down next to him and let him cover her with the blankets, the warmth of his body slowly spreading through hers. He regretted his years away from Ghent, from her. It was good to know his feelings mirrored hers. And yet, what would have become of her if Sebastian had never left? Where would she be now: working at Aux Quatre Vents, or some other place like it? Perhaps she would have become Mrs Pieters, running a modest household in a respectable district of Ghent, instead of the Astrid Christyn Hotel. She would have got rid of the old weaver's house and all its contents, for sure. Sebastian was the last person in the world she would have lured into that line of work.

'I don't think your friend likes me, by the way,' he said. His chin was hooked over her shoulder, the stubble rough against her skin.

'Who, Saskia?'

'She said you didn't need me and that I should clear off – words to that effect.'

'Saskia can be very . . . protective. And she doesn't trust men, in general. Her sisters all married unhappily.'

'So that's it.'

'You remember the dance at the opera house?' Adelais had never planned to tell anyone, but she couldn't help herself. 'I think she put something in my drink.'

'What?' Sebastian was laughing.

'I think she drugged me.'

'You're serious?' He sat up. 'Why would she drug you?'

Already Adelais wished she hadn't mentioned it. She didn't want to think about ugly things. 'I don't know. Maybe she thought it would be funny. Or maybe she wanted to keep me from you.'

'Me? Why?'

'So I wouldn't get my heart broken.'

Sebastian exhaled a long breath and lay down again. 'How did you find out?'

'It was just something she said.' Captain Toussaint and his boss were in her head now, trespassing on her happiness. 'I could be wrong.'

'Have you asked her about it?'

'What good would that do? She'd deny it. I still wouldn't know and she'd hate me for suspecting her.'

Sebastian shook his head. 'So you suspect her in secret and that's better?'

'It was ages ago. She's grown up a lot since then.'

Sebastian's fingers found the nape of Adelais's neck. She closed her eyes as they pushed gently through her hair. 'For the record,' he said, 'I wouldn't have broken your heart for anything.'

Adelais took his hand and brought it to her lips. 'So you say. How do I know? You could be like Mr van Roy.'

Gently Sebastian rolled her over so that she was facing him. 'I'd never lie to you, Adelais. To other people, yes. But not you. It would be madness.'

'I know. I was joking.' She kissed his hand. The scent of his skin was comforting.

'No secrets then, you promise?'

Adelais held him close. She was glad at that moment that he could not see her face, the hot blush on her cheeks. 'I promise,' she said.

The children at Sebastian's school were putting on a play to mark St Nicolas Day, and Sebastian had to go back to Antwerp to help make scenery. Adelais took him to the station on the Vespa.

'I'll be back as soon as the holidays start,' he said, as he climbed off.

Adelais told him he had better come back or she would hunt him down, like Cary Grant was hunted in *North by Northwest*, but it was a film Sebastian hadn't seen.

'What do you want for Christmas?' he said, but the train for Antwerp blew its whistle and he had to run before Adelais could think of an answer. Riding back through the city, it occurred to her that she had no answer. She didn't want anything, at least anything that could be bought in a shop. She had done enough shopping to last a lifetime. Most of her purchases were still hidden away behind nine locks, untouched.

Nadia was on the front desk when she got back to the hotel. Mrs Hofman was there too, complaining. She had turned up in the dining room half an hour after breakfast was over and asked to be fed. The kitchen staff, who had already started preparing for lunch, had refused.

'An omelette with spring onions,' she said. 'Anyone would think I wanted lobster thermidor. Mind you, I know a good few places would have done that for me. Because *they* know how to look after their customers.'

Nadia offered to go and make the omelette. Adelais took over the front desk. There was no sign of Saskia, but she usually stayed away on Sundays. Adelais was glad. She didn't know what to say about Sebastian. It was too soon to pick over what had happened. The thought of it made her feel warm inside, and for now that was all the clarity she needed.

When Nadia returned, Adelais went up to the first floor. On Sundays, the cleaning had to wait until the afternoon, although Hendryck always left the bar in good order. She went from table to table, empty-ing the ashtrays and picking up discarded cocktail napkins. The air was heavy with the smell of stale smoke. She opened the windows and let a breeze blow through the room. From her place behind the bar, Great-Aunt Magdalena stared out at the winter sky, lips pursed, keep-ing her thoughts to herself – except it wasn't Great-Aunt Magdalena. It was the portrait of a stranger they had bought from a junk shop in Roeselare.

— Forty-eight —

The Federal Engraving Bureau was being stripped bare. Major de Smet hardly recognised it. The movers had not stopped at the cabinets, the shelving and the furniture: they had unscrewed the workbenches from the floor, removed the lampshades and the light bulbs, and rolled up the linoleum. On his way in, he saw a man loading a stack of varnished lavatory seats into the back of a truck. He wondered if the porcelain was next.

Monsieur Meunier had gained some weight and lost some hair since de Smet's last visit, but his office was largely unchanged. The rug was rolled up, books and files were lying in stacks around the room, tied up with string, but his desk and chair were still in place, as well as the bright lamp that he had used to examine the bureau's daily output. More importantly, the safe was exactly where it had always been.

'Tell me the procedure again, from the moment you arrived in the morning.' De Smet stood in front of the desk. There was nowhere for him to sit.

Meunier sighed. He could see no point to this line of inquiry. His own theory was that Verlinden, the dead nightwatchman, had been mixed up with communists and had fallen foul of them, for one reason or another. 'It was the same every day, Major. I'd let myself into the office with my key – I was always the first to arrive. I'd open up the safe, take out the plates and designs for the day, and check that they were all there. Everything goes in the ledger, without exception.' He brought his hand down on a thick black tome that lay on his desk, as if about to swear on it. 'Then one of the senior staff would collect them.'

'They weren't in here when you used the safe?'

Meunier shook his head. 'I never unlocked the safe unless I was alone. Not that I didn't trust my staff, but one can't be too careful.'

'And at the end of the day?'

'At the appointed hour, the plates and designs would be brought back to this office, checked once again against the ledger, and stored in the safe as before.'

'How long did that take?'

'I'm sorry?'

'Checking the items against the ledger, how long did it take?'

'It would depend on the volume of work in progress. Not long usually. It was just a matter of counting.'

'And you always did that yourself?'

Meunier hesitated. 'Yes. Yes, almost always.'

De Smet nodded to himself. *Almost always.* It was just as he'd thought. 'And that would be here? Everything would be laid out here, on this desk?'

'That's right.'

'Then you would open the safe and put everything back in.'

'Correct.'

'Once you were alone.'

Meunier nodded. 'Of course, yes. Once I was alone.'

'Show me.'

'I'm sorry?'

'Open the safe.'

'There are no plates in there, not any more.'

'All the same.'

Meunier sighed again, louder. He spun round on his chair and turned his attention to the massive steel safe that was sunk into the wall.

De Smet took a couple of steps to his left. From there, he had a clear view of the director's stubby fingers on the dial.

That would have been how it all began, the moment of inception. De Smet could picture it perfectly: Monsieur Meunier on the telephone, the receiver tucked under his ear, preoccupied, in a hurry to get home for the evening – he had tickets for the opera perhaps, or friends coming round for dinner – putting the plates and the designs back in the safe while one of his trusted engravers was still standing there, on the other side of the desk. The combination was secret knowledge. The engraver wasn't supposed to have it. There hadn't been time to make a plan: he would have memorised the numbers on instinct. De Smet had to admire the opportunism.

Right now, the safe in Meunier's office contained only a cash box and a single set of designs.

'For a new teaching certificate,' Meunier said, dropping them onto his desk. 'Our last job on the premises. The Ministry of Education wasn't after anything elaborate, of course – not too worried about forgery. It would have been nice to go out with something more illustrious.'

De Smet unrolled the design. The paper was waxy and stiff. There were two layers, although one was almost blank except for the state emblem. 'A thief could use these designs to make his own plates, couldn't he?'

Meunier seemed convinced that the major was wasting his time. He took the opportunity to count the contents of the cash box. 'If he had the necessary skills, and the right materials, and if he could somehow make his plates before anyone noticed the designs were missing – and all that without being observed, then yes, I suppose he could.'

Meunier closed the cash box and looked over his shoulder with a smirk on his face.

'Which means he worked at night,' de Smet said.

Meunier's smirk vanished. 'At night? Where would he do that?'

'I'm guessing here, right where you're sitting. That's where I'd do it. Less danger of being disturbed. I don't think the lock on your office would be much of an impediment for a craftsman who works in metal. And if he had the safe combination . . .'

Meunier eased himself back from the desk, a look on his face between disquiet and distaste. 'It's impossible. It takes weeks to make a plate – months sometimes. How would they come and go without being seen? It's absurd.'

De Smet handed back the designs. 'He only had to manage it once: once in, once out. He broke out the night of the fire. That was the point of it: to cover the noise of a window being demolished. And sometime before that, a few weeks in fact, someone got him in – through the door.'

'People don't just walk in here, Major,' Meunier said. 'They need identification. Even tradesmen, even plumbers.'

'I remember a press event here, a month before the fire, when the new designs were announced,' de Smet said. 'The place was full of photographers and journalists.'

'All of them with the appropriate accreditation, which would have been checked.'

De Smet saw no need to answer this point. Judging from the sweat on Monsieur Meunier's brow, even he could see that if a man could forge banknotes well enough to fool most of the tellers in Belgium, forging a press pass was not going to present a challenge.

Somewhere in the bureau there had been a hiding place, big enough to conceal a man and whatever he needed to survive. De Smet went through the building, carrying a torch, Monsieur Meunier walking ahead, pointing out the irrelevant and the obvious as they went, like a reluctant tour guide.

An attic space under the roof showed promise. There was enough room, even a small circular window in the end wall. But it was a long drop to the landing below, and manoeuvring the ladder would have been noisy and difficult, especially in the dark. De Smet lifted the floorboards in what had been a meeting room, though the furniture and the pictures were now gone. He found enough space underneath for a man to conceal himself, provided he didn't move an inch. A few days there would have left him crippled.

The cellars were bare and well lit. De Smet went around the walls, checking for anything untoward, but found nothing: the brickwork was solid and in decent repair. The biggest room housed some of the old brewing equipment: copper piping, grimy vessels made of wood and steel, a stack of quarter-barrels playing host to a family of mice.

'Well, that's everywhere,' Meunier said. 'If it's all the same, I really must get back to—'

As if to prove his point a telephone started ringing above them.

Partly hidden behind the stack of barrels was an old mash tun. De Smet remembered seeing it before, though he had hardly given it a second glance. In the top of the rusted steel cylinder there was a hatch, through which the ingredients would once have been added. It was just big enough for a man to slip through, provided he was slender.

'You go ahead, monsieur,' he said. 'Answer the telephone. It might be important. I'll only be a minute.'

Meunier grunted and made his way back up the stairs. When he was gone, de Smet went to the mash tun and shone his torch through the hatch: he saw a blanket, scraps of paper, what looked like a bundle of rags. Something shiny reflected the beam of the torch. De Smet fished it out with a handkerchief. It was a glazed earthenware bottle. The label advertised a brand of genever.

There might still be fingerprints on the glaze, physical evidence tying Lennart de Wolf to the scene, perhaps his brother-in-law as well. In a court of law it might be vital to establish how the de Wolf family business got started: with murder. All that remained to be found were de Wolf's plates. No doubt his daughter could help with that.

De Smet stood alone in the darkness, picturing the conclusion of the hunt: the pale, handcuffed defendant, the guilty verdict, the sentence. But what then? He shone the torch at the gaping hatch. *What then?* A few column inches in the newspaper, certainly. A pat on the back from a chastened Colonel Delhaye perhaps. If he was lucky, an offer to stay on at Federal Police Headquarters for another year, in the interests of saving face: a temporary truce between the new brooms and the old guard. A bigger clock when they finally got rid of him. Then nothing.

And the de Wolf girl? Seven to ten years later she would be free, perhaps sooner than that. Forgive and forget. She would recover the money she had hidden in numbered bank accounts or write her story and live well on the proceeds. He could picture her visiting him in his poky flat, in the interests of research, old adversaries reconciled. She would feel sorry for him, living alone with only his memories and his old cases for company. When they were done talking, she would promise to come and visit him again, and fail to keep her word.

De Smet shook his head. It was not going to happen that way.

—— Forty-nine ——

On Monday evening, Adelais packed the new batch of notes into a shoulder bag, and rode the Vespa north towards the docks. A letter addressed to her had arrived at the hotel that morning. It read simply:

Monday 10pm
'Safari'
2 Zeilstraat
Muide-Meulestede
C

It had rained in the afternoon. The wind that blew in her face was clinging and raw. Adelais followed a set of tramlines for one kilometre, until they brought her to the water, then crossed over the Muide Bridge. The district on the other side was crammed into a narrow tongue of land between the ship canal and the three biggest docks in the city. At the end of the cross-streets, the dim red lights of cranes and moored vessels hung motionless in the sky. A municipal police car went past on the quayside, but the traffic had already thinned to a trickle. Nothing moved on the narrow pavements.

Safari turned out to be a bar. It stood on the corner of Zeilstraat behind frosted windows, its faded sign painted in zebra stripes. Adelais parked the scooter and went inside, her arrival announced by the clack of a heavy bead curtain strung across the doorway. Inside it was dark and smoky. Around the walls were booths, each equipped with a table and a light with an orange shade. The benches were covered in brown vinyl. A man at the bar looked Adelais up and down and turned away. There was no sign of Uncle Cornelis.

Adelais tightened her grip on her shoulder bag and walked over to an empty booth. Music was coming from a loudspeaker over her head. The guitar rhythms were intricate and strange, and the singer sang in a language she could not understand. There were no other women in the place, and no space to dance. A clock above the bar read five minutes past ten. She wondered why they were meeting here, and how long she was supposed to wait.

A skinny young man appeared, wearing a purple batik shirt. He tamped out a cigarette and wandered over. 'What'll it be?'

'The lady isn't staying.' Uncle Cornelis was standing behind him, dressed in the same patched blue coat he had worn last time, but with a black woollen cap pulled down over his forehead. 'I'll take a beer.'

'Two beers,' Adelais held up two fingers so that the barman could not be in any doubt. He shrugged and went back to the bar.

Uncle Cornelis slid into the booth. 'I suppose we have a minute or two.' His gaze fell on the shoulder bag. 'How did you get on?'

'It's done.'

'All of it?'

Adelais nodded.

'As if you'd let me down.' Uncle Cornelis waited for the beers to arrive, then reached across the table.

Adelais took the bag off her shoulder, but hung on to it. 'You have to tell me something. It's important.'

Uncle Cornelis frowned and sat back. From somewhere upstairs came a raised voice, a woman shrieking, angry. A door slammed. 'We need this deal, Adelais, for the future. You trust me, don't you?'

'It's not the deal I want to know about.'

'Then what is it?'

Adelais looked down at the shoulder bag resting on her lap, at one hundred and fifty thousand francs, expertly forged. 'Pauwel Verlinden.'

Uncle Cornelis remained silent.

'You know who I'm talking about, don't you?' Still Uncle Cornelis said nothing. 'My mother used to visit his grave. She put flowers there. Why did she do that? The grave of a man who died ten years ago?'

Uncle Cornelis shook his head. 'I didn't know she'd been doing that.'

'She tried to keep it a secret. I don't think even my father knew.'

'That's something, at least.'

'Why? Why did she do it?'

'There isn't time now, Adelais.'

'I know about the fire in Anderlecht. What did my mother have to do with it?'

Uncle Cornelis picked up his glass, and put it down again without drinking. 'Some things it's better not to know. And you don't have to know this. Why should you carry the burden, when it's not your fault?'

Adelais tightened her grip on the shoulder bag. Uncle Cornelis knew better than to think she was bluffing. He sucked his teeth for a moment, before relenting with a heavy sigh. 'I blame myself, Adelais. I should never . . . I should never have let her get involved. We needed another hand and we didn't trust anyone else. Family, you know?'

Adelais felt the blood begin to drain from her face. 'Involve her how?'

At last Uncle Cornelis took a drink. Adelais could sense the wheels going round in his head, trying to decide what to tell her, what to hide.

'All Odilie had to do was smash through a window, once the commotion started.'

'You mean the fire, don't you?'

Uncle Cornelis nodded. 'A diversion, that's all it was. That was my job, start a fire in an empty warehouse.'

'What about my father?'

Uncle Cornelis nodded. 'Lennart was inside. He spent three weeks in there, inside the bureau. It was a feat of endurance, what he went through: working all night, hiding by day, not making a sound. Think of it, every night for the best part of a month, in winter. And the work was good, Adelais. I was afraid it would go to pieces, but it didn't.' Uncle Cornelis smiled. 'You're a lot like your papa in that way. You get the job done, no matter what. That's how I know he'd be proud of you.'

Adelais shook her head. The old fear was there. She wanted to tell Uncle Cornelis to stop.

His voice softened. 'The best engraver in Flanders, Adelais, and they wouldn't give him work because of the war, because he helped make banknotes during the occupation. They called him a collaborator, but he had to make a living. He had a young family. He had—'

'Tell me what happened.'

Uncle Cornelis frowned. 'When the work was done, he had to get out of the building. The window was the only way, but he couldn't break it from the inside. There'd have been all the wrong kinds of questions.'

'How did Verlinden die?'

Uncle Cornelis looked at his watch. 'You should get going now. I don't want to have to introduce you. There's no need.'

'*Tell me.*'

Uncle Cornelis ran a hand across his mouth. These were things he had never intended to share, but Adelais had him cornered. 'All right. At first, everything went fine, like clockwork. The other two had already made it to the car, but then I got held up. I had to take a detour to avoid being seen. Your mother came looking for me, thought I might have hurt myself because I'd been up on the roof. Verlinden saw her from a window. He was already inside the warehouse, rescuing a cat or something stupid. Odilie panicked. The fire was on the other side of the building. She thought she was buying us some time, a minute or two. She thought Verlinden would break out. She couldn't know the man was going to pass out from the fumes. It was just bad luck.'

Adelais's mouth was dry. For a moment, she thought she was going to faint. 'She locked him in, didn't she? She locked him in.'

Uncle Cornelis put a hand on her arm. 'She didn't know, Adelais. She couldn't have known.'

Adelais wasn't listening. She was imagining Verlinden's death, the terror as he tried in vain to escape the inferno, the engulfing flames, the singed and charring flesh – as her mother would have imagined them a thousand times since that night: a prelude to the fires of Hell that would one day consume her damned soul.

But there was more. The truth unspooled in her mind. Adelais could not stop it. Her father would have said no to Uncle Cornelis's plan. Maybe he resented his treatment, but he wasn't a criminal, and Adelais's mother was God-fearing, devout. They would have needed persuading, motivation. So Adelais had been recruited, to break down their resolve. Poor Adelais, who had been dealt a cruel hand in life. Poor little Adelais, who had done nothing to deserve such bad luck, and who had no future without treatments the de Wolfs could not afford. *If I had such a daughter, there is nothing I would not do for her, nothing I would not risk.*

The plan had cost Pauwel Verlinden his life and guilt had descended on the de Wolfs like a plague. It had taken her mother and her father, leaving Adelais alone. Uncle Cornelis's plan had destroyed her family, and what had she done? She had gone along with it, completed it, put it at the centre of her life.

Uncle Cornelis had said her father would be proud.

'Odilie didn't mean any harm,' Uncle Cornelis was saying. 'It was just bad luck, like I told her, one of those things that . . . happen. An innocent mistake.'

Adelais pulled her arm away. Didn't he see? That innocent mistake had destroyed her mother's life. She looked into Uncle Cornelis's eyes, but saw no trace there of the same anguish, no shame for dragging his sister into a criminal scheme for which she was utterly unprepared. She saw only ruefulness at life's unpredictability and other people's inability to accept it. For the first time, Adelais saw into his soul: it was unyielding, cold.

A car pulled up outside. Adelais heard its doors open and close. Uncle

Cornelis straightened up. 'You should go now. You don't need to meet these people.' He gave Adelais a smile and lowered his voice. 'We'll be all right, you and me. We don't make mistakes.'

Adelais threw her beer in his face. She dumped the shoulder bag in his lap and walked out of the bar. A couple of men passed her outside the door. She did not look at their faces.

— Fifty —

Sebastian Pieters was having a dream in which Marie-Astrid, his one-time fiancée, had locked him in a bathing hut and was laughing with her lovers on the other side of the door. He was woken by the sound of his landlady shouting up the stairs.

'Mr Pieters? Mr Pieters!'

The alarm clock read seven o'clock and it was dark outside. In his dream, he had been naked. He quickly checked beneath the covers and was grateful to discover he was still wearing his pyjamas.

'Mr Pieters, the telephone!'

The telephone was in the front hall. For a fee, paying guests were permitted to use it for outgoing calls, but Mrs Goethals made it clear that the number was to be given out sparingly, and on no account to tradesmen. She was a landlady, she said, not a bellboy.

'I'm coming!'

It entered Sebastian's head that the call might be from Marie-Astrid. But what could she possibly want with him? If she was hoping they could get back together the answer was going to be no.

The room was cold. He pulled on his dressing gown and hurriedly searched for his slippers. He found one of them under the bed, but the other was nowhere to be seen. He went down the stairs barefoot. Mrs Goethals's door closed with a bang. The receiver was on the hall table.

'Hello?'

'Sebastian? It's me.'

'Adelais. Thank God.'

'I'm sorry, it's early. I was afraid I'd miss you.'

'It's fine. I'm just glad you're not . . .' Sebastian coughed. 'I'm glad it's you. Is everything all right?' There was a pause on the line. Sebastian felt his stomach squirm. 'Adelais?'

He heard her take a deep breath.

'Sebastian, if I asked you if we could begin again, if we could wipe away everything that's happened since you left Ghent, all of it, what would—'

'I'd say, I wish we could.'

'And if that meant going away, you and me, somewhere far away, without telling anyone, at least for a while, and going soon – very, very soon – what would you say then?'

'What are you talking about?'

'*What would you say?*'

A dustcart went by outside, rattling the windows. Sebastian heard a creak behind Mrs Goethals's door. She was listening, of course. He lowered his voice. 'Just tell me what to pack.'

She knew where to go. She had seen it in films: a place where people found themselves, where they made a fresh start. Two thousand years of history put things into perspective. She had checked the flight timetables before she called Sebastian. Now she rode into town and bought the tickets at a travel agent. In one week's time their plane would take off at eleven o'clock in the morning from the airport at Zaventem. Sebastian would meet her at the check-in desk.

After the travel agent, Adelais went to the house on Schoolstraat. She took her father's old leather suitcase from the cupboard under the stairs and put it on the kitchen table. One suitcase was all she could take with her. Everything would have to fit inside it, everything she wanted to keep.

She collected the family photographs from the front room and removed them from their frames: pictures of the grandparents she remembered, and the ones she had never seen; her mother and father on their wedding day, her mother with extravagantly curled hair, holding a bouquet and beaming, her father, smooth-faced, handsome; ten-year-old Adelais wearing a veil and a pair of white gloves; six-year-old Adelais grinning at the camera, showing off a missing tooth. One by one, the photographs went into the suitcase. She thought of her mother returning from Africa to find them missing, but in her heart she knew that was never going to happen. Nothing less than a lifetime of penance could stave off eternal punishment.

Adelais went up to the bedroom where her parents used to sleep. Her mother's clothes were still hanging in the wardrobe: dingy floral dresses and dark heavy coats. In a drawer she found a jewellery box. There wasn't much inside: a silver broach, a ring encrusted with garnets and a string of pearls. A memory came back to her from childhood of her mother putting them around her little daughter's neck, telling her not to suck them if she didn't want to choke. Adelais had been fascinated by the way they seemed to give off their own light. The pearls and the jewellery box went into the suitcase.

There was a smaller wardrobe in Adelais's room with her old clothes inside. She hadn't worn them in years. Her blue dungarees were hanging next to half a dozen skirts and dresses: muted colours and long skirts. In the past, she had worn each one of them a hundred times at least. It was a lifetime ago.

She collected some books, her old notebook with the red cover, the dozing China cat that served as a piggy bank, and the leasehold contract for the house at 37 Sluizeken, which was still hidden under the mattress. Last, she took down the picture from above her bed, which her father had given her on the night of her eleventh birthday: his hand-tinted etching of an old stone bridge.

Adelais checked her watch. Time was running out. She had arranged to see a notary at three o'clock and it was already half past two. She had decided to make the Astrid Christyn over to Saskia. A fresh start meant giving it up for good. There was no other way. And Saskia couldn't hate her for running away when that was her parting gift.

When Adelais had finished going through the house she closed the suitcase and carried it out through the back door, pausing to take one last look at her father's workshop, at the place where she had seen him so often, at the scratched bench and the worn chair, the tools still lying there, ready for use. The clocks on the wall had stopped.

——— Fifty-one ———

It wasn't like Adelais to be gone all day, with no explanation. Saskia began to wonder what was wrong, and why she hadn't been told about it.

'I saw her go out this morning,' Nadia said from behind the reception desk. She was due to help out in the dining room, but there was nobody to take her place.

'She didn't say when she'd be back?'

Nadia shook her head. The telephone rang. 'She seemed in a hurry.'

The afternoon was busy. A party of six arrived from Germany. The builders were working on the bathrooms in the stable block and wanted decisions on the taps and fittings. The telephone rang constantly. The hotel was going to be busy over Christmas, and every new inquiry involved a lengthy to-and-fro. Three times Hendryck climbed a stepladder to change some bulbs in the ballroom chandelier, and three times he had to climb down again to help handle the calls.

Adelais had been different lately. She tried to hide it, but something had changed. She went about her work in the normal way, but she never had time to chat, to plan, to share a joke, as she had before. Her appearances in the ballroom were brief, and even when she was dancing to a favourite waltz, a glazed look would come over her, as if she had other things on her mind. She loved dancing. It wasn't like her.

Saskia could pinpoint the moment when things had changed: it had happened after the federal police showed up at the hotel. It had been a nasty surprise to discover the gendarmes had been watching, tracking the counterfeit notes, getting closer, but the threat had been dealt with and they were no longer in danger. Their precautions, their defences, had held up. Saskia wondered if she should have been more reassuring.

Underneath it all, Adelais had always been afraid. Her fragility was one of the things Saskia liked about her. She was the perfect playmate: clever and adventurous, but also vulnerable, and in need of reassurance. Saskia had never got bored with her, as she had with most of her friends, and she doubted now if she ever would. She could picture them sharing a house one day, when the Astrid Christyn was sold and they were rich. Adelais had never refused Saskia anything and she wasn't going to start now.

It was well into the evening by the time Adelais pulled up on her scooter. Strapped to the back was an old brown suitcase.

'What have you got in there?' Saskia said.

'Mementoes.'

The hall was bustling. The German party were gathering for their foray into the city. Taxis had been ordered.

'We could have used some help today, it's been—'

'I'm sorry,' Adelais said, and vanished into the office.

As soon as the Germans had gone, Saskia followed her. 'I was worried, Adelais.' She was determined to sound reassuring. 'I thought something had happened to you: another accident. The roads are . . .'

Adelais had opened the safe. After another good week, it was well stocked with cash. She began laying out notes on the desk.

'Ninety-eight thousand, seven hundred and twenty francs,' Saskia said. 'Do you want to see the ledger?' Adelais's cheeks were flushed and her hair was damp across her forehead. 'You know, you're going to have to tidy yourself up if you're going to dance tonight.'

'I'm not.'

'Disappoint our guests, it doesn't matter.' Saskia bit her tongue. She didn't want an argument. 'You look famished. You should eat something.'

'I'll get something from the kitchens.'

Adelais was still counting out the money, placing it into separate piles, her every movement charged with a nervous energy.

'What are you doing? I told you how much is there.'

'I'm not counting. I'm checking the five hundreds.' Adelais lowered her voice. 'For Patershol francs.'

'We've always kept them separate, you know that.'

'Gamblers walk out of here with Patershol francs, but then they come back again, don't they? They could bring the notes with them and we might not even notice.'

'It's a small risk.' Saskia folded her arms. 'You're worried about it now? Why?'

'I just thought of it.' Adelais put the money down. 'There are some things I need to tell you.'

'Go on, then.'

'Not here. At the weaver's house, later. It has to be there.'

So, it was Patershol business. 'What is it? The gendarmes again? Are we in—'

'No. We won't have to worry about them. I'm going to make sure of that, once and for all.'

'How?'

'*Later.*'

'But this is nothing bad, right?'

'No, it's nothing bad. It's good. Very good.'

It was several years since Salvator de Smet had put on a dinner jacket, but on leaving headquarters that afternoon, it had struck him that it would be inappropriate to show up at the hotel in his uniform. Everyone, guests and staff alike, would assume he was there on official business. His appearance would attract attention and there was always a chance that someone senior from Ghent's municipal police would be there. They'd want to know what had brought him back.

It was dark by the time he reached the outskirts of Brussels. Low cloud hung over the city, reflecting the pallid glow of the street lights, until the city was behind him and darkness enveloped everything that wasn't in the beam of his headlamps. He put on his police radio and turned the dial, searching the airwaves for music. What he found – guitar bands and boy singers – did not appeal to him and he turned it off again. He tried to recall the music that had been playing on his first visit to the Astrid Christyn, when he had danced with Miss de Wolf. He had enjoyed that dance, her body close to his. He enjoyed the prospect of many more.

His old Juvaquatre was noisy and sluggish. It had never bothered him before, but he would have felt better arriving at the hotel in something more impressive. He could have afforded a better car if he had received the promotion he deserved, and the rise in salary that would have gone with it, but he had always steered clear of the politics required, the flattery and backstabbing that preceded every upward step.

What he had always cared about was his work: the pursuit, capture and punishment of swindlers and fraudsters, that particular brand of criminal who took his fellow citizens for fools, who abused their trust. Except that this time, it was different. This time, he wouldn't leave it to the system to administer justice. For once, he would take care of that himself, in a way that guaranteed *his* satisfaction, that answered *his* needs. The state – its bureaucrats and time servers – had abused his loyalty. He owed them nothing.

Oncoming cars and lorries swept past him with hypnotic regularity, throwing bands of light across his face and arms. With each pass, he felt himself drawing closer to a new life, free from the constraints of duty. Soon there would be no going back.

At last he crossed over the River Scheldt and turned north towards Laarne. A grey smudge on the western horizon briefly betrayed the location of Ghent, until it was lost beyond the trees that crowded the road. It was a relief when he glimpsed the Astrid Christyn in the distance, and the tall cone of lights beside the gate. They beckoned to him, the way Christmas beckons to a child.

After a dance or two they would talk, in private. It would be his regrettable – no, painful – duty to tell Miss de Wolf that more counterfeit notes had been traced to her hotel. The information he had received, but not yet shared, would be sure to prompt the most thorough investigation of the Astrid Christyn, its staff, its owner, and her complete financial history. The federal authorities would leave no stone unturned. She would be under grave suspicion all the while. At the same time, he would let her see that he was conflicted, torn between his duty to the law and his deep admiration for her. In warning her of what was about to take place, he had already risked his career.

Miss de Wolf was no fool. She would understand: he alone could keep disaster at bay. He wouldn't have to say it. All the same, he wanted to see her persuade him, deploy every charm at her command to lead him astray. He would have her that night – nothing less would do – but how much more satisfying it would be if she played the seductress. The alternative was blackmail. But blackmail was transactional, vulgar. Vulgarity did not belong at the Astrid Christyn Hotel.

He would spend the night in Miss de Wolf's bed and when he woke up in the morning it would be as her lover, as the count to her countess. If she came to feel trapped by the arrangement, as perhaps she would in time, he would remind her that the penalty for the crimes she had committed was lengthy imprisonment, and that the prison of their private arrangement was a lot more comfortable than most.

He was picturing the elegant bedroom, the four-poster bed, Miss de Wolf slumbering naked in it, when a scooter turned out of the hotel driveway into the beam of his headlamps and buzzed past him. He recognised the rider. It was as if she had ridden right out of his thoughts, intent on escape.

The music was late starting because the pianist's bicycle had a puncture and it took him a while to fix it. Albert covered on the accordion, but without the piano, his music took a melancholy turn, which put people off dancing. Adelais put in an appearance at the bar, but left again after dinner, just as they were getting ready to open the gaming room. Saskia wanted to follow her right away, but somebody had to see to business.

She wondered what Adelais could possibly have to tell her that would qualify as good news.

At nine o'clock, she went to the office to collect the float: the usual thirty thousand francs. She opened the safe and counted out the money. Adelais hadn't found any Patershol francs. All the cash was clean. Saskia closed the safe again and got ready to go. That was when her gaze fell on the flight timetable open on top of the desk.

Flights from Brussels to Milan, to Naples, to Rome and to Venice. The timetable was only good until the end of the year. Saskia had never been to Italy and she was quite sure Adelais hadn't either. The two of them had certainly earned a holiday, but a trip just before Christmas, *over* Christmas? They couldn't possibly go, not both of them. The Astrid Christyn was going to be packed. There was too much to do, too much money to be made.

Saskia switched off the light and left the office. There was nothing to worry about: just Adelais enjoying a pipe dream. They could take a break later, in the new year perhaps, when things were quiet again. They would take a week in Venice and ride through the canals in a gondola. Or they could head off to Milan and go shopping. She couldn't imagine Adelais going anywhere without her. Who could she possibly go with? Who did she have left? Only her mother, and she had gone to work for Christ in Africa.

Renilde was already in the cage, gossiping with Nadia across the counter. When they gossiped, it was usually about men: the few they liked the look of, the many they found ridiculous. To make a point – it wasn't clear what – Renilde took hold of the bars and shook them, like a prisoner in a Western.

'Don't do that, for God's sake,' Saskia said. 'They're only screwed in.'

The women fell silent. The pianist had arrived and dance music had started up in the ballroom. A handful of guests had gathered at the bar. More would arrive soon. Saskia slapped the money down and pushed it under the window. 'Thirty thousand.'

'Is Miss Adelais coming down tonight?' Renilde said, as if Adelais's room was upstairs, as befitted a countess, instead of downstairs beside the kitchens.

'She's had to go out.'

'Again?'

Nadia giggled.

'What's the joke?'

'Nothing.'

Renilde was counting the money and grinning at the same time.

'Then why are you both laughing?'

Renilde tidied the stack of notes and put it away in the drawer. 'Nadia thinks Miss Adelais is in love.'

'What are you talking about?'

'That young man who was getting the tour last Saturday. Sebastian something? I hardly saw him, but Nadia says, he and Miss Adelais—'

'You're talking shit!' One of the guests at the bar looked round. Saskia hadn't meant to shout. 'That was Sebastian Pieters. He's an old . . . acquaintance of ours. Miss Adelais wasn't even pleased to see him. She couldn't wait for him to leave.'

Nadia and Renilde looked at each other, eyebrows raised. It was as if they had just heard something so absurd it was better left unchallenged. Saskia understood. She placed a steadying hand on the counter. 'Why? When *did* he leave?'

Nadia giggled again. Saskia wanted to slap her.

Renilde straightened the necklace at her throat. 'Early on Sunday, I heard. They went off together on her scooter.' She suppressed a grin. 'They looked tired.'

Nadia thought this was hilarious. Saskia remained rooted to the spot. She smiled and shook her head, as if it was all too silly, as if none of it mattered, as if it were beneath her to care. 'You two,' she said, and walked away down the main stairs to the lobby.

People were coming through the front door. A blast of cold air hit her in the face. She turned away and headed into the kitchens. The kitchen staff were clearing up after dinner, steam rising from sinks of soapy water, the room noisy with a clatter of plates being stacked and stowed away. She took the corridor to the servant's room where Adelais slept and opened the door. Adelais hadn't locked it.

The bed was half made. Saskia pulled back the covers. The bottom sheet was creased and bunched up in the middle. It gave off a faint musky smell. She grabbed the edge of the mattress and tipped it over, sheets, pillows and all, onto the floor.

Adelais left her scooter in the yard. She pulled off her helmet and made her way carefully along the dock. It had started to rain. She could hear the drops falling on the river. Darkness shrouded everything but a solitary street light on the bridge upstream.

Inside the old weaver's house she unlocked the door on the ground floor, and took down the drawing that was pinned to the back of it. *Me, Aged 7.* She stared at the child in her red dress, at her wide, grinning face, and folded the picture away into a pocket.

In the room above, she went to the sinks at the back and turned on the taps. The special inks were oil-based and thick, but they would flush away into the drain, if she mixed in the washing solution she used to clean the presses. The empty tins she could take away with her, a few at a time. The lithographic and intaglio machines were not incriminating. They left no impressions of their own on the notes, but each letterpress character had a unique signature. The blocks of type went into a bag. She would drop it into the Handelsdok later, along with all the plates. She knew a good spot, where stacks of rusting rails and sleepers hid the quayside from view.

She watched the fatty globules of ink swirl around the sink. Soon there would be no tangible connection between the weaver's house and the millions of counterfeit francs being passed around the country. There was the ground floor and the cellar, piled high with the goods she had not managed to give away. But what did they indicate, beyond an addiction to shopping? They would not come after her for that. When the time came to tell Sebastian what she had done, how she had really come by the Astrid Christyn, it would all be in the past.

She made her way to the top floor and opened the safe. There were sixty thousand Patershol francs on the top shelf. They would have to be destroyed somehow. She stuffed them into her pockets. The stock of esparto paper would be harder to get rid of. There was a whole crate's worth, still unused – too much to be loaded onto the scooter. And it was bulky, conspicuous. She decided to dump it into the river outside the house. Esparto paper was made from grass. It would rot away in a few weeks, or a few months. Tonight was a good night for it: rainy, moonless. No one would see her.

She opened the window. The paper came in packets of two hundred and fifty sheets. She could throw them into the river from where she was, one packet at a time. But what about the noise? The wind was getting up, but not enough to cover it.

She put a couple of packets inside the sleeping bag and dragged it behind her down the narrow stairs. The bag hit each step with a heavy thud. She reached the dock. Everything was still except for the splashing of the rain on the river. Nothing moved on the bridge. She pulled out the first packet of paper and dropped it into the water. It sank at once and vanished. She took a pace to her left and reached into the bag again.

'Good evening, Miss de Wolf.'

The second packet of paper landed at Adelais's feet, and burst open.

'Esparto, I assume. Does this mean you've no more use for it?'

She knew his voice. She had heard it in her dreams. He was standing at the corner of the house, holding a cigarette. 'Major de Smet.'

'Forgive my arriving unannounced. As you can see, I'd anticipated a more formal setting.'

Adelais could just make out that he was not in his uniform, but an overcoat over a dinner jacket. She had no idea what it meant. 'What are you doing here?'

De Smet walked to the edge of the dock and scooped up a loose sheet of paper. 'I'd be curious to know how you got hold of this.' He sniffed at it. 'Italian paper would have been an easier option. Their esparto's less durable, but easier to procure. But you opted for French, like the Bank of Belgium.' He shook his head. 'Such attention to detail.'

Adelais shuddered. 'I don't know what you're talking about.' She couldn't do any better, knowing it was all over, that this was the end. She glanced at the river, at the black water. There was nowhere to run.

De Smet pulled up his collar. 'Shall we go inside? We could catch our deaths out here.'

The door was open. She couldn't stop him. All she could do was follow. There was no sign of any other officers. De Smet seemed to have come alone. And why the evening dress? Even through the dread, it came to her that something wasn't right.

De Smet went into the first room and put on the light. He went to the box marked *Lokeren* and opened the lid. The scarf and the wooden horse had been left at the boys' orphanage, but everything was still just as Adelais had found it.

De Smet pulled out a lace tablecloth. 'Here we are: the retail operation. Very labour-intensive and time-consuming. Almost a full-time job, I expect.' He dropped the tablecloth and went to the box marked *Tournai*. A decorative wall plate with a floral pattern brought a fleeting smile to his lips. 'The gaming was a much slicker operation. Was that your idea or your father's?'

'My father had nothing to do with it.'

De Smet's face was pale and lined, but his eyes were keen. 'I believe you. Craftsmen are perfectionists, but they tend to lack ambition.' Carefully he replaced the plate in the box. 'The presses, they're upstairs, I suppose?'

He went up to the first floor without waiting for an answer. Adelais

371

had left the door unlocked. De Smet went from machine to machine, running his hands over the surfaces, stooping to examine the mechanisms, like a prospective buyer. One of the taps was still running, ink washing away down the drain. Adelais turned it off. Another week and she would have been gone, free, able to start a new life. But she'd had her share of good luck and it had finally run out. She wished de Smet would arrest her, if he was going to.

'Show me the plates,' he said. 'Or are they in the river too?'

She did not have it in her to fight, to protest, to delay. Major de Smet could summon an army of gendarmes to tear the house apart. They would find everything. She left the sinks and went up the stairs to the top floor. Her limbs felt heavy, a numbness creeping over her, as if the answer to her predicament was to sleep. If she slept, she might wake up and find that de Smet had never been there, that she had dreamed it all. She might wake up with Sebastian beside her, his warm body, his smooth skin – and in that moment it struck her that the night they had spent together was the only one they would ever have.

She knelt down in front of the safe and dialled the combination: 20.4.47. She had given the picture to her uncle. She could hear his voice: *My little wolf.* But where was he now? Safely over the border in Holland was her guess. Ever since the police had seen his face, hadn't he let her take all the risks? Wasn't he, underneath the smiles and the confidence, a coward?

She opened the safe: the plates were wrapped up on the bottom shelf. It wasn't until she held them in her hands that she noticed the Beretta was not with them.

De Smet took an eyeglass from his pocket and screwed it into his eye, the way Adelais's father used to examine the insides of a watch. He unwrapped the plates and held them up to the light, one after the other. The intaglio plates interested him the most. 'Originals,' he said, 'in all but name. Monsieur Declercq was right: these could have gone to the Bank of Belgium and no one would have said a word.'

When he was done, de Smet wrapped up the plates and carefully placed them back in the safe. Adelais didn't understand. The plates were vital evidence. Wasn't he going to take them away?

'There's no doubt about it,' he said, 'your father was a remarkable craftsman, as skilled as any engraver in the country. It was a shame they shut him out – an injustice, in fact. Tell me: when did he start to teach you?'

'Teach me?'

'Printing. Forgery.'

'He never taught me. He never set foot here. He was . . .' But what was he? Innocent? Scared? 'He's dead now, anyway.'

'And your uncle too, I understand.'

Nothing in de Smet's tone suggested he thought otherwise. Adelais nodded.

'You were alone, weren't you, after you mother left? Working in a bar by the docks.' De Smet noticed the boxes of paper and flipped back one of the lids. 'You weren't looking at much of a future. Then suddenly . . .' He gestured at the room, the house. 'Opportunity. A chance to change everything. You didn't let it go to waste. That *would* have been a crime, wouldn't it?'

Was de Smet toying with her? Adelais wished he would stop.

He took out some paper and flipped his thumb along the edge. The esparto was crisp and stiff. It made a distinctive, high-pitched sound. 'You didn't steal from anyone, not really. Your notes were so good they simply vanished into the system, a modest increase in the money supply. Even the Bank of Belgium couldn't complain. You barely made up for what people left in their laundry.' He looked at her. 'Isn't that so?'

'I don't know.'

De Smet sighed. 'Sadly, the authorities won't take any of that into account. They're jealous of their privileges when it comes to printing money, even money as good as yours.'

Adelais could not stand it any more. 'Are you going to arrest me?'

De Smet closed the box and stood looking at her, his hands in his pockets. He stepped close, frowning. She could smell his cologne, the damp wool of his coat. 'I've given my life to the law, Miss de Wolf, but law and justice aren't always the same thing. I've learned that.'

A glimmer of hope. Had she misunderstood? De Smet seemed to be offering her a way out. 'I don't . . . What do you—'

'A young woman of such character and beauty, such *purpose* . . .' The back of de Smet's fingers brushed against her cheek. They were cold. 'Can I throw her to the wolves? Can I let her life be ruined? Should I risk throwing away my own for her sake? I'm at a loss, Miss de Wolf. What should I do?' He pushed his cold fingers through the hair at the nape of her neck. 'I'm afraid the decision will have to be yours.'

Adelais shuddered. This was why de Smet had come alone, dressed for an evening of entertainment. 'Let me go.'

De Smet smiled. 'I might do that, if you persuade me.'

'No, I meant, *let me go!*'

She pushed him away. He stepped back, stared at her, seemingly astonished, affronted. 'Perhaps you need more time to think. I don't want to rush you.'

He stepped closer again. Without warning, he yanked one arm behind her back. His right hand found her throat. She fell back against the wall, her stick clattering to the floor. She felt de Smet's dry lips against her skin, a hand pushing against her breast.

'*No!*'

He pulled her to him, stared into her face. 'I'm beginning to think you aren't that clever after all, Miss de Wolf. I can't tell you how disappointing that is.'

Where was her strength? Where was her power to fight? He spun her round and pushed her against the armchair, his hands busy under her clothes. 'Now, let's start again.' With all his weight, he forced her down, face first.

She could scream. She opened her mouth, tried to force out the sound. Would anyone hear her? Would anyone come? She took a deep breath.

A swoop of movement behind her, a sharp, violent crack. De Smet's grip loosened. He let out a growl of shock, of outrage. Adelais turned in time to see Saskia swing at him again. The pistol from the safe was in her hand. The blow caught the side of de Smet's head. He fell to his knees. Saskia hit him a third time, connecting with the base of his skull. He crawled away from her, gasping, and collapsed.

Saskia stooped over him. There was a trickle of blood on de Smet's temple. He made no sound. She prodded him with her foot. 'Major de Smet, isn't it? I thought we'd done with him.'

'Saskia?'

But it couldn't be Saskia. The fury, the violence, it came from a stranger.

Saskia smiled – more of a twitch than a smile – and drew the back of her hand across her mouth. 'He's unconscious.' Adelais went to embrace her, but Saskia simply held out the Beretta. 'Your turn.'

'What?'

'Shoot him.' Saskia was shaking, pale. She wouldn't meet Adelais's gaze.

'What are you talking about?'

Saskia pushed the gun closer. Adelais could smell the metal and the oil. 'Go on. It's your turn. I don't have to do everything.'

'Are you mad? I'm not going to shoot him.'

De Smet moaned, coughed. Feebly, one of his legs kicked out behind him.

Saskia sighed, her eyes closing. 'It's all right. He followed you. And he came alone. That means nobody knows he's here.'

'Saskia, we can't—'

'Look, I know what we have to do. I worked it all out while I was hiding. We wrap him up in something. There's rope downstairs and blankets.'

'Saskia—'

'We put him in his car and drive out of the city, and you follow on the scooter.' Saskia was talking fast, almost as if she was talking to herself. 'We throw him in one of the canals. The Ringvaart. There are lots of empty stretches, not a house for miles. No one would see. Then we drive the car far away, and hide it in an old barn or something. With any luck someone will steal it – we should leave the keys inside. Nobody will find it for weeks, if ever. We'll be . . .'

Adelais reached up and took the pistol. 'Saskia, we have to call an ambulance. We have to tell the truth.'

'What?' Saskia stared at her. Her eyes were wild. She laughed. 'Are you serious?'

'I'm sorry.'

'No, no, no. We're . . . we're *fine*. We just have to keep our heads. We do this, this one thing, and . . . and then we go back to how it was. We go back to the Astrid Christyn and carry on like before. No one will know, and we can just forget it, like . . . like . . . Because he deserved it – he deserved it, Adelais – and we had no choice. *No choice.*' Saskia looked up. 'And that'll be the end of it, Adelais. We won't have to think about it ever again.'

Adelais shook her head. 'That won't be the end of it. There'll never be an end. Believe me, I know.'

Saskia stared at her. Her face was a picture of scorn and disbelief. 'That's *stupid*. You still want to be a good girl, do you? Well, it's too late. We've come too far.' Saskia reached for the pistol. Adelais pulled it away. 'I'm not paying for your mistakes, Adelais. Not this time.'

'We've both made mistakes, Saskia.'

'No, no. You. *Your* mistake.' Saskia nodded at de Smet. He was still moving, trying to drag himself towards the window. 'He followed you. You *let him* follow you. Maybe you'd have noticed if you hadn't been dreaming about Sebastian Pieters and your romantic little getaway.'

'For God's sake, this isn't the time.'

'You were going to leave, weren't you? Leave *me*. That was the "good news" you had for me, wasn't it? That you were leaving with that . . . ridiculous boy.'

'That doesn't matter now. We have to call an—'

'You promised me you wouldn't have him back. I made you promise and you promised. And now . . . It's so *stupid* of you, Adelais. He *left you*. Just like everyone else, like your mother, and your father. They all left you, all of them, except me.' Saskia jabbed a thumb against her chest. 'I'm the only friend you've ever had. And now you want me to go to prison so you won't have a conscience. Well, that's not going to happen. I'm going to deal with this problem and you're going to help me.'

Saskia made another grab for the pistol. Adelais tried to hold on, to tighten her grip. Saskia elbowed her hard in the chest. Adelais lost her footing, fell to her knees.

Saskia wrenched the gun free. 'Stupid,' she said. 'Stupid.'

She advanced towards de Smet. He had managed to get onto his side. One arm was clawing uselessly at the air, like a drunk's. Saskia looked at the gun, found the safety catch, flipped it off.

'Saskia, no!'

Saskia looked back. 'This is your fault, Adelais. You should have let that stupid boy drown.'

She stood over de Smet and raised the Beretta. De Smet rolled over onto his back. His eyes were open.

'*Saskia!*'

Adelais felt the gunshot like a blow to the head, one strong enough to split bone. It was all over now. No way back. They were murderers, always would be, forever.

She forced herself to look. De Smet wasn't dead yet. He was still moving. He had managed to get up on one knee. It was Saskia who stumbled. She turned to Adelais and held out her left hand. It was red with blood. Then she fell.

De Smet's gun had been in the pocket of his coat. He held it now where Adelais could see it. He blinked, tilted his head to one side, coughed, and took aim.

Adelais sprung forward, not caring how she connected, if the bullet went through her, only wanting to tear at him, to hurt him. She hit de Smet as he was trying to get up on both feet. He staggered backwards, helpless against her fury, her driving strength, and crashed through the glass.

Adelais held on to him, holding him tight as they fell into the darkness, cheek to cheek, as if they were dancing. The last thing she felt before the water engulfed her was the jolt of de Smet's skull smacking down on the edge of the dock.

— Fifty-two —

Major de Smet had been missing for three days when a call came in from Assistant Commissioner van Buel in Ghent. De Smet's body had been recovered from a narrow stretch of the Leie River in a rundown district of Patershol. At the time, police divers had been looking to recover a firearm used in a fatal shooting nearby.

'Several head injuries, enough to render him unconscious. We think he might have fallen from an upstairs window.'

Toussaint sat down, aware suddenly that he was in de Smet's chair, sitting where de Smet always sat. Van Buel's words struck him as faintly preposterous. De Smet couldn't be dead. He was here, an almost tangible presence. Toussaint would not have been surprised to see him walk through the door.

'Who was shot?' he said.

'Female, early twenties. We just identified her as Saskia Helsen. She worked at the Astrid Christyn Hotel.'

'The Astrid—What was her name again?'

'Helsen, Saskia. Her father's a doctor here. Well off.'

Saskia. She had flirted with him the night he and de Smet had gone to the hotel. She had been playful and curvaceous – just his type. He might have taken her telephone number for future use, if he hadn't suddenly felt ill for some reason, and been forced to make a dash to the gents. Now she was dead, shot. And de Smet had been on the scene. He hadn't said a word about going back to Ghent. If he had been there on federal police business, why hadn't he told anyone?

'Did you find the gun?'

'We found two: a Beretta, loaded but not fired, and a Browning automatic.'

De Smet's gun was a Browning. Toussaint's choice had always been a Beretta.

'And?'

'The fatal shot came from the Browning. Major de Smet's finger was still hooked around the trigger guard.'

'That doesn't mean—'

'The bullet's a match.'

Toussaint could see the headlines already, tales of vice and murder among the federal gendarmerie. How were they going to go down in the new department, with the new men in charge? When it came to de Smet, Toussaint was already tainted by association. This could only make things worse – unless the whole business could somehow be tidied away, neutralised.

'Where did this happen exactly?'

'37 Sluizeken. Business premises, some sort of printing operation. The building's owned by a property company in Antwerp: Haeck Maris NV.' Toussaint wrote down the name. 'They own a lot of the land in Patershol. Low-rent properties, leased out mostly.'

'So who holds the lease?'

'We're still trying to find out.' Van Buel's tone was wary. Federal officers, turning up unannounced on his patch, murdering the daughters of eminent citizens, Toussaint could see how that might cause resentment. 'Do you know why de Smet was in Ghent?'

'No, I don't,' Toussaint said.

'He was dressed like he was going to a party.'

'Maybe I should come down.'

'Maybe you should.' Van Buel sniffed. 'Clear up your own bloody mess.'

Colonel Delhaye reluctantly allowed Toussaint to spearhead the investigation. He left that afternoon and drove to the address in Patershol. A municipal officer was on guard outside. The whole place had been taped off. Toussaint identified himself and made his way along the narrow dock. The river slid past, fast and high, swollen by the recent rain. A picture flashed through his mind: de Smet's body being dragged out, lifeless. Above him, a tall window on the top floor of the house showed obvious damage. Shards of glass littered the boards below.

Toussaint went straight up to the top floor. The position of Helsen's body had been marked on the floor in chalk. The shape was an indistinct blob. Only the lower legs and feet were unmistakable. In the middle, on the bare boards, there was a large, dark stain, the size of a dinner plate. According to van Buel, the bullet had gone clean through the dead girl's heart. It was like de Smet not to miss.

Across the room, a safe stood open. If there had been anything inside, it had been removed as evidence. Toussaint had been expecting a love nest, a hideaway, but nothing about 37 Sluizeken was romantic.

On the floor below he found the presses: lithographic, intaglio, letterpress. He did not need to see banknotes. He knew what the machines were for. De Smet had finally found the place, after eight years of searching: the heart of the Tournai Forger's operation. It was a place he himself had imagined a thousand times, though in his mind it had always been dark, subterranean, remote. Why had de Smet kept the information to himself? Why had he come alone? It was contrary to police procedure. His superiors would want to know if de Smet had come to make an arrest, or a deal.

Down in the cellar, another officer – a new recruit, by the look of it – was at work, making a list of all the items in the boxes and labelling them one by one. He was going to be there for weeks, given the scale of the task.

'We're working on the assumption these are stolen goods, sir,' he said. 'It'll be a business returning them all.'

Toussaint took a porcelain shepherdess from one of the shelves. The glazed face wore an anxious expression. 'You don't have to worry about that. They're not stolen.'

The new recruit looked puzzled. 'Then what are they doing here, sir?'

Toussaint put the shepherdess back. 'It's what my boss used to call a retail operation, for what it's worth. It's over now anyway.'

He left the house and drove to municipal police headquarters. Van Buel handed him a file. Among the reports inside were black-and-white photographs of de Smet's body on a slab. Toussaint stared at the sunken eyes, the slack mouth, and it seemed to him that he was looking at a stranger, that in spite of all the years they had worked together, he had never really known de Smet at all.

'We found out who holds the current lease,' van Buel said.

'I'm guessing Miss Adelais de Wolf.'

'How did you know?'

'She and Helsen were in business together. Have you found her?'

Van Buel shook his head. 'No luck at the hotel. She has another address in Sint-Amandsberg.'

'And?'

'All we found there was a pile of wet clothes.'

Nadia arrived at the Astrid Christyn at a quarter to eight and tried her best to concentrate on sorting the post as usual. Most of the staff were still in shock, but Hendryck, who had found himself in charge, had impressed upon everyone the importance of carrying on as normally as possible. So far, they had just about managed it.

The municipal police had given them the news the day before, although they had refused to go into details. Instead they had questioned several members of staff about Miss Helsen's movements, including where and when she had last been seen. It was obvious that foul play was suspected. They asked about an address in Patershol that nobody had ever heard of. They also asked to see Miss de Wolf, after which they asked a lot more questions about where she might have gone. It was hard keeping up appearances. Every time Nadia saw another member of staff, it took a lot of willpower not to stop and talk, to express her disbelief. It was as if she had been forced to take a vow of silence, like a nun.

The morning newspapers arrived. Nadia glanced through them, looking for the story. There was nothing in *De Standaard*, and nothing in *Het Volk*. She had just picked up a copy of *Het Laatste Nieuws*, when another police car pulled up outside. This time the driver was a gendarme. Nadia recognised him: he was tall, with a long face and a nasty scar along his jaw.

'The acting manager, please,' he said, without introducing himself.

Hendryck was fetched from the dining room, where he had been helping with breakfast.

The gendarme produced a piece of paper. 'My name is Captain Toussaint. I have a warrant to search these premises.'

'Search? What for?' Hendryck said.

'Information. In particular, we're anxious to locate Miss Adelais de Wolf. You've still not heard from her?'

Hendryck slowly shook his head. Nadia could tell what he was thinking: that maybe Adelais had suffered the same fate as Miss Helsen and they just hadn't found her body.

'I'll start with her office,' Toussaint said. 'I take it she has one?'

Hendryck led the way. The door of the office closed behind them. Renilde came downstairs and hovered by the front desk. 'What's happening?'

'They're after Miss Adelais.'

'*After* her?'

Nadia hadn't meant it to sound that way. 'I mean, she's missing.'

'What happens if she's . . . if she never comes back?'

'I don't know.' Nadia smiled sweetly at a couple of guests coming out of the dining room. 'Just get back to work, will you?'

Five minutes went by before Toussaint and Hendryck emerged from the office. Toussaint crossed the lobby in a hurry and went straight to his car. He had a document in his hand.

'He made me open the safe,' Hendryck said. 'I told him there was only cash inside, but that didn't stop him. He went through the lot. I watched him like a hawk, mind you.' He tapped the side of his nose. 'Didn't like the look of him, truth be told. With some people, you can just tell.'

'He took something. What was it?'

'A flight timetable. He seemed to think that was interesting, for some reason. God knows why.'

The gendarme's car pulled away. Hendryck returned to the dining room. Nadia forced herself to carry on sorting the mail. She tried not to think about Miss Adelais, lying undiscovered somewhere, dead. She hadn't just been a boss. She'd been a friend. Nadia found she had tears in her eyes. She could live to be a hundred, but she'd never work for anyone like that again.

Among the letters was a brown paper packet. There was no stamp. Nadia blinked. Her name was written on the front in capital letters.

She looked over her shoulder and opened the packet. It contained a battered paperback book. Inside the back cover was a letter in a small blue envelope. But the letter was not addressed to her.

The telephone rang. Absently, Nadia picked up the receiver. 'Astrid Christyn Hotel.'

'Nadia?' She recognised the voice at once. 'Did you find the package?'

GHENT: HOTELIER SLAIN

Last Tuesday night municipal police were called to the scene of a fatal shooting in the district of Patershol in Ghent. The victim was identified as 21-year-old Saskia Helsen, youngest daughter of Dr Ralf Helsen, a professor of physiotherapy and university lecturer.

Miss Helsen worked at the exclusive Astrid Christyn Hotel, a popular nightspot that opened last year in the countryside east of Ghent, and which has rapidly grown to be a favourite among visiting celebrities.

Staff contacted by *De Standaard* were unable to suggest a possible motive for the killing.

Police are appealing for witnesses to come forward. In particular they are anxious to interview Miss Helsen's colleague at the Astrid Christyn, Miss Adelais de Wolf, daughter of watch-mender Lennart de Wolf (deceased), previously of Sint-Amandsberg, Ghent. Miss de Wolf has not been seen since the night of the shooting, and fears are said to be growing for her safety.

— Fifty-three —

Captain Toussaint closed his copy of *De Standaard* and hurled it into the bin. He had expected reports of the case to appear somewhere, somehow, but not for a few more days, and certainly not with a reference to Adelais de Wolf. The reporter hadn't got that from the Helsen family. One of van Buel's people must have let that particular cat out of the bag. De Wolf would go to ground now, knowing the police were actively searching for her. She would find a way to skip the country that didn't involve handing over her passport, if she hadn't done that already.

The best chance of catching her had always been at the airport. She had been planning to travel, had even written down some prices on the back of the flight timetable she had left on her desk. Lieutenant Masson had spent the last day on the telephone, going through passenger lists for every flight out of Belgium this side of February. But de Wolf wouldn't risk flying now, not once she saw the newspapers. Even if she missed today's report in *De Standaard*, other papers were bound to take up the story. The celebrity angle pretty much guaranteed it. Meanwhile, Colonel Delhaye wanted answers: he wanted to know what de Smet had been doing in Patershol, and how badly the reputation of the gendarmerie was going to be damaged when the facts came out. If Toussaint could prove that de Smet had sacrificed his life in the line of duty, tracking a notorious criminal operation to its source, things might not look so bad. For that, he needed an arrest, and ideally a confession.

Toussaint decided it was time for a drink, but before he could escape from the office, Lieutenant Masson came hurrying down the corridor, clutching his notebook. A day on the telephone to airlines hadn't dimmed his enthusiasm for police work, but it had made him hoarse.

'Sir, Miss A. de Wolf bought two tickets to Rome last Monday, one way from Zaventem. The other ticket's in the name of a Mr S. Pieters.'

Toussaint hardly had the heart to tell him that it was too late, thanks to *De Standaard* and van Buel's idiots in Ghent. 'Rome,' he said. 'Very nice too.'

Masson looked confused. 'Sir, the flight's scheduled for eleven o'clock on December the 10th.'

'What?'

'December the 10th, sir. That's today.'

Toussaint looked at his watch. It was gone ten o'clock. 'Shit.' He hurried back inside the office and picked up his gun. 'Call the airport. Tell them who we're looking for and send a couple of men after me.'

'Yes, sir.' Masson went straight to the telephone.

'Tell them no sirens and no bloody ruckus. She sees us first, she'll be gone.'

'Understood, sir.'

Toussaint pulled on his coat. 'Miss de Wolf may be a lot of things, but she isn't blind.'

The traffic was heavy and Toussaint had to use the lights and the horn to make it to Zaventem in twenty-five minutes. He had never seen the airport busier. As he pulled up, several coachloads of people were crowding through the main entrance, lugging suitcases and children. Taxis were double-parked halfway along the kerb. He pulled over at the first available space and radioed back to headquarters.

'De Wolf hasn't checked in,' Masson said. 'Nor has Pieters.'

'Damn. She's not coming.'

'Flight's delayed, sir: one hour. If she rang the airport, she'd know that.'

Lieutenant Masson, looking on the bright side.

'I guess we'll see.'

The terminal was just a few years old: three blocks of concrete, glass and steel, with a check-in area easily twice the size of the ticket hall at Brussels-Centraal. A pair of escalators on the right led up to a mezzanine, where a crowded cafe offered a view across the runway and the check-in desks below. The Alitalia desk was halfway along, a sign that said ROME suspended above it. Flight information clattered on the boards, cutting through the hubbub of voices.

Toussaint bought a newspaper at a kiosk and loitered at the edge of the mezzanine, trying to look like a passenger killing time. The queue for Rome was down to a handful of people. It was almost lost between much bigger queues for London and Frankfurt. At the end of it stood a young man in a raincoat, carrying a suitcase. He kept looking at his watch. A businessman came hurrying towards the Alitalia desk, ticket in hand. The young man gave up his place. He wasn't queuing, he was waiting for someone. Toussaint felt his pulse quicken. Maybe the young man was Pieters. He clearly wasn't expecting to travel alone.

A pair of federal officers came through the doors. They spotted Toussaint and gave him a nod. One stayed by the door. The other went to the gate marked EMIGRATION. It was ten minutes to eleven. A voice came over the tannoy: a flight to Paris was boarding. The young man looked at his watch again. Whoever he was waiting for, they were late.

Just below the mezzanine, a little boy in a pushchair started wailing. His mother handed him a teddy bear. The child took the bear and hurled it across the floor. When Toussaint looked up again, he saw that the officer by the doors was signalling to him. He pointed into the crowd. Then Toussaint saw her: a blonde woman in a raincoat, making her way towards the Alitalia desk, walking purposefully, fast. The young man turned to greet her.

She should have changed her plans, Toussaint thought. Now he had her.

He dropped the newspaper and ran. At the bottom of the escalator, the toddler stopped mid-wail and stared at him, open-mouthed, as the gendarme barged his way through the crowd.

At the Astrid Christyn Hotel, Mr and Mrs Hofman were in their room, packing in readiness for an afternoon departure. Mrs Hofman's clothes were spread out on the double bed, but she had bought too many new items for everything to fit inside her suitcase. She had been forced to take her husband's as well. Mr Hofman's things had gone into a laundry bag, borrowed from the hotel.

'We've been here almost a fortnight and I haven't seen anyone famous,' Mrs Hofman said. 'I thought there were meant to be film stars.'

'I suppose it's not the season,' Mr Hofman said. 'We'll come back when the film festival's on.'

'Knowing my luck, it'll be booked up.'

Mr Hofman placed his hands on his young wife's shoulders. 'That can't happen if we own the place.'

'Own the place? Is it for sale?'

'I'm assured it is. And if we own the place, we'll be the hosts, my dear.'

'Like Miss de Wolf is now?'

'Exactly.'

Mrs Hofman considered this for a moment. 'I want to meet some directors. They might discover me. I'd like to be in films. I don't think it can be all that hard, if you have the looks.'

'And you certainly do, my dear.'

Mrs Hofman allowed her husband to massage her neck. 'More than Miss de Wolf. She has a limp anyway. Who wants to see that?'

'No one. Shall we buy it then? I think the Astrid Christyn would be a very tidy addition to the portfolio.'

Mrs Hofman sniffed and walked over to the bureau beside the bed. 'All right. But you'll have to get rid of the staff. They're all terribly rude and lazy.'

'Consider them sacked.'

Mrs Hofman opened the top drawer and began rummaging around inside. Then she opened the drawer beneath and rummaged around in that. 'Where is it? Bernard?'

'Where's what, my dear?'

'My passport.' Mrs Hofman's rummaging became more and more

frantic. 'My passport. Call the police!' She pulled out the drawer and emptied it onto the floor.

'The police? My dear, just—'

'It's not here. It's gone, it's gone. They've stolen it. I'm telling you: someone's stolen my fucking passport!'

The other officers had already got there. One of them was holding the blonde woman by the arm, making sure she didn't get away. The other was checking her boyfriend's papers. He looked utterly bewildered.

Passengers on either side of them were staring. Someone took a photograph with an electric flashgun. The light burned into Toussaint's retina, so that for a few seconds all he could see was a large brown blob.

The second officer handed over the boyfriend's passport. 'Sebastian Pieters, sir. Flying to Rome, he says.'

But Toussaint wasn't looking at Sebastian Pieters. He was looking at the young blonde woman. He recognised her from his visit to the Astrid Christyn Hotel, but her name wasn't Adelais de Wolf. She had been the croupier at the roulette table where he had lost all his money.

'You? What are you . . . ? What the hell's going on?'

'Hello again, Captain,' Nadia said brightly and gave him a smile that, under different circumstances, he might have regarded as a very good sign.

Up on the mezzanine, a young woman in an old coat and an old woollen hat sat watching the commotion from a table in the cafe. She had been wearing sunglasses to shield her eyes from the sunlight lancing in through the glass walls, but now she took them off, so that she could get a better view of the commotion down below. She had already seen Nadia hand over the paperback book, moments before the police arrived, and seen Sebastian tuck it into his pocket before reaching for his passport. Now the two of them were being led away for questioning by Captain

Toussaint, questioning that would not take very long, since neither of them had any significant information to reveal.

She got up and walked to the rail at the edge of the mezzanine. She watched Sebastian Pieters being led through the crowd, an officer following on behind with his suitcase, leaving the terminal through one of the big glass doors. She hurried to the edge of the platform, so that she could catch a last glimpse of him getting into the back of a police car. For a moment, the silhouette of his head was visible through the back window. Then the police car pulled out, blue lights turning silently, and drove away.

She stood staring at where Sebastian Pieters had been, oblivious to the clatter of the boards and the announcements over the tannoy. For a long time, she did not move at all.

Eventually a woman in Sabena livery tapped her on the arm. 'Excuse me, Mrs Hofman?' she said. 'I think they just called your flight.'

—— Fifty-four ——

Cornelis Mertens telephoned from the back of a bar in central Rotterdam. The notary had been expecting his call.

'The buyer's lined up,' Cornelis said. 'Time to start on the paperwork. Strike while the iron's hot.'

A couple were sitting by the window, sipping frothing glasses of beer. It was only lunchtime, but Cornelis decided it would be a good idea to celebrate once the wheels were in motion. The only question was what to order? It was too early for spirits, but this wasn't the kind of establishment that stocked champagne.

Klysen started talking, but his words were obscured by a series of loud beeps on the line. Cornelis fumbled in his pocket and pumped some more coins into the slot.

'I just checked with the other notary – Jan Nielandt – and, apparently, it all went through on Friday. He went down to Brussels for the signatures.'

'What? What did you say?'

'It's all gone through.'

'What's gone through?'

'The sale. What are we talking about?'

'*What sale?*'

Klysen sighed. 'Of the Ribaucourt hunting lodge, now known as the Astrid Christyn Hotel.'

'No, no. That's impossible. What are you . . . ? My niece hasn't sold it, not yet. I told her—'

'I'm afraid she has,' Klysen said. 'As of December the 7th, she's no longer the legal owner. Like I said, I've already checked with the notary concerned. It's all signed and sealed.'

For a moment, Cornelis was speechless. The couple by the window were laughing, as if they were in on the joke, the joke that was on him.

'Wait a minute,' Cornelis said. 'How much did she sell it for? How many millions?'

There was a thud, followed by a rustling of papers. Klysen came back on the line. 'No millions at all.'

'What? But that's—'

'The sale price is right here: one Belgian franc.'

When the call was over, Cornelis went and sat down at the bar.

'What'll it be?' the barman said.

'Cognac. A double.' But Cornelis knew he was going to need more than that.

The barman glanced at the clock. 'That kind of day, is it?'

Cornelis did not answer. He reached into his pocket for cigarettes. His fingers brushed against the little bronze wolf he usually kept there. He took it out and placed it in front of him. The wolf had its head back and its jaws were open wide, as if it were howling at the moon.

A grim smile crept over his face. He shook his head. By the time the barman returned with the cognac, he was laughing out loud – although the barman couldn't be sure if he was really happy or not, because soon there were tears running down his cheeks.

Hendryck sent a taxi to meet them at the station and had the staff assemble in the lobby to greet the new owner. He himself waited impatiently at the top of the steps, bouncing on the balls of his feet, his breath condensing in the chilly air. There was nothing left of the snow that had fallen the previous week, but the sun was breaking through the clouds, bathing the walls behind him in golden winter light.

The taxi turned into the gates at half past two and made its way up the drive. Hendryck straightened his tie and tapped on one of the glazed panels of the door, to make sure everyone inside was ready. When the taxi pulled up, he walked down the steps and opened the passenger doors.

'Mrs Verlinden, my name is Hendryck. I'm the acting manager. It is my great pleasure to welcome you to the Astrid Christyn Hotel.'

Liesbeth Verlinden climbed out onto the gravel. Her son Nikolaas, who had been sitting next to the taxi driver, was out next. Last came Emeline Verlinden. She was pale and hung on her mother's arm.

Nikolaas Verlinden looked up at the building. His mouth, to Hendryck's satisfaction, fell wide open. 'This . . . this is even grander than the Leopold.'

'The Leopold?'

'The hotel where Mama cleans and makes beds.' Nikolaas glanced at his mother and decided he ought to elaborate. 'She makes them very well.'

'Then we'd better make sure we do the same,' Hendryck said, tapping the side of his nose, 'or she'll know.'

He led the family up the steps and into the lobby. Liesbeth Verlinden said nothing. She stared at her surroundings, blinking, as if expecting it to vanish at any moment, or reveal itself to be a trick. Hendryck introduced the staff and kept up a stream of explanatory chatter – the history of the building, the routine of the hotel, the calibre of the guests – as much to cover the silence as anything else. Finally, he opened the doors onto the terrace, so that the Verlindens could get a proper view across the grounds.

Nikolaas did not wait for an invitation: he tore across the terrace and down the lawn. At the ornamental pond he stopped and shouted for his sister: 'Come on, Emmi, let's explore!'

Emeline left her mother and hurried after him. When Liesbeth Verlinden and Hendryck finally caught up with them, the children were on the swings, swooping back and forth through the air. There was a rosy blush on Emeline's cheeks and she was laughing.

Nadia had arrived at the airport with a verbal message from Adelais: she was sorry she could not meet him, but it was now impossible. She hoped to explain herself to him one day, but there wasn't time now. That was it.

Over the hours that followed, Sebastian repeated the message several times at Federal Police Headquarters. He also answered a large number of questions that were actually a small number of questions, rephrased in a large number of ways. When it became clear that he really didn't know where Adelais was, had no idea what she'd been doing on the night of 5 December, and could shed no light whatever on the operation at 37 Sluizeken, he was at last allowed to leave.

Captain Toussaint wouldn't explain what it was all about. He would only say that Adelais might be in a position to assist with police inquiries, and that he was anxious to speak to her. It was vital Sebastian let him know at once if she got in touch again. Sebastian said he would, without meaning it. He asked what had happened to Nadia and was told she had already left. Sebastian had the impression that she had not been much help either. She was just an employee at the hotel, carrying out instructions.

Sebastian took the train to Ghent. Mrs Goethals would still have his room in Antwerp, which was paid for until the end of the month, but the thought of returning there alone, of carrying on as before as if nothing had happened, was more than he could bear. He still did not understand why Adelais hadn't met him at the airport. Nor did he understand how she had come to be of interest to the police. Sitting in the crowded carriage, his suitcase on his lap, the feeling grew that he was in some way to blame. He had been away from Adelais too long. Without her, his life had come adrift – he knew that. Maybe hers had too. Fate had brought them together beneath the Sint-Joris Bridge. Maybe Fate didn't like being ignored.

He was a few minutes from the city when he remembered the book Nadia had given him at the airport. In all the excitement, he had forgotten about it completely. He pulled it from his pocket: it was his old copy of *The Yellow Dog*. He and Adelais had started it together years before, when he was in hospital, but they had never finished it. Why had she sent it back to him now, after all this time? Did he want him to read it? Or was it her way of saying there was no going back to the past, after all, no picking up where they had left off?

Inside the back cover, he found a letter in a small blue envelope. His name was written on the front.

Dear Sebastian,

I expect you will hear some things about me over the days to come, stories and rumours. Some of them will be true, but not the worst of them — this I swear. All the same, I cannot go with you now, as I had hoped. I wanted more than anything to spend my days with you. Since we met, I am not sure I have ever wanted anything else. But we cannot live in a dream, and I cannot drag you into the life that I have made. It would make you wretched and unhappy, and I can't bear the idea of that. Your life will be better without me.

I have one last thing to ask of you and it is this: curse me, if you want, but don't feel sorry for me, and don't worry about me either. If I have learned anything, it is that I can fend for myself very well.

Forgive me if you can.

With love always,

Adelais

Sebastian's train slid through the southern districts of Ghent. The sun had set and the streets were deep in shadow. He wished he could write back to Adelais, and tell her she was wrong: that he would always be happier with her than without her, no matter what kind of life she had, no matter what she had done. But how could he write back to her, when there was nowhere to send the letter?

He got off at the station and set off on foot for his parents' house in Zuid. By the time he had crossed the road, his mind was made up: maybe Adelais needed him and maybe she didn't, but there was only one way to find out. He had lost her once before, after she had saved his life, but it hadn't taken long to find her again. If he could do it ten years ago, he could do it now. He would find a way, somehow. They would finish *The Yellow Dog* together.

He looked up at the sky. A passenger aircraft was passing high overhead, the sound rolling like distant thunder. He stopped to watch as it climbed towards the south, the roar of the engines slowly fading, the tail lights growing smaller and dimmer until they disappeared at last among the stars.

Acknowledgements

I would like to offer my sincere thanks to Christopher Zach for his close reading and comments on the first draft, Nicola Barr and her colleagues at The Bent Agency for their advocacy, Kate Fogg and Liz Foley for their backing, Katherine Fry for her meticulous copy-edit, and my editor Katie Ellis-Brown for her sensitive work on the manuscript and her support throughout.

Credits

Vintage would like to thank everyone who worked on the
publication of *THE HOUSE WITH NINE LOCKS*

Agent
Nicola Barr

Editor
Katie Ellis-Brown

Editorial
Liz Foley
Sania Riaz
Anouska Levy

Copy-editor
Katherine Fry

Proofreader
Alex Milner

Managing Editorial
Graeme Hall

Contracts
Emma D'Cruz
Gemma Avery
Ceri Cooper
Rebecca Smith
Anne Porter
Rita Omoro
Hayley Morgan

Design
Yeti Lambregts

Digital
Anna Baggaley
Claire Dolan
Brydie Scott
Charlotte Ridsdale
Zaheerah Khalik

Inventory
Nadine Hart

Publicity
Bethan Jones
Mia Quibell-Smith
Amrit Bhullar

Finance
Ed Grande
Samuel Uwague

Marketing
Sophie Painter
Lucy Upton
Mairéad Zielinski

Production
Konrad Kirkham

Polly Dorner
Eoin Dunne

Sales
Nathaniel Breakwell
Malissa Mistry
Elspeth Dougal
Tracy Orchard
Jade Perez
Lewis Gain
Nick Cordingly
Kate Gunn
Maiya Grant
Danielle Appleton

Rights
Catherine Wood
Lucie Deacon
Lucy Beresford-Knox
Beth Wood
Maddie Stephenson
Agnes Watters
Sophie Brownlow
Amy Moss

Audio
Hannah Cawse

About the Author

Philip Gray studied modern history at the University of Cambridge, and went on to work as a journalist in Madrid, Rome and Lisbon. He has tutored in crime writing at City, University of London, and serves as a director at an award-winning documentary film company, specialising in science and history. He lives in London.